PENGUIN BOOKS

The Hangman's Song

James Oswald is the author of the Inspector McLean series of crime novels. The first six, *Natural Causes*, *The Book of Souls*, *The Hangman's Song*, *Dead Men's Bones*, *Prayer for the Dead* and *The Damage Done* are available as Penguin paperbacks and ebooks. He has also written an epic fantasy series, *The Ballad of Sir Benfro*, which is published by Penguin, as well as comic scripts and short stories.

In his spare time he runs a 350-acre livestock farm in north-east Fife, where he raises pedigree Highland cattle and New Zealand Romney sheep.

D1422198

The Hangman's Song

JAMES OSWALD

PENGUIN BOOKS

PENGUIN BOOKS

UK | USA | Canada | Ireland | Australia
India | New Zealand | South Africa

Penguin Books is part of the Penguin Random House group of companies
whose addresses can be found at global.penguinrandomhouse.com.

First published in Penguin Books 2014

001

Copyright © James Oswald, 2014
All rights reserved

The moral right of the author has been asserted

Set in 12.5/14.75pt Garamond MT Std
Typeset by Jouve (UK), Milton Keynes
Printed in England by Clays Ltd, St Ives plc

ISBN: 978-1-405-93126-7

www.greenpenguin.co.uk

MIX
Paper from
responsible sources
FSC® C018179

Penguin Random House is committed to a
sustainable future for our business, our readers
and our planet. This book is made from Forest
Stewardship Council® certified paper.

This one's for Zos, Dregs, Fergus, Felix
and of course
'Doctor' Eleanor Austin

I

'The important thing is to get the drop right. Nothing else matters, really.'

He stands on tippy-toes, balanced on the precarious chair, hands behind his back like a good boy. His fingers are trembling slightly, as if in anticipation, but he's not struggling. I knew he wouldn't. Not now. He wants this, after all.

'Of course, to work that out I need to know your height, your weight, your build.'

I tug at the rope. Good, stout hemp; none of that nylon rubbish for a job like this. Getting it over the beam was a struggle, but now it's secure, ready. His eyelids flutter as I slip the noose over his head, gently snug it around his neck past his ear, let the excess loop over his bare shoulder.

'Height? No, height is easy, as long as you're not wearing platform shoes. Clothes can be deceptive though, make a thin man seem fat. And then there's build.'

He doesn't respond, but then why would he? He's not here any more. I can see the movement of his eyes under closed lids, the flick, flick, flick as he watches something far off in his mind. I reach out, run the backs of my fingers down his cheek, his arm, the muscles of his taut stomach. He is young, so young. Barely a man yet and the world has already dragged him down. Young skin is so soft and pure, not corrupted by the cankers and blemishes of age. A pity the same cannot be said of young minds. They are so fragile, so hopeless.

'Muscle is so much denser than fat. A well-muscled physique will weigh more than a lazy body. It is essential to take that into account.'

The spirit shivers in me, drinking deep from the well of despair that fills this room. There is nothing here worth saving, only the joy of release from a life not worth living.

'A handshake is usually enough. You can tell so much from a person's hand, their grip. I knew as soon as I met you how long a piece of rope we would need.'

I let my hand drop lightly down, stroking him with my nails. He rises to the occasion, ever so slightly, a soft moan escaping from his lips as I reach in, cup his barely dropped testicles, tickle them with my fingertips. The touch is both exhilarating and revolting, as if some tawdry sex act could ever be as intimate as what we have, this man child and me.

He shivers, whether from cold or excitement I will never know. I withdraw my hand, take a step back. One second, two, the pressure builds as the spirit rises within me. I see the rope, the knot, the chair, the table. Clothes neatly folded and placed on the bed a few feet away.

There is a moment when I push the chair away. Anything is possible. He floats in the air like a hoverfly, trapped in that instant. And then he is falling, falling, falling, the loops of rope untwining in lazy, slow-motion rolls until nothing is left.

And then.

Snap.

'You sure about this, Tony?'

Detective Chief Inspector Jo Dexter sat in the passenger seat of the Transit van, staring out through a grubby windscreen at the industrial wasteland around Leith Docks. Street lights glowed in orange strings; roads to nowhere. The first tinge of dawn painted the undersides of the clouds, marching north and east across the Forth to Fife. The high-rises that had sprung up along the northern shoreline were dark silhouettes pocked by the occasional light of a shift-worker coming home. This early in the morning there wasn't much activity, least of all from the dark bulk of the freighter they were watching. It had docked two days ago, a routine trip from Rotterdam bringing in aggregates for the new road bridge. As if they didn't have enough rock and sand in Scotland already. A team had been watching around the clock ever since, acting on information thought to be reliable. Beyond the unloading of a large quantity of gravel, nothing interesting had happened at all.

'According to Forth Ports, she sails on the tide. In about two hours' time.' Detective Inspector Anthony McLean checked his watch, even though the clock on the dashboard told him it was almost five in the morning. 'If nothing happens before then, we've been played for fools. I dare say it won't be the first time.'

'Easy for you to say. You're not the one having to justify the overtime.'

McLean looked across at his companion. He'd known Jo Dexter of old. She'd joined up at the same time as him, but had hit the promotion ladder early. McLean was happy for her, though he preferred his own niche; a career of chasing prostitutes and pornographers had hardened Jo Dexter's once pretty features so that she looked far older than her thirty-nine years. Vice did that to a person, he'd been told. And now he was finding out first hand thanks to bloody Dagwood.

'Well, you're the one reckoned the tip-off was good.' The temperature dropped by several degrees. Even in the darkness, McLean could see that this was the wrong thing to say, no matter how true it was. The letter had appeared in his in-tray on the first day of his secondment to Jo Dexter's team in the Sexual Crimes Unit. It didn't have a stamp on it, and no one knew how it had got there. Nevertheless, the information in it showed that whoever had written it knew a great deal about the sleazy underbelly of Edinburgh's sex industry, and the final nugget had concerned a highly organized people-smuggling operation and this very ship.

'It's just that normally these things happen in container ports. How the hell do you smuggle people off a boat like that without being seen?'

'Your guess is as good as mine.' McLean switched his focus away from his temporary boss, across the empty yard to where a large box van had appeared at the security gate. After a short pause, the guard let it through. It continued its slow journey around the seemingly random

4

piles of rocks, sand and other unidentified materials that were the port's stock-in-trade, headed in the general direction of the ship.

McLean picked up his radio set, called the guardhouse. 'Who was that?'

'Catering firm. Provisions for the ship's galley. Guess they've got to eat, aye?' The guard sounded bored. Hardly surprising given his shift.

'They check out OK?' McLean asked.

'On the roster, aye.'

'OK then. Keep your eyes peeled for anything unusual.' He put the radio back on the dashboard as the box van arrived at the ship's side. In the semi-darkness, with nothing to compare it to other than the distant buildings, the ship had seemed small. Now with the van alongside, McLean could see just how big it was, high in the water without its ballast of rock.

'You think they might try something here?' Jo Dexter stretched as best she could in the confined space. She'd have been better off in the back, were it not for the half-dozen officers already in there, snoring gently.

McLean picked up the binoculars he'd appropriated from stores earlier that day, focused on the box van as the driver got out. A single lamp lit the steps leading up from the dockside to the deck, casting more shadow than anything else.

'Even if we weren't here watching, nothing gets out of this bit of the port without the excise boys checking it. There's no way they'd be able to smuggle anyone out unless they'd paid somebody off.'

'Stranger things have happened, Tony. What can you see?'

The driver opened up the back of the van and clambered into the darkness. After a moment he jumped back out again, grabbed a box and carried it up the steps. At least that's what McLean assumed he'd done. The way the van was parked, it obscured the foot of the steps, and the top was in shadow. Only a small part in the middle was visible, and by the time he'd adjusted the focus, the driver was gone.

'A man unloading groceries, by the look of it. Yup. There he goes again.' Movement at the back of the van, and the driver once more grabbed a box, heading for the steps. McLean flicked the binoculars up a fraction, and caught a fleeting glimpse of someone before the darkness swallowed them. It wasn't much, but there was something wrong. He couldn't put his finger on it; the way the driver moved, perhaps?

A moment later and the figure passed across his view again, heading up the steps with a baker's tray in its hands. But that couldn't be right, could it? How had he missed the driver coming back down the steps? Unless there were two people in the van. That would make more sense anyway.

Another figure cut across the narrow pool of light, this time carrying a large cardboard box, struggling under its weight and bulk. McLean squinted through the binoculars, wishing the magnification was better. This figure seemed different from the first and second. There couldn't be three people working the van, could there? And how much in the way of provisions did a cargo ship need to make the crossing from Leith to Rotterdam?

Dropping the binoculars back onto the seat, McLean

started the engine, slammed the Transit into gear and shot forwards. Beside him, Jo Dexter grabbed for the handle above the door, too stunned to say anything.

'Not smuggling them in. Taking them out. Wake up you lot. It's time to go to work.' McLean shouted to the team in the back. A couple of muffled grunts and a high-pitched yelp were all the answer he got as he accelerated as hard as he could, covering the distance to the ship in less than a minute. The back of the box van was open, and as he swept round behind it, the Transit's headlights threw aside the shadows, revealing what was inside.

'Go! Go! Go!' The team burst out of the back of the Transit, fanning out and securing the van. A commotion up on deck was followed by a shout of 'Armed police. Drop your weapons.' McLean and Dexter watched from the Transit as a large cardboard box fell from above, twisting once, twice, before smashing against the concrete of the dock in an explosion of oranges.

It was over in seconds. The sergeant in charge of the armed-response team came over to the Transit and signalled the all clear. McLean didn't need to hear it; he could see with his own eyes. Out of the back of the box van they began to clamber into the light. Pale, almost cadaverous some of them, scantily clad despite the cold and all bearing that same terrified expression. A dozen or more young women, no more than girls, really, though their faces showed they'd seen more than any girl their age should ever see.

'Well, that's not quite what I was expecting.'

McLean leaned back against the cool concrete wall

outside the back of the station, watching as the last of the young women was escorted into the station. Dawn had already painted the overcast sky in oranges and purples, promising rain for later on. A quick glance at his watch showed that it was almost shift-change time. Not that he worked shifts any more.

'Not what I was expecting, either.' Jo Dexter pulled deeply on the cigarette, held the smoke for just long enough for it to do its worst, then let it spill upwards as she let her head clunk lightly against the wall. 'Remind me about that tip-off again?'

The letter. McLean reached into his jacket pocket and pulled out the photocopy the forensics team had given him. He knew that they'd not managed to lift anything from the original, but he still wasn't allowed to have it back. It didn't matter, the words were still the same. Date, time, place, ship name, it was all there. He even had a suspicion he knew who had sent it, but it wasn't a suspicion he cared to share. He tapped the edge of the folded-up paper against his hand.

'It all checked out. You know that as well as I do, otherwise we'd never have got this lot authorized.' He nodded at the Transit van as the last of the armed-response team jangled back into the station, Kevlar body armour unstrapped and dangling.

'You're right. I thought it was legit. But this? Trafficking prostitutes away from the city? Taking them to Rotterdam and then God only knows where.' Dexter shook her head, sucked once more on the cigarette as if the answer might be in there somewhere. The smoke billowing out into the lightening air gave up no answers.

'I . . .' McLean began, but was interrupted by his phone buzzing in his pocket. It had been on silent all through the stake-out and arrests. A quick scan of the screen showed an instantly recognized number. Dexter must have read something from the expression on his face, said nothing as he took the call. It wasn't a long one, not even time enough for her to finish her cigarette.

'Bad news?' she asked through a haze of smoke.

'Not sure. I have to go.' He saw the scowl forming on Dexter's face. 'Won't be long. It's just . . . I have to go.' And he scurried off before she could stop him.

3

McLean didn't even wait for Doctor Wheeler to greet him, just started off down the corridor and expected her to keep up. He'd known her what . . . almost six months? Quiet, competent and impossibly young for someone with such a detailed knowledge of the human brain, she had given him hope that Emma would recover eventually, promised to let him know as soon as anything happened.

And now something had.

The guilt had been there ever since her abduction, when poor, mad Sergeant Needham had smashed her over the head, and all because he'd let Emma get close to him. He'd visited her every day, even if it was sometimes only for five minutes. He'd watched her, as he'd watched his grandmother before, wasting away bit by bit, her mind somewhere else, her body kept alive by machines. Day after day, the hope being ground away like a mountain succumbing to the onslaught of weather. Slow, but inexorable. He'd been steeling himself, rebuilding the walls that she'd been the first in a decade to breach. Hardening himself for the time when he'd have to bury another.

But something had happened.

'You said on the phone there'd been a change?'

'Indeed there has, Inspector. But you mustn't get your hopes up. She's still unconscious.'

The route to the ward was imprinted on McLean's

memory, but he still had to run the gamut of patients out and about, trailing drips on wheeled stands or revealing more flesh than it was comfortable to see through skimpy backless gowns. Even though it felt like he'd spent half of his life in them, he still couldn't get used to hospitals; their smell of disinfectant, bodily fluids and despair. The institutional beige walls didn't help, and neither did the bizarre collection of artworks hung along the corridors. No doubt chosen by some psychotherapist with a view to creating the optimum healing environment. Either that or a six-year-old child.

'Unconscious is not the same as in a coma though. She's going to come round soon.' Was that a desperate hope in his voice, or just weary resignation?

'I believe so. Yes. And yes, you're right, unconscious isn't the same as coma. The brainwave patterns are different for a start. There's more happening. She's shifting to something more akin to sleep.'

They had reached the door to the ward, but before McLean could push on through, the doctor reached out and stopped him.

'Inspector . . . Tony. You need to face up to the fact that there could be permanent damage. There almost certainly will be permanent damage.'

'I know. But this happened because of me. I'm not going to abandon her now.' McLean was about to open the door when it pulled away from him of its own accord. A startled nurse stood on the other side.

'Oh, Doctor. I was just coming to look for you. The patient's started talking. I think she might be about to wake up.'

Just like McLean's grandmother had been for the eighteen months it had taken her body to die, Emma was surrounded by the machinery that kept her alive. She had been propped upright, her shrunken form pale even against the white pillows of the hospital bed, her unruly mop of black, spiky hair tamed by some well-meaning nurse, far longer than she would ever have worn it. As he approached, McLean could see the change in her in an instant. Her eyes fluttered under eyelids, twitches in her face almost reminding him of her mischievous smile, then creasing into a frown. And all the while she muttered, quiet whimpers of terror. He was about to take her hand as he had done every day since she'd been brought here, but before he could, Doctor Wheeler once more stopped him.

'Best to wait just now. A touch could bring her out too quickly. Let her come at her own pace.'

'What's happening to her? She looks scared.'

'Difficult to be sure, but she's probably reliving the last few moments before she was knocked out.' Doctor Wheeler consulted the clipboard at the end of the bed, then pulled a pager out of her pocket. McLean hadn't even heard it ping. 'Gotta go. I'll check back as soon as I can.'

It was a special kind of hell, sitting there, watching the emotions skim across Emma's face, wondering what it was that Needy had done to her. Just the bash to the skull, or had there been something more? McLean found it hard to recall the events clearly himself. Too much smoke inhalation and blows to his own head. Too much dealing with the past he thought he'd finished with but which didn't want to let him go.

'Oh my god. No.'

The voice was barely more than a whisper, but it was hers. McLean looked around to see if any of the nurses in the ward had noticed. They were busy with the other patients and their machines. He reached out, about to take Emma's hand where it lay on the covers, fingers flexing minutely. Before he could, she drew her hand away.

'No, no, no, no. No!' Louder now, and Emma started to shake. Her heart rate monitor pinged a warning, but still the nurses were oblivious. McLean went to stand, meaning to get some help, but a tiny hand whipped out and grabbed him by the wrist, surprisingly tight. He snapped his head around as Emma sat bolt upright, eyes wide open.

'It took their souls. Trapped them all. They were lost. I was lost.'

And then the grip was gone. Her eyes flipped up into her head and she dropped back into the pillows. McLean could only watch as the nurses gathered around, alerted by the motion. He couldn't move, could only stare at Emma's face as they bustled around her, checking monitors, adjusting drips, whispering urgent messages to each other. Did this happen whenever a patient woke from coma? Was there some procedure they followed?

Slowly, the commotion died down. Everything that could be checked had been checked. The patient was asleep, heart rate steady. It was going to be OK. Everything was going to be fine. Still he sat and watched, oblivious to the passing of time. Minutes, hours, he didn't really care. This was his fault, after all. He wasn't going to shirk that responsibility. Not now. Not ever.

She woke more slowly the second time; colour coming back to her cheeks as her breathing changed from deep and regular to shallow and swift. Her eyes opened slowly, a hand reaching up to her head as if feeling for the damage that had been inflicted. Then she noticed the tube taped to her arm, the needle.

'It's OK,' McLean said, hoping to fend off the panic with a familiar face and voice. 'You're in hospital. You've been unconscious.'

Emma slowly rolled over, her head too heavy for the wasted muscles in her neck to control. She squinted against the light, even though it was muted in the ward, and it took her a while to focus on him. Even longer for her to speak. He'd hoped for a smile, but was rewarded only with a frown. Her voice, when it finally came, was cracked and dry. The words as terrible as they were inevitable.

'Who are you?'

4

'We've got sixteen girls who between them seem to speak about eight words of English, a Dutch captain screaming blue murder, Leith Ports chewing my ear off about a freighter that was meant to leave at dawn, and you go running off just because of a phone call. Jesus Christ, Tony. No bloody wonder Dagwood wanted shot of you. Five hours you've been gone. What took so bloody long?'

Jo Dexter stood in the middle of the main room housing the Sexual Crimes Unit, arms folded across her front. She looked as if she'd been waiting for McLean to come home, like an errant child. Any moment now she was going to start tapping her foot.

'It's Emma. She's woken up. I had to be there. Sorry.'

'Shit. There you go again. I can't even give you a proper bollocking, can I?' The DCI slumped back against an unused desk, dropped her hands to her sides. The room was almost empty, just a couple of PCs on the back shift manning the hotline phones and pretending they weren't playing Words with Friends on the vice squad special computers; the ones that weren't blocked from the worst of the internet. 'How is she?'

'It's . . . complicated.' McLean pictured the scene in his mind. That face he had watched for almost two months now, suddenly come back to life only to be covered with confusion and fear. 'She doesn't remember anything. Well, apart from her name.'

'You need time?' McLean could see that Dexter really didn't want him to say yes. Like everyone else, they were permanently short-staffed. That was why he was here, after all.

'No. She's going to be in the hospital a while yet. Think I'd rather throw myself into the job right now. Otherwise I'm just going to fret.'

'Fine. Well, you and DS Buchanan can make a start on processing these girls then. We can't keep them in the cells much longer. Immigration'll be here soon, and I'd like to find out who put them on that ship before they get here.'

'Why were they taking you onto that boat? Where were you going?'

McLean sat at the table in interview room one, the nice one where they put people who were 'helping the police with their enquiries' rather than the more skanky holes where the low-lifes were questioned. Opposite him, the young woman stared at her hands, folded in her lap. Her long blonde hair had a natural curl to it that was almost hidden by the layers of grease and grime. Her face was thinner than a supermodel's, sharp cheek bones poking out through skin the colour of curdled milk. Her eyes were sunken pits, the traces of bruising yellowing them like some weird attempt at alternative make-up. He was fairly sure she understood everything he was saying, but like all her companions from the van, she was playing the silent act.

'Were you trying to get home, was that it?'

She looked up at him then, fixed him with a stare from her grey-blue eyes that left no doubt as to just how much of an idiot she thought him. Still she didn't speak, scratching at the inside of her left elbow with the long fingernails of her right hand. The track marks were easy to see, but old.

'Look, I know you speak English. I know you've been working as a prostitute somewhere in the city. I know that probably wasn't your idea. You thought you were coming here to get a job cleaning, or maybe working in an office. But the men who brought you here had other ideas, didn't they.'

Alongside him, Detective Sergeant Buchanan shifted in his seat impatiently. McLean tried to suppress a grimace, but something must have shown on his face. The girl looked straight at him, flicked her eyes across to the other detective and back again, then raised both eyebrows. It was the briefest of interactions, but it was the most he'd got out of any of them so far. Eight down, seven still to go.

'You couldn't get us some coffee could you, Sergeant?' McLean voiced it as a question but even the dumbest of officers should have realized that it was a command. Buchanan opened his mouth as if to say something, then closed it again with an echoing pop. He dragged his chair backwards as he stood, the noise setting McLean's teeth on edge. Ambled slowly to the door and paused before opening it.

'Black, no sugar for me.' McLean tried not to flick his head in a gesture of dismissal, but he might have failed a little.

Buchanan left the door open. Whether on purpose or because he lacked the basic motor skills to close it, McLean didn't want to guess. He got up, closed it, and sat back down again. The young woman said nothing, but her eyes followed him all the time. Only when he was back in his seat did she finally speak.

'You're not like the others. I've not seen you before.'

Her voice surprised him. He had assumed she was from Eastern Europe, but she spoke with a Midlands accent.

'I'm on secondment. Filling in while they decide who gets to be promoted.'

'You must have fucked up pretty badly to get sent here. What did you do?'

What did I do? My job. Only it was bloody Dagwood who got made up to acting superintendent when we broke open that cannabis operation, and he didn't want anyone around pissing on his chips. McLean kept silent, studied the young woman's face for a moment, trying to see past the Slavic features that had made him jump to such an erroneous conclusion earlier on.

'The other girls. They from England too?'

'Nah. Most of em's Poles, Romanians, think I might've heard some Russian spoke too. Don't really know them that well. We only got picked up a couple days ago.'

'Picked up?'

'There an echo in here?' The young woman pushed back her greasy hair, scratched at the side of her nose, sniffed. For an awful moment McLean thought she was going to spit on the floor, but she swallowed instead. He wasn't sure which was worse.

'There were sixteen of you in that van, being loaded onto a ship bound for Rotterdam. Normally we have to deal with people coming the other way. I'm curious as to why you were being trafficked out of the country.'

'You not even going to ask my name?'

'Would you tell it me if I did?'

'It's Magda. And yeah, I know that's Polish. My grampa came over in the war and never went back.'

'So what's the score then, Magda? Why were you being sent overseas?'

'Cos I speak Polish, probably. Cos of the way I look. Mebbe they thought I was like all the others. Mebbe I tried to tell them and got a smack in the face for my trouble. Mebbe they didn't care who I was. Long as they get the numbers.'

'Numbers for what, though? Where were they taking you?'

Magda gave him an odd, quizzical look, as if she couldn't quite believe what she was hearing.

'You know I'm a whore, don't you? You know what that is, y'know, apart from the whole sex for cash thing?'

McLean didn't answer. He wasn't quite sure he could.

'Means I'm a piece of meat, dunnit. Owned and traded. I get passed from one pimp to the next and I don't get any say in that. Who'm I gonna complain to anyway, the filth? Ha, that's a laugh. You lot either don't give a fuck or just want a free one. I got no rights, no protection. Just a habit needs feeding and only one way to feed it. So when Malky says I'm going with Ivan now, I don't argue. Cos what's the fucking point, eh?'

'You don't know where they were taking you.'

'Top marks for the inspector.' Magda clapped her hands together in mock applause. For a moment something like the ghost of a smile spread across her face, and then the door clicked open. DS Buchanan appeared, arse first, carrying two mugs of coffee. By the time he'd turned around and placed the mugs on the table, Magda's face was blank, eyes down, staring at the hands folded in her lap, fingers worrying at the scars of track marks on her inner arms. It was almost as if the whole conversation had been no more than a dream.

'Thanks. Not having one yourself?' McLean picked up the mug with black coffee in it, nudging the other one carefully across the table to Magda. Buchanan opened his mouth, looked at the two mugs, then shut it again. He pulled out his chair and sat down heavily.

'You don't know where they were taking you.' McLean tried to pick up the threads of the conversation, even though he knew he was in for a struggle. 'But you know who took you. Who's Malky, Magda? Who's Ivan?'

Buchanan looked sideways at McLean as he spoke the young woman's name, a quizzical eyebrow raised. McLean wondered if he could find some other way to send the sergeant away. He was clearly not helping.

'Malky'd be Malky Jennings. Typical lowlife scumbag runs a dozen hookers out of Restalrig.'

Maybe helping a bit. 'Go on,' McLean said.

'He's small beer. We usually let him get away with a caution if he pushes too far. Known quantity, if you get my meaning. We lock him up and who knows what'll float up to take his place. He has his uses.' Meaning he was someone's informant. Or supplier.

'And Ivan?' McLean directed his question at Buchanan, but looked at Magda. He couldn't catch her eye though; she was finding her lap increasingly fascinating, those marks on her inner arm more itchy by the minute.

'Ivan, I haven't a fucking clue.'

'Magda, who's Ivan?' McLean let the question hang in the silence that followed, just watching the young woman across the table. She kept her gaze down for long seconds, the only sound the scrit, scrit, scrit of her fingernails on the flesh of her inner arm. She'd be breaking through soon, adding to the scars already there. Perhaps finally realizing what she was doing, she stopped, raised her head and fixed him with a stare through her lank blonde ringlets. There was something more than anger and defiance in that stare. There was fear. And then the quickest of flicks across to the detective sergeant and back. Then she dropped her head and said no more.

'Tell me about Malky Jennings.'

McLean leaned against the wall by the whiteboard in the SCU main office, looking out over a cluster of empty desks. The blinds were drawn on the windows at the far side of the room, slants of sunlight painting stripes onto the grubby carpet tiles. This wasn't a place people generally liked to spend much time in; you never knew what new degradation or atrocity was going to appear next.

'Not much to tell, really. Scumbag just about sums it up.' DS Buchanan lounged in the one good chair in the office, feet up on his desk. Observing the small team at the SCU in the few days since he'd arrived, McLean recognized the Alpha Dog, or, perhaps more accurately, the frustrated Beta Dog, lording it over the junior ranks but never quite having the nerve to challenge for the top spot. He was an old-school copper, which in the case of Grumpy Bob was a good thing; less so with Buchanan. Where DS Laird affected an air of laziness but got the work done, Buchanan was the kind of policeman who always seemed busy, but was actually doing bugger all.

'We got a file on him?'

'Should have.' Buchanan made a show of taking his feet off the desk, pulled his keyboard towards him and started tapping away. McLean pushed himself off the wall and came around to see what appeared on the screen.

'Malcolm Jeffrey Jennings.' Buchanan poked a greasy finger at the glass. 'Thirty-six years old. Lives in one of the tower blocks down Lochend way. He's got form for drugs, but strictly small time. Mostly he runs prostitutes in that area. Nasty little shit. Violent, but he's bright enough not to hit them in the face. Prefers a baseball bat to the ribs, way I hear it.'

McLean peered at the image on the screen. A thin, ratty-faced man peered back. Narrow, long nose, broken sometime long ago. Hair in lank, greasy straggles down to his shoulders. Eyes set just that little bit too close together, giving his face a permanent angry frown. Deep bags under them suggesting some form of habit, barely under control.

'And we tolerate this why?'

Buchanan sighed, clicked the cursor on a series of thumbnail images taken by a surveillance team. The first showed Malky Jennings walking along a street with a woman beside him. McLean hadn't noticed in the mug shot, but Jennings liked to dress flamboyantly. Not necessarily with any sense of style, but the purple velvet smoking jacket and ruff-necked shirt were certainly noticeable.

'Malky's a known quantity. We keep an eye on him, haul him in if he gets too far out of line. But there's no point locking him up. He's not the problem.'

McLean scanned the top of the list of convictions and cautions. 'He looks like a big problem to me.'

Buchanan snorted. 'You're new here, so you wouldn't understand.'

'No, I don't. Explain it to me.'

'OK then.' Buchanan put on his best school teacher voice. 'Malky Jennings is a scumbag, but one whose behaviour we can predict, possibly even control to a certain extent. Lock him up and someone else moves in on the territory. Someone we don't know anything about, maybe. Someone trying to make a name for themselves, establish their place. That means violence and disruption, and that makes the Chief Constable unhappy. So we leave Malky Jennings well alone.'

'Lesser of two evils.' McLean understood the concept, but that didn't mean he had to like it.

'Now you're getting it.'

'There's just one thing you seem to be missing though. This Russian fellow, Ivan or whatever. He's a new player, right?'

Buchanan nodded. 'Looks like it.'

'And he's taken a whole load of Malky's prostitutes, put them on a boat headed for the Continent and God knows where after that.'

Again with the nod. McLean could almost see the thoughts linking themselves together in Buchanan's head.

'So at the very least we need to talk to Jennings and see what's going on, wouldn't you think? Bring him in and let's make him sweat a bit. If we're giving him our tacit approval, then he can bloody well give us something back in return.'

5

'Is that a genuine weejy board? Christ, I thought those things went out in the seventies.'

She's not the prettiest girl he's ever met, but there's something about her he finds impossibly attractive. Maybe it's her hair, cut like his mum would have had it back when she was that age. Or perhaps it's her easy smile. Not a 'come and get me, boys' flash of the teeth, but a selfless sharing of genuine joy. She's always happy, and that's so rare. It's almost infectious, though it would take more than a winning smile to lighten his mood these days.

Of course, it helps that she's weird. Everyone loves weird.

The evening started well. Just a few of them out for a drink after work, winding down at the end of another shitty week. Some lucky bastard's leaving do, otherwise he'd not have bothered. He's not a big drinker – can't afford it – but there's a certain sad fun to be had watching the girls slowly lose control. He's not interested in exploiting their drunkenness for anything so tawdry as sex; that's not his style at all. What would be the point, anyway? He's still got to work with them, day in, day out. Most of them think he's gay, and he's never really bothered to correct them on that. It's not true, of course, but women seem to be far more comfortable around a gay man.

And then they'd met this strange, mad, intoxicating

woman. He wasn't really sure whose friend she was, or whether she'd simply attached herself to their party. She reminded him of someone, but he couldn't put his finger on the name. Every time he thought he'd got it, she'd caught him looking at her and flashed him a knowing smile. And every time he looked into her eyes it was as if his brain switched off and had to reboot.

Someone had suggested going to a club, but no one was keen. There were pubs that stayed open pretty much all night, but they'd had enough of pubs. Like him, she was on soft drinks anyway. He'd noticed that and she'd noticed that he'd noticed. They'd shared a smile then. And she'd suggested they all come back to her place.

Put like that it sounded corny. A come-on, but not a come-on. Not unless she was hoping to have an orgy with all five of them. That was his nervousness showing through, to think about sex at a time like that. Of course, sex was the furthest thing from her mind, this strange, intoxicating woman. She wanted something different from them. A séance.

'Automatic writing has been a favourite of mediums for thousands of years.' She lays the board out on the table, places the planchette in the centre. He can't help noticing that this isn't an ancient artefact. The wood is shiny with varnish, not age, and the letters are clearly machine-stencilled. The company logo 'Hasbro' in tiny letters in one corner is a bit of a giveaway.

'It's not the board, silly. It's what's going on in your head.' She smiles again, slaps him gently on the arm. That's something else he's noticed about her. She likes to touch. A light brushing of the fingers here, a firm hand

26

on the arm there. It's almost as if she doesn't know she's doing it. He doesn't think the others have noticed, anyway. But then they're all half cut, tucking into the bottle of wine she found in the cupboard under the sink in her kitchen.

'OK then. What are we meant to do?'

'First we all need to sit in a circle and hold hands. Here.' She holds out her left hand to him, fixes him with a stare that can't be denied. Before he knows it, he's in her grip, with Mandy from Accounts on his other side. The others all join together too, without any of the joking and complaints he would have expected. An expectant hush falls on the gathering.

'Spirits from the other side, hear our call. We have questions and seek your wisdom.'

Is it his imagination, or is the room just that little bit colder? And were the corners of the room always so dark and shadowy? Did they always move like that?

'Come to us, spirits. Answer our call. Is there anybody out there?'

The planchette, shaped like a tiny wooden heart with a hole hacked through the middle of it, moves slowly across the board. Scrape, scrape, scrape of wood against wood as it inches towards the circle marked 'Yes'. He stares at it for long moments before realizing that none of them are touching it. He looks sideways at her, unable to break the bond that links them all together in their circle. For the first time since he was a wee boy waking in the darkness of the middle of the night, he feels genuine fear. She is hunched over, her eyes squeezed tight shut, her lips moving as if she is speaking some silent language. It's impossible to shake the feeling that there is something in the room with them. Some*one*.

Too late, he realizes that there is. Looming out of the shadows on the far side of the circle. Only there is no circle now, no weird, happy, smiley girl. No Ouija board. Just him and a face with eyes of fire. A devil's grin splits in two, all teeth and sharp, pointed tongue, lips as red as fresh-spilled blood. It speaks a voice from far away and long ago. A voice that opens up the darkest depths of his soul, lays bare his hopelessness and despair.

'You are mine.'

6

Against all the odds, there was a parking space just a few yards away from the front door to Emma's tenement. McLean had picked her up from the hospital earlier; with her mother in a care home in Aberdeen, there was no one else to do it, and he couldn't face the thought of her taking a taxi. Given the way she'd looked out the window all the way across town, it was probably just as well. He was reminded of a small child on her first visit to the big city. Eyes wide at each new wonder, mouth hanging ever-so-slightly open.

'Is this it?' she asked as he parked the car and killed the engine. No spark of recognition at all.

'Yup. This is it. You've been renting it since you came down from Aberdeen about eighteen months ago, remember?'

She looked along the street, eyes gliding over her own front door as if it meant no more to her than any other. 'Nope.'

'Well, let's go inside. See if you recognize your stuff.'

Emma had been skinny to start with, but two months on a drip had left her skeletally thin, and weak with it. The hospital had tried their best since she'd woken; regular physiotherapy sessions and the stodgiest food McLean had seen since his school days, but still she moved like someone twice her age. He had to suppress the urge to put his arm out and help her. That, he had already learnt, just pissed her off. Some things were still the same about her, he was pleased to see.

'This one.' He pointed at the door she was about to walk past. 'Here.'

He dug the keys out of his jacket pocket and handed them over. The little plastic gnome hung from the key ring, its hair a bright pink shock of colour. She looked at it with the same intense fascination she'd shown on the journey over, but showed no interest in the keys.

'This is mine?'

McLean nodded.

'I have no recollection of it at all. Did I buy it? Did someone give it to me? Did you give it to me?' With this last question Emma stared at his face, examining his features in a way that McLean found deeply disturbing. It was a look he knew well. One he had used in many an interrogation over the years. She even left the silence hanging, waiting for him to fill it and condemn himself with the answer.

'Not guilty, your honour.' He held up his hands in denial. 'Are you going in or not?'

Emma frowned in confusion for a moment, then seemed to notice the bunch of keys hanging from the fascinating key ring. 'Oh. Right.' Pause. 'Umm. Which one is it?'

It had been like this for almost three weeks now. Doctor Wheeler felt that Emma was improving all the time, but McLean couldn't see it. Yes, there were occasional flashes of the old Em, but mostly there was this uncomfortable, awkward person who didn't seem to know much about anything at all. She had latched on to him with such an intensity that at first he'd thought it was something of their relationship coming back. But as the days had passed and he'd done all he could to help her recuperate, so he'd begun to suspect that she clung to him because his was the first face she'd seen on waking. Even now there were times when he caught her staring at him with something closer to fear than anything else. She didn't treat him like an equal, didn't act like an adult. It was almost as if the blow to her head had regressed her to a child.

'Here, let me.' He reached for the keys. She shrunk away from him, just a little, then realized what she was doing and checked herself. Almost reluctantly she handed over the key ring, fingers clinging to the little gnome as he pulled it away. He selected the right key, slid it in the lock and opened the door.

Inside was dark. What little light that could make it through the grimy window halfway up the stairs was swallowed up by a large, dead pot plant on the windowsill. McLean had been here a couple of times a week since Emma had been taken to hospital, checking her mail and making sure the flat was OK. In all that time he'd never seen the plant watered and only now it occurred to him that this might be because it was hers. She paused on the stairs as they passed it, feeling a leafy frond between bony fingers. For a moment he thought it might be sparking a memory, but she just shook her head and moved on.

She didn't recognize her front door, and when he pushed it open to let her into the apartment, she hesitated on the threshold, peering in as if expecting monsters. McLean stepped inside and reluctantly Emma followed. If this was meant to start the process of bringing back her memories, as the good doctor had suggested, then it didn't seem to be working.

'I'll make some tea.' He left her standing in the hallway. 'Why don't you have a look around. I've done my best to keep the place clean and tidy.'

'You said I rented this place.' Emma had followed him into the tiny kitchen and now stood close as he filled the kettle. 'Who's been paying the rent whilst I was . . . you know?'

'Don't worry. It was all taken care of.'

'I must owe you a lot of money.'

The assumption that he'd paid for it all was correct, but it surprised him she'd made it nonetheless. Technically she was on sick pay and there were damages due for being injured in the line of duty. Either the Scenes Examination Branch or the police should have been picking up the tab, but in the end he'd just taken it on himself. It was much easier than waiting for the internal bureaucracy to run its course, and it wasn't as if he couldn't afford it.

'It's not a problem. You've got to get better first.' The kettle popped off, steam billowing out into the frigid air. The whole apartment was cold, now he thought about it. Tucked down in a narrow street, away from the sun. Perhaps he should have had the heating on.

'I knew there was something I should have got. Milk.' McLean opened the fridge in the hope that magic pixies might have put some there, but they were on holiday this week. 'You mind your tea black?'

'Not much of a tea drinker, really.' Emma stepped back into the hall, pulled open the bathroom door and peered in. 'So this is where I live, then?'

'Yup.'

'What about you?' She closed the door, turned to face him with a stare that was almost the old Emma. Almost, but not quite. 'You live here too?'

McLean felt a reddening about his ears and wasn't quite sure why. 'No. I live over the other side of town.'

'But you and me. We were . . .'

'Yes. Not for long, but . . . Yes.'

'That's so weird.' She opened the bedroom door, paused a moment and then darted in, grabbed the stuffed animal toy off the bed, hugged it to herself. 'Potamus! I remember him. Mum bought him for me when I was eight. Christ, that feels like it was just a couple of years ago.'

She kept the stuffed hippo with her as they moved into the living room. The largest room in the apartment, it was filled with mementos, books, photographs. As far as McLean was aware, even the furniture had moved down from Aberdeen with her, so if anything was going to jog her memory, this should. Emma stood in the middle of the room, looking slowly around. Then she noticed the low bookshelf by the window, its top lined with photos in frames. She picked one up, showing herself and a bunch of young women McLean didn't recognize, peered at it, shook her head and set it back down again. The same routine went for all the others until finally she got to the one of her mother.

Grey-haired and frail, the old lady slumped in a high-backed armchair that looked too big for her. She wasn't smiling, wasn't even looking at the camera properly. Something in her eyes had died long before the photograph was taken. McLean only recognized her because he'd travelled up to Aberdeen to introduce himself, try somehow to explain to Mrs Baird what had happened to her daughter and assure her that he'd do everything in his power to speed her recovery. What he had found had been a husk, a 65-year-old body with no mind. Emma had told him her mother was in a care home; what she'd failed to mention was the severity of her dementia.

'This looks like my gran, only different.' Emma placed the photograph back down on the bookshelf, one finger caressing the glass as she slowly turned away. 'It's my mum, isn't it?'

'She's had Alzheimer's for seven years. She's getting the best care possible.'

'Why don't I remember any of this? The last thing I remember about Mum is talking to her about going to college. I was seventeen. I don't even know how old I am now.'

'Do you really want me to tell you?'

Emma walked across to the mantelpiece and stared at her reflection in the mirror hanging over it. 'No. It'll just depress me. Why can't I remember?'

'It'll come back. Give it time. Doctor Wheeler said . . .'

'I know what Doctor Wheeler said. But she doesn't have to live with it, does she?' Emma swept one arm around in an arc encompassing the room. 'She doesn't have to live in a place filled with stuff I don't remember buying. Or worse, photographs of people twenty years older than I remember them.'

'You want to go somewhere else? I've got a spare room. You're more than welcome.' The words tumbled out before he'd really considered them. It sounded almost like he was asking her to move in with him. The thought filled him with conflicting feelings; hope and despair. And guilt. There was always guilt.

Emma took one more slow look at the living room, eyes finally settling on him with a desperate stare. 'Please.'

It took almost an hour to get across town, fighting the traffic chaos caused by the construction work for the trams. By the time the car crunched over the gravel and came to a halt at the back door, the afternoon was almost gone. McLean was grateful that Jo Dexter had given him the time off, but sooner or later someone was going to phone him and drag him back to the station.

'Just the one spare room?' Emma asked as they walked towards the house. She seemed more relaxed here somehow. Perhaps it was easier being somewhere she wasn't expected to recognize anything. McLean was searching for a suitable reply as he opened the door, but something large and furry trotted out, twining itself around Emma's legs, tail high and purring like a badly tuned engine. He felt a moment's irrational jealousy. Mrs McCutcheon's cat had never shown him that kind of affection.

Emma bent down, stroked the cat. It nudged her hand, rubbing the side of its head on her arm, tail quivering with pleasure at meeting an old friend. She picked it up and it started to nuzzle at her face. And then McLean saw tears in the corners of her eyes.

'There was a fire. Everyone was killed. Only the cat survived.' She turned to face him. 'The cat and you.'

'There you go. Extra towels in the airing cupboard. I'm not sure how comfortable the bed is, but the sheets are clean.'

McLean stood just inside the guest bedroom, pointed at the door across the way that led to the en-suite bathroom. Emma sat on the end of a king-size bed looking as pale as the white sheets as she stared around the room. It was one of five spare bedrooms in the house, not counting McLean's own room and his grandmother's. Or the old box-rooms up in the roof where in times past the servants would have slept. Not for the first time he wondered why he kept the place. It was way too big for him.

'It's very nice. Thank you.' Emma fiddled with the strap on her bag. Awkward. Beside her, Mrs McCutcheon's cat had leapt onto the bed and was pawing at the bedding, purring as it nuzzled her free hand.

'I'm just across the landing. Shout if you need anything. I'll leave the light on.' McLean cringed at his words, treating her like a child. But in some ways that's what she was. Scared, alone, unsure of anything. He couldn't begin to imagine what was going through her mind. Only that she didn't seem to remember much that had happened since she had turned sixteen.

'Tony?'

He turned in the doorway as he was about to leave. Emma pushed the cat aside, stood up.

'We had something, didn't we?'

An image in his head, unbidden. Lying on a cold bed, staring up at the ceiling. Rolling over to see spiky black hair poking up out of the top of the hogged duvet. A hand reaching out, touching his side. Warmth as the duvet and the body it contains envelope him.

'Yes. We did.'

Another image. Older. A body lies in the dark, cold

36

water, naked and splayed out. Long dark hair tugged by the current into a fan like seaweed. A loss as deep and wide and cruel as the gaping cut across her neck.

'You're a kind man.' Emma was suddenly very close, her hand touching his, those dark eyes staring straight at him. He saw her face properly for the first time in months. Those eyes sunken in their sockets like a junkie three days into Cold Turkey. Her cheekbones pushed up through grey skin as if trying to escape something terrible inside. And her hair, once spiky with a life of its own, now hung lank around her scalp, streaks of white mixed in with the black. But she was still Emma. There was a spark in her he recognized. Damaged, flickering, but there.

She reached up, lightly touched the side of his face, stood on tiptoes as she leaned forward to kiss him. And then she stopped, just inches away. A shudder ran through her, she dropped her head into her hands, started to shake. McLean went to touch her, but something stopped his hand before he made contact.

'You'll be OK.' He tried to make the words as soft and reassuring as possible, but she still flinched at them, as if he'd slapped her. Mrs McCutcheon's cat jumped down off the bed, scowled at McLean in a way that only cats can, and started to weave itself in and out of Emma's legs until she bent down, stroked it, picked it up. The two of them stared at him until he felt uncomfortable. It didn't take long.

'If you need anything, just ask.' He stepped backwards out of the room, leaving Emma to close the door behind him. Time, that was what Doctor Wheeler had said was needed. Time and stability. Well, he'd try to give her both, but in the morning he was going to have to start looking for help.

Something woke him in the dead of night. One moment McLean was asleep, the next he was fully awake, staring up at the darkness and the shapes of his fading dream. He strained his ears, searching for the sound that had woken him. A cat yowling outside perhaps, or a car horn in the distance. He glanced over at the bedside table. 3.14 a.m., according to the red glow of the alarm clock. At the same time as he registered the meaning of the numbers, he heard the lightest of creaks, a floorboard outside his bedroom. And then the door latch clicked.

There was no light from the landing, just the feeling of air displaced. Soft footfalls on the threadbare carpet and then a body pulled back his duvet, clambered into bed beside him. Emma smelled at once familiar and deeply different. There was an antiseptic quality to her, as if after spending months in hospital her skin had absorbed the aroma completely. The arm that reached across his chest was stick-thin and bony. She pulled herself tight to his side, nestled her head against his shoulder, shivered slightly in her heavy cotton pyjamas. After a couple of moments, she started to mutter under her breath. He couldn't make out the words, but she sounded scared.

McLean lay perfectly still, unsure quite what to do. There was nothing sexual in Emma's behaviour, not like her earlier awkward advance. This was more like a child climbing into bed with a parent because something in the darkness has terrified it. He tilted his head gently, tried to listen to her voice. It sounded different, almost foreign. In the dull glow of the alarm clock he could see that her eyes were tight shut. After a while, the words drifted away to silence, her breathing slowed and she relaxed into proper sleep. How long was it since he'd bade her good night? How long had she lain alone and frightened in a strange room? And how the hell was he going to get any sleep himself with her lying there? And yet he didn't dare move, couldn't bring himself to disturb her.

A flicker in the darkness, shadow upon silent shadow. His eyes darted to the dresser, sitting in front of the window. A different kind of black filtered in from outside, tinged with a distant orange glow of the night-time city. In its diffraction he saw an outline, the unmistakable shape of Mrs McCutcheon's cat. There was no way he could see in the gloom, but he knew it was watching him.

Watching them both.

7

It had to come sooner or later, that much McLean knew. He wasn't a betting man, but it was going to be either Ritchie or MacBride. Grumpy Bob could cope with pretty much anything Dagwood threw at him, and the newly promoted Acting Superintendent Duguid still had some small respect for Bob Laird. Either that or fear; Grumpy Bob knew where a surprising number of bodies were buried.

Bad enough Dagwood being in charge of CID, but until the Powers That Be decided how Scotland's new Single Police Service was going to work, he was running the whole station – uniform, plain clothes and civilian staff. If he'd been insufferable before, it was as nothing compared to him now. Dagwood had always been of the 'management by bullying' school, and with no one to keep him in check, morale was taking a battering.

In a way, Dagwood had done him a favour sending him over to the SCU, although McLean knew damned well that had never been his intention. It meant that he didn't have to deal directly with the man on a daily basis, although there was still a mountain of paperwork to get through. For some reason he couldn't quite fathom, he seemed to be in charge of the overtime rosters for half a dozen investigative teams, even though he wasn't actually running any of their investigations himself. Dagwood had made it quite clear early on in his tenure that he didn't trust McLean to run a sweepstake, let alone something as complex as a murder enquiry. Hence he had been placed under the watchful eye of DCI Dexter. Which was why he was currently sorting through sixteen sets of interviews, none of which yielded any useful information. DS Buchanan was supposed to be following up the lead on Malky the pimp, but so far he seemed to have gone to ground. The phone was a welcome distraction.

'McLean.'

'Umm. Sir. Sorry to call you. Didn't really know who else I could ask.'

So Detective Constable MacBride had been the first to break.

'What's the problem?' McLean set aside his report and leaned back in his chair.

'I'm looking into a suicide. Apartment down in Trinity. Bloke hung himself.'

'Hanged.'

'What?'

'Hanged, Constable. A picture is hung, a man is hanged. Who's the senior officer in charge?'

'Erm, that'd be me, sir.'

Bloody brilliant. True enough MacBride was a competent detective, but he was just a constable, and not long in plain clothes either. If there was a dead body, there should have been a detective inspector involved at the very least.

'Where's Ritchie?'

'Dag– . . . Err . . . Acting Superintendent Duguid's got her organizing the door-to-doors on the missing school-girl search.'

Which should have been uniform's gig.

'OK. What's the problem with this suicide then?' McLean rubbed his face and stifled a sigh. Looked at the reports in front of him, the mound of papers teetering over the edge of his in-tray. 'No, forget that, Stuart. Give me the address and I'll come have a look for myself.'

The posh bit might have been home to Edinburgh's judges and lawyers, but time was you wouldn't have dared walk through the back end of Trinity in uniform on your own. Even a pair of beat officers might find themselves in a sticky situation if the locals were in the mood for a fight. Parts of it were still bad, but the money pouring into Leith had begun to filter out sideways now, spreading middle-class civility like spilled extra-virgin olive oil as it went. Nowadays the violence stayed behind closed doors, more often emotional rather than physical though there was plenty of that too.

The address was for a small development just off the Ferry Road. McLean couldn't really tell what the building had been before it had been gutted and turned into flats, only that it had never been intended for habitation. Whoever had done the work had been looking to maximize profits though; the individual apartments were tiny.

An ambulance blocked the entrance to the parking bays behind the building, so McLean left his car on a double yellow line behind a familiar mud-and-British-Racing-Green Jaguar with a 'Doctor on Call' sticker shoved in the windscreen. A pair of bored-looking paramedics were loafing around at the bottom of a set of stone stairs leading up to the first floor of the old building. They nodded at McLean as he passed, either recognizing him or not caring if anyone approached what might be a crime scene. At the top of the stairs, a uniform PC guarded the door with almost as much professionalism. She struggled to attention as she saw him.

'Inspector. Sir. I'm sorry. No one told me. I thought . . .'

'Don't worry. I'm not really here.' He stopped, looked around. Saw no battered white Transit van. 'And neither's SEB by the look of things.'

'They're on their way, sir.'

'What's the situation, then? Who found the body?'

'I'm not sure, sir. You should probably see DC Mac-Bride. He's inside with the pathologist.'

'Body's still here, I take it.' McLean nodded at the paramedics, didn't wait for an answer.

The door opened onto a narrow hall. Little more than a corridor with delusions of grandeur. There appeared to be four apartments shoe-horned into this tiny space, but only one had a gaggle of people clustered around its open doorway. McLean recognized Tracy Sharp, assistant to the city pathologist, Angus Cadwallader. No doubt the man himself was inside.

'Is it safe to go in?' McLean stopped at the door, peered through. Doctor Sharp might have been wearing a white coverall, but the assembled constables were in uniform. No latex gloves, no over-boots.

'Don't think you could contaminate the scene any more than it's already been, Tony. Come on in.' Angus Cadwallader stood in the middle of a small, open-plan apartment. There wasn't much in the way of furniture, just a futon, a couple of bookshelves and a desk shoved into one corner.

The chair that should have gone with the desk lay on its side in the middle of the floor alongside a small table. Above it, the old roof was opened up, exposing sarking board, purlins, joists and beams. A stout rope had been slung over one of these, its other end wrapped in a professional-looking noose around the neck of a naked and very dead young man.

Death had not been kind to him. His eyes bulged, and a swollen blue tongue poked out between his lips, shiny crinkles of saliva running off it down his chin and onto his chest as if slugs had been crawling over him. The shock of the hanging had loosened his bowels and made a nasty mess of the threadbare rug that covered the polished floorboards.

'So, a suicide then.' McLean wrinkled his nose as he got closer.

'Certainly looks that way,' Cadwallader said. 'No sign of a struggle, no obvious marks to suggest he was forced. His hands aren't tied.'

McLean peered closer, and sure enough the young man's hands hung loosely by his side.

'Was there a note?'

'On his computer.' This from DC MacBride, who was hunched over the desk. He was wearing latex gloves, McLean noticed.

The computer was a small laptop, tethered to the desk by an external keyboard and mouse. The desk itself was as far removed from McLean's own as to hardly warrant the same name. It was tiny, like everything else in the apartment, and it was as tidy as a cleaners' convention. There were no papers strewn across it, no piles

44

of reports in the in-tray awaiting attention. No in-tray for that matter. Just a clear expanse of fake wood. He pulled a pair of latex gloves from his pocket, squeezed his hands into them and slid open the top, narrow drawer.

'I had a look already,' MacBride said. 'There's not much to see.'

It was true. The drawer held pens, neatly lined up and sorted into colours. A pair of small scissors, a stapler, a ruler. Nothing out of the ordinary. The drawer below yielded a lined A4 writing pad and some envelopes. The bottom drawer held a hole punch and a couple of power adaptors for mobile phones, the cords neatly tied as if they'd never been used.

'What about this message then?' A screensaver image looped and twirled mesmerically about the screen until MacBride nudged the mouse. The image steadied to a word processor, a few words typed out, the cursor blinking as it waited for more.

Ive had enough. There's no reasen too go on. The world hates me well it can do without me now. To whoever finds me, Im sorry. Good bye.

'That it?'

'That's all there was when I got here.'

'We know who he is?' McLean looked back at the naked man.

'Neighbour says he's Grigori Mikhailevic. Doesn't know him well.'

'That who found the body?'

'Aye. Door was open as she walked past. Says she didn't come in, and I'm inclined to believe her.'

'Where's she now?'

'Back in her flat. PC Gregg's with her.'

Sandy Gregg. Poor woman. Well, at least she wouldn't have to do any talking. McLean looked around the apartment. It wasn't just the desk that was tidy; everything had a place and everything was in its place. What little furniture there was sat square, aligned with the walls. Even the table upon which the chair had been balanced was centred neatly. Perhaps that was a necessary adaptation to living somewhere so small, but he'd seen places smaller still where chaos had been allowed to reign. No, this was the apartment of a tidy man. Meticulously tidy. Anally retentive, as the Freudians would have it. And there he was, hanging from a stout hemp rope slung over his own beam.

'We're done here, if you want to cut him down.' Cadwallader straightened up from his crouch with an audible popping of bones.

'Your crime scene, Constable. I'm not here, remember.' McLean nodded at MacBride.

'Oh. Right. Yes. Carry on, Doctor Cadwallader.'

'Any more thoughts, Angus?' McLean asked.

'Well, if it wasn't suicide it was a very good fake. If I had to put money on it now, I'd say he killed himself. I'll run blood tests in case he's been given something to make him compliant, check one or two other things at the PM. But I'm not seeing any evidence of foul play here.'

'But you think there's something fishy.' McLean turned to DC MacBride.

'It's hard to put my finger on it, sir, but there's something not right. I'd like to look into it some more, but you know what Duguid's like. He'll want this written up and forgotten by the end of the day.'

'We wouldn't want you going out and finding new crimes to investigate. Just think what that would do to the statistics. Let alone the budget.'

'I don't know, sir. It's just . . .'

'I think you're right, there's something hooky here. This is a man who arranges his pens by colour and lines things up so they're nice and square. There's no mess in here at all, no clutter. That sort of person doesn't hang himself, it's too prone to things going wrong. That sort of mind isn't normally suicidal at all. More likely to be homicidal, especially if the neighbours don't put their recycling in the right bin.'

'So you think I should keep looking?'

McLean watched as the two paramedics manhandled the body onto the stretcher they had wheeled in, careful to avoid the mess on the rug.

'Yes. And I'd start with that laptop. The note's a joke. It's impersonal, could've been written by anyone. And it's riddled with typos and spelling mistakes. I'll bet you a purple beer token there's not a single error in any of the other documents on there.'

8

The door to Chief Superintendent McIntyre's office was closed; that was the first thing that McLean noticed. For three years it had stood ajar, no barrier between the chief and those who worked under her. Janice's desk now stood unattended and cleared of anything that might be deemed personal. Jayne McIntyre's open-door policy had been one of the few positive things about the station, but now she had moved to better things, or at least he hoped so. Anything to do with the setting up of the new Police Service of Scotland was a double-edged sword. McLean couldn't begrudge her the chance to progress up the greasy pole, but there was part of him that wished she was still here, or at least that the person who'd been promoted to fill her shoes was less red-faced, balding and generally useless.

Taking a moment to compose himself, he knocked quietly on the door, waited for the gruff 'enter' and then did as he was bid.

Acting Superintendent Charles Duguid had taken no time to impose his own lack of style on McIntyre's office. The casual area, with its bookshelves, coffee machine and curiously uncomfortable armchairs, was gone, replaced by a wall of whiteboards and a long conference table. The pictures on the wall were gone too, presumably to Tulliallan. Neutral ground for the new HQ so that no one region could dominate. As if that wasn't going to happen anyway. Duguid hadn't bothered to replace them yet, no doubt finding comfort in the discoloured patches they had left on the walls. The desk itself was the same one McIntyre had used, but where under her tenure it had usually been heaped with papers, reports and other signs of busy-ness, now it was almost clear. And behind it, scowling at McLean as he finished his telephone conversation, the man of the hour.

'What is it, McLean?' Duguid made no effort to hide the impatience in his voice.

'You wanted to see me, sir. The duty sergeant –'

'That was hours ago. Where the hell have you been?'

McLean suppressed the urge to look at his watch. He was fairly sure Sergeant Dundas wouldn't have sat on the message for more than a few minutes, and he'd been in his office for the past two hours trying to make some sense of the overtime figures foisted on him by one of Duguid's own investigations.

'Well, you're here now, I suppose.' Duguid leaned back in his enormous leather chair. That was new, and expensive by the look of things. A pity he hadn't bothered to provide one on the other side of the desk. McLean stood with his hands behind his back, trying not to let his temper rise. That was, after all, exactly what Duguid wanted.

'I've been reviewing your cases since your promotion.' Duguid nodded towards a closed brown folder that was pretty much the only thing on his desk. There was nothing on the outside to indicate that it was what he said it was, and judging by its thinness, it was more likely a review of Duguid's own caseload, but McLean said nothing. He knew better than to provoke the beast this early in the conversation.

'Not much of a clear-up rate, is there. Not many arrests and convictions. When was the last time you gave evidence in court?'

'A couple of years ago. The Broughton Post Office raid.'

'You were still a sergeant then.' It wasn't a question. McLean resisted the temptation to add 'Detective.'

'So, since making inspector you've put how many criminals away?'

That depends on how you count, doesn't it? The drug bust that gave you your bloody promotion was effectively down to my lead, so you could say something of the order of two dozen awaiting trial just at the moment. And there's the small matter of the forensic photographer who was posting crime scene photos on the web. I caught him, but you took the credit for that one, even after you'd tried to pin it on someone else. McLean bit back the obvious retort.

'There's Christopher Roberts. He's in remand right now. The PF's finalizing the case.'

'Ah yes. Roberts. The unlikely child snatcher. He claims he was coerced, I understand. Put in an impossible position by a very powerful and influential man. A man who should have been arrested for murder, abduction and many other things. What happened to him, McLean?'

'As I understand it, sir, his bodyguard killed him. Poetic justice, I'd say.'

'Of course you would. And no doubt you'd say it was

poetic justice that the bodyguard died a week later in hospital. You were the last one to visit him before that, I'm told. And the doctors aren't really sure what killed him.'

Don't rise to it. Don't give him the satisfaction.

'If you're unhappy with my performance, sir –'

'Of course I'm bloody unhappy with your performance, McLean. Why do you think I asked you here?'

Because you're a prize arse who likes to bully people and I'm the only one who dares to stand up to you? 'I assumed it was to allocate me a new case, sir. I understand there's a gang of pickpockets have been working the festival. Organized, probably East European and tied into something larger. I know it's sergeant work, but then I don't really expect anything more complicated from you, sir.'

Duguid's already florid face reddened. 'With that attitude, McLean, it's hardly any surprise. You've no respect for authority, and every time you start investigating someone they end up dead.'

'With respect, sir –'

'Don't give me any of that shit. Gavin Spenser, dead. Alison Kydd, dead. Needy –' Duguid broke off. So that was it. Three months on and still the enmity. Forget the fact that Sergeant John Needham had abducted, raped and murdered three women, tried to kill a fourth. He was an old-school copper and they stood up for one another.

'Would it have been better if he'd gone to trial, sir? After what he did?'

'He'd have been found insane.'

'And that would have been OK, I suppose.'

'Dammit, McLean. You're just trouble wherever you

go. I don't know why McIntyre put up with you, but I'm sure as hell not going to.' Duguid picked up the folder, flipped it open. 'What were you doing over at that suicide case in Trinity?'

It took McLean a moment to process the change of direction. 'What?'

'The suicide. Chap hung himself. Why were you poking your nose in there when you're meant to be helping Jo Dexter out in Vice?'

'I wasn't "poking my nose" in anywhere, sir. DC Mac-Bride was appointed SIO. He's only a constable.'

'What of it? The way I hear, it was suicide, plain and simple. Even left a note. Doesn't take a detective inspector to fill out an incident report, does it?'

McLean suppressed the urge to sigh. It was like dealing with a particularly obstinate toddler. 'A person died in unnatural circumstances, sir. At the very least, the Fiscal will want a basic investigation. DC MacBride thought there was something unusual about the case. He called it in so he could get a second opinion. No doubt a sergeant would have done, but there weren't any available. I was going that way anyway, so I thought I'd drop in and see what he was on about. Turns out he was right.'

Duguid's eyes narrowed, a sure sign that he was trying to think. 'What do you mean, he was right?'

'There's a lot about the hanging that doesn't add up, sir. Enough to make me suspicious.'

'And we're going to pay for this hunch-following how, exactly?'

'I wouldn't call it a hunch, sir.'

'No, you wouldn't. But that's what it is. And we don't

have the budget to go digging where there's nothing to find. The PF doesn't want to waste money on lengthy enquiries either. If it looks like a duck and sounds like a duck, then it's a duck, McLean. Now get MacBride to write up the report and file it.'

McLean held his breath, just for a few seconds. Duguid stared at him from the other side of the desk, his face a mottle of crimson and white. There wasn't really much point arguing with the man when he was like this, and besides, he had somewhere else he needed to be.

'If you say so, sir.'

'I do. Now get out of here. Some of us have work to do.'

A hubbub of quiet noise filled the echoing hall of the sale room, the collected murmurs and whispers of over a hundred punters settled into ranks of chairs lined up to face a stage at the far end. A simple lectern stood to one side, a stand to the other presumably for books to be placed upon. Fortunately there was little mention of the man whose books were on sale, and no photographs. Perhaps it was the notoriety of the collection, or maybe antiquarian book sales were always like this. It was the first time he'd ever been to one, so McLean couldn't be sure. He wasn't even sure why he'd come at all.

The sale catalogue had plopped through his letterbox a month or so earlier. At first he'd thought it was some kind of cruel joke. Then he'd noticed that it had been addressed to his grandmother, not him. Yet another mailing list woefully out of date. Donald Anderson's shop on the Canongate had already been sold and was apparently going to become a trendy wine bar. Now it was the turn of his substantial collection of rare and ancient books. The money raised, so the introduction to the catalogue stated, was to go to the Sick Kids Hospital and the Zero Tolerance campaign. Such had been Anderson's last wishes, conveyed to his solicitors just the day before he died.

McLean hadn't read any more than that, consigning the catalogue to the bin in the corner of the kitchen where all the junk mail went to die. But something about it had stuck with him, and two days later he'd fished it out again. Every so often he'd find himself idly leafing through it as he drank tea at the old kitchen table, wondering what possible use he might have for an obscure sixteenth-century hagiography or a bound fragment of an illuminated manuscript from an unverified source but thought to be of the St Kilda school. He had noticed a first edition of Gray's *Anatomy* that looked like the sort of thing Angus Cadwallader would have loved, but why he'd noted the date and time of the sale in his diary and made sure the afternoon was free, he had no idea. Even less so why he'd actually come along.

'Inspector. What a pleasant surprise.'

McLean looked around to see a large woman approaching. At least he thought she was a woman, though she had the largest hands he'd ever seen. She wore the sort of outfit you might expect to be taking tea in Jenner's on a weekday afternoon, an overemphasis on tweed and heavy makeup. She was either wearing a wig or had spent the entire morning at a very skilled hairdresser's, one who most likely trained in the 1950s. Still slightly bemused to be at the sale, it took him too long to make the complex series of connections to a name.

'Madame Rose.' He nodded, shuffling sideways in his seat as she dropped herself indecorously beside him, too close for comfort. Not she at all. He. McLean remembered now, the so-called medium and fortune-teller with the shop at the bottom of Leith Walk. She'd helped . . . dammit, he'd helped out with the ritual killing cold case a year or so back. Had a vast collection of occult rubbish, including many ancient books, tucked away at the back of the shop. Madame Rose was also a friend of Jayne McIntyre, which had to count for something he supposed. He wondered how they'd met.

'Just Rose is fine.' Madame Rose settled into the seat, which creaked in protest at his considerable bulk. 'I must say I didn't expect to see you here. What with your connection to Anderson and all.'

'I never really expected to come here myself.' McLean tapped the rolled-up catalogue against his leg, considering the possibility of getting up and leaving. A few minutes earlier he might have got away with it. Now, having been recognized, it would only draw attention.

'And yet here you are. Had your eye on anything in particular?' The medium nodded at McLean's rolled-up catalogue. 'There's some rather wonderful first editions of Wendell's *Treatise on Babylonian Magic*. I do hope they don't go for too much. Rumour has it they once belonged to Aleister Crowley.'

A red-faced gentleman in a too-tight suit appeared at the lectern before McLean could say anything in reply, or make good his escape.

'Good afternoon, ladies and gentlemen, and welcome to this sale of rare and antiquarian books, the collection of the late Donald Anderson.'

The auctioneer lost no time in getting stuck into the collection, rattling off quick descriptions of each book as it was placed on a stand beside his lectern by a pair of assistants. Bidding was brisk, with some pieces fetching quite ridiculously large sums of money. So much for a double-dip recession.

Sitting beside him, McLean could feel Madame Rose twitch with each new sale, as if he were a football fan at a cup final. The medium hadn't bid for anything, seemed just to be there to watch. Every so often he would make little notes in the catalogue. Names of who was buying what.

'Lot thirty-two. Gray's *Anatomy*. First edition, published London in 1858 by J. W. Parker. Not in brilliant condition, but originally the property of a Mr A. Conan Doyle according to the inscription in the front. That has not been verified, although it is entirely possible. Who'll start me at five hundred pounds? Five hundred? No? Four hundred then? Three hundred and fifty? I don't need to remind you that there are no reserves in this sale, but all proceeds are going to a good cause. Three hundred then. Surely someone? Thank you, sir.'

McLean look around to see who had made the first bid, then realized that it was him.

'Three hundred I've got. Who'll give me three-fifty. Yes? Four?'

And so it went on. Someone across the hall was in for a fight, but McLean had decided he wanted this book. So he kept upping his bid. When the hammer finally came down he discovered he'd paid almost fifteen hundred pounds, plus auctioneer's commission, for a book that probably had nothing to do with Sir Arthur Conan Doyle whatsoever.

For some reason he didn't care.

'You come very highly recommended, Miss Nairn. Do you have much experience working with younger patients?'

She had arrived not long after he'd come home, deflated after the curious excitement of the sale room. Her feet crunching up the gravel drive had given him a few moments' notice before the doorbell rang. At first he'd thought she was lost; she certainly didn't look like the kind of person who lived in this part of town.

He'd forgotten about the appointment, of course, but the letter from Doctor Wheeler was legitimate, so he'd let her in, ushering her into the library for an impromptu interview. It was either there or the kitchen, and that seemed just a little too informal. From the CV sent by the hospital, he'd been expecting someone perhaps a little older than the young woman sitting opposite him, perhaps a little less, what was the word, Gothic? No, that wasn't right. She had more of an Earth Mother thing going, but with black leather DMs that laced almost up to her knees and piercings in places that surely weren't meant to be pierced. Still, there was no denying her credentials. Or his desperation.

'I started off in trauma rehabilitation, Detective Inspector. Most of my patients were in their teens or twenties. Motorbike accidents, a few soldiers injured in Iraq or Afghanistan.'

So she'd done her homework too. That was a good sign, wasn't it? McLean knew better than to judge someone purely by their outward appearance. Emma herself was hardly conventional.

'Did Doctor Wheeler tell you about Miss Baird's condition?'

'A little, but she's bound by patient–doctor confidentiality. I understand Emma has some memory loss, she was in the ICU for several months. Other than that, not much. Is she here?'

'Upstairs.' McLean glanced at the ceiling. In truth Emma had hardly come out of her bedroom in the days since she'd arrived, apart from her regular early-morning visits to his own room, his own bed. He'd lugged a television up there for her, but judging by the gaps in the bookshelves, she was filling her time mostly with reading. She ate the food he put in front of her, but he didn't think she helped herself to anything whilst he was away at work. He was pretty sure she'd not left the house, except for the two appointments with Doctor Wheeler back at the hospital. It had been at the last one where he'd broached the subject of a full-time carer. Miss Nairn was, he hoped, the answer.

'If you don't mind me asking, what's your relationship with Emma?'

Cut right to the chase, why don't you?

'She's my girlfriend. Was. Is? I'm not sure. She was abducted, possibly drugged, certainly had a very severe blow to the head. About four months ago. She was in a coma for almost two months. When she finally woke up she couldn't remember anything about the last fifteen years.'

Miss Nairn uncrossed her legs, leaned forward in her high-backed armchair. She wore a thin tie-died skirt over black leggings, white T-shirt and a suede leather jacket. Her blonde hair had been cut tight to her scalp, the furrows on her brow as she frowned reaching up into the short fuzz.

'That sounds unusual, for physical trauma. Has Emma seen a psychiatrist?'

'Not yet, but it's early days.'

'Early days, yes.' Miss Nairn tapped at her cheek with a finger, making a hollow pop, pop sound. 'So what is it you want me to do, Detective Inspector?'

'Whatever you can, really. I can give her a roof, a bed, feed her, but Emma needs company and I can't give up work to look after her while she recovers.' Even as he spoke the words, McLean saw the lie in them. He didn't need to work at all. If Miss Nairn saw the lie too, she didn't let on.

'And you think a carer specializing in physical-trauma victims is what she needs?'

'You were Doctor Wheeler's suggestion. If you don't think you're right for it, I'm sure she can give me other names.'

'No, no. I think I can help.' Miss Nairn levered herself out of the chair and McLean realized how he'd been played. If nothing else, she was smart. That had to be worth something.

'You're OK with doing this full time? Staying here?' McLean asked.

'It's usually the best way. And it looks like you've got the space.' Miss Nairn smiled, half twirled around, her outstretched arms taking in the over-large room. Her skirt flared out like a flamenco dancer's, a brief moment of exuberance before it settled back down against her legs. 'Shall we go and meet Emma then?'

9

'You got a minute, sir?'

McLean looked up from the report he'd been trying to force into his brain for an hour. The elfin, freckled face of Detective Sergeant Kirsty Ritchie peered around the door-jamb, not trusting itself to commit fully to a relationship with his office.

'A minute, an hour. Anything's got to be better than this.' McLean dropped the sheaf of paper onto his desk, where it nestled in amongst many others of its kind. He thought that Dagwood had sent him off to work in the SCU, but that hadn't stopped the acting superintendent from passing on every half-baked criminal psychology paper that came his way as well. Read, digest, condense into little words for the hard of thinking.

'I've been working with Stu– . . . DC MacBride on the suicide case. You know.' Ritchie leaned against the door, still not actually entering the office.

'I visited the scene, yes.' And got a bollocking for it. 'What did you make of it?'

'The scene? I think he's right. There's something odd about it.'

'But you can't be more specific, right?'

'Yeah. And that's what's bugging me.'

'You want to go deeper? Do a profile on the victim?' McLean dug around in the recesses of his memory for anything specific about the case. Came up with less than he'd have liked. 'Did we have a name for him?'

'Grigori Mikhailevic, according to his neighbour. Lithuanian. Of Russian descent if that name's anything to go by. Apparently he was over here studying accountancy. I guess that's enough to turn anyone to suicide.'

'Family?'

'Working on it. I've put in a call to the embassy, but you know how long it can take to get a response these days, especially if they think it's a suicide.'

'You haven't told them you think it's suspicious?'

'Well, that's the problem, isn't it. I can't.'

Ahh. So that's what it's about. 'Let me guess.' McLean raised a finger in the direction of the ceiling and the floor above. Not that the office in question was immediately over his own; that would have been far too demeaning for Dagwood.

'As far as he's concerned it's a simple case of suicide. He's already chewed MacBride's ear off once for even calling out SEB without asking first. Wants it written up and filed away ASAP.'

And they made this man acting superintendent. Put him in charge of an entire station. McLean slumped back in his seat, resisted the urge to bury his head in his hands.

'I know. He chewed me off a strip just for going along to have a look.'

'He does know that any dead body has to be investigated for foul play?' It was a question, but not one that should have needed answering. McLean just shrugged.

DS Ritchie looked over her shoulder into the empty

corridor beyond, as if expecting the object of their scorn to appear at any moment.

'I've not been here long, sir. But if you want my opinion, I think he's struggling to cope. He shouldn't even have been made up to super, let alone put in charge.'

'You won't find me disagreeing with you, Kirsty, but there's not a lot I can do. I'm just a humble detective inspector. It was hard enough dealing with him when he was just a DCI himself.'

'What about McIntyre? Is there nothing she can do?' There was a desperation in Ritchie's question, like a small child about to scream 'but it's not fair!'

'Last time I spoke to Jayne she was running to stay still. The phrase "poisoned chalice" comes to mind. This whole Police Scotland is a bugger's muddle and no mistake.'

'Aye, I thought as much.' Ritchie's face dropped, as if the last hope had died and unremitting hardship was the best she could expect from now on.

'What's he got you doing, then?' McLean asked.

'Anything. Everything. Mostly running around after DI Spence. That and responding to every petty burglary call that comes in like I was a beat constable. Not much actual detecting, though.' Ritchie nodded at McLean's desk. 'Paperwork. Lots of it. Beginning to wish I'd stayed up in Aberdeen.'

McLean looked at the piles on his desk, up at the clock on the wall. He'd been reading for at least three hours. Wasting time. 'Is MacBride about?'

'Down in the canteen last I saw him.'

'OK. Go and get him. I'll meet you out the back in ten minutes.'

'Where're we going?' The spark of intrigue in Ritchie's face was worth the trouble McLean knew he was inevitably going to get himself into.

'The City Mortuary. Let's see if Angus has had a chance to look at this dead Lithuanian student.'

McLean paused at the door to the CID room where all the detective sergeants lived, wondering whether going in was a good idea or not. Sooner or later word would get upstairs, and then there'd be consequences. On the other hand, if his instinct was right, and young MacBride's hunch was good, there was every chance a murder was about to go uninvestigated just so the crime statistics would look good. A sophisticated and well-planned murder at that, which meant either that there was more to Grigori Mikhailevic than was immediately apparent, or someone had acquired a taste for killing. Neither option was particularly appealing.

Or, of course, it was a suicide and he was going to look a right tit.

A series of desks cluttered up most of the space, reminding him more of a school room than an office. Perhaps it was the way they all faced the whiteboard wall. Or maybe it was the mixture of the hard-working and the semi-comatose sat at those desks that reminded him of hot summer afternoons and Latin declension. Detective Sergeant Carter was in earnest conversation with some uniform PCs and barely looked up as he walked in. A couple of other sergeants glanced around from their desks, phones clamped to their ears, eyes slightly wide with the fear of being caught looking at naughty pictures hidden inside a textbook. Both of them hung up without a word when they saw who it was had interrupted their afternoon; no bollocking from Dagwood today, no need to pretend they were busy.

McLean spotted his quarry over in the corner, feet up on his desk, face bathed in warm sunshine from the large window. Grumpy Bob had the look about him of a man who has fallen asleep reading a report. His balding head was tilted back, mouth slightly open, eyes tightly shut, but as McLean approached, before he could even say anything, the detective sergeant had swung his legs off the desk, scooped up his report and begun leafing through the upside-down pages. Then he saw who it was.

'Oh, it's you, sir. I thought . . .'

'Dagwood that bad, is he?'

'Don't get me started. He pops in here about once every bloody five minutes. No wonder he never gets anything done.'

'Well, you never know. HQ might even choose someone before Christmas. Then again, they might decide to make his position permanent.'

'Oh Christ. Don't.' Grumpy Bob groaned at the thought. Behind him, McLean heard several others.

'You got a moment, Bob?' he asked.

'If it gets me out of here, aye.'

'Well, it might. You know that suicide DC MacBride's been investigating?'

'Aye.'

'Well I want you to have a look at it too. Go over his report. Stick your nose in at the scene if SOC are finished with it.'

'Give it the benefit of my many years of experience, you mean.'

'That's the one. Just keep it low profile.'

Grumpy Bob raised his eyes heavenward and frowned. 'I take it this is not a sanctioned use of investigative resource.'

'Not exactly, no.'

'Nae bother, sir. I'll get right on it. Got to be better than wading through all this pish.' Grumpy Bob thwapped the sheaf of paper down on his desk. 'New procedures for community policing, my arse.'

'Aye, well. You can get off it and go have a nosey. On the quiet'd be best, but if Dagwood finds out and kicks up a fuss, tell him I sent you.'

'Oh, don't you worry about that, sir. I will.'

Hidden away down the Cowgate in the bowels of the Old Town, the City Mortuary was an easy place to overlook. That might have been the idea behind putting it there, of course. No one likes to be confronted by their mortality. A fresh breeze blew in off the Firth of Forth, whistling as it picked up speed down the narrow, canyon-like confines of the street. Throwing rubbish around their feet like playful paper dogs as they approached the entrance.

McLean held open the door, then followed Ritchie and MacBride into the air-conditioned lobby. The little party barely got a nod from the security guard; he'd seen them often enough before. They scribbled their names on the visitor pad anyway, before heading into the cool interior.

Angus Cadwallader was two-finger typing at an ancient computer in the office off the examination room when

McLean rapped his knuckles on the open door. The pathologist looked around, peering over half-moon spectacles, eyes taking a while to regain their focus before a broad smile spread across his face.

'Tony. It's been ages. I was beginning to think I'd done something.' He cast an eye over McLean's shoulder to the two officers standing behind him. 'The team's all back together, I see.'

'Not quite. Grumpy Bob's off down to Trinity. I thought the rest of us deserved a break from the office. Wondered if you'd had a chance to look at our Hanged Man yet.'

'And you decided to walk rather than phone? Things must be bad.' Cadwallader grabbed a pair of latex gloves from a box by the door, then led them through to the cold store. A bank of stainless steel refrigerator doors, about two foot square and each with a heavy handle, were set into one wall. Behind each, a body awaited, ready to give up its secrets.

'This one, I think. A pity Tracy's not here. She knows where everyone is.' Cadwallader opened a door, slid out a long shelf with a corpse on it, draped in a white sheet. Rolled back, this revealed the face of the young man McLean had last seen dangling from a stout hemp rope. His face was still distorted, his neck mottled with bruises.

'Grab that trolley will you, Constable.' Cadwallader pointed across the room. Startled, DC MacBride complied, and together they transferred the cadaver on its tray to the examination table through in the next room.

'You've done him already,' McLean said as the pathologist rolled the sheet down further. A brutal Y-shaped incision across the dead student's chest and down to his crotch had been sewn up with delicate care, no doubt the work of the missing Doctor Sharp.

'Yesterday. I'm still waiting on the results of the tox screening to come back. I was making a start on the report when you arrived.'

'The edited version?' McLean nodded at the young man on the slab, wondering why Cadwallader had wheeled him out.

'In a word, odd.'

'Odd?'

'Yes. Odd. I couldn't put my finger on it at first. But see here.' The pathologist lifted one of the dead student's hands up, splayed out the fingers. They were puffy and red where blood had pooled in them as they hung at his sides after death, but otherwise they looked well enough kept. The nails were trimmed neatly but would have needed doing again in a week or so. Had their owner not died.

'What am I looking at?' McLean asked. Behind him he could sense DS Ritchie leaning in for a closer look. No doubt DC MacBride was backing off. No fan of the dead, he.

'It's what's not there.' Cadwallader put down the hand and picked up the other. Here the fingernails were pared right back, the pads of the fingers thick.

'A guitarist.' McLean turned to MacBride, surprised to find him watching closely. 'Was there a guitar in the flat, Constable?'

'I think so, sir. I can check.'

'You're missing the point, Tony. Either that or being deliberately obtuse.' Cadwallader put the hand back down, rolled the white sheet back over the body. 'I've checked those hands thoroughly and there's no sign of any damage to the fingers. No splinters or wood fragments at all. It's just about possible he might have got that rope up over that beam without damaging his hands, but it's unlikely.'

'It's not much to go on though, is it?'

'On its own, no. But you saw his nails. They were quite clean, but it's amazing what gets left behind even after a good scrub. I could tell you a fair bit of his history over the twenty-four hours leading up to his death going by what was under those nails. Probably longer if I had the time and resources. But there was one thing very notable by its absence. No hemp fibres.'

For a moment McLean wondered what cannabis residue had to do with anything, but then the penny dropped.

'The rope.'

'Exactly, Tony. The rope. Your man there may have hanged himself, but if he did, then someone else put the rope up over the beam and around his neck.'

News had obviously run ahead of him. McLean could tell by the way the few other plain clothes officers he met on his way up to the third floor looked at him like he was a marked man. It was a stare he was all too familiar with; that mixture of anger that he'd poked the hornets' nest and relief that the little buggers were going to be focusing their attention on someone else for a change.

Duguid's office door was open, and McLean almost walked straight in as he would have done back when Jayne McIntyre was in charge. A self-preserving sixth sense stopped him. That and a quiet 'ahem' from the desk to one side of the door. He looked around to see a pale-faced constable manning the barricades.

'He's, um, expecting you, sir.'

McLean raised an eyebrow. 'Anyone else had a strip torn off yet?'

'I couldn't say, sir. DS Laird was in earlier though.'

Poor old Grumpy Bob. Well, he'd been dealing with the likes of Dagwood for long enough to develop the necessary thick skin. McLean took a deep breath, then advanced upon the open doorway. Across the room he could see the object of his scorn hunched over his desk, peering myopically at the screen of a tiny laptop computer. He rapped lightly on the door frame. Acting Superintendent

Charles Duguid stopped what he was doing, looked up and scowled.

'About bloody time. Come in and shut the door.'

McLean did as he was told, approaching the desk like a man who wasn't in fear of his life. Better to close on your enemy fast.

'The Leith suicide. Did I not make it clear I wanted it wrapped up quickly?'

McLean nodded, said nothing.

'And yet you asked DS Laird to go and check it over again today.'

McLean shifted slightly, stopped himself from fidgeting. Again said nothing.

'And now I hear you've taken DC MacBride and DS Ritchie down to the mortuary for . . . what exactly?' Duguid's scowl deepened. 'For Christ's sake. You're meant to be working with Jo Dexter in the SCU. Is Edinburgh so chaste you've got time to go nosing into every suicide?'

'It –'

'There's plenty of work for all of us without you sniffing out more, McLean. Don't go complicating things. It's a simple case. Young man couldn't face it any more, hanged himself. End of.'

'It wasn't a suicide sir.'

Duguid's stare hardened, his face starting the journey from red to purple.

'What the fuck are you talking about? There was no evidence of foul play. I've read the report. Have you?'

'Sir, I've just been talking to the pathologist. There's no trace of fibres from the rope under his nails. He didn't touch it. That means at the very least he had an accomplice. Someone helped him.'

Duguid let out a noise halfway between a sigh and a roar. 'It's never easy with you, McLean. You can't leave well enough alone, can you.'

McLean held his tongue. No point deliberately poking the bear, especially now he was in charge.

'I don't know what arrangement you had with Jayne McIntyre, but from now on it will be proper channels. You understand? No new investigations without approval. We don't have the manpower to go playing every hunch. You know our budget's being cut like everyone else's.'

'I understand, sir. Which is why I came to see you as soon as I knew there was something amiss.'

'Dammit, McLean. Are you listening?' Duguid thumped the desk in time with his words. 'Proper channels. You report to DCI Brooks. He decides whether or not to take it up with me. You deal with the sergeants, they deal with the constables. Chain of command. Christ, what did they teach you in Tulliallan?'

How to think for myself. Obviously a lesson you missed.

'I'll speak to DCI Brooks right away, sir.'

'No, McLean, you won't.' Duguid slumped back into his expensive leather chair. 'You're here now. I'm not so bloody stupid as to send you off around the houses. Brooks will only come bleating back to me like the rest of them.'

'It won't take much manpower, sir. DC MacBride's done a good job so far. He and Bob Laird can do the legwork. I'll keep an eye on progress, make sure they're not

72

spending too much time on it. We just need to find out a little bit more about the victim. Speak to his friends, fellow students, tutors.'

'Contrary to what gets said in the canteen, I do know how to run an investigation, McLean.'

Yes. And it mostly involves having someone else do all the work and then taking all the credit. 'Sorry, sir. I just meant it shouldn't take more than a few days.'

'Make sure it doesn't.' Duguid nodded a dismissal and turned back to his laptop. McLean breathed out a silent sigh of relief and turned to leave.

'Oh, and McLean?'

'Sir?'

'Don't think this gets you off Sex Crimes. You want the work, fine, but you're reporting to DCI Dexter as well as John Brooks. Don't come running to me if they expect you to work twenty-four hours a day.'

He's happy to get out of the club. Pounding noise they call music, strobe lights threatening to induce epilepsy, drinks costing half a day's wages for a single round. He's never seen the attraction of the places. You can't even talk to anyone; it's all by eye contact, a smile, a nod. Is it any surprise a bloke can get confused? Take the wrong message from a throw of the head?

Not that it's a problem this time. There's a crowd of them leaving all at once, bubbling out into the cool night street like school kids at the bell. Only they're school kids with a nice dull alcohol fug and ears that don't hear too well, enveloped in a warm fuzziness that's almost unsettling. There'll be whining in the morning. Tinnitus by the time he's forty, if he's that lucky.

He doesn't really know where they're going. Christ, he doesn't even know half of the people in the group. But there's Kizzy and Len and a couple of girls he recognizes from the college. The others all seem friendly enough. Either that or they're on something. Someone mentions a place nearby. Was it another club or someone's house? He hopes it wasn't another club. He couldn't really face that.

Maybe it's the cold air, but he can't really focus on anything. Or is it that he can only focus on one thing at a time? He doesn't feel drunk. Not like he's felt drunk before. Not like those wild undergrad days when he'd stagger back from the pub in the wee small hours, stiff-legged, trying to use the lines between the paving slabs to keep himself straight. Usually failing. And besides, he hardly had anything. Couldn't really afford it. But there's the group, and then there's a house. A bottle getting passed around. Wine? Laughter, smiling faces. Blink and he's somewhere else. Blink and there's a hand on his forehead, eyes gazing deep into his own. Blink and they're still there, burrowing into his soul. Blink.

Home. His home? Yes, he thinks so. Or is this a dream? It feels a bit like a dream. Is there someone here with him? He can't see anyone, but he can hear a voice in his head calming him, reassuring like his mum that time he had the flu. Maybe that's it; he's got the flu. That would explain why he's naked. Getting ready for bed. Sleep would be good; sleep cures everything. There's no worrying about the lack of cash when you're asleep. No fretting about the bills mounting up, the drudgery of a life that's fallen so far short of all the promises he was made. No wondering when the axe is going to fall. Wouldn't it be wonderful to sleep for ever. To fall into that warm, sweet, dark embrace and never leave.

The ground far, far away. His feet on a precarious chair. Hairy like a Hobbit. There was a girl once, long ago, said she loved him for his feet. But she left him all the same. What would she think of those feet now? Those hairy legs?

The voice calls to him. Is it her? It tells him to step off the chair. Just jump off and everything will be fine. There's something around his neck, a light pressure resting on his shoulder, brushing the skin of his naked back. But that's

75

OK. He doesn't need to worry about that. He doesn't need to worry about anything any more. Just a quick bend of the knees and jump down to the ground. Falling, falling, slow like they decided they didn't need gravity after all.

12

'Jesus wept. What is that smell?'

McLean stood at the entrance to a narrow alleyway running down the back of an anonymous row of prefab concrete garages. It was a place where things went to die: bits of old car, rusted beyond recognition; rotting mattresses, springs escaping like metal insects; an exercise bike bent as if it had been in a collision with a truck; the inevitable purloined shopping trolley. Mostly it was decaying black bin bags, ripped open by seagulls and urban foxes. Chip pokes, foil containers scraped clean of their biryani and saag aloo, pizza boxes stained with grease. Here and there a used condom, as if this foetid hole were the perfect spot for a bit of romance. And in amongst it all, thrown out with the rest of the trash, the decomposing body of a man.

At least, he assumed it was a man. It wasn't easy to tell from what was left. No doubt finding them tastier than rancid pizza, the foxes had taken his fingers down to stubs, and something had eaten away at his face. It had to be a man's body, though. No self-respecting woman would dress up like that.

'Putrefaction, Tony. Enzymatic breakdown of the body's cells. Bacterial decay. And I dare say the garbage doesn't help.' Squatting close to the dead body, the city pathologist, Angus Cadwallader, lifted a flaccid arm and inspected what was left of a hand. McLean stayed put at the end of the alley, to avoid contaminating the crime scene, of course. Although if truth be told he was more worried about ruining his shoes. He doubted forensics would get anything useful from here.

'What's the prognosis then? You think you can save him?'

Cadwallader levered himself back up to his feet and picked a careful route back from the body. His white overalls were stained a riot of greens and browns around his legs, black wellingtons slimed with things best not thought about. 'I can't be hugely accurate until I get him back to the mortuary, but given the weather we've been having lately and the state of the insect life living inside his mouth, I reckon he's been there at least a fortnight.'

McLean took a step back and turned slowly on his heels. The garages were surrounded on all sides by squat, six-storey tower blocks. Ugly concrete and pebble-dash, each apartment with a wide balcony affording views across the Forth. Or the back of the next block if you were unlucky. At least half of the balconies had washing draped on airers or dangling from railings. Many hundreds of people lived here, looked out these windows, saw what was going on. For two weeks, no one had come forward to report the rotting corpse chucked out with the bin bags.

'He was covered up, aye?' McLean asked the uniform sergeant who'd first greeted him when he'd arrived on site.

'Reckon so, sir. That many foxes round here these days, they must've dug down and pulled him up.'

'How'd we find out about him then?'

'Anonymous tip-off. Probably someone round here got

sick of the stench.' The sergeant nodded in the direction of the nearest flat as another squad car drew up. A couple of uniforms were trying to placate a small mob of garage-owners, no doubt anxious to know when they could get back in and dispose of all the stolen goods and pirated DVDs that were hidden inside. It might be an idea to use the body as an excuse to search all the lock-ups in the close, but they'd need a lot more manpower if they were going to do that. A riot squad too.

The short figure of DCI Jo Dexter climbed out of the squad car and ducked under the cordon tape. McLean watched her size up the whole site as she approached. Her eyes darted from tower block to parked car to garage and finally to the group of people standing at the opening to the narrow alley.

'One for us, Tony?'

'Not sure. I thought you might want to take a look. It's not pretty, mind you.'

Dexter gave him the sort of look his grandmother had reserved for the times he said something really obvious. He held the stare for a couple of seconds before conceding defeat.

'Over here then.' He pointed at the alleyway and the two of them stepped carefully into the shade, as close as they dared.

'He's certainly dead,' Dexter said. The body lay on its back, sprawled almost as if it had fallen into the soft embrace of the bin bags. Or more likely been thrown.

'SEB haven't been yet. Not sure I want to be the one to tell them they've got to go through all this shit.'

'Waste of time anyway. He wasn't killed here.' Dexter

inched closer, testing each footfall as if she were creeping over thin ice. 'Why'd you think it was something for us?'

'The jacket he's wearing. Look familiar to you?'

Dexter took one more step forward. Swore. It could have been because she'd trodden in something that meant her shoes would have to be incinerated, or it could have been that she, too, had been looking through mug shots that morning.

'Malky Jennings?' McLean asked as they both retreated from the alleyway.

'Malky fucking Jennings,' Dexter echoed. 'Either that or someone's nicked his clothes.'

'Subject is male, Caucasian. One metre seventy-three tall. Extensive damage to the extremities, most likely from wild animals. Decomposition consistent with having been dead for at least two weeks, given current weather conditions.'

McLean stood some distance off from the examination table as Angus Cadwallader dictated his observations into the microphone slung from the ceiling. Doctor Peachey was on hand as witness to the proceedings, with Doctor Sharp assisting as she ever did. He felt like a gatecrasher at a very exclusive party.

'Can you narrow that down at all?'

'Ah, Tony. You always ask, even though you know what the answer will be.' Cadwallader pulled open the deceased's mouth, shone a light into the depths within. 'I've sent off a collection of the more interesting insects we found inside him at the scene. There's an entomologist at the university who's a marvel with bugs. She'll be able to tell you to the hour when the eggs were laid. Probably who the father was too. But it takes time.'

'What about cause of death, then?'

'You want me to speculate, or would you rather I carry out this post-mortem first and then tell you?'

McLean bounced on his feet, didn't answer. Cadwallader was right, of course. He always was. The only reason for being down here in the mortuary was to get away from the station for a few hours. There was nothing to be gained from watching the gruesome spectacle of Malcolm Jeffrey Jennings being cut open, his most intimate secrets revealed. If it really was Malky Jennings of course, lying there on the slab. Identification was going to take a while, even if the corpse had been wearing those distinctive clothes. They'd need to run DNA, and that could take days. Even dental records might be a challenge. From what little he knew of Jennings, visits to the dentist were fairly low on his list of priorities, and someone had mashed his face in anyway. Perhaps he needed to attack the problem from a different direction.

'Let me know if anything unusual comes up, will you?'

Cadwallader looked up from the corpse, frowned. 'You not staying to the end?'

'No. I've got a better idea.'

'Oh yes? What?'

McLean grinned as he reached for the door handle. It wasn't often he found something to be cheerful about these days. 'I'm off down the East End to see if I can find me a prostitute.'

*

Mid-afternoon was the wrong time of day, of course. No one would be plying her trade on the streets at this hour unless she was really desperate and stupid. On the other hand, you had to be pretty desperate to be in this line of business. Stupidity? Well, there were different kinds.

The address Magda had given when she was processed turned out to be a fourth-floor flat in one of the seventies concrete blocks that backed onto the square and lock-ups where Malky Jennings had been found. If it was Malky Jennings. Scaffolding clung to the frontage like a parasite, but there was no sign of workmen. Just a bucket on a rope, looped over a winch at the top and tied away out of easy reach.

The entrances to the flats on the fourth floor were spaced along a long concrete walkway, open to the brisk wind off the Firth of Forth. Fine in the summer, when a breeze kept away the stench of the courtyard below. In the winter, with a cold north-easterly throwing wet snow against anything more than a few feet high, it must have been miserable. Pity the poor buggers who lived on the next two floors up. As he approached the one he was looking for, McLean saw why the scaffolding was there. The rough harling on the parapet running along the outside of the walkway had succumbed to years of Edinburgh's coastal weather, cracked away to reveal loose bricks behind it. The missing workmen had knocked out a fair few of these, no doubt clearing back the rot before repairing the wall. He peered over the edge at the car park far below, felt his muscles tighten involuntarily. It was a long way down.

McLean was about to knock when he realized he'd

come alone, what that meant. He should have found a uniform PC, or better yet DS Ritchie, to accompany him. She was good at this sort of thing, and it always helped to have a female police officer with you. It added balance. But he had to admit he'd been avoiding the station recently, falling back into bad habits. Anything to avoid Duguid, Brooks or more often the pleading of his fellow officers for him to do something about it, please, for pity's sake. Replace 'it' with whatever asinine thing one of his superiors had done that particular day.

Movement further along the walkway caught his eye. The door to the neighbouring flat stood open and a young girl sat outside on the concrete. She was playing with a pair of naked, armless dolls, and as she looked up, McLean could see that her face was grimy, her hair matted in places. She gave him an adult's scowl and returned to her play. One to mention to social services? Or would they just scowl at him themselves and tell him to mind his own business? Probably.

The door opened almost before he'd knocked on it. A middle-aged woman stared at him, not who he'd been expecting. She was shorter than Magda, not much more than five foot tall. She wasn't dressed particularly like a prostitute either, although he didn't really know what a prostitute dressed like when she wasn't working. Jeans, a hoodie maybe. Comfortable slip-ons. This woman looked more like someone who worked in an office. Slacks and a blouse, sensible jacket, heavy handbag slung over one shoulder. She gave McLean a look almost as unfriendly as the little girl.

'What you want?'

'Is Magda Evans in?'

The woman turned, shouted into the depths of the flat. 'Magda! I thought you said you'd packed that in.'

A distant voice, coming closer. 'What? What you talking about?'

Magda appeared, barefoot, stained jogging bottoms and a sweatshirt two sizes too big for her. Her quizzical expression turned blank when she saw McLean standing in the doorway. 'Oh. It's you.'

'You know him? One of your Johns?' The short woman managed to fit a long list of derogatory comments into that one word.

'Polis.'

If anything, the short woman's expression grew even frostier. She crossed her arms over her chest. 'Can't youse lot leave her alone, aye? She's no doin' that any more. Not for you. Not for anyone.'

An inkling of what was going on began to form in the back of McLean's brain. He recalled how Magda had reacted to DS Buchanan, how much more willing she was to talk to him without the other officer present. And the short woman, well, his best guess was social services or some shelter. Maybe he should have phoned ahead. Here he was dealing with things as if this were a murder investigation, but there was more to it than that.

'Detective Inspector McLean.' He held up his warrant card so that the short woman could see it. Let her know that he wasn't afraid of her being able to identify him. Could work two ways, he supposed. 'I wanted to have a word with Magda about Malky Jennings. That's all.'

If his words had reassured the short woman, she gave

no sign of it. Magda's face changed at the name, a look of anxiety creeping over her Slavic features. She stood perfectly still, as if frozen by indecision.

'Look, I don't know who you are.' McLean addressed the short woman. 'But I assume you're some kind of helper. I need to talk to Magda, either here or at the station. If it's here, now, then you're welcome to sit in and observe. But I'm dealing with a murder investigation here, and I've not got a lot of patience right now.'

'Murder? Malky's dead?' Magda spoke quietly, but McLean could hear the hope in her voice.

'Someone's dead. It might be him. I'm trying to find that out.'

'Well you'd better come in then,' the short woman said.

Her name was Clarice Saunders, pronounced the way Anthony Hopkins does it. She worked for a charity rehabilitating former sex workers, or at least that was what she told McLean once they were settled in Magda's sitting room. It could have been a wonderful place to live, with a floor-to-ceiling window giving views across the city towards Arthur's Seat and the castle that anywhere else would have been worth hundreds of thousands of pounds. Here, in the Schemes, surrounded by the junkies, the unemployed and the just trying to make the best of their lives with what little they had, a nice view counted for nothing. The single-glazing, rattling in the wind, didn't help. Neither did the mould blackening the corners, reaching up from the floor and down from the ceiling; the flaking paint on the window frames; the peeling strips of faded flock wallpaper. Magda's furniture had seen better days, too. Probably in the mid-seventies from the look of it. But the mugs in which she brought them tea were clean, and the packet of biscuits was within its sell-by date, just.

'Tell me about Malky Jennings,' McLean said once Magda had taken a seat. She perched on the edge, knees close together, legs tucked to one side like a debutante. Her nails had been painted in alternating shades of red and gold but the varnish was beginning to crack and flake away.

'What's to say? He's a toerag who likes to beat up women. You reckon he's dead? I say not soon enough.'

'He was your pimp, right?'

Clarice let out a sharp little bark of a humourless laugh, like a terrier poked.

Magda took a long drink of her tea before replying. 'He owned me. Like I told you back at the station. Right up until he sold me to that Russian.'

'How does that work?'

Another long pause. 'He told me when to work, who to go with, how much to charge. He took all the money and let me sometimes have a little back for food. If he didn't think I was working hard enough, he hit me. If he thought I was trying to hold back some money, he hit me. If he felt like it, he hit me. Never the face, you understand. Always here, here.' She touched her sides lightly. 'You can still give blow jobs even if your ribs are broken.'

'Why did you stay with him? Why –'

'– didn't she go to the police?' Clarice finished a different question to the one he'd been going to ask, but not all that different. 'You're new to the Sex Crimes Unit, aren't you, Detective Inspector. You don't really know how it works.'

'I'm beginning to get an idea.'

'You arrest someone like Malky Jennings, another wee shite pops up to take his place. Only first he's got to make his name, ain't he? So he puts his fists about a bit. Maybe picks on one girl and puts her in the hospital. Keeps everyone else in line.' Clarice perched on the edge of the tatty sofa, knees together, elbows planted firmly on them, hands cupped around her mug of tea as she leaned forward earnestly. 'Your lot know this, so they don't arrest people like Malky Jennings. Turn a blind eye. Maybe in exchange for a few favours. Information. Wouldn't surprise me if there was cash involved too. Off the books.'

McLean cast his mind back to the series of interviews, the sullen young women, tight-lipped and nervous. How none of them had said anything much at all, except Magda and then only when DS Buchanan was out of the room. Was it really like that in the SCU? He couldn't believe Jo Dexter standing for that kind of nonsense. At least not the Jo Dexter he'd known back in training college. No doubt it was something he'd have to look into, and no doubt it would make him unpopular, but that wasn't really why he was here.

'Tell me more about Malky, Magda. What was he like, physically?'

' He was average height I guess. Skinny. Big nose. Bad teeth. He used to wear these flash clothes, like he thought he was something out've the movies, you know? Only he wasn't nothing special. Just another violent shit of a man.'

'Could you identify him?' Christ, how to put this delicately. 'If you couldn't see his face?'

Magda's brow creased, then her mouth split in a meagre grin. 'Did he fuck me, you mean? Do I know what his scrawny little body looks like? Yes, inspector, he did fuck me. But he wasn't really one for cuddling and intimacy, you know? More a throw you against the wall and bang you up the arse kind of a guy. That or a quick face-fuck with a knife at your throat.'

Sounds charming. McLean fidgeted with the folder he'd brought with him, the case notes so far and photographs of the body. It was beginning to look like this was a dead end, at least for now. No point trying to find out why someone might have killed Malky Jennings if they didn't know for certain he was dead.

'That him?' Magda pointed at the folder. 'Can I see?'

'It's not a pretty sight. If we could ID him from his mug shots I'd not be here right now.'

'I'm not squeamish, Inspector. Show us.' Magda reached out for the folder. Reluctantly, McLean opened it up, selected a full-body shot from the mortuary. Naked and laid out on the slab, the corpse was pale and mottled, skin yellowing around the bloody stumps that had once been hands, sightless eyes staring out from lids chewed away by something that didn't care what it ate. He handed it over, noticing that Clarice strained forward to try and get a look herself, then recoiled in shock.

Magda's reaction was slower, more measured. Her eyes darted over the A4 print, sipping at the details one at a time before going back for more. Her frown came back, and she peered closer still, her nose almost touching the page before she finally went to hand it back.

'It's him. About as certain as I can be from a photo.'

'How can you tell?'

'He has a scar, down here.' Magda pointed to her crotch. 'I gave it to him. Reckon I should be able to recognize it again if I see it.'

13

'Well, that's a pretty positive ID on Malky Jennings. I think we can safely say it's him.'

McLean dropped his coat over the back of the chair currently sat in front of the desk they'd given him in the SCU office. It wasn't the same, comfortable chair that had been there when he'd left that morning; that was groaning under the weight of DS Buchanan at the other end of the room. He'd nick it back when the sergeant left, early as usual, and so the game would continue until he managed to get out of the place altogether.

'Who confirmed it?' DCI Dexter asked from her perch on the edge of one of the several empty desks. The SCU control room was large, dark and empty. As far as he could tell, there were only about five officers working full time in the place, and they tended to avoid it if they could. Behind the chief inspector's head, a whiteboard had acquired some photographs of Malky Jennings in his final resting place, and laid out on the mortuary slab. A few half-hearted early-investigation questions had been marked in. Across the room, the board for the white slave trafficking investigation was fuller, but held much less promise.

'One of the girls we picked up off the boat.'

'You trust the word of a pro?' Jo Dexter raised an eyebrow in mock incredulity.

'She's no love of Jennings. And she was able to identify a unique body marking. On account of she was the one gave it to him in the first place.'

DS Buchanan snorted. 'What'd you offer her in return?'

McLean turned on the sergeant. 'What do you mean?'

'These girls aren't our friends.' Buchanan paused just long enough to be rude before adding, 'Sir.'

'No? That's not what I'm hearing. Some of them seem to be very friendly indeed. To some officers.'

Buchanan's face hardened, his joy at McLean's apparent naivety turning quickly into anger. Suspicions confirmed then.

'You reckon she's reliable, this witness of yours?' DCI Dexter pushed herself off the desk, neatly blocking the space between McLean and the sergeant.

'I think so, yes. She's trying to get out. Being sold into white slavery may have changed her priorities a little. She was with a Clarice Saunders when I met her. You've come across her, I take it.'

This time DS Buchanan's laugh was more of a guffaw. 'The midget? Aye, we've all heard of her. Interfering wee busy-body.'

McLean peered around Jo Dexter to where Buchanan was still sitting at his desk, but the sergeant had his head turned away, fascinated by whatever he was reading.

'You got a moment, Tony?' Dexter asked, nodding towards the door. He followed her out, across the corridor and into her own office. She closed the door firmly behind them, then dropped wearily into her seat, indicated for McLean to take the other one.

'I don't think Pete likes you.'

'Well, if half the things I've heard about him are true, I don't much like him either.'

'Oh they're true. I've no doubt about that. Old hand like him's bound to be a bit bent.'

'And you're OK with that?'

'OK's a strong word. I think it's the least bad alternative.'

McLean rubbed at his face, not sure what to say.

'Look, I know why you've been sent here, Tony. Can't say as I didn't see it coming.'

'Far as I'm concerned this is my punishment for calling Dagwood an idiot to his face. On balance I think I'd rather be here than having to deal with him. Sadly I have to do both, it would seem.'

Jo Dexter slumped back in her seat. 'You really did call him an idiot then.'

'Well he is. And it was my lead that cleared up the cannabis-farming operation, for all the good it did us. But he got the promotion.'

'You sound like a little boy, you know.'

'Oh I'm not bitter about that. Not really. I don't want promotion. I just wish they'd give the job to someone who actually knows what they're doing.'

'Dagwood's cannier than you give him credit for. He sent you here, after all. What is it he always says about you, Tony? You over-complicate things? Something like that.'

'And he over-simplifies. I don't . . . Oh.' Stupid, really. He should have seen it straight away.

'He wants to shake things up here. He's known Pete Buchanan for decades, knows all about how the SCU works, the compromises we make to get results. And he doesn't like it. So he chucks you in here like a grenade. And who benefits when it all explodes?'

'But surely there must be a better way of doing things than . . .' McLean tailed off, trying not to think too hard about exactly what was being done already.

'If we had unlimited resources, yes. If people weren't prepared to pay for sex, maybe all the hookers would find better jobs elsewhere. Maybe there wouldn't be drugs in the Schemes if there was work for everyone. But there isn't. Policing by containment, that's the best we can hope for here. We tread a fine line, and the last thing we need is someone coming in and trampling over all that.'

'I can't turn a blind eye if an officer is taking bribes, Jo. Whatever form they come in.'

Dexter stared at him, her hard face pinched.

'I know. And I shouldn't either. Christ, I'd like to clean this operation up, but there's never a right time. We implode and who knows what's going to happen on the streets?'

'Worse than letting the likes of Malky Jennings operate because we're scared what might come along if he's put behind bars? Worse than rounding up prostitutes and shipping them out to the Middle East to be slaves?'

'Aye, well. About that.' Jo Dexter straightened in her chair, the confessional over. 'This pro of yours, you've got some kind of rapport with her?'

'Jesus Christ. She's not a "pro". She's a young woman with a name, a history. She made some shitty decisions in the past, now she's trying to change.'

'OK. OK. Sorry.' Dexter put her hands up in mock defeat. 'I get your point. Really, I do. But whatever she is, you've got something going there. She won't talk to anyone else, but she might talk to you.'

'You think she knows more than she told us already?'

'She didn't tell us anything, Tony. Neither did any of the others. But they know exactly who took them and why. We need to find this Russian, whoever he is. That should be our top priority.'

'What about Malky Jennings?'

'What about him? He's dead, Tony. You think it's any coincidence he was killed just a few days after his girls have been lifted off the streets?'

'Find the Russian, find who killed Malky. You think it'll be that easy?'

Jo Dexter gave him a weary smile. More like a hopeful grimace, really. 'I never said it'd be easy, Tony. Just do what you can, eh?'

'There is no Russian. You know that, right?'

McLean put down the phone, fresh from speaking to some loon at Serious and Organized in the vain hope that they might both have something helpful about the prostitute-smuggling operation, and be prepared to share it. So far it didn't look good on either count, though there was always the chance his initial enquiry would kick something off and he'd be passed a melodramatic brown envelope in a dark car park sometime. He looked up from his temporary desk in the SCU main office, over to where DS Buchanan was pretending to work.

'What d'you mean?'

'There's no Russian. We'd have heard of him already if

there was. That whore of yours made him up. She's given you something that'll keep you running around for days. Meantime she gets a bit of freedom, chance to find a new pimp.'

'You know her? Magda?'

A moment's hesitation. Not much, but enough for McLean to see the lie coming. Buchanan shook his head. 'Her? No. But I've seen the type plenty.'

'Her type?' McLean didn't try to keep the disdain out of his voice. Couldn't see the point.

'Aye. She's a serial escaper. Stuck in the life, tries to get out. Probably succeeds for a while thanks to someone like your new friend Clarice.' Buchanan made a meal of the name. 'Only thing is, she doesn't know how to operate without a man like Malky telling her what to do. Sooner or later, usually sooner, she'll come crawling back to her old haunts. There'll be a new Malky in charge then, of course. Who knows, we might even have broken him in.'

McLean shook his head. 'You think this is all just a game, don't you.'

'Well it is, isn't it? And one we can't win.'

'So why d'you stay at it? Why not get a transfer out?'

Buchanan shrugged. 'Tried it. Didn't like it. Ended up crawling back here.'

'Hey, Tony. You any idea what time it is?'

He'd been heading out of the station, walking to his old car. Tapped the name in his phone book without thinking, forgetting that his oldest friend had moved to California three months ago, along with his new wife, to take up a very lucrative professorship at a very prestigious university. It wasn't until he heard Phil's voice that he realized what he'd done.

'Come off it, Phil. You're what, ten hours behind?' McLean glanced briefly at his watch. 'Even you should be up by now.'

'You're forgetting the delights of scientific research. I've been up all night checking Assays. Only got to my bed about an hour ago.'

He knew it was a lie, at least the Assays bit. Still, what was the point of having friends if you couldn't lie to them?

'Sorry. Been pulling a few all-nighters here too.'

'Let me guess. You wanted someone to have a pint with and hit speed dial. I knew I shouldn't have let Rachel put our new number into your phone.'

McLean considered pretending there'd been a different reason for his call, found he really couldn't be bothered. 'Something like that, aye. It's been a shitty few days. Shitty few weeks if I'm being honest.'

'You should book yourself some holidays. Come over here and visit. We've got a spare room. You can even see the beach, if you stand on a chair and crick your neck.'

It was very tempting. Hell, he could just hand in his notice and walk away. Except that he knew he'd never do that. 'I'd love to, Phil, but it's complicated. What with Emma and everything.'

'No change, I take it.' Even thousands of miles away, Phil's concern was as genuine as it was a knife to the guts. Had he really forgotten to tell his best friend?

'Christ, did I not say? She woke up, about a month ago.'

'A month! Jesus, Tony, have you any idea what Rae's going to do to me when I tell her? How is she?'

'It's . . . complicated.' McLean settled into the car seat, phone clamped tight to his ear and started telling the tale. He'd hoped he might get a pint and a blether, but right now he'd settle for one of the two. Worry about how he'd not spoken to his best friend in over a month some other time.

Mrs McCutcheon's cat stared up at him from the middle of the kitchen table when McLean let himself in through the back door. It was late, he was tired and the last thing he wanted was to have an argument with a cat.

'You really shouldn't be on there, you know,' he said, shucking his coat off one arm whilst he dropped the pile of case files that he'd foolishly agreed to look over onto the nearest chair. The cat held his gaze for just long enough to let him know it was considering what he'd said, then jumped elegantly from the table and trotted out through the door to the front hall.

The light was on, and the sound of music leaked from the closed door to the library. His brand new Linn stereo system was in there, along with a couple of dozen vinyl LPs he'd picked up in the months since his flat had burned down. Christ alone knew how long it would take to rebuild his collection, amassed over a lifetime and something he'd always meant to catalogue. Perhaps it didn't really matter; it wasn't as if he ever had time to sit and listen to music any more.

The other thing that was in the library, of course, was his whisky. And that was something he felt he deserved, especially after a day like today. What he didn't really want was to have to spend time with people. Old habits died hard, and he'd lived alone for so long. It was a struggle adjusting to having two young women under his roof. Still, needs must when there was a dram at stake, and if he was going to make it through the case files, perhaps more than one.

Emma was sitting on the floor, cross-legged and with her back to him when he opened the door. Jenny Nairn slouched on the sofa, reading a book. She looked up almost guiltily as he entered, that flicker across her eyes something he'd seen countless times in interview rooms. Emma must have noticed it too, as she looked around, straining her neck rather than getting up. A big smile spread across her face when she saw him.

'Tony! We were just talking about you. How was your day?'

An endless round of meetings, paperwork and management issues that meant he'd done no actual investigative work at all. Hence the case files that had followed him home. 'Same as usual.'

'You never were a good liar.' Emma levered herself up off the floor, hopped over and gave him a hug, a chaste kiss on the cheek.

'You ladies get up to anything interesting while I was gone?'

'Jen's been making me do crossword puzzles and stuff. It's meant to work my brain, apparently.'

'She's making good progress.' Jenny put her book down, took her stockinged feet off the cushion and placed them carefully on the floor. Her movements were supple, careful. She reminded McLean of a cat. Nothing done without careful consideration. 'Tell Tony about the camera,' she said.

'Oh god, yes. I almost forgot.' Emma hurried over to the antique writing desk at the far end of the room, came back with a clunky old digital SLR camera he dimly remembered his grandmother buying, around about the same time she'd discovered the delights of the internet.

'Where'd you find that?'

'I was going through the desk, looking for a pen.' Emma's face dropped. 'I hope you don't mind.'

'Not really, no.'

'But the thing is, I know how to use it. See.' Emma popped off the lens cap, twisted a few knobs, put the camera to her face and took a picture. The flash starred his eyes, so McLean had to blink to see the image on the small screen on the back. He looked like he was sucking on a lemon, but then he'd never liked having his photo taken.

'Very nice,' he lied.

'Not that, silly.' Emma's thumbs tapped at the tiny buttons on the back of the camera, flicking from menu to menu with the dexterity of a teenager on an Xbox. Things happened that McLean couldn't begin to understand, but the image changed, turned black and white, cropped, swivelled.

'I know it inside out. It's like I've had one for years, used it every day. But I don't remember ever owning a digital camera at all.'

McLean thought back to the first time he'd met the SOC officer, at a crime scene in Merchiston, snapping away like a paparazzo at a celebrity wedding. She was a dab hand with photo-imaging software, too; a skill that had almost seen her locked up, accused of posting crime scene photographs on dodgy websites.

'You're a trained crime scene photographer.' McLean knew as he said the words that they were the wrong thing. It was so difficult to know how to deal with Emma these days. Her mood swung back and forth like a small child at a birthday party.

'Yes, but I don't remember.' Emma waved the camera about like a club. 'It's like there's this other person inside me who knows all sorts of stuff, but she never talks to me. Just steps in and takes over when it pleases her.'

'Perhaps you need to let her. Encourage her.'

'Actually, that's not a bad idea,' Jenny said. 'You should take loads of photographs. We can make a project of it. Get you outside a bit.'

Emma looked nervously at the window, even though the curtains were drawn. 'Outside?'

'You'll be fine, Em.' Jenny stood up and took the camera. 'We'll start in the garden. You can take pictures of the birds. We won't go any further until you're happy, OK?'

Emma nodded, even though she didn't look happy. As soon as outside had been mentioned the life had fled from her. The sky still seemed to terrify her.

'I think it's probably bedtime anyway.' Jenny handed the camera to McLean, took Emma's hand like she was a child. Unlike a child, she didn't throw a tantrum, just muttered a quiet 'Night' and allowed herself to be led out of the room.

*

Much later, a hefty dram consumed and most of the case files at least skimmed over, McLean glanced at the clock on the mantelpiece. One in the morning was not such an unfamiliar time to him, but it was still late. He knocked back the last of the whisky, stacked the files neatly on the desk and headed for bed.

The hall was dark, no lights on in the rest of the house, so that when he switched off the library light he was plunged into darkness. Shapes re-formed slowly as his eyes adjusted, the ever-present orange glow of the night-time city filtering in through the skylight high above. The dark didn't bother him, not in this house where he'd grown up. He knew all its secrets, the feel of the air in different rooms, the way the floorboards creaked as he walked over them. In the almost-black, with just the faint, distant roar of the city as a background noise, this was his place. He didn't need lights to know it.

The door to Emma's room was closed, which was a relief. It had been a few days now since she'd climbed into his bed for security, like a child frightened of the dark, but her mood swing earlier, and the mention of going outside, had worried him. It wouldn't surprise him at all if he woke to find her alongside him again.

He trod quietly across the landing, the reflected glow of the clouds shining through the big glass skylight over the stairwell, casting evil shadows of deeper black, twisting sinister shapes out of the banisters. His own room was at the far side, opposite Emma's, and as he reached for the door handle, he noticed something out of place. Froze.

When she'd taken on the job of Emma's full-time carer,

Jenny Nairn had insisted on taking one of the attic rooms, rather than any of the main spare rooms that McLean had offered. He wasn't sure why; maybe the opulence bothered her. Or maybe she felt that as a hired help she should of course live in the servants' quarters. Perhaps she felt a need to be above everyone else and looking down. Whatever her reasons, now she was sitting on the narrow back stairs leading up to her room.

'Thought you were never coming up. You work too hard, Inspector.' She pushed herself upright, stepped from the shadows towards him. For a moment he wondered whether this was some kind of awkward advance, but she stopped just outside his personal space.

'You could have come and talked to me downstairs. If there was something you wanted to ask.'

'Nah. You were busy. Looked like you wanted some time to yourself too.'

Nothing could have been further from the truth, really. What he wanted was the company of the Emma Baird he'd met all those months ago. Someone he could go down the pub with, forget about the slow torture that was work in a station run by Acting Superintendent Charles Duguid and his band of cronies. But he couldn't have that, of course.

'Not really,' was all he managed to say. 'This about Emma, I take it?'

'Yes. No. Sort of.' Jenny studied her fingernails for a moment. 'It's kind of, well . . . I don't really know you, but you seem open-minded, right?'

McLean said nothing, wishing she'd get to the point.

'It's just, I've got this idea of something that might

help. Help Em, that is. Only most people, if I mentioned it to them they'd scoff.'

'Doctor Wheeler thinks highly of you. That counts for a lot in my book. If you think there's something that can help Emma, please don't hold back.'

'You sure? OK. Well I was going to suggest you try hypnotic regression therapy.'

Of all the crazy ideas that had skimmed his mind, this wasn't the most loony. At least not quite. 'Hypnosis. As in Derren whatsisname? Brown?'

Jenny's shoulders slumped. 'There you go. It's so hard to shake the old magic trick aspect of it. Hypnosis is a well-researched therapeutic tool. And Doctor Austin is the most skilled hypnotherapist I've ever encountered. She helped me, way back when my folks died. I really think she could work wonders with Emma.'

McLean stifled a yawn born only from lack of sleep. He didn't know much about Jenny's background beyond the basic checks he'd done before hiring her, but the news of her parents' death struck a chord. No stranger to him, that experience. She worked well with Emma and, despite her rather unorthodox appearance, didn't seem the type to suggest something lightly.

'You say Doctor Austin. This is a qualified practitioner?'

'Eleanor's a psychiatrist, yes. She has a private practice in the New Town and teaches at the university.'

'OK. It's not something I'd normally consider, but I'll run it past Doctor Wheeler at Emma's check-up tomorrow. If she's happy, then we'll go see your Doctor Austin.'

'Thank you, Inspector. You won't regret it.' Jenny's face

broke into a wide grin, her teeth flashing white in the semi-darkness. She darted forward, grabbed his hand and squeezed it for a moment in a peculiarly old-fashioned gesture. Then without another word she turned and scampered up the black, narrow staircase to her attic room.

14

'Well, this is all a bit of a fucking mess, isn't it.'

McLean stared out through the grimy windscreen at the long line of traffic not in any way moving down Queen Street. Digging up the roads to put in tram tracks had been one of Edinburgh Council's more inspired ideas. Buggering up the procurement contracts in true civil service fashion so that the job was going to take twice as long was just the icing on the cake. There were times when the city just ground to a halt, and this seemed to be one of them. He suspected the traffic wasn't what was bothering his old friend though. Sat beside him in the passenger seat, Grumpy Bob was for once living up to his name.

'Dagwood making life miserable again?'

'He's a walking disaster area, breaking up teams for no bloody reason. You know what he's got Ritchie doing now?'

McLean did, but he knew better than to get in the way of one of Grumpy Bob's rants.

'She's down in the basement doing Needy's old job. Filing. I mean, for fuck's sake. She's a detective. What's that all about?'

'It's only short term. A week at the most.' McLean indicated, turned down towards the Colonies, got a hoot of the horn from another frustrated driver. Serve him right. Idiot had been half asleep and missed his chance.

'You know as well as I do why she's been sent there and it's got bugger all to do with them needing a sergeant at short notice. There's half a dozen would've come back out of retirement to do the work part time.'

'You think he's really that vindictive?' McLean was going to use the word petty, but thought the better of it. He was searching the corners of the buildings, looking for the street sign whilst at the same time trying to avoid driving into the back of another car.

'What do you think? First thing he did when he took over. Jayne McIntyre's seat wasn't even cold and he'd split up our team. Sent you off to the SCU? Young MacBride running around after Spence like he's a sergeant with years under his belt.'

'He's not making you work for a living is he, Bob?' McLean found the street he was looking for, slowed down as he saw the blue and white tape across the road.

'Ach, you know what I mean, sir. He's just changing things 'cause he can. Fucking us around 'cause we pissed him off. Great man management that is.'

'You're not telling me anything I didn't already know, Bob. Not a whole lot I can do about it though.' McLean killed the engine, climbed out of the car. They were in a tiny street, both sides blocked in by neat terraces of houses. Once upon a time these three-storey buildings would have been single residences, the basement levels the realm of servants. Now they were all split up into as many flats as the landlords thought they could get away with. Tiny little bedsits shoe-horned into rooms that had been small by the standards of the New Town to start with. All the activity seemed to be focused around an upper flat, reached by a flight of stone steps from the pavement. McLean showed his warrant card to a uniform PC who looked about twelve. 'Who's SIO?' he asked.

'Umm. You, sir?' The PC looked confused.

OK. Start again. 'Who's in charge of the crime scene?'

'I'm not exactly sure, sir. Detective Constable Mac-Bride's inside. He seems to be giving orders.'

And so it begins. The breakdown in the chain of command.

'This is a dead body we're dealing with here, Constable?' Grumpy Bob asked the question before McLean had the chance.

'Aye, sir. Hanged hisself.'

'And they sent a detective constable to take charge? No sign of DI Spence or DS Carter? Anyone else?'

'No, sir. Just Stu– . . . DC MacBride. Duty doctor's been too.'

Bloody marvellous. McLean looked around the street, the rows of wheelie bins, the gates in the metal railings where steps led down to basement flats, the tightly parked cars with their permits proudly displayed, the gathering faces at windows.

'Right, well, I guess it's up to me then. I want this cordon moved further down the street. Take in the houses either side of the crime scene. I want to know who owns all these cars. I want a list of all the neighbours, this side and across the road. And I need someone to go and tell everyone who's rubbernecking to get back inside. We'll start interviewing as soon as I've seen the body. OK?'

The constable stared slack-jawed, rooted to the spot by the impossible list of tasks.

'Well, get on with it, lad. Don't stand there like you're wanting your arse kicked.' Grumpy Bob stepped in with his size nines. With what might have been a frightened yelp, the young officer jumped to attention, then scurried off in search of help.

'Right then. Let's go see what we've been saddled with, shall we?' McLean said, and headed up the stairs.

There wasn't a lot of room in the tiny flat, and most of it was taken up by the body dangling from a rope tied up in the skylight. Judging by the smell and what little McLean could see as he approached, the deceased had been there quite a while.

'Another suicide?' he asked by way of a greeting. Detective Constable MacBride turned a little too quickly and almost tripped over his own feet, wobbling precariously as he tried not to touch the body. The look of worry on his face eased as he realized who had spoken.

'Oh, thank Christ for that. You back from Vice then, sir?'

'No, Constable, and it's the Sex Crimes Unit, as well you know.' McLean gave the constable a reassuring grin, even though he didn't much feel like it. 'And I'm not here. Just cadged a lift from Bob, OK? He'll be SIO on this one.'

MacBride nodded, he was quick on the uptake that way. Might make sergeant soon, inspector in a couple of years if he was unlucky. He turned back to the body, flattening himself to the wall to make room for McLean and Grumpy Bob to see.

'Looks like a suicide, sir. Jammed a broom handle in the skylight, threw the rope over it, stood on a chair at the top of the stairs. There's even a note through in the room there.'

'But you don't like the look of it.' McLean took a step closer to get a better view of the body. It was male, that much was obvious enough. Judging by the smell, the bloating and the discoloured skin, it had been hanging for weeks rather than days. Flies buzzed around the corpse, a few battering themselves against the glass skylight, most happy to be locked in with such a prize.

'The pathologist been yet?' Grumpy Bob asked.

MacBride shook his head. 'Just Doctor Buckley.'

'Well, we can't do anything here until Angus has done his bit.' McLean scanned the narrow hallway, seeing just two doors leading off it other than the one they'd come in through. 'Where's this note then?'

'This way, sir.'

MacBride inched past the hanged man, careful not to disturb the body. McLean followed, trying not to breathe as much to avoid the stench as anything. Grumpy Bob stayed back. 'I'll just wait, in case Cadwallader turns up, aye?'

As if he wouldn't be able to find the body by himself. 'Fine, Bob,' McLean said. 'Fewer of us in here the better. You know what SEB are like if we contaminate their nice clean crime scenes.'

The door on the right-hand side of the hall opened onto a bedsit room scarcely big enough to stun a kitten. A single bed, unmade, was rammed into one corner, a cheap Formica-topped table within easy reach of it forming a desk of sorts. The only chair in the place was lying on its side in the hallway, not far from the dangling feet of the hanged man. A narrow window peered out through years of grime onto the back of the terrace and the slow-moving

Water of Leith. Underneath it, a kitchen sink, electric water heater and two-hob cooker all filled a space only marginally bigger than a tea tray. The dirty plates in the sink had begun to grow some interesting new life forms, but looking around the tiny room, McLean suspected that was only because the deceased had not been discovered for a week or two. Generally, the place was shabby, cluttered, but not dirty.

'The note's here, sir.' MacBride stood beside the table-cum-desk, studiously not touching anything. A pile of textbooks were wedged up against the wall, the little coloured tags on their spines telling of overdue library tickets. Alongside them, a stack of cheap spiral-bound notebooks and an elderly mobile phone, a broken tin pencil case with a random collection of cheap pens in it. All had been moved to the sides to make space for the single sheet of paper, green biro spelling out the last confused thoughts of a man about to hang himself.

There is no hope, only blackness.
I can see no point in going on.
To whoever finds me, I am sorry.
Farewell, cruel world.

'It's a bit melodramatic, isn't it?' McLean leaned close, inspecting the page for any marks without actually touching it. The notebook it had been torn from lay on the top of the pile, the leaky plastic pen alongside. Everything was very neat, almost perfectly lined up square. He turned and scanned the room again; shabby, not chaotic, but neither was it somewhere an obsessive lived.

A noise from outside dragged his attention back to the door through to the hall, the unmistakable sound of the city pathologist, Angus Cadwallader, arriving on the scene.

'Oh good Christ, Bob. Not another one?' Two footsteps on the wooden steps and then, 'Oh shit. Tracy!'

McLean rushed to the door, fairly sure what sight was going to greet him. Sure enough, frozen in tableau, Angus Cadwallader and his assistant Tracy Sharp stood in the hallway, with Grumpy Bob silhouetted behind them by the daylight outside. Closer still, the body hung from its stout hemp rope. As he watched in horrified fascination, its head slowly shifted sideways and up, as if the hanged man were trying to look his dissector in the eye. And then with a horrible sucking, tearing sound, like pulling a foot from wet mud, it sheared off completely, rotted flesh of neck no longer able to hold the weight of the body beneath it, vertebrae snapped by the drop that had killed him. The body didn't so much fall as slough to the floor, exploding in a mess of foetid liquid, a water bomb balloon filled with diarrhoea that splattered over walls, doors, pathologist and assistant alike. McLean sprang back, gagging at the smell as the rope, released of its tension, flipped the severed head in a neat arc through the open doorway. It landed with a horrible thud, rolled over once and came to a halt at his feet, dead eyes staring sightlessly upwards. He stared back, aware of nothing but the noise behind him as Detective Constable MacBride threw up on the threadbare carpet.

The stench of rotting flesh was still in his nostrils three hours later as McLean sat in a chair in Doctor Wheeler's office, Emma beside him. No one had mentioned it, but he was sure they could smell him. Just too polite to say anything.

It had taken almost two of those hours just to get out of the tiny little bedsit room. Once the body had exploded all over the hall, he and DC MacBride had been effectively trapped; no way out except to wade through a morass of decaying flesh and noxious fluids. Angus Cadwallader had done his best to inspect the remains in situ as quickly as possible, but removing them had proven tricky. In the end one of the neighbours had produced a ladder and they'd climbed out of the window. McLean had sent the constable back to the station for a shower and a change of clothes, with the advice that he might want to think about burning those he had been wearing. There hadn't been time for him to do the same, even with Grumpy Bob ably handling the crime scene. McLean had barely made it to the hospital on time, meeting an anxious Emma and scowling Jenny Nairn in the lobby with minutes to spare.

'These are remarkable. Very good indeed.' Doctor Wheeler shuffled slowly through a pile of photographs printed off earlier in the day. Not only could Emma handle a camera like a professional, she had taken to the photo-editing software like a teenager with a new video game. The results were costing him a fortune in printer ink and glossy paper, but it was worth it to see the spark in her eyes as she worked.

'You've been going outside, I see,' Doctor Wheeler added. 'Is this a park somewhere?'

'The garden,' McLean said. The doctor made no reply,

merely raised an eyebrow and peered more closely at the photograph.

'There's a squirrel lives in that tree.' Emma leaned forward, tapping the photo. 'Mrs McCutcheon's cat tries to catch it, but it's too quick for her.'

'Mrs McCutcheon?'

'Her?'

McLean and Doctor Wheeler spoke at the same time. Her question was understandable, his less so. He'd never given the cat a name, true. And he would always think of it as Mrs McCutcheon's cat. But he couldn't recall ever telling Emma that. Nor had he any idea what gender it was.

'You've been visiting a neighbour?' Doctor Wheeler asked.

'Ah. No. Mrs McCutcheon lived in the ground floor flat in my Newington tenement. She . . .'

'She died in a fire.' Emma's finger slid from the photo, her hands slowly coming together in her lap. Her voice was different, an echo of her old self. 'It was so sad. Only one of her cats survived. Tony took it in. Like he took me in.' She looked sideways at him and a shiver ran through McLean's whole frame. Was that how she thought of him? As the man who took her in and gave her a roof over her head? It was true, in a way. But it was also deeply depressing. They'd had so much more, and now she thought of him as . . . what? A cross between a knight in shining armour and a parent?

'Well, these are very good anyway.' Doctor Wheeler shuffled the photographs into a pile, banging the edges against the desk with a little more noise than was necessary.

'You're making progress. And it shows us that the memories are still in there somewhere. We just need to find the right stimulus to shake them free.'

'Did you have something in mind?' McLean asked. Alongside him, Emma had retrieved her stack of photos and was leafing through them as if no one else was there.

'Ah, the detective's leading question.' Doctor Wheeler smiled. 'As a matter of fact I did. Something a bit unusual, I'll grant you, but a colleague of mine over in Glasgow's used it a couple of times with good results.'

'What are you suggesting?' McLean had a horrible feeling he knew already.

'It's called cranial-electro stimulation therapy,' Dr Wheeler began.

'Shock therapy.' It wasn't a question.

'Not exactly, no.' Doctor Wheeler's voice changed, taking on the tone McLean suspected she used on her students. 'Not like *One Flew Over the Cuckoo's Nest*. That's electro-convulsive therapy. ECT. That would be counter-productive in that it's designed to eliminate behaviours and tends to destroy memories. What we're trying to do is stimulate Emma's brain into rebuilding the lost connections.'

'But you still want to pass an electric current through her head.' McLean slumped back in his chair, let out a long noisy breath. He'd thought maybe some new drug, something behavioural.

'You're sceptical.'

'Does it show?'

'Just a bit.'

He thought about the odd conversation the night

before. 'Probably no worse than what Ms Nairn suggested last night.'

Doctor Wheeler gave him an odd little look, half a smile, half a frown. 'Let me guess. Hypnotherapy.'

'You think it's hogwash?'

'No. quite the contrary. It's a useful part of the recovery process, especially where memory loss is concerned. It would probably be good for Emma, certainly shouldn't do her any harm.'

'I sense a but in there.'

'So easy to read?' Doctor Wheeler shrugged. 'It's not so much the what as the who. I take it Jenny's talking about Doctor Austin.'

'That was the name.'

'Well, Eleanor's good at what she does. I'll give her that much. Silly of me, really. We had a bit of a falling out many years ago, which is probably why I wouldn't have suggested her myself. But she helped Jenny, many others too.' Doctor Wheeler shook her head as if trying to dislodge something stuck there. 'No. You'd be as well taking Emma to see her.'

15

'Why were you even there, for fuck's sake?'

Chief Superintendent McIntyre's office, early morning. McLean tried to focus on Duguid, not stare past him at the pattern of rain on the window. Too easy to be swept away by the endless motion, tune out the droning noise of that voice. It was a skill he'd perfected through innumerable endless morning briefings as a sergeant, but now was not the time for it, no matter how much he wanted to just ignore his superior.

'You were meant to be assisting Jo Dexter with a murder enquiry, not swanning about poking your nose into messy suicides.' Duguid grasped the sheaf of paper that was Grumpy Bob's initial report on the hanged man as if the act of terminal desperation had been meant only for his personal inconvenience. McLean held his tongue, kept his eyes on the acting superintendent, just the occasional sideways glance about the room. No matter what the man did to the place, it would always be Jayne McIntyre's office as far as he was concerned. A place where problems were shared, dissected, solved.

'Are you even listening to me, McLean.'

'Yes, sir. I'm sorry about the suicide scene. I wasn't meant to be there, but I was getting a lift across to HQ when the call came in. It was on the way, we thought it would be a five-minute detour.'

Duguid sneered. 'That old Morse-mobile of yours not working then?'

It took a while for McLean to realize what the acting superintendent meant. He'd not been using his grandmother's old Alfa much; it wasn't really suited to modern cities with their gridlocked traffic. Somewhere on his list of things to do was buy a new car; he couldn't carry on living across town without one. It was just that pretty much everything else on the list was higher priority.

'Why do I fucking well bother, McLean?' Duguid dropped the mangled report back onto the desk, ran a bony, long-fingered hand over his face and through his hair, like a face-hugging alien. 'You're determined to stick your nose into every little investigation going.'

'With respect, sir. I don't think this is a "little" investigation at all. If you've read the report you'll know that DS Laird thinks it's suspicious. Might not be a suicide at all.'

'Oh Christ. Here we go again. Haven't I heard this before? You said there was something hooky about the last suicide but we couldn't find anything. God only knows how many man hours we wasted interviewing the poor bastard's friends and they all said he was depressed as fuck.'

McLean gritted his teeth. Why couldn't the man see? It was plain as the knobbly lump on the end of his red nose.

'I know what they said, sir. I've read DC MacBride's interview transcripts. Mikhailevic wasn't happy, true, but there's a long way between that and stringing a rope up, looping it round your neck and jumping off a chair you've balanced on the edge of a table. And no one's been able to explain how he did all that without getting any rope fibres under his nails.'

Duguid stared up at him with his piggy little eyes, an expression on his face of utter bemusement. 'I just don't get you, McLean. Suicide note – check. Suicidal tendencies – check. None of the neighbours saw or heard anyone else. What more do you need to convince you that he killed himself? A fucking home video?'

'I'd be the first to admit it's tenuous, sir. But I thought we were supposed to investigate crimes. If Grigori Mikhailevic didn't commit suicide. If someone –'

'If someone what, McLean? If someone somehow managed to string him up without him struggling? If someone persuaded him to write a suicide note, climb up on a chair, jump off to his death? Have you heard of Occam's Razor? Educated man like yourself, I'd have thought you would.'

'To be honest, sir, I'd accepted Mikhailevic's death as suicide. Not happy about it, but I get that we don't have limitless resources. I don't consider the time we put into investigating it a waste, either. We'll put that down to different priorities, shall we?'

Duguid opened his mouth to speak, the red anger rising in his face. McLean cut him off before he could start.

'But yesterday's hanging opened up a whole new angle. There were too many similarities for it to be coincidence. They both used the same phrase in their notes: "To whoever finds me, I am sorry."'

'That's hardly enough to launch a murder enquiry,' Duguid scoffed.

'No, sir. It's not. But it's not a normal thing to find in a suicide note. Generally speaking the last thing these people are doing is thinking about the impact of their actions on others. I think we need to consider the possibility that these two suicides are connected. I'd like DS Laird and DC MacBride to reopen the Mikhailevic case, combine the two investigations. Just in case there's some sort of suicide pact going on. You know, like happened down in Wales a few years back?'

Duguid fell silent. Were it not for the drumming of rain on the window, McLean felt sure he could have heard the cogs turning slowly in the acting superintendent's brain. He stood still, hands clasped behind his back, almost at attention. Said nothing while he waited. No point rushing a decision out of Dagwood; you'd only end up regretting it.

'Not Grumpy Bob, no,' Duguid said eventually. 'He's part of Spence's team on the Braid Hill investigation. Technically MacBride is too. You want to look into this suicide so desperately, do it yourself.'

Ah yes, the notorious Braid Hill flasher. Not seen since the students went down for the summer holidays. Just the sort of high-profile, manpower-hungry investigation that needed a detective inspector, a detective sergeant and a detective constable to pursue. Nothing to do with the fact that a certain acting superintendent lived just across the road from the last reported sighting.

'What about DS Ritchie?'

'What about her? She's busy.'

'You've got her running the evidence store, sir. She's an experienced detective sergeant. She transferred down here from Aberdeen to help with investigations, not piss around in the stores. It's bad enough you being shifted to admin without losing anyone else from CID. We're short enough as it is.'

Duguid looked up suddenly at McLean's words, sharp enough to catch the veiled compliment, searching for the joke but not finding it.

'What about the evidence store? We need someone with half a brain to run it.'

'Bring Tam Ferrers out of retirement, or Pete Dundas. He made enough noise about having to quit before his time anyway.'

Duguid's stare narrowed as he considered the idea, as if his hatred for McLean was warring with the realization that it was a sensible suggestion. McLean decided it was time to play his trump card.

'If you bring an ex-copper back in on contract, it's a direct cost, sir. You can run it through the admin budget rather than payroll.' Not as if he'd wasted a morning discussing it with Heather in HR.

'Very well.' Duguid gave his head the lightest of nods. 'You can break the news to her yourself. And set up something with Human Resources to get a replacement in.'

Of course, because it's every detective inspector's job to sort out the station's admin staff needs. McLean nodded back in acknowledgement, turned to leave.

'And McLean.'

'Sir?' He didn't turn around.

'I want this done by the sergeants and constables. Use PC Gregg or someone else from uniform. There's plenty wanting a shot at being a detective. None of your hands-on, sticking your nose in everywhere stuff. You're an inspector now. You manage the investigations. Direct. Leave the grunt-work to those on a lower pay scale.'

'Sir.' Another nod. McLean ground his hands into fists

and willed himself calm. He left the office without another word, closed the door firmly behind him. He'd got what he wanted; it was just a shame it had come at such a high cost.

'I don't know what you did to get me out of there, sir, but I owe you big time.'

Detective Sergeant Kirsty Ritchie sat in one of the uncomfortable chairs in the CID room, leaning back against the wall. She'd only been in the evidence store a week, but already she had taken on the pale and unhealthy pallor of those who dwelled underground.

'Me? I didn't do anything.' McLean feigned ignorance as he set to cleaning the scribbled notes of a long-abandoned investigation from the whiteboards that filled one wall of the room. He thought he'd been clever, stopping by the major incident room and nicking a whiteboard eraser and a handful of pens, but time had welded the ink in place. Now he was doing his best with a damp cloth he'd found in amongst the detritus around the coffee machine in the far corner of the room. He suspected it was meant for drying up mugs. If so, no one had explained to the detectives who used the place that they were supposed to wash them first.

'That's not what I heard. And there's no way Dagwood could've come up with the idea of bringing back Sergeant Dundas from his retirement.'

'And yet there it is. His own idea, fully formed and costed in his head.' McLean polished a coffee smear from the now usable whiteboard and took a step back. Where to start? He took a red marker pen out of his pocket and wrote 'Grigori Mikhailevic' in capital letters at the top. Pulling out another pen, blue this time, he reached across to write the next name a couple of feet away. Paused.

'The second hanging. What was his name again? Paul Sanders? Pete?'

Ritchie dropped her seat back down, pulled the folder off the desk beside her. 'Patrick Sands. Twenty-five years old. Works in a call centre off Leith Walk. Studying part time for his banking exams.' She gave a little snort of disbelief. 'I didn't even know there was such a thing.'

'Every day's a good day when you learn something new.' McLean wrote the name down and stepped back again. So far the only thing linking these two was the fact that they were both written on this board here in the CID room. Now all they had to do was fill in the big blank space between them.

'Where do we start?' Ritchie asked, standing beside him now. She had the Mikhailevic file in one hand, tapped the corner of it lightly against her chin. McLean caught that slight whiff of perfume off her and realized he'd not smelled it for a while now. Duguid had done a fine job of ripping his team apart.

'There's a list of Mikhailevic's friends and co-workers in there.' He pointed at the folder. 'Don't worry, it's not long. Contact them all and see if any of them know Sands.'

'I'll get on it. What have we got on Sands so far?'

McLean picked up the other folder, slimmer even than the one Ritchie was holding. 'Bugger all. Name, place of work. Not much else. MacBride did what he could, but he's got a lot else to deal with.'

'He going to be helping us with this one?'

McLean let out a long sigh. 'It would make sense. He was the first detective at both scenes. But like I said, Mike Spence has got him running around after every call that comes in. And Dagwood said no. See if you can get PC Gregg to help, or one of the other more resourceful uniforms.'

Ritchie gave him a sceptical look. 'What about Grumpy Bob?'

'Did I hear someone calling my name?'

McLean and Ritchie both turned at the same time, narrowly avoiding a nasty collision. Grumpy Bob stood in the doorway, a newspaper tucked under one arm, coffee mug in the opposite hand. Little tendrils of steam wafted off the top, bringing a warm, rich aroma to the room. Not from the canteen then.

'Morning, Bob. You still working that burglary case?'

'Got the little toerag down in the cells as we speak, sir. Can you believe he tried to flog some of his ill-gotten gains across the road.' Grumpy Bob nodded towards the window in an approximation of the direction of the pub used almost exclusively by police officers just off their shift.

'Surely nobody's that stupid,' Ritchie said.

'You've not been in Edinburgh long, lass. We take pride in the idiocy of our petty criminals.' Grumpy Bob dropped his newspaper onto his desk, pulled out the chair and sat down. He took a long slurp of coffee, staring at the white-board all the while.

'Mikhailevic. That's the chappy hanged himself, aye?'

McLean nodded.

'And Wee Paddy Sands would be the one we had to scrape up off of his own floor yesterday.'

McLean resisted the urge to ask who Bob thought 'we' was in this statement, since as far as he was aware, the detective sergeant had kept well away from the clean-up operation. 'That's the one.'

'What makes you think there's a connection?'

'Come on, Bob. Two hangings in quick succession? Similar profile to the two victims? The same phrase used in both suicide notes?'

'The same rope, too.' Grumpy Bob grinned and for a moment, McLean was a wet-behind-the-ears detective constable again.

'You noticed that.'

'I noticed that, aye. And it's not just any old rope either. Good solid hemp, three-quarter inch thick. You got photos in those folders?' Grumpy Bob pushed himself out of his seat like a much younger man, reaching for the reports. He shuffled through the first one, coming out with a couple of glossy sheets, stuck them to the whiteboard under Mikhailevic. By the time he'd finished, Ritchie had done the same for Sands. McLean stood back, watching them at work.

'You'll only get that at a ship's chandler's.' Grumpy Bob tapped at one of the photographs showing a close-up of the rope still tight around the victim's neck. The second picture was just the rope laid out, the knot still tight. 'There's only a couple in the city, probably worth paying them a visit.'

'While you're at it, see if you can find an expert on knots,' McLean said. The two sergeants stopped what they were doing.

'Knots?' Grumpy Bob asked.

'Knots. Yes. I don't know much about them. Sure I couldn't tie one of those hangman's nooses, but they look very similar to me. Everything else is circumstantial so far, but if we can show that these two knots were tied by the same person . . .' McLean let the sentence go unfinished, stared at the two photographs, that all too familiar chill forming in his gut as the implications of what he was seeing started to build.

16

McLean found Jo Dexter at her desk, poring over some photographs that would almost certainly get anyone else arrested, should they be found in their possession. It looked like she was comparing images to see if the same child appeared in more than one. The scowl on her face when she looked up as he knocked at the door showed just how little she enjoyed the task.

'Thought you were coming in earlier,' she said by way of greeting.

'I was, but I had to go and see his majesty first. Seems I'm now working Vice and Homicide. It's a good thing I don't need to sleep.'

Dexter tried to smile at the joke, but it didn't really sit well with the job she'd been doing. Everyone referred to the Sexual Crimes Unit as Vice, except the poor bastards working there. Nothing glamorous about dealing with paedophiles and rapists day in and day out. Never mind the prostitution and all its associated ills.

'Still buggered sideways till Tuesday?'

'Something like that. I don't know whose brilliant idea it was to put Dagwood in charge, but they'd better make a decision soon about a permanent station head.'

'What if they decide to give it to him?'

McLean looked at the DCI's face, searching for any

hint that she was joking. Finding none. 'They wouldn't. They couldn't. Could they?'

'They thought he was good enough to fill in.'

'Yes, but that was just temporary. I mean, Jayne had to move out sharpish when . . .'

Now the smile, a wicked cracking around the eyes. It was a tired one though, as if the possibility of Superintendent Charles Duguid, not acting, was too terrible even for the darkest of comedies.

'What's he got you working on then?' Dexter shuffled the photographs back into a pile, pushed them into a brown folder where she wouldn't have to look at the one on top. At least not for now. McLean told her about the two suicides by hanging, DC MacBride's initial suspicions and the anomalies that had come to light after just a brief investigation.

'I can see why he's not happy throwing a lot of man-power at it,' Dexter said after a while. 'I mean, it sounds suspicious to me, but in the end it's a couple of lonely blokes with no prospects both deciding to top themselves the same way. You'll probably find there's been a documentary about a hangman on the telly recently. Something like that. Just bad luck it struck a chord with both of them.'

McLean rubbed at his eyes. 'Thanks for the support.'

'Hey. I'm just saying. You may be right.' Dexter held her hands up in surrender. 'Anyways, I'm guessing that's not what you came to chat about.'

'No, I was wondering where we were with Malky Jennings. I missed the morning briefing.'

'Wouldn't've made any difference if you'd been there.

Nothing's changed. We've as much chance of catching whoever did him as I have of making Detective Super. Acting or no.'

'Interviews all done?'

'Aye. Every single apartment in that square. Even the ones that look out the other way. Half the folk living there are on the dole. They'd've been in all day watching telly. Or stoned out of their heads. Nobody saw a bloody thing.'

'And he was killed somewhere else, dumped in the night?'

'That's what the SOCOs and your pathologist friend think. Beaten to death with a stick or a bat and then thrown into the garbage pile at the back of the lock-ups. No real surprise he was there; half his pros live in those apartments.'

McLean thought of Magda Evans in her mouldy fourth-floor flat, standing at that floor-to-ceiling window and looking down as someone beat her pimp into a pulp. Or had she already been on her way to the boat then? He'd got more information out of her than anyone else so far. Perhaps he should go and talk to her again. Might be worth speaking to that charity wifey as well, if he could remember her name. Sanders or something.

'You've got that look on your face again, Tony. What're you thinking?'

'Just what you said. Half his pros live there. Might be worth having another chat with them.'

'I'll get Pete onto it. He knows everyone down there.'

'That might not be the best idea.' McLean pulled up a chair and sat down. He knew this was going to be difficult; no reason for it to be uncomfortable too.

'What is it with you and him? You don't like his methods? He gets results.'

'He scares people into giving him what he wants. From what I've heard that's not always information. I'd not be happy working with someone who took that sort of thing if it was offered, let alone demanding it with menace.'

'Like I said, he gets results.' Dexter sat back in her chair, shoulders slumped. 'I don't like it any more than you do, but it gets to you, this job.' She swept a weary hand in the direction of her desk, the envelope filled with pictures of young children having their innocence stripped away along with their clothes. 'Some of us just get bitter, drink too much. Others get it out of their system in different ways. Pete Buchanan has been here longer than anyone.'

McLean shook his head. 'It's no excuse. And it's no help here. You saw how those girls we took off the boat clammed up when he was interviewing them. They're not going to help us if he's about.'

'And you think they will if it's just you?'

'No. But they might if I get Clarice Saunders in.' Judging by Dexter's expression he'd got the right name.

'Jesus, Tony. Dagwood said you'd be a breath of fresh air in the place. He didn't say anything about a tornado. You want to bring that woman in here?'

'I want to find out who killed Malky Jennings. I've a suspicion it's the same people who pulled all those women off the streets and put them on a boat to the Continent. Next stop the Middle East and Christ alone knows what.'

'And all Clarice Saunders will want to do is tear a strip off any officer she can buttonhole for more than two minutes.'

'If Buchanan's the best we can do then maybe she's got a point. Look, we can do this at my own station, use some of the CID sergeants. New faces.' McLean stopped speaking, aware that Duguid would have a fit if he found out. Dexter stared at him, silent for what felt like an hour. He said nothing, just met her stare and waited.

'Fine,' she said eventually. 'Bring Little Miss in. Interview your girls without any of us to help.'

'Thank you.' McLean stood, opened the door. Dexter waited until he was just about to leave before speaking again.

'Just don't blame me when it all blows up in your face.'

The CID room was empty when McLean popped his head round the door several hours later. The whiteboard had begun to fill up, evidence of some work going on at least. He had to hope that Ritchie and Grumpy Bob were off interviewing friends and associates of the late Patrick Sands, or maybe following up something from the pathology report.

Thinking of it, McLean realized he'd not seen anything about Sands since his partly liquefied remains had been scooped up and taken away for closer examination. That was one post-mortem he was pleased not to have had to witness. But it was frustrating nonetheless. Being split between two teams meant he couldn't concentrate fully on either. Nor could he give Emma the attention she really deserved.

Without realizing it, McLean had entered the room and crossed to the whiteboard. Grumpy Bob's and Ritchie's desks faced each other close by, and he started to scan the papers lying on them for anything that might look like a pathologist's report. He almost jumped when the door opened across the room, starting like a guilty schoolboy. But it was only DC MacBride who entered.

'Afternoon, Stuart. You seen the path report for Sands?'

'Erm. Couldn't rightly say, sir.' MacBride looked very uncomfortable, as if he were a child recently scolded.

'Someone been picking on you, Constable?'

MacBride's cheeks went pink, his forehead shining like a beacon. He was going to have to work on that if he wanted to make a good interviewer.

'It's Dagwood, isn't it. Let me guess. He told you not to work on any of my cases, and if I bullied you into it to let him know. Am I right?'

'Actually it was me, but the sentiment's the same.' Mac-Bride spun around as the door he'd just entered pushed open. He was so close that it almost caught him on the chin, not that the man behind it would have cared.

'Come on, MacBride. Out the way.' Detective Chief Inspector John Brooks blundered into the room, closely followed by his sidekick, Detective Inspector Michael Spence. Or Little and Large as they were universally known in CID. Behind them, a gaggle of DCs clustered nervously, no doubt awed by the presence of such powerful men.

'I thought you were working Vice these days, McLean.' Brooks dropped his heavy frame into the nearest available chair, glanced up at the whiteboard. 'Oh yes. Your pet theory about the suicides. Charles did mention something now I think about it.'

Charles. McLean stifled a laugh. As if Brooks hadn't

spent his entire time in CID calling Duguid every name under the sun. Now they were best buddies and on first-name terms. Or maybe he was just trying to impress the new recruits.

'You know me, sir. I don't like unanswered questions.'

'Problem is you see questions where there aren't any, McLean. Don't you. And you just keep on asking them regardless of the cost.'

'I prefer to think of it as being thorough. Sir.'

'Well go and be thorough somewhere else then. I need this room for a briefing.' Brooks nodded at the assembled constables, all of whom were staring at him like first-years in front of a prefect. Except MacBride, McLean noticed. He at least had the decency to look embarrassed.

'Unless of course you'd like to sit in and give us the benefit of your thoroughness.' This from Little Detective Inspector Michael Spence. Until he'd said it, McLean might have considered staying to listen, if only to annoy Brooks. On his own, Mike Spence was OK, but something of the toad crept into him when he was with his boss. Together they could be as catty as schoolgirls and he really wasn't in the mood for being on the receiving end of that.

'It's OK. I wouldn't want to get in the way.' McLean turned his back on the detectives, caught MacBride's eye as he left. 'You see DS Ritchie, let her know I'm looking for her, aye?'

MacBride nodded, but said nothing. McLean left him, sitting with the others and yet painfully apart. Well, the lad was going to have to learn about politics if he wanted to go anywhere.

17

He doesn't really know why he's come here. Well, that's not true; there's the pain, that's the main reason. But this isn't a place for pain, not exactly. The hospital's for pain. They give you drugs that don't really take it away, just make you not care about it so much. Except that he does, care that is. He can feel it, even through the stupefying, thought-muddying fog of medication. The grinding of bone upon bone, the stretch of scar, ripping deep inside muscle, the impossible weariness of constantly feeling his whole body falling apart.

'Jonathan. Welcome. I've heard so much about you. Please, take a seat.'

He folds himself into the chair as gently as possible. Even so his skin screams at the touch of soft cushion and old leather. Somewhere deep inside he knows that it can't really hurt, not sitting in a chair, but that part of his brain is no longer wired to the rest of him.

'You were in an accident, they tell me. Badly hurt.'

He tries to focus on the person speaking to him, but the words take him straight back to that day. He remembers it all, cannot help living it over and over again. The screeching noise like an animal mortally wounded, brakes locked, rubber on tarmac. It only took seconds but he pictures it in years. The slow inevitability of it all is almost as bad as the pain. Tiny details present themselves: the expression on the driver's face, more annoyance than surprise; the pattern of cracks in the windscreen that will shatter and rend his skin to mincemeat; the broken wiper arm that will knife him like a jealous lover, vent his spleen.

'You've been in a lot of pain, yes? Even though your body has healed, it still troubles you.'

He isn't healed. Not nearly. He can hear the shotgun cracks as his bones pop, feel the wind rush out of him as the van hits. He is flying through the air, helpless as the street bin rushes up to meet him. Better if he'd not been wearing his helmet. Then it would have been over quickly.

'I can help you. I can make the pain go away.'

A touch, light on his hand. It sends shivers of purest agony pulsing through his arm. He looks up, sees no face, no body attached to that point of contact. Just two eyes, blazing like the headlights that took away his life. Something surges through him, a force that would be impossible to resist, even if he wanted to resist it. But he doesn't. This is why he came here, after all. To be rid of the pain. To be rid of it all.

'You are mine!' The voice is triumphant, gloating almost as if it has won some great victory. He no longer cares. Longs only for it to end.

'Yes. I am yours.'

18

He'd been expecting something different. McLean wasn't really sure what; maybe a bit more mysticism, some occult paraphernalia, even a picture of Paul McKenna or something. Instead the offices of Doctor Eleanor Austin were light and airy. More Feng Shui than Doris Stokes. They had sat in a room that could have been the reception area for a dentist or an accountant, plied with coffee and pleasantries by a young assistant who had introduced himself as Dave. The wait had been short, and now they were in the therapy room with Doctor Austin herself. She was older than he'd thought she'd be. Much older than Doctor Wheeler, certainly. And yet she held herself with the poise of a younger woman. She sat in a high-backed leather armchair on one side of a low table. Emma had a similar seat to herself and he was relegated to a sofa arranged along one wall so that he could see and be seen by both of them.

'So tell me, Emma. What's your most vivid memory from before the . . . trauma?'

'I'm not really sure. It's all such a blur.'

'That's the recent past. We'll get to that. Tell me something that you remember from a long time ago. Home, perhaps. A birthday, or maybe Christmas?' Doctor Austin's voice was soft, calm, reassuring, with the slightest hint of a sing-song lilt to it, an accent McLean couldn't place.

'I never liked Christmas. Mum was always sick, and Dad . . . I don't want to talk about Dad.'

Emma was still pale, even this long after coming out of her coma. The high-backed chair she sat in almost swallowed her, making her look even more like the child he sometimes thought she had become. As far as he was aware, no actual hypnotism had taken place yet; this was just a getting to know you session.

'What about university then? I understand you went to Aberdeen, read biology.'

'I don't remember. I mean, yes. I understand on some level I must have. I know a lot about it. Just don't know how I know, if you know what I mean.' Emma's voice had begun to take on that edge McLean had become all too aware of. The tone that said she was verging on panic as she tried to sort the memories in her head. He'd tried gently questioning her himself, teasing out details and helping her build a trail in her mind back to where they'd originally come from. It usually ended badly. He couldn't begin to imagine what it was like, to know something but not know how you knew. To understand that a large chunk of your life was missing. He'd be treading on the edge of terror himself, if it had happened to him.

'OK. Let's leave that for now.' Doctor Austin was obviously sensitive to the mood too. Then again, you'd have to be in her line of work, surely. It was all about the empathy, after all. 'We'll try something different.'

'Are you going to hypnotize me?' Emma asked.

'Not straight away, no. I just want you to relax. Close your eyes. Listen to my voice.' Doctor Austin began to recite a slow, quiet litany, her voice even softer than it had been before. It took him a while to make out the actual words, longer still to realize that he, too, had closed his eyes. With an effort, McLean opened them. The room turned darker, and colder too. An involuntary shiver ran through his body. Emma had almost disappeared into the back of her chair, her head drooped, eyes closed, arms folded loosely on her lap. Opposite her, Doctor Austin was in complete contrast, ramrod stiff, upright, chin jutting out. Her eyes too were closed, but McLean could see flickering movement behind the lids as if she were reading some script off the inside of them. She crackled with an energy that was both reassuring and alarming. He shook his head, not realizing until he did that it was fuzzy, as if he'd been drinking on an empty stomach. With the motion, the room brightened, the scene shifted almost imperceptibly, Doctor Austin's words drifted away to nothing.

'Did you fall asleep, Tony?'

McLean shifted his gaze at the question. Emma was no longer sitting in her chair, but had somehow stood and crossed the room to where he was sitting without him realizing. He looked up at her with a mixture of confusion and surprise. She loomed over him, the ceiling light making a halo of her spiky hair, and she was smiling at him with a grin that went right up to her eyes. It was the first time he'd seen her smile like that since she'd woken in the hospital, and it filled him with hope that chased away the strangeness of the past few minutes.

'I did? I guess I was more tired than I thought.'

'Can we go home now?' Emma turned a little, towards where Doctor Austin was still seated, and the effect of the lights disappeared. Without the halo, the smile, she was once more the frightened little girl in a woman's body. Her whole posture was different, hunched into herself as if she had no self-confidence.

McLean hauled himself out of the sofa, knees protesting as if he'd been sitting there for hours. A quick glance at his watch, but no, only twenty minutes had passed since they'd been ushered into the room by Dave.

'Are we finished?' he asked Doctor Austin.

'For now, yes.' The doctor stood, touched a hand lightly to Emma's elbow and steered her towards the door. 'I'll need to see you again in a few days. Then we'll try a little hypnosis.'

McLean followed the two of them out of the room, through the reception area where Dave was forcing coffee and biscuits on another customer. He felt removed from the scene, as if his hearing were dulled by listening to loud music, but as he stepped out of the building into the street and the clear, bright sunlight, the noise of the city returned, enveloping him like the embrace of an old friend.

The downside of taking the morning off to see Emma through her session with the hypnotherapist was that he had a mountain of paperwork waiting for him when he finally arrived at the station. McLean had taken the unusual step of closing his office door in the hope that nothing would disturb him. Now an unpleasant electronic imitation of an old-fashioned bell broke his concentration as he fought to understand a set of overtime forms that appeared to have no bearing on any of his active cases. He dropped the sheaf of papers and reached gratefully for the phone, noting the flashing light for the front desk.

'McLean.'

'Ah. Glad I caught you, sir. There's a fellow down here asking for you by name.' Sergeant Murray was working the desk this afternoon, it would seem.

'You couldn't be a bit more specific could you, Pete?'

A short pause as if the desk sergeant were trying to find the right words. 'It's, errr . . . personal, sir.'

Oh bloody hell. 'OK. I'm on my way.'

McLean hung up, took a quick look around his office in an attempt to fix it in his mind. It wouldn't be the first time he'd been called away on a false errand only to find on his return that things had been moved. He could lock the door, of course, but somehow that felt like ceding victory to his tormentors before the game had even begun. And there was always the possibility this was a perfectly genuine matter requiring his personal attention. A slim possibility.

The station was quiet as he strode the corridors, which either meant everyone was out fighting crime or they were all avoiding him. He pushed through the security door into the reception area, seeing a well-dressed elderly gentleman with a large leather Gladstone bag. No one else had seen fit to bother the police at that precise moment, and a quick glance over his shoulder showed that Sergeant Murray was nowhere to be seen. Ah well, might as well play along.

'You wanted to see me, Mr . . . ?' McLean approached the elderly gentleman, who looked up, startled by the voice. He was thin, long-fingered bony hands folded neatly across his lap, head somehow too large for his body. His suit fitted perfectly, but whereas on a younger man this would flatter, on him it only emphasized how much he needed a really good meal. McLean had seen enough cadavers to know better than to use the adjective cadaverous lightly, but this time he felt it was perhaps justified.

'Detective Inspector McLean?' The well-dressed man stood up as if his muscles had been replaced with rubber bands. Standing, he was taller than McLean had been expecting. He held out a hand to be shaken. 'Jeremy Scranton. From Garibaldi and Sons.'

'The tailors?' McLean took the hand, surprised to find it was warm and not mortuary cold.

'The same. I've come for your measuring, as arranged. Would you like to do it here, or is there somewhere a little less, ahem, public? I've brought some material samples for you to consider as well.'

It didn't take a genius to work out what was going on. McLean looked back over his shoulder to the reception desk, hidden behind its screen of bullet-proof glass. Sergeant Murray was nowhere to be seen, which rather confirmed that he'd been in on the joke. Like most pranks, it was hilarious to the people who'd thought it up, and no doubt they'd be sniggering at how well they'd fooled him, but this poor old man had done nothing. He'd come here, taken up his precious time, expecting to be paid, and now he was going to have to go back to his shop empty-handed. Worse, if McLean ever wanted to buy something from Garibaldi and Sons, who were by all acknowledgement the finest tailors in the city, if not the whole of Scotland, then he was going to have to do some serious apologizing.

Or he could just go with it, and get a nice suit into the bargain.

'Thank you so much for coming, Mr Scranton. Please, follow me.'

A parcel sat on the kitchen table waiting for him when McLean let himself in late. He fully expected to get a couple of fine suits out of the prank, but being measured up had taken a lot longer than he'd anticipated. And the paperwork he'd been avoiding all day had still needed doing after Mr Scranton had left.

The house was quiet, even Mrs McCutcheon's cat barely stirred from its place beside the Aga, just lifted its head and fixed him with a beady stare for a moment before going back to sleep. He strained his ears for sounds that anyone was still up, but at this hour he doubted it. The clock in the kitchen suggested it was more tomorrow than today. So much for work–life balance.

One good thing to be said about having two women living in his house was that there was always food in the cupboards. Jenny was a vegetarian, something that had not come as much of a surprise to him, and Emma had taken her cue. Consequently most of what was in the fridge could be labelled under the broad term 'salad' and everything in the cupboards looked distressingly healthy. There was beer though, and wine. Through in the library there would be whisky too. He set about making himself a cheese sandwich, debating long and hard before adding a couple of lettuce leaves and a smear of mayonnaise. Poured himself a glass of Riesling from the bottle he'd started yesterday and took his spoils to the table.

The parcel was a little larger than A4, and as thick as a box file. His name and address were on a label printed out and stuck across the front, but there were no franking mark or stamps. Taking a bite of sandwich, he pulled the parcel towards him, turned it over. The name of an old city auction house had been printed on the back, and at the sight of it he remembered. The auction of Donald Anderson's books, the curious impulsion to buy this copy of Gray's *Anatomy*, purportedly from the collection of Sir Arthur Conan Doyle.

'A nice lady dropped it round earlier.'

McLean twisted round in his seat, sending a slice of pain up his neck in the process. In the shadows by the door through to the hall stood Jenny Nairn. He'd not heard her come in; a quick glance showed bare feet poking out from the legs of her sweatpants, hoody with the hood down on top, arms folded as she leaned against the wall. Her nose ring glinted in the light, her eyes dark shadows that were hard to see. How long had she been standing there watching him?

'I say lady.' She pushed herself away from the wall, padded into the light. 'But he was plainly a man dressed as a lady. You have strange friends.'

'Madame Rose. She . . . He runs a, well, I'm not sure what you would call it. A psychic centre, I guess. Palm reading, Tarot cards, that sort of stuff. Out of an old flat down Leith Walk. He's also something of an expert on medieval books and manuscripts, especially the more esoteric stuff. Not sure I'd describe him as a friend. He brought this round himself?' McLean hefted the parcel.

'Just winding you up. Everyone knows Rose.' Jenny

grinned as she drew out a chair and slumped into it. 'He dropped in back of six. Think he was a bit disappointed you weren't home.'

'That makes two of us.' McLean took another bite of his sandwich, carefully peeled open the parcel and slid out the book inside. There was a bill of sale from the auction house and a handwritten note.

'May I?' Jenny nodded at the book.

'Sure.' McLean handed it over.

'You went to see Eleanor today,' Jenny said.

'Doctor Austin? Yes.'

'I'm so glad you did. She helped me out when my folks died. Don't think I'd be here if it wasn't for her. She'll sort Emma out, don't you worry.'

'Your folks?' The words were out before McLean remembered. 'Oh yes. You said. I'm sorry.'

'No worries.' Jenny tapped a slender finger on the cover of the book as she spoke. 'It was a few years back now. Christ, near enough ten. You deal with it. Move on, y'know?'

'As it happens, I do. Sort of. I was four when my parents died. My gran raised me. Here in this house. Seemed somehow appropriate given I was born here.'

'Here? In this house? For real?' Jenny's face cracked into a wide grin as she echoed his words. 'How'd that happen? Your mum not trust doctors?'

'Far from it. Gran was a doctor. Ended up a pathologist, but she was working as a GP when I was born. She wouldn't hear of my mother slumming it in some hospital.'

'So which room, then? Where did the great Detective Inspector Tony McLean take his first breath?'

The question surprised him, not so much for its personal nature as for the wild-eyed enthusiasm that had come over her. He'd not thought about the facts of his birth in years; well, it wasn't something you dwelt upon, really. He remembered his gran bringing it up at dinner parties or whenever he invited a girl home. Her little way of embarrassing him to show she cared.

'Oddly enough, it was in the attic. Mum was up there doing all the sorts of things pregnant women are told not to do when they're close to term. I arrived earlier and quicker than expected. Gran just rolled her sleeves up and delivered me on the attic floor. That's how she tells it, anyway. Told it, I should say.'

Jenny's smile faded slightly. 'You miss her. Your gran.'

'She was more of a mum than my mother ever had the chance to be. But like you said, we deal with it, move on.' He shook his head slightly, trying to dislodge the feeling that he was lying to himself. No doubt sensing the awkwardness, perhaps feeling it herself, Jenny opened up the book near the back and started leafing forwards. McLean watched her for a moment before realizing he was still holding the note Madame Rose had written to him.

My Dear Inspector, it began. *I trust this finds you well. I hope to speak to you in person, but if you are not around then this note should suffice for now. My investigations have, alas, yielded little to corroborate the signature in the front of this book. It is of the correct type and age for a medical student of that time, and if Donald had it in his collection then it is likely he thought it genuine.*

McLean stopped as he read the name. Donald. So informal, as if he and Madame Rose had been friends. But then there was really no reason why they should not have been. Anderson was older, of course, but he'd been another expert in the same small field. They'd have known each other well. McLean shook his head, dispelling the train of thought, and returned to the note.

The grapevine informs me that your paramour is returned to consciousness. I would be the last to indulge in idle gossip, but I trust that Miss Baird fares well and is making a speedy recovery. You and I both know the malign influence to which she was exposed, however, and you have unique experience of the evil that can come of it. It is my most fervent hope that her encounter was brief and has led to no permanent harm, but should you suspect otherwise, please know that you need only ask and I will do all in my power to help.

Ever yours

Madame Rose

'Arthur Conan Doyle. Who'd've thought it?' Jenny Nairn snapped the book shut as McLean stared at the note and its curious contents. He placed it on the table, then laid the bill of sale on top of it, though he couldn't really be sure who he was hiding it from.

'We don't know it's real,' he said eventually, taking the book back and opening it up. The dedication and signature were there on the top of the first page. Just the sort of place a young and impecunious student would mark his valuable possession.

'We don't?' Jenny arched an eyebrow. 'It looks like his signature, doesn't it?'

'That's easily faked. Apparently the ink too. There's a big market for Conan Doyle memorabilia, particularly in the States. Something like this could fetch a lot of money if it were verified.'

'But that's not why you bought it, is it.' It wasn't a

question, which was just as well. McLean looked at his half-eaten sandwich, the red lettuce leaves poking out through the cheese and mayonnaise like a bloody gash in dead, white flesh. His appetite vanished, and even the glass of wine had lost its appeal. He felt suddenly very tired.

'You should go to bed. It's late.' Sitting beside him at the kitchen table, Jenny sounded just like his grandmother. An impressive feat given her age. He couldn't argue with her logic though, started to clear up his plate and glass.

'I'll sort that out, don't worry.' Jenny took them from him, bustled over to the sink.

'I didn't hire you as a maid, you know.'

She ignored him, carried on acting like one. 'She's in your bed again. Emma.'

McLean sighed. It was difficult to sleep with her there. He'd been alone so long before she'd forced her way into his life, and he couldn't help remembering her warmth, her vitality, her intoxicating scent. Having her so close, so intimate and yet unattainable was a special kind of torment.

'There's not many would put up with that. Not without taking advantage.' Jenny came back to the table, picked up the book and the two sheets of paper all together, slipped them back in their packaging and handed them to him. 'You're a good man, Tony McLean. Don't spoil that.'

And then she walked past him, bare feet silent on the floor as she disappeared into the darkness of the hall.

19

Way too early in the morning, McLean stifled a yawn as he waited for the foul-tasting coffee from the office vending machine to have some effect. The interview room was cold, which helped a bit. If the heating didn't kick in soon though, he was likely to slip into a hypothermic coma. The clunks and gurgles from the tiny radiator suggested it was trying, at least.

The door clicked open and the cheery face of Grumpy Bob peered through. 'You ready, sir?'

'Aye, Bob. Send them in.'

The door pushed wider to let in two women. Magda Evans wore jeans torn at the knee and a padded bum freezer jacket, gold with little sparkly flecks in the material. She'd tied her hair in a messy wedge on top of her head and stood upright, as if a great weight had been taken off her shoulders. She towered over the diminutive form of Clarice Saunders, swaddled in a long black woollen overcoat.

'Thanks for coming in, both of you.' McLean stood and motioned for them to take the seats on the other side of the table. Unexpectedly, Magda took the extended hand, shook it vigorously. Her touch was warm, a welcome bit of stolen heat in the chill room. McLean studied her face in the instant of that contact. She had less makeup on than the last time they'd met, and she looked healthier for it. Or maybe it was just the knowledge that her pimp was dead and she might actually escape the life she'd lived.

'This is about Malky Jennings?' Magda seemed reluctant to release his hand, so McLean tugged it gently away. Clarice had already sat down and was staring at the two of them like a disapproving parent.

'Among other things, yes. Please, sit.' He pointed at the chair and waited until Magda complied before taking his own.

'Any chance you could rustle us up some tea?' Grumpy Bob stood in the doorway. He nodded at the request, pulling the door closed behind him as he left.

'No second officer as witness?' Clarice asked.

'This isn't a formal interview, Ms Saunders. You're here because you agreed to come in. I can record things if you want.' McLean pointed at the tape machine on its shelf just in case she didn't know how it was done.

'And if we hadn't agreed to come in? Would you have arrested Magda again?'

'Again? I wasn't aware we'd arrested her before.'

'You held her here for twenty-four hours. After she'd been abducted and shoved in the hold of an old boat bound for God knows where.'

'That was the other thing I wanted to talk to Magda about, actually.' McLean shifted his gaze from the stern, tiny woman to her companion, knowing full well that it would take more than that to shut her out.

'I already told you all I know about that, Inspector.'

'I don't doubt that you believe that, Miss Evans, but I'd like to go over the events one more time, just in case we missed something. First though, Malky Jennings.'

'Malky Jennings. What of him?'

'Let's not beat about the bush. You hated him for what he did to you, aye?'

'You're not suggesting Magda here –' Clarice butted in. McLean cut her off before she could get into full flow.

'No, Miss Saunders, I'm not. Otherwise this interview would be under caution and there'd be another officer present. I know Miss Evans here had as much motive to kill Jennings as anyone. Any of his prostitutes had plenty of motive, but I don't think any of them killed him, OK?'

'He was a total bastard.' Magda's voice was quiet, matter of fact. 'But then all men are. Most men, maybe.'

McLean let that slide. 'He had control over you though, didn't he. Fixed you up with drugs, stopped you from going elsewhere. I've heard he was a violent man. Very possessive.'

'It sounds like you knew him better than most, Detective Inspector,' Clarice said. McLean ignored her again.

'You tried to leave him a couple of times though.' The sheet on Magda Evans was surprisingly short for someone who'd worked the streets in Edinburgh for as long as she had, but there was a pattern to the cautions she'd been given. Two separate occasions when she'd been found far off her normal patch. One short stint in a notorious Marchmont massage parlour that had been just a little too blatant even for the city council's laissez-faire policy, another incident in Sighthill. Both far from Restalrig and the little empire of Malky Jennings.

'He always found me though. Didn't matter how far I ran.'

'How did he know where to look?'

Clarice snorted a dismissive little laugh. 'You don't know much about how these people operate, do you, Inspector.'

'Like I said, he had control over you. And he had connections.' McLean slumped back in his chair so that his focus was no longer solely on the ex-hooker. 'He was low-level, true, but he dealt drugs and pimped a dozen, maybe fourteen prostitutes in and around Restalrig. And we let him, I'm sorry to say.'

'Can I get that in writing?' Clarice was actually smiling. It made her look slightly mad.

'Sadly I don't speak for the entire police service, Miss Saunders. I do disagree with the way things have been run here, but I also have to follow orders. Malky Jennings was largely left to his own devices because he was a known quantity.'

'This isn't anything I didn't already know.' Clarice Saunders' smile had gone, now she had her serious face on. 'I've been trying to help these women for ten years now, and every time I've reported the likes of Malky Jennings to you lot, there's been minimal response. Pulled in for questioning, maybe a fine for possession. Never anything about the women he regularly beat black and blue.'

'And you'll know why we did it, too, Miss Saunders.' McLean addressed his next question directly to Magda. 'Would you have testified against him in court if he broke your ribs?'

Her lack of response was answer enough.

'No, you wouldn't. I don't blame you, if I'm being honest. You put him away, he's out again in six months, a year. Like you said, he always managed to find you. Don't suppose it'd be just your ribs he broke the next time. And while he's away, who takes over? How do they go about asserting their authority?'

'So what? You just give up? You let the likes of him run the place? I thought you swore an oath to protect and serve?'

McLean hadn't the heart to correct Clarice Saunders on that point. It was a fair summary of what he'd thought the job was about, after all.

'Let's just say I don't like it, OK? But it's true. Malky might have beaten his girls around, but he stopped anyone worse from coming along and putting them in the mortuary. Now he's gone and I really need to know who's trying to take over his patch.'

A long silence filled the room. Earlier on in the interview, McLean hadn't been able to avoid Magda's stare, but as the conversation had turned to Malky, so her gaze had dropped. Now even her head was bowed and her shoulders slumped.

'Magda's put that world behind her, inspector.' Clarice Saunders reached over and placed a hand on her companion's arm. 'She doesn't know. Doesn't want to know.'

'You think that was wise, sir? Going all confessional on them like that?'

Grumpy Bob leaned against the wall in the corridor outside the interview room. He had a mug of tea clasped in his hand and a rolled-up newspaper shoved under his arm. A uniform PC had taken Magda Evans and Clarice Saunders out through the back, where McLean had organized a taxi to take them home.

'My Gran always told me it was best to tell the truth, no matter how painful.'

'Aye, but she didn't work for the polis, did she.'

'Not directly, no. Not sure what she'd have made of all this, either.'

All this. A nice, easy way of summing up a godawful mess. Despite her initial enthusiasm for the interview, and the different location, Magda Evans had managed to give them zero new information. McLean wasn't fooled by Clarice Saunders' stories either. Maybe the charity worker believed her new best friend was making a break from her old life. Maybe it was even true. But it didn't take a genius to see that Magda knew damned well who had muscled in on Malky Jennings' patch, and she had a very good idea who'd taken her and the other girls onto that boat. Chances were she knew why they'd picked her, too, and the story about her being half Polish didn't wash.

'So what's next?' Grumpy Bob asked. McLean eyed him up, the tea, the paper.

'Looks like you're set for a session in an empty incident room, if you can find one.'

'That depends on whether you can make me a better offer or not.'

'How're you getting on with the Braid Hill investigation? Keeping you busy?'

Grumpy Bob's answer was to pull out his newspaper and flip it open with his one free hand. The headline was easy enough to read. 'Flasher Caught!'

'Students back already?'

'Post-grad. They never really go away. Stupid bugger tried to climb over a garden wall in his flasher mac. Didn't realize it was topped with smashed glass until it was too late. He's in the hospital now. Not going anywhere in a hurry. Not on his own two feet, anyway. Probably won't be fathering many children either.'

McLean winced, but only briefly. 'So you're at a bit of a loose end right now.'

Grumpy Bob lifted his mug to his mouth, took a noisy slurp of tea. 'Mebbe. Why?'

'Ritchie's off on some bloody Police Scotland thing, but she left me a list of ship's chandlers who stock hemp rope. Thought I might go and see if any of them recall seeing either of our hanged men.'

The Captain's Rest sounded more like the name of a seaside pub than a place you'd buy bits and pieces for your yacht. There was no mistaking what it was once you approached the place, though. Stacked on the pavement outside the door, rolls of blue nylon rope, buoys, wicker lobster pots for the tourist trade and heavy ironmongery dared the casual thief to have a go. The windows displayed more expensive and easily pocketed equipment, shielded from the sun by a thin film of rumpled yellow cellophane on the inside of the glass. If you wanted to buy a dead wasp, this was clearly the place to come, too.

Inside was everything McLean expected. Head-high shelving formed narrow aisles, funnelling the shopper towards a wooden counter at the back. Deep-sea fishing gear hung from hooks on the ceiling, along with shackles, ratchets, pulleys and other impressively engineered gear he had no name for. Over to one side a rack of heavy-duty wet-weather clothing gave testament to the reality of sailing in the Firth of Forth and North Sea. No high fashion here, just survival in an environment where exposure could kill you in minutes.

Behind him, Grumpy Bob closed the door with a jingling rattle from a collection of karabiners hung on the frame, then set off into the shop to look at a stack of charts and navigation aids. McLean squeezed himself down the nearest aisle, stepping over a cardboard box that had escaped from the shelves, and approached the counter. At first he thought there was no one in, but a shuffling noise from under the wooden counter-top turned out to be a very small man with a great profusion of bushy, white hair, most of it on the lower part of his face and neck. The captain, no doubt.

'Good morning, sir. What can I do for you today?'

'I was wondering, do you sell hemp rope?'

'Ah, the old-fashioned kind. Much the best for the older boats. What is it you sail, sir? You look like a clinker-built man to me.'

McLean fished around in his inside jacket pocket, brought out his warrant card and a couple of photographs.

'Actually I'm not a sailor at all. I'm investigating a couple of suspicious deaths.'

The shopkeeper retrieved a pair of ancient wire spectacles from a chain around his neck, placed them on the end of his nose and peered at the warrant card. He stared at the image, then up at McLean, then back at the image. For a moment McLean thought he was going to carry on like that for ever.

'McLean, McLean. Any relation to Johnny McLean?

Has a twin-master in South Queensferry. Did the round-the-world a couple of years back.'

'Not that I'm aware of, no.' McLean retrieved his warrant card.

'Are you sure? You look like him.'

'Quite sure. About the hemp rope?'

'Oh yes, of course. We stock some quarter inch, half inch, three-quarter and inch. Anything bigger we'd need to order up from the manufacturer. It's foreign, of course. Comes from India. Seems like we don't make anything over here these days.'

'Quite.' McLean laid out the photographs on the counter. Grigori Mikhailevic and Patrick Sands. 'Both of these men bought three-quarter-inch hemp rope recently. You recognize either of them?'

'It's not a crime, selling rope you know.' The shopkeeper took up the photograph of Mikhailevic and gave it as close a scrutiny as he had McLean's warrant card. His spectacles were scratched almost opaque and smeared with greasy fingerprints. How he saw anything through them was a mystery, but something must have got through the mess.

'This one I recognize.' He put Mikhailevic down and picked up Sands. 'Came in and bought twenty metres of three-quarter inch, oh, a month back? Bit more probably.'

'And the other?'

'Never seen him in my life.'

'Twenty metres. That's what, sixty feet?'

'More like sixty-five.'

'Good length that.' Grumpy Bob sauntered up to the counter. 'What would you do on a boat with twenty metres of rope?'

'Depends on the boat, really,' the shopkeeper said. 'You'd not use it for sheets, right enough. But you might use it to tie up a smaller craft. Course, most people buying rope don't want it for boats, do they. Not everyone comes in here's a sailor. You gentlemen, for instance.'

'You say you recognize this man, Grigori Mikhailevic?' McLean held up the photograph to attract the shop-keeper's attention before he launched into another random segue.

'Aye, didn't know that was his name. Don't think he sounded foreign, mind. I'd remember something like that.'

'You remember how he paid? You have any record?'

'Probably cash. Why?'

'I was hoping you might have been able to pinpoint the sale,' McLean said. 'If we know when he bought the rope, we can trace his movements immediately before and after. I'm trying to build up a picture of his movements.'

'He hanged himself, didn't he. The shopkeeper grim-aced. 'Not much else you can do with that much good three-quarter-inch hemp on dry land.'

He bent down below the counter again and came out with a large hard-bound ledger. Dropped the spectacles off his nose, licked an index finger and began leafing through the pages.

'My boy wants me to put all this on his damned com-puter, but I find this much easier to work with.' It didn't take long for him to find what he was looking for. He spun the book around so McLean and Grumpy Bob could see.

'There you go. Two months ago. Cash sale. That's your chappy, God rest his soul.'

*

Of the two other chandler's shops on the list, only one stocked hemp rope and hadn't sold any for months. Nylon, it would seem, was the thing these days. Only old bufties insisted on the traditional stuff. They'd visited a couple of big hardware stores as well, just in case, but it seemed to be very much a niche product. The afternoon was winding out towards evening as McLean and Grumpy Bob crawled through the traffic on the way back to the station. A whole day of successfully avoiding Duguid and in the meantime doing some actual detective work. It felt good; a change from the dull drudgery of constant staff management, report writing and time wasting.

'Where're we going with this, sir?' Grumpy Bob sat in the passenger seat of the pool car McLean had managed to secure by luck more than good judgement. Not for the first time it occurred to him that life would be much easier if he just bought a proper car for himself and used that, like every other detective he knew.

'Not exactly sure, Bob. But we know now when and where Mikhailevic bought his rope.'

'Aye, but two months ago? He didn't kill himself till what, three weeks ago? Why'd he hang on to it for so long?' Grumpy Bob grimaced at the unintentional pun, but let it slide anyway.

'I don't know. Maybe he meant to kill himself two months ago, then had second thoughts.'

'I guess so.' Grumpy Bob stared into the middle distance, a clear indication that he was thinking things through. 'That kind've makes it more likely this is just a simple suicide though, doesn't it?'

'How so?'

'Well, I'm no expert, but I'd imagine if you'd decided to do that, to hang yourself, you'd need to get some rope from somewhere. That shop's not far from his flat, so chances are he'd have known about it. He goes in there, buys it with cash, takes it home. Has second thoughts maybe, leaves it under the bed for a while. Comes home after a particularly shit day and does the deed. No need for any complications, really.'

'You're forgetting one little thing though, Bob.' McLean feathered the brakes, coming to a halt at the end of a long line of stationary cars. The pool car was a pig to drive, its clutch heavy, gearbox notched as if it had been driven by monkeys all its short life. Probably not far from the truth. 'He bought twenty metres of rope. Sixty-five feet, near as doesn't really matter.'

'And he only used thirteen to hang himself.' Grumpy Bob got it.

'Exactly. So where's the rest? Wasn't in his flat, so did he give it to Sands? And who buys rope for someone else to hang themselves with? How does that even work?'

'You think there's some kind of suicide pact going on here?'

'We don't even know if they knew each other. There's nothing obvious to link them. Well, apart from the hanging of course.' Dip clutch, release handbrake, ease forward a few more feet. Maybe one of those new-fangled semi-automatic gearboxes he'd read about. It would certainly make driving in the city easier. 'Give forensics a call, see if they can match the two pieces. Problem is, even if they do match, that still only makes twenty-six feet. Where's the other forty?'

'Christ, you really think there's more of them out there?'

McLean eased the clutch out again as the lights turned green, mistimed it, stalled. Behind him the horns started before he could even get the engine going again. He really needed to get himself a car. Anything was better than this heap of shit.

'I really don't know, Bob, but we need to find that rope.'

20

A note on McLean's desk belied the quiet that had settled over the station by the time he and Grumpy Bob got back in. 'See me tomorrow, first thing. D.' First thing was underlined twice, never a good sign where the acting superintendent was concerned. McLean screwed it up and threw it in the bin, took a quick look at the piles of reports and overtime sheets that had been placed where some poor bastard of a secretary had obviously hoped he would see them when he sat down. No chance of that, not now. He closed the door on the trouble that would only get bigger, and went off in search of something more enjoyable to contemplate.

The quiet extended to the CID room, only two desks occupied by detectives. DC MacBride was on the telephone, furiously scribbling down notes and occasionally nodding his head in agreement with whatever was being said on the other end. DS Ritchie looked up from her computer screen as he entered.

'Hive of activity here,' McLean said.

'DCI Brooks has taken the team off to the pub to celebrate.' Ritchie snapped shut the notebook she'd been transcribing onto the computer and slumped back in her chair.

'The Braid Hill Flasher, I heard. Hardly cause for a piss-up though.'

'Not that. They caught the gang that's been hitting post offices over in the West End. Three of them holed up in a flat in Comely Bank. They had the whole street blocked off, sent in an armed-response team. It'll be all over the evening news.'

McLean thought about the note on his desk upstairs. 'This come in before or after Dagwood knocked off for the day?'

'After, why?'

'I've got a bollocking diaried for tomorrow, first thing. Maybe he'll have a change of mind.'

'That'll be DS Laird, sir.' McLean looked around. Detective Constable MacBride had finished his telephone call.

'What's Grumpy Bob done this time?'

'Gone off with you when he was supposed to be working with DI Spence. Least that's what I heard in the canteen.'

McLean pinched the bridge of his nose and let out a heavy sigh. He'd never really been sure why people did that at times of stress or exasperation, but oddly enough it helped.

'You get that list of friends and co-workers for the two suicides?'

DS Ritchie swivelled in her chair and looked at Mac-Bride, by way of passing on the question. McLean rolled his eyes at her.

'What? Dagwood said you weren't to use him for your investigation. He said nothing to me. I'm just delegating my workload to the available detective constables. Aren't I, Stuart?'

And this is what happens when you promote a detective chief inspector beyond his level of competence. 'OK, then. Has anyone got a list of friends and co-workers for the two suicides?'

'Here, sir.' MacBride held up a sheet of paper. It was split into two columns, one for Mikhailevic, one for Sands. None of the names were repeated in both columns, but that was hardly surprising as there were only half a dozen in total.

'So few?'

'That's all I've been able to come up with so far. Neither of them were exactly sociable.'

'You've spoken to their workplaces? Their bosses?'

'Mikhailevic was a student, but he had a job in a bar on Leith Walk. Sands was working in a call centre, some online bank outfit. He was a temp, paid through an agency, but he'd been there almost a year. Apparently he was studying for his banking exams. According to his manager it'd be a miracle if he ever passed them. Diligent but unimaginative was the exact phrase he used.'

'Sounds perfect banker material to me.' McLean looked at the list again, checked the time. 'Mikhailevic worked in a pub, you say?'

'The Bond Bar, down the bottom end of Leith Walk.'

'Well then, since DCI Brooks obviously didn't see fit to include you in his celebrations, I think I'll have to buy you both a drink.'

The Bond Bar was one of those places old men went to nurse grudges, a pint of heavy and a wee nip of an afternoon. The smoking ban had cleared the air inside, but nothing could get rid of the miasma of stale beer, body odour and mould that hung about the place. Early evening and a dozen or so punters were staring at a screen showing some indeterminate football match. It wouldn't be a long wait to be served.

'What you having?' McLean asked Ritchie while at the same time trying to catch the barman's eye. DC MacBride, perhaps with an eye on his future in the police service, had politely turned down the opportunity to go for a drink, claiming he had a mountain of paperwork to process. McLean couldn't blame him, really. If Dagwood was generous with anything it was with his animosity to anyone who helped those he didn't like.

'I'm guessing a white wine spritzer's not going to cut it here.' Ritchie stared across the bar at the rows of optics behind. Cheap spirits and a couple of prize bottles of malt whisky arranged on a deep shelf with smeary shot glasses and postcards from the Costa Del Sol. There might have been a bottle of wine in the chiller cabinet under the till, but there was no telling how long it had been open.

'Best stick with the beer.' McLean pointed at a fake pump handle as the barman finally sauntered up, scarcely taking his eyes from the football. 'Two pints of Eighty Bob please.'

They took their dubious prize to a table as far away from the screen as possible, McLean making sure his back was turned to the flickering lights. He hefted his glass, said 'cheers' and took a long drink, watching Ritchie do the same. The Eighty Bob wasn't bad. Which was to say it was cold, wet and not particularly sour. He wasn't sure it had any discernible flavour either.

'How was the task force? You know all there is to know about Police Scotland?'

'About as much as anyone, I guess. Which is to say bugger all, really.' Ritchie took another long swig. 'Christ, I didn't realize how much I needed that. Thanks.'

'You're welcome. Though I'd rather have gone somewhere a bit more upmarket.'

'Yeah, it's not exactly the most welcoming of places. I presume we're here to talk to the barman.' Ritchie nodded at the dour man, absent-mindedly polishing a glass with a stained bar mat whilst he watched the television. 'Why the wait?'

'Three reasons. One, he'd be less likely to help us if we just came in and started asking questions. Two, half time is in about five minutes. All these people will want another drink, and then there'll be about ten minutes of men called Brian discussing the game so far. We're far more likely to hold his attention then.'

'Didn't know you were a footie fan, sir.' Ritchie raised a thin eyebrow. They'd never really grown back properly since the fire she'd dragged him out of.

'I'm not. Can't stand watching sport, to be honest. But it helps to know how the other half live, eh?'

'What about three then?'

'Three?' McLean lifted his pint, took a long deep draught before continuing. 'Three was I really needed a drink.'

The referee called half-time five minutes later. McLean watched as the collected punters headed either to the toilets or to the bar before returning to their tables in readiness for the second half. After her initial thirst, Ritchie had slowed down, but he'd more or less finished his own pint. Ah well, it was all in the line of duty. He threw back the last of it and went in search of another.

The barman was a little more friendly this time, in the same way a room at minus eighteen is a little warmer than a room at minus twenty.

'Two more, aye?'

McLean nodded, waited for the drinks to be poured, handed over a ten-pound note.

'Grigori Mikhailevic. Used to work here on the late shift,' he said as the barman handed over his change.

'What of him?' Back down to minus twenty.

'I was wondering if you knew him at all.'

'Why?'

McLean produced his warrant card. 'You know he hanged himself?'

'Aye, I heard that. Didn't much surprise me, like.'

'What, miserable was he?'

'No' exactly miserable, but he didn't say much, ken? Kept to himself.'

'Was he a good worker?'

'Good enough, I suppose. Turned up, did the job. Didn't complain. Just never went out of his way, ken? No' a great one for the chatter.'

'What about friends? He ever meet people here?'

The barman made a noise that sounded exactly like 'Ppphhhttt'. Shook his head. 'Not that I remember.'

'You ever see this man before?' McLean slid the photograph of Patrick Sands across the bar. The barman peered at it, but didn't pick it up.

'Nope,' he said after just long enough a pause for McLean to trust he was telling the truth. In the mirror behind the bar he could see the television screen, footballers running back onto the pitch.

'Well, thanks anyway.' He picked up the two pints, turned to go back to the table where Ritchie was staring at her smartphone with an expression of horror on her face. No doubt some impossible demand from their gallant leader. Christ he wished Jayne McIntyre would come back.

'There was one time, now I think of it.'

McLean did a one-eighty, managing somehow not to spill any of the semi-precious liquid. 'Aye?'

'That's right. I remember now, ken. Not long before he . . . Well. He was here wi' a lassie.'

'A young woman?'

'No' so young, ye ken. Thought mebbe she was his mother at first, but the way they was carrying on. And him being foreign and all, well, she didn't look like she was Russian.'

'You remember when this was?'

'I dunno. Couple of days before his last shift?'

'You remember what she looked like?'

The barman's eyes flickered away towards the television screen, back again. 'Quite tall, aye? Bit of grey in her hair. She had a long coat on. Black, I think. They sat over there where you're sitting just now.'

He pointed, and McLean turned to look. Ritchie was still glowering at her phone. When he turned back, the barman had picked up his glass and cloth, eyes glued to the television where the match was back in play. Well, it was more information than he'd hoped for, even if he didn't know what it meant. He nodded a quick 'thanks' to the barman, receiving the most minimal of grunts by way of reply, then set off across the empty bar towards Ritchie. She looked like she needed a distraction.

'Get anything?' She asked as McLean plunked her pint down beside the now-empty glass.

'Depends what you would consider anything.' He told her about the conversation with the barman, the mysterious older woman.

'Lecturer, tutor? Could be almost anyone. I don't suppose they have CCTV in here.'

'Doubt it, and even if they did they'd be unlikely to have kept recordings from that far back.'

'But you think she's important, don't you.'

'We're working on the assumption these two suicides are linked, aye?'

Ritchie nodded, said nothing.

'And we know that Mikhailevic hadn't handled the rope he used, so someone must have helped him.'

'Could've been Sands. If the two of them knew each other. You know. One helps his mate hang himself, then goes home and tops himself.'

McLean could see by Ritchie's expression that she didn't really believe it. Too far-fetched.

'It doesn't really stack up. Sands would stay close if he was going to do that. Not traipse halfway across town before hanging himself. He must've died before Mikhailevic, too. The way he was.'

'So we're looking for a third party.' Ritchie took a sip of

her beer, placed the glass back carefully on the dog-eared beer mat, exactly central.

'It's an avenue of enquiry, and this woman Mikhailevic was seen with is a loose end. Anyway, we can go and talk to the college tomorrow. Maybe we'll get lucky and find a tall, greying lady in a long dark coat there.'

Ritchie grimaced. 'Erm, not me, I'm afraid. Got an email from Dagwood. He wants me at Tulliallan for eight. More bloody Task Force Action Groups or whatever pish they come up with next.'

McLean put his glass down before he broke it. The pettiness of the man never ceased to amaze him. 'Don't suppose you feel like calling in sick?'

'And have him come round my flat to check?'

'Fair point. I'm sorry, Ritchie, this is my fault.'

'It's not your fault he's a dick. Sir,' she added.

'Aye, but it's my fault he's picking on you and MacBride. Christ, I wish Jayne McIntyre was back.'

'I'll drink to that,' Ritchie said, and raised her glass.

They didn't stay much longer at the Bond Bar; it wasn't really the place for a session, and Ritchie had to be up early for her trip to Tulliallan the next day. McLean watched her head off towards the New Town and her tiny flat before shoving his hands in his pockets and walking in the opposite direction. He'd probably flag down a taxi before long, but it was always good to walk, especially when you had things to think about.

It wasn't long before he realized he'd picked up a tail; the man wasn't exactly trying to hide it. McLean slowed, hand clasping his mobile phone as he allowed his pursuer to catch up. He had a sneaking suspicion he knew what this was all about.

'So you're the idiot went round to see Razors MacDougal about his daughter, eh?'

'What of it?' McLean looked at the man walking alongside him. Say what you liked about the Scottish Crime and Drug Enforcement Agency, they enjoyed their cloak and dagger. No doubt this loon with his long dark overcoat in the autumn, wearing shades even in the half-light of the gloaming, had been watching and waiting for a chance to approach unseen. Too easy to just phone. Or stick something in the internal mail system.

'Takes some balls, I'd've thought. Going into the house of a man like that and accusing him of sexual assault on his only child.'

'Is that what you wanted to talk to me about? MacDougal? Only I've not seen him since we closed the case.'

'Nah. MacDougal's low priority right now. We're keeping an eye on him, mind. And you too, McLean. He likes you, for some reason I can't begin to fathom. That might be useful to us sometime.'

'So this is about Ivan the Russian then.'

'If he even exists.' The SCDEA officer swung his arms like a soldier marching. Quite likely he was ex-Services. 'It's an odd one, I'll give you that much. People smuggling's nothing new, but normally they're coming over here. Not often we see a bunch being freighted back the way. And it's not as if they were prime meat, either.'

McLean stiffened at the words. Bad enough getting that attitude from an old dinosaur like Buchanan, but a young Turk from the drug squad ought to know better. On the other hand, he had a point. None of the young women they'd pulled off the boat had been remotely healthy. The word 'used' sprung to mind.

'You say "if he exists". You really have no idea about him?'

'Not a Scooby, mate. But we'll be looking into it. The boss don't like it when stuff happens he hasn't sanctioned. Know what I mean?'

McLean didn't, but decided not to say so. 'You'll let me know what you find out?'

'If I can. Depends what we turn up.' The SCDEA officer tapped the side of his nose with single finger, a gesture McLean felt singularly inapt for the occasion. 'Be seeing you, Inspector. But don't expect to see me.' And with that he turned down a side street to nowhere. McLean paused for the briefest of moments, shook his head at the idiocy of it all, then carried on his long walk home.

21

Edinburgh was full of them, tiny little institutes and further education colleges trading on the name of the bigger universities. Grigori Mikhailevic had, according to DC MacBride's notes, been studying accountancy at a place called Fulcholme College, based in Newhaven. Its centre of operations was a large detached house, the front garden flattened and laid to tarmac. Wide stone steps led up to the front door, with an impressive sign beside it claiming accreditation from a body McLean had never heard of.

Inside was much like any of a thousand large houses dotted across the city, once the homes of prosperous merchants, bankers or clergy. The only real difference between this place and his Gran's house was that he didn't have a reception desk set up in the hallway. He was disappointed to see the receptionist was a young man, not the greying, tall lady he'd hoped for. It was never that easy.

'Can I help you, sir?'

McLean showed his warrant card. Before he could say anything, the receptionist had picked up a phone and hit a button for an internal call.

'Professor? There's a policeman here. Detective Inspector McLean.' He palmed the microphone end of the hand-piece, looked up. 'It's about Grigori?'

McLean nodded, pocketing his card as he looked around. Four closed doors, each with a modern plastic plaque screwed to the dark wood. Room 1, Room 2, Room 3, Room 4. They didn't go in for creativity much at Fulcholme, it would seem. Stairs climbed up the back wall, past a mezzanine window, chest-height dark-oak panelling sucking the light out of everything, even on this bright summer morning. The most notable thing about the whole place, however, was the complete lack of students. He'd have expected at least one or two to be loitering around the hall waiting for a tutorial to start; there were sofas arranged around an empty fireplace that looked to be just for that purpose.

'Professor Bain will be with you in a minute, Inspector.' The receptionist hung up his phone at almost the exact moment one of the doors clicked and swung open. A round-faced man appeared from Room 1, saw McLean and approached with hand extended. His hair was white, and grew only from the sides of his head and his ears.

'Terrible business, terrible.' Professor Bain gave McLean's hand a vigorous shake. 'Come to my office, please. Trevor, can you organize some coffee? You do like coffee don't you, Inspector?'

McLean found himself being bustled into Room 1, which turned out to be a large study. At one end, surrounded by floor-to-ceiling bookshelves, a desk had been positioned to give commanding views out of the window onto the back yard. At the other end, near the door to the hall, a couple of sofas and four armchairs clustered around a low table. A flipchart board stood to one side, scribblings from the last tutorial group still evident on the final page.

'Please excuse the mess. Here, have a seat.' Professor

Bain indicated the armchairs before dropping himself onto a sofa. 'I must say, I'm surprised to see a detective inspector out here. It's about poor Grigori, you say.'

'You call him Grigori. First name. He was popular here, I take it.' McLean sat on the edge of the armchair, unwilling to trust himself to its depths. He wanted to maintain eye level with the professor, not be talked down to like an undergrad.

'I try to be on first-name terms with all my students, but, yes, Grigori was special. A model student in many ways. And a nice person, too. Always ready to help his classmates. If they needed it, that is.'

'I'd very much like to talk to them, if I could.'

'Shouldn't be a problem. They're all in lectures right now. But why the interest? I mean, I'm glad you're investigating, of course. But poor Grigori took his own life, didn't he?'

'Yes, at least we think so. But there are remarkable similarities between his death and that of another young man at much the same time. Tell me, does the name Patrick Sands mean anything to you?' McLean slid the photograph out of his pocket and handed it over. Professor Bain studied it a while before handing it back.

'He doesn't look familiar. But then I see so many faces come through here every year. Sands, you say? I'll ask Trevor to check the register, see if we have anyone of that name on file.'

'Thanks.' McLean took back the photo. 'Tell me, Professor Bain, were you surprised when Mikhailevic killed himself?'

There was the tiniest of pauses before the answer. 'Yes, I think I was. But do we ever really know people?'

'He was doing OK in his studies?'

'Top of his class. A very diligent student.'

McLean remembered the tiny bedsit flat, the neatness of the place, the pens lined up in their drawer. 'What about fees? Did he have money problems?'

'His fees were all paid up for the year. Grigori wasn't rich, but he worked hard. I think he had a job in a bar? I'm sure money was tight, but not enough to drive him to suicide.'

'What about family? He was from Russia, I understand. Did he miss them?'

'Lithuania, actually. But of Russian descent. He never mentioned his family though. If he missed them, he didn't say. I don't think that would be reason for killing yourself anyway. No.'

'And yet when I asked you if you were surprised by what he did, you hesitated.'

'Did I?' Professor Bain looked down at his feet, then back at McLean. 'I suppose I did. It's difficult to put it in words. Grigori was . . . Well, distant isn't right. But there were times when he would just disappear into his head. He'd be sitting there, like you are, contributing to the tutorial group one moment, and then the next you'd ask him a question and he'd not hear you. It was almost like a kind of epilepsy. A little seizure if you like. But instead of going into convulsions, he'd just stop.'

'Did he realize this was happening?'

'Well, there's the thing, Inspector. I'm not sure he did. Or if he did he didn't want to admit to it. That's the only time I've seen him depressed though, when I asked him if he was all right.'

*

Students really were getting very young these days. McLean had thought MacBride was fresh-faced, but Grigori Mikhailevic's tutorial group made the detective constable look ancient by comparison. The group was not large; just five other students appeared to be studying for whatever accountancy qualification Fulcholme College could offer. McLean felt he should maybe find out, but as he interviewed the group he was increasingly convinced this was a dead end in the investigation.

There were three women and two men, all foreign though none from Mikhailevic's country. All of them spoke English so fluently it shamed his pathetic schoolboy French. None of them knew Mikhailevic well, it seemed.

'Did you never go out for a drink after tutorials? Go clubbing at the weekends?' McLean pitched the question to the whole group, he could see no point in interviewing them separately. One of the women, Claudia from Spain was how she'd introduced herself, seemed to have appointed herself as spokesperson.

'No, no. Grigori was always working. Working here on his studies, working in that horrible little bar. We asked him, did we not, Eva?' This, directed to one of the other young women, received a nod of assent from the whole group. 'But he didn't have much money. And I think he was a bit shy, you know.'

'Did he ever meet anyone here? A woman perhaps. Or maybe he mentioned something?'

A vigorous shake of the head from Claudia, followed by something that was almost a laugh. 'No. Not Grigori. He would never do something like that. He would die of shame.'

'What about his family back home. Did he ever mention them?'

'We never really talked much about that sort of thing.'

'But he helped you? With your studies, when you were struggling?'

Claudia rolled her eyes as if such a suggestion were madness, but Eva spoke before the older woman could say anything.

'He helped me, from time to time.'

'Go on.' McLean tried to make his voice sound encouraging.

'I couldn't, how do you say it, get to grips with value added tax.'

You and me both, McLean suppressed the urge to say. He let the silence linger until Eva felt the need to fill it.

'Grigori spent some time explaining it to me. He was very bright, and very kind.'

'Did you talk about other things?'

'Not so much, but I think there may have been something going on. Just before he . . . You know.' No one seemed able to say the words 'hanged himself'.

'Why do you say that?'

'Well, I don't know. It's just that he was different. Not more cheerful, particularly. Grigori was never very cheerful. But he acted like he had purpose. Does that make sense?'

Like a man who has decided he's going to take his own life. A man who finds a certain sense of peace in the short time between making the decision and carrying out the act. Or maybe a man who has met someone who has a profound effect on him?

'And he was different in his routine, too.' The third young woman spoke finally and McLean revised his opinion of her nationality. Edinburgh born and bred, if he was any judge. 'He left here earlier, got in later. It was only a few days, but he was such a creature of habit. I thought maybe he'd met someone. Y'know, like, a girlfriend. Only, well, Grigori? It didn't seem likely. He was so shy.'

The phone rang, vibrating in his pocket as he stepped out of the building and into the mid-morning sun. Overhead, seagulls wheeled and screamed, which made it hard to hear what was being said at the other end of the line.

'McLean.'

'Ah, Tony. How delightful. I was expecting the answering machine.' The clipped tones of Angus Cadwallader.

'It's your lucky day, Angus. My phone is both working and switched on.'

'So it would seem. Might be your lucky day too.'

'Oh aye?'

'Your two hanging victims. Mikhailevic and Sands. I've got some interesting lab test results just in.'

'Interesting how?'

'Interesting as in something rather unusual was going on in their brains when they died. Both of them have abnormally high levels of dopamine in their systems.'

'You think they were drugged?' McLean stopped. 'Someone maybe slipped them L-Dopa?'

'Would that it were that simple.' Cadwallader paused and over the screeching of gulls McLean could hear the sounds of the examination room in full swing. Perhaps the pathologist really had been hoping for the answering machine. 'Look, any chance you could pop round the mortuary later on this afternoon? I've a shed load of PMs to do, but I think you'll want to see these results.'

'I'll do that, Angus. But you know I won't be able to concentrate now, what with you tantalizing me like this.'

'Well, sorry about that. Must dash. See you later.' And the phone went dead.

McLean paused beside his old Alfa. Stared at nothing in particular as he tried to remember his old university days and neuropsychology lectures. Dopamine levels. Weren't they tied into suggestibility? He'd need to phone Doctor Wheeler. She'd know.

'Nice car, mister.'

The voice jarred him out of his thinking, a young boy on a BMX bike hurtling down the pavement in contravention of lord only knew how many health and safety laws. McLean smiled to himself, opened the door and climbed in. It was a nice car, he had to admit. Just bloody useless for his line of work.

Midday traffic was relatively light on the outskirts of the city, but the sun high in the sky cast a merciless heat over everything. McLean watched the temperature gauge rise past the central point and on towards the red, despite managing to keep some airflow over the radiator as he drove along. So the old Alfa might have been designed for Italian summers, but somewhere in the intervening forty years since it had been built, the cooling system had lost most of its ability to actually cool.

The heat was seeping into the cabin too, warm air flowing through the ventilation ducts despite the lever being pushed as far over to cold as it would go. He had the windows wound down on both sides, not an easy feat when you don't have electric motors to do the work for you. Even so it was sweltering, worse when he had to stop for traffic lights.

Thoughts of ice-cold air conditioning were cut short by the buzzing of his mobile phone where it lay on the passenger seat. It had fallen face down when he'd thrown it there, so he couldn't see who was calling. Probably Cadwallader with more complications. No hands free, but there was a gap in a line of cars parked along the side of the road. He pulled over, grabbed the phone before it went to voicemail.

'McLean.'

No voice at the other end, just a noise McLean couldn't immediately identify. Then a clattering as if the phone had been dropped. Distant voices, male, harsh, the words unintelligible, their intention all too obvious from the tone. Then a woman's voice shouted in pain. More noise of things being broken. A scream.

McLean stared at the screen. It was a mobile number, not one stored in his address book or anything he recognized. Scrabbling in the glove box he found a notebook and pen, jotted it down. He pushed the button for speakerphone and listened in horror as someone was systematically beaten at the other end. Should he listen in for clues, or hang up and try to find out where this was happening?

A second's indecision was punctuated with another scream. It was a woman being beaten, of that much he was certain. How many women had his mobile number and weren't in his address book? Immediately he thought of Emma. Had someone broken into the house and disturbed her? But both hers and Jenny Nairn's numbers were in his phone's memory.

The sound of something hard hitting a sack of wet potatoes. Who else, dammit? Not Ritchie; and all the DCs would be using Airwave sets. It had to be a civilian. Someone who might find themselves in danger. Someone he'd given his number to. His card.

Shit. McLean killed the call as the screams faded to low moans. Flicked through his address book until he found another number. It rang once, twice. Come on.

'This is the Sexual Crime Unit –' McLean killed the call as it went to answerphone. Where the hell was everyone? He thumbed through his contacts list until he found another number, hit dial, listened as it rang. Hoped to God it wouldn't be another message.

'Aye?' DS Buchanan's voice was gruff, almost as if he were out of breath from running.

'Thank Christ for that. McLean here. Have you got a mobile number for Magda Evans on file?'

'Magda who?'

Oh for fuck's sake. 'Magda Evans. Come on, man, you remember. The prostitute we took off that boat. The one who ID'd Malky Jennings.'

'Oh right. Her. Why, you fancy one, do you?'

McLean ground his teeth. 'Sergeant Buchanan. Do you or do you not have a note of her mobile number? Be careful how you answer that question if you want to continue being a sergeant.'

Silence for long seconds. In his imagination McLean

could still hear the wet slapping sound of a body being repeatedly hit with a blunt object.

'Aye. I've got it here in my notebook.' Buchanan reeled off a number. It was the same as the one that had called him. 'What's this about then, sir?'

'She's just phoned me. Sounds like she's being beaten to a pulp. Where are you right now?'

A pause, then Buchanan answered. 'Sighthill. Got a call out on a kiddie fiddler hanging around the school playground. Don't think there's anything to it. Just someone spreading rumours.'

'Well get over here sharpish. Tag a squad car if you have to. And call control. I want backup at Magda Evans's flat by the time I get there.'

McLean didn't wait for an answer. He dropped the phone onto the passenger seat again and pulled out into the traffic. U-turn to the sound of mixed horns, he had a moment to wish he had a pool car; one with the hidden blue lights in the front grille. On the other hand, the Alfa was light, nimble and fast. He floored the throttle, best speed to Restalrig.

It didn't come as a huge surprise to find that there was no squad car waiting for him when he arrived at the block of flats. McLean parked as close as he dared, locked his car and sprinted to the stairs. Halfway up he realized he was heading without backup into a situation best described as perilous. Where the hell was that squad car?

He stopped on the walkway below Magda's floor, peered down at the cars parked below. His Alfa stuck out like a sore thumb, but as yet had drawn no attention. Then again, the residents of this block hadn't noticed a dead body a hundred yards away until he'd started to smell so bad even the urban foxes wouldn't touch him any more, so why should they notice this? Not much he could do about it anyway.

Peering up at the underside of the walkway above, he strained his ears for any noise of a fight. It was impossible to make out anything over the howl of the wind all around, and he couldn't see the front doors of the flats from where he was, the scaffolding obscuring the view even more than the damaged parapet wall. He was going to have to go in.

The walkway on the fourth floor was empty this time; no small girl playing with a doll with no arms. He checked the doors as he approached, but they were all closed, lace curtains or blinds drawn against the prying eyes of casual thieves. A silence and stillness settled on the scene as he approached Magda's front door. There was a dusty imprint of a boot where it had been kicked in, the security chain hanging uselessly from the jamb. He stopped by the window that looked onto the small hallway inside, peered in around the edge. It was hard to make out anything. Nothing moved.

McLean checked his watch. Twenty minutes since he'd called in. Where was that bloody squad car? The wind swirled dust around his feet in little eddies, and was that a groan from inside? In his mind he heard the sounds from the phone call, the thwack of something hard being smashed against something soft and wet. A baseball bat like they'd used to beat Malky Jennings to death? He couldn't wait any longer for backup, he had to go in.

The door pushed open silently. The thin rug had rucked up as if something had been dragged towards the open door at the far end. The living room if he remembered correctly. McLean stepped carefully over the splinters, keeping as silent as possible as he crossed the hallway and sneaked a look.

It hadn't been the most tidy of flats to start with, but now it was like a war zone. The sofa had been turned over, its cushions ripped open and foam padding spread all around; the coffee table was smashed, a broken chair leg poking out through the shards of the glass top; the television lay face up, the screen scratched and torn. Something had been smashed hard enough against the glass wall that it had cracked and crazed, star-patterns radiating out from a bloody smear.

There was no sign of Magda.

No sign of anyone. McLean picked his way carefully through the mess, into the kitchen beyond. Whoever had been to the flat had kept their work to the living room, in here was tidy by comparison. At least until he looked down. Blood smeared across the cheap lino, towards a door at the other end. He followed it, careful not to step in anything. Pulled on a pair of latex gloves before opening the door. Beyond was a short corridor, lit only by narrow lantern lights above a couple more doors. Bedrooms, presumably. The flooring here was cheap carpet, but the blood smear continued to the end, a similar mark along the wall just below shoulder height, where someone might place a hand to steady themselves. It stopped at the far end of the corridor. A neat hand print marked the painted wood with blood like some plague warning.

It was the bathroom, of course. Where else would she go in the state she was in? McLean pushed the door open, eyes following the blood smear across the floor to the shower. Magda had crawled in, huddled against the wall with the shower curtain pulled down off its rail across her. At least he assumed it was Magda. It was difficult to tell by looking at her face.

Her eyes were puffed closed, black and red. Her nose wasn't so much broken as exploded. Blood and mucus and cartilage smeared together in a glutinous mess. Her cheeks were gashed deep, the same knife cruelly carved a cross-hatch pattern in her forehead, but it was her mouth that was the worst, slit at either end in the Joker's rictus smile. He couldn't tell whether she was alive or dead. A part of him wished it was the latter; these were not injuries that were going to heal well. That had no doubt been the point.

'Magda?' He knelt down close as he dared, not wanting to spook her. 'Magda? It's Detective Inspector McLean. You phoned me.'

Her right hand clasped the shower curtain tight, her left arm was plainly broken. Still clothed, it was impossible to tell the extent of her other injuries, though he was in no doubt they were severe. McLean was about to lean in and check for a pulse when she stirred, breathed out a bubble of blood and spit through her ruined lips. Moaned in soft pain. He stepped back, nothing he could do for her here.

'Help's on its way.' He remembered the squad car that should have been there fifteen minutes earlier, checked his phone to see if there were any new messages. Nothing. Where the hell were they? He was reluctant to leave her, but he was bugger all use standing there staring at her. He had to do something.

A towelling dressing gown hung on the back of the bathroom door. He carefully tucked it around Magda's shivering body, then retraced his steps to the front door, dialling the station as he went.

'I need an ambulance here right away. And where's the backup that was meant to be here half an hour ago?' McLean peered out and down to where his Alfa was beginning to draw a crowd of ne'er-do-wells. He was about to yell at them when they scattered anyway. Then a squad car appeared from around the side of the neighbouring block, lights flashing lazily on its roof.

22

The City Mortuary was a haven of tranquillity after a long and hectic day. McLean stepped from the oven-like heat of the Cowgate into the air-conditioned chill and let out a sigh of relief. There might be complications here, but at least no one would be chewing his ear off about staffing costs, or complaining about his methods.

The examination room was empty, the stainless steel tables clean and shiny, the tools that looked like they should have been in a carpenter's workshop all tidied away. McLean found Angus Cadwallader in the open-plan office adjacent, still wearing his green scrubs and two-finger typing at an elderly computer. His assistant, Tracy, looked up as he rapped on the frame of the open door.

'Ah, the prodigal son returns.' Cadwallader wheeled around on his chair, the grin on his face turning to a worried frown. 'Good God, Tony. You look like you haven't slept in weeks.'

Until his friend said it, McLean hadn't really considered himself tired. Now it had been mentioned, he wondered how he'd not noticed. He rubbed at his eyes and stifled a yawn.

'It's been a very long day, and I've not been getting much sleep lately either.'

'Oh aye? Emma keeping you up late, is she?'

'Not in the way you're thinking, Angus.' McLean

explained about the late-night visitations, stressing their entirely Platonic nature. For once the pathologist refrained from making any obvious joke.

'I'm sure she'll get better. It just takes time.'

'I don't know, Angus. It seems like there's a bit of her missing. If that makes any sense?'

Cadwallader didn't answer that, which was perhaps for the best.

'What about these test results? Abnormally high dopamine levels, you said.'

'Yes, of course. I was forgetting.' Cadwallader twirled his chair back around to the computer screen and tapped away at the keys for a few uncertain seconds before looking up at his assistant. 'Tracy? How do I get the path lab screen up again?'

Tracy caught McLean's eye and shook her head in despair before hauling herself out of her seat and around to her boss's computer. A couple of clicks was all it took. 'There you go,' she said.

'It was so much easier when it was all paper based.' Cadwallader fetched a pair of half-moon spectacles from where they hung on a slim cord around his neck, placed them on his nose and leaned close in to the screen. 'Ah. Here we are.'

McLean stared at the columns of figures and chemical symbols. 'What am I looking at?'

'Here.' Cadwallader stabbed at the screen, leaving a smear of what McLean hoped was grease on the glass. 'This is the first one, Sands. Dopamine levels off the scale. Serotonin's quite high as well. Same here with the second one, Mik– . . . whatsisname.'

'So Sands was the first victim,' McLean said. 'Thought that was probably the case.'

'What gave it away?' Cadwallader twirled his chair around again, this time leafing through a stack of papers flowing out of his in-tray.

'Oh, you know how it is. Hang around with pathologists long enough and you pick up a few tips here and there. The putrefaction got me thinking, though.'

'Yes, he was a bit ripe. Unlike your Russian fellow.'

'Lithuanian.'

'Eh?'

'He was Lithuanian, not Russian. Of Russian descent, I think is how it was explained to me.'

'Yes, well. Russian, Lithuanian. It's not important. What is important is that he died second, like you suspected. The other fellow'd been hanging for at least a couple of weeks beforehand. Makes you wonder about the neighbourhood though, if no one noticed the smell until he'd been decomposing for a fortnight. Possibly even a month.'

Brilliant. More complications.

'But that's not important.' Cadwallader tapped the screen again. 'This is important. This profile in one suicide would be interesting but not enough to be suspicious. You get outliers in any population and anyone who puts a noose around his neck's got some pretty hooky brain chemistry going on. But two? Well, that starts to look like an outside influence to me.'

'They were drugged?'

'If only it were that simple, Tony. Well, it is that simple. L-Dopa, like you mentioned on the phone this morning.

Very good at raising dopamine levels. But there's one small problem.'

'Only one?' McLean raised a quizzical eyebrow.

'Quite. But back to the matter in hand. L-Dopa leaves traces, not least of which is a paper trail. None of them are here.'

'So what else could account for these results?' McLean squinted at the screen again. It still didn't make any sense to him. 'You said serotonin was high too? What does that mean? My neurobiology's a bit rusty.'

'It means they were both very relaxed. That's the serotonin. And very suggestible, judging by the dopamine.'

'So what you're saying is that someone could have just told these two to go hang themselves and they were so laid back they'd have done it?'

'Pretty much, yes.'

'So how did they get like that? What were they given?'

'As far as I can tell, nothing. Their own brains produced those levels. Both of them.'

An anxious-looking Jenny Nairn met him in the kitchen as he let himself in an hour later. McLean had driven home straight from the mortuary, not wanting the hassle of going back to the office. He'd have to write up everything Cadwallader had told him, though he had a nasty suspicion it wouldn't be enough to sway Duguid from his cost-cutting.

'Something up?' The agitation on Jenny's face instantly brought up dreadful scenarios. And where was Emma anyway? Normally the two young women were joined at the hip.

'It's Wednesday. Remember?'

Wednesday. Of course. Jenny's night off. He'd left that morning before either of them were up, and if he was being honest with himself, had hardly considered what day of the week it might be. It wasn't as if he was counting up to the weekend or anything.

'Sorry. Completely forgot.' He glanced up at the clock on the wall. Ten past seven already. 'You want me to give you a lift into town?'

'In that old bucket of yours?' Jenny shook her head. 'No, it's OK. I've got a cab booked. Should be here any minute. I was just getting a bit worried about having to send him away.'

'You should've phoned. I can get a bit carried away with the work sometimes. Not used to having people at home.'

'I had noticed.'

'How is she today? You two get up to any mischief while I was away?'

'She's been photographing things again. That camera's something of a lifeline for her right now. We spent most of the day up in the attic going through old trunks of clothes and stuff.' Jenny paused, no doubt considering what she'd just said. 'You don't mind, do you?'

'God no. It needs clearing out. Some of that stuff belonged to my great-grandparents. There's probably boxes there that haven't been touched since before the war.' Or at least in the twenty-five or more years it had been since he'd grown out of playing up there in amongst the dust and spiders' webs.

Lights played across the window, accompanied by the crunch of wheels on gravel. 'Your taxi,' McLean said, as if there were any doubt. 'Look, I'll be late going in tomorrow morning, so don't worry about rushing back.'

'Thanks. I'll bear that in mind.' Jenny grabbed her bag and headed for the door.

'Going anywhere interesting?'

'Maybe. We'll see. Friend of mine runs a séance group. You know, Ouija boards and astral projection. She's as mad as a coot, but a lot of fun. Especially when there's been a bottle or two of wine consumed.'

'Well, be careful.' McLean wasn't sure whether he should be taking her seriously or not. That was the problem with Jenny Nairn. Her sense of humour was so dry it could be used to cure leather.

'Oh I will. Have no doubt about that, Inspector.'

'Please, Tony's fine,' he said. But she was already gone.

He found Emma in the library, hunched over the computer. She'd obviously been there for hours, daylight slowly leaching out of the room as dusk set in. The glow from the screen painted her face pale, emphasizing how sunken her eyes still were, how angular her cheekbones. He stood silent in the doorway for long moments, just looking at her as the tumble of the day ebbed away from his mind. Absorbed in whatever task she was doing, she was almost the Emma of old; that streak of rebellious obsessiveness was obviously a trait that had established itself early on in her life. It was, he realized, both what had allowed her to break through the barriers he'd put up after Kirsty's death, and what had attracted him to her enough to let her get close.

Something must have broken her concentration. She

looked up and saw him standing there in the doorway. A grin spread slowly across her face, but it wasn't the welcoming smile of a friend, or a lover, so much as the delight of a child.

'You're back.' She didn't stand up, or run across the room to give him a hug. Whatever was on the screen held her fascination too much for that.

'I'm back,' McLean confirmed. 'And Jenny's just left. What're you doing there?'

'Don't like Jenny any more' was all he got by way of response to the question. Emma's gaze flicked back to the screen, then to him again, as if she were fighting to maintain her attention.

'You don't like her? I thought she was your best friend.' McLean flicked on the lights, though whether it was that or the suggestion that made Emma pout like a teenager he couldn't tell. He walked across the room to the drinks cabinet, artfully hidden behind a fake bookcase, poured himself a glass of whisky then went to see what she was finding so fascinating. She wrinkled her nose at the smell as he put the glass down on the desk, but shuffled over a bit anyway so he could see what was on the screen.

'More photos?' A series of thumbnail images arranged across the page, dark and difficult to make out at this resolution. 'I thought you were up in the attic playing costumes.'

That got him a nudge in the ribs, not too hard but sore nonetheless. It was an oddity of Emma's condition that whilst she often behaved like an eight-year-old girl, if you treated her like one it rarely went well.

'Not playing. Looking for stuff. And taking photographs. And talking to the ghosts.'

The statement was so matter of fact, McLean didn't at first register it. He was still staring at the tiny thumbnails when it finally sank in.

'Ghosts?'

'Mmm hmm.' Emma clicked the mouse and a full-size picture came into view. 'Ghosts, see?'

It was the attic, that much he recognized. There were several rooms up in the roof space of this big old house. One was a servant's bedroom, now occupied by Jenny Nairn. In olden times it would have been shared by more than one serving girl. Alongside it at the top of the narrow stairs was a tiny washroom; a luxury indeed for a time when most servants would have been expected to use the facilities in the coach house. That was now the garage, but had also housed the male servants before the First World War. Back when a house this size would have employed at least five full-time staff. The final room was what McLean had always referred to as the attic; one large, long room with a couple of skylights and a narrow slit window at the gable end. It was where unwanted stuff went to die, and Emma had captured that well in her photograph. There were the stacks of boxes and trunks bearing the initials of long-forgotten ancestors; the heavy old oak wardrobe he had no idea how anyone had managed to get up there. He'd spent many a wet winter afternoon searching for the door in the back that would take him to Narnia. Across from the wardrobe, an old leather Chesterfield sofa and a couple of armchairs had been the *Tirpitz* and Lancaster bombers to his young imagination. They didn't appear to have moved an inch since the last great battle, but neither were they empty as he expected.

Three wispy white figures sat on them, staring at the camera. You couldn't exactly call them people, but neither were they something to do with the lens, some light flare or reflection.

'What on earth?'

'I told you, silly. They're ghosts. Look.' Emma clicked through a half dozen more photographs, each showing a different angle on much the same scene. In some of the pictures there were only one or two figures. But they were always there, like someone had run across the view on a long-exposure shot.

'How did you do this?' McLean asked after a while. 'Is it some kind of software manipulation?'

That got him another jab to the ribs. 'They're ghosts. Spirits.' Emma paused for a minute, stopped looking at the screen and turned to him. 'And you can see them.'

'Well, yes. I mean, I can see something. Ghosts if you say so.'

'No, I mean you can actually see them. Like here and here and here.' Emma jabbed at the screen, setting it to a perilous wobble.

'Umm. Isn't that the whole point? You showed me the pictures.'

'But Jenny couldn't see them. Or she wouldn't see them. Sometimes I think she's just humouring me. Just being nice 'cause she's paid to. She swore blind there was nothing in these photos but the furniture and boxes.'

McLean bent down to get a better look, staring long

and hard at the image with its curious misty lines. He couldn't have said exactly what it was he was seeing, something from an age when photography was new and people believed in faeries, perhaps. But there was something on the photographs. Of that he was sure. Of course, it could have been an elaborate joke; wouldn't have been the first one Emma had played on him. Her posture and the palpable feeling of excitement radiating off her made it unlikely though. This close, he could feel her warmth, smell the scent of shampoo in her hair. He pulled away before he lost himself in it.

'So what are these ghosts doing up in the attic?' The question was only half joking, though he didn't realize that until he'd asked it.

'Nothing. They're just memories.' Emma clicked on the little x in the top corner of the screen and the ghostly images disappeared.

23

Patrick Sands hadn't been the most popular of employees. That at least was the impression McLean got from talking to his team boss at Chartered Eagle Bank. It was a typical downtown call centre, just off the London Road. Driving past you might mistake it for a DIY warehouse or a cash and carry store. Only the lack of windows at ground level and the omission of any car parking spaces gave the game away. McLean and Ritchie had arrived early for their appointment, but their contact, Ashley Coombes, hadn't mentioned anything about it. She'd welcomed them in and been nothing but helpful. He only wished all interviews were as easy.

'So the last time he came to work was two months ago. Didn't anyone say anything? Try to find out where he was?' McLean sat in a surprisingly comfortable low-backed leather armchair in a small office off the main hall of the call centre. An expensive-looking machine had given him a very nice cup of coffee and the woman sitting opposite him, separated by a low table, had apologized profusely for the lack of biscuits, having spent five minutes searching through every cupboard in the room just in case.

'Patrick came to us through a temping agency. We contacted them about him, of course, but they just sent a replacement.'

'How long had he been working here?' Detective Sergeant Ritchie asked the question, which was just as well since McLean was enjoying his coffee too much.

'He started here on January 3rd. Here. I've made a copy of his file for you.' Coombes picked up the slim brown folder she'd brought in with her and handed it to Ritchie.

'What was he like, as a person?' McLean reluctantly placed his empty cup on the table, wondered idly if it would be rude to ask for another.

'Quiet, I guess. Competent. He got on with the job. We've taken on a few of the temps as permanent employees. Offered it to him, but he wasn't interested.'

'And yet he was studying for his banking exams.'

'Was he? I didn't know that.' Coombes looked genuinely surprised.

'Would you say he was depressed at all?' McLean picked up his coffee cup, rolled it around in his hand then realized what he was doing and put it down again.

'Not especially, no. Here, let me.' Coombes took the cup over to the machine, punched some buttons to produce more coffee. 'Like I said, he was quiet. He didn't socialize much with the rest of the team. After hours, you know. Sometimes they all go off to the pub together, but Paddy would always just go home.'

'Paddy?'

'That's what everyone called him, yes.' Coombes paused, a slight frown rippling across her forehead as a thought scuttled through her mind. 'Now I think about it, he wasn't really all that happy about it.'

'Probably not enough to make him commit suicide though.'

'No, I guess not.' The frown disappeared, replaced by a smile. 'How's the coffee?'

'Lovely.' McLean raised his cup. 'I don't suppose we could have a quick chat with his co-workers?'

'Umm. Here? Now?' The frown came back.

'It won't take a minute. I can speak to them at their desks if it's easier.' McLean swallowed the last drop, put the cup down on the table. 'I just want to see if anyone noticed anything strange in the last few days he was here.'

The open-plan office echoed with a hundred different voices, a study in desperate busy-ness. Most of the workers were seated in front of large flat-screen monitors, heads down and concentrating on selling mortgages, personal loans, insurance or whatever it was the bank did. At one end of the hall a large screen displayed the number of calls currently being answered, and the number stacking up to be dealt with. The air was filled with a sense of desperation so thick you could almost taste it. Or maybe that was just the odour of sweat and unwashed bodies.

Coombes led them to a far corner, where ten or so people worked in a space blocked off by low partitions. The rest of the room was similarly split up, reminding McLean of nothing so much as a livestock market, beasts waiting nervously for their turn in the ring, or the short walk to the killing house.

Everyone was busy when they arrived; no one looked up to see the new arrivals. Coombes stood in the middle, peering over shoulders at screens as if the rapidly changing pages meant something to her. There was a moment's indecision as she tried to decide which of two calls were going to end soonest, and then she dived in, tapping a young man on the shoulder. He clicked a single key on his keyboard before swivelling around in his chair to face them all.

'John, can you spare a moment?' As if the poor bastard had any choice. He nodded, eyes flicking from Coombes to McLean to Ritchie and back to Coombes again.

'These two police officers want to ask everyone about Paddy Sands. It won't take a moment.' The last was not a question so much as a statement, and seemed to be directed at the two detectives rather than the hapless John.

'You worked with Sands?' McLean asked.

John nodded.

'Where did he sit?'

John pointed. 'Over there. It's Steve's station now.'

'You talk much?' Even as he asked, McLean realized it wasn't the most intelligent of questions. No doubt if you spent enough time in this place you'd get used to it, but he was having a hard time filtering out one voice from the constant babble.

'Break time, maybe. Sometimes on the afternoon shift it's a bit quieter.' John glanced quickly over his shoulder at the big screen.

'You ever go out after work. The pub or something?'

'With Paddy? Nah. He wasn't really into that.'

'What about the last few days he was here? Was he different in any way?'

'Couldn't really say. We all have off days, y'know?'

'Who sat next to him? Same people as now?' He nodded his head in the direction of the workstation now occupied by Steve.

'Nah, was Jen. She left about a week before Paddy. And Charlie there sat on the other side.'

McLean was about to go and speak to Charlie when the young woman sitting next to John tapped her keyboard, slipped off her headset and swivelled around to face him.

'There was that one night Paddy came out with the rest of us. Must be, what, couple months ago?'

John looked momentarily confused, then the light came on behind his eyes. 'Aye, that was right, Maeve's leaving do. I think he was a bit soft on Maeve.'

'Him and every other person in here with balls.' The young woman shook her head. 'Except for Ben, of course.'

This was obviously an in-joke at Ben's expense, whoever Ben was. Both of them laughed anyway.

'You all go somewhere together then? For this leaving do. Sands as well?'

'Oh God, I don't remember much,' the young woman said. 'Had the day off after, so I drank more than was probably wise. I think a bunch of them went off after the pub but I was well gone. Last I saw Paddy he was talking to Jen.' She shook her head. 'No, that can't be right. Jen'd left by then, hadn't she?'

'Yeah, but she came back for Maeve.'

'And this was just before Sands left?' McLean asked.

John scratched at his cheek for a moment before saying 'Yeah. Couple days maybe. It all blurs into one after a while, mind.'

'I can imagine. And thanks, you've been a great help.'

McLean left the two of them to their calls, turned to where the young man called Charlie had been pointed out to him. All the people working here seemed to be young. Or maybe he was just getting old. Charlie was staring intently at his screen, fingers battering away at his rackety keyboard as he spoke into the microphone dangling just in front of his lips. Busy. And probably wouldn't have any great insights into the state of Patrick Sands' mind.

'Are we done here?' Coombes took his hesitation as a cue to move the distraction away from her workforce. McLean couldn't bring himself to be annoyed. Time was money in these places, after all, and she had given him two cups of very good coffee.

'I think so.' He let her lead them towards the exit.

'There was one thing,' he added as they reached the door. 'There was a young woman worked alongside Sands for a while. Left a bit before he did.'

'Jen. Yes. What of her?'

'I was wondering if you could tell us how to find her.'

Coombes looked a little askance, as if McLean had asked her what her preferred sexual position was. 'I can't hand over confidential personnel information like that, Inspector. Not even to the police. I'm sorry.'

'I understand, of course. Perhaps you could point me in the right direction though. Was she another temp? What's her full name?'

'Oh. Right. Yes. She was a temp. Worked for the same agency as Paddy. They might be able to contact her for you, I suppose. And it's Nairn, her surname. Jennifer Nairn.'

24

'So this is where you work. It's nice.'

Jenny Nairn didn't try to hide the irony in her voice as she lounged back in her uncomfortable plastic chair. The interview room was probably the best available, but it was still a small room in a police station. And whilst this might be an informal session, it was still 'helping the police with their enquiries'. The easy-going young woman McLean had shared his house with for the past month had disappeared almost as soon as he'd suggested she might like to make the trip down. Now she was almost as unhelpful as Emma in one of her more childish moods.

'Miss Nairn. I understand that you worked at Chartered Eagle Bank, in their call centre in London Road, for the first four months of this year.' DS Ritchie asked the question. She had a long list that she and McLean had put together for the interview. Now he sat silently beside her, all too aware of the awkward situation he was in. Technically Jenny wasn't a suspect, but the fact that he was her current employer would no doubt give Duguid something to complain about when he read the report. If he read the report, though of course this would be the one, the only one, that he did.

'What of it?'

'Did you or did you not work at Chartered Eagle bank?'

'Yes, yes. I did. Shithole that it was, I worked there.'
Jenny tipped her head back, tilting the chair onto two legs,
pushing as far as it would go without losing her balance.

'Why? I thought you were a registered care nurse.'

'Yeah, well. There's not always jobs for registered care
nurses, are there. I'd been looking after an old bloke in the
New Town up to Christmas, but he died. Money was a bit
tight so I took the call centre job to tide me over.' Thump
as the chair came back down. 'Look, is this important?
Only I can't see how.'

Ritchie almost recoiled, stopped herself at the last
moment. 'Sorry. You're right. Not important. This isn't
really about you, so much as Patrick Sands.'

'Yes, Tony mentioned that.' Jenny looked straight at
McLean. The way a shark might look at a passing fish. A
smile that was all teeth.

'You worked in the same team as him. Alongside him in
fact. You must have talked.'

Jenny gave a little humourless laugh. 'You been to that
place, right?'

'We have, yes.'

'Well, you'll know there's not much time for idle chit-
chat. Even when the calls were light, Ms Coombes didn't
like us talking too much.' Something about the way Jenny
pronounced Ms as Mzzz suggested she hadn't much cared
for the woman. It was perhaps not all that surprising.

'Is that why you left?'

'No. I left because I was fed up. That and a friend
of mine at the hospital told me about a carer's job that
might be coming up. You know, coma patient woken with

memory loss? Needing full-time care while she recovers? Ring any bells?'

'Tell me about Patrick Sands then.' Ritchie quickly changed the subject.

'Not much to say, really. Paddy was nice enough. Shy. He didn't hang out with everyone after work much, but then neither did I.'

'Did he struggle with his shyness?'

'How do you mean?'

'Did it depress him?'

Jenny made a sour face. 'What am I, his therapist?'

'I don't know. Were you? You have a degree in psychology. Maybe he asked you for help. Maybe he made a pass at you. I don't know. I'm trying to find out what sort of a person he was, not criticize you.'

Round one to Miss Nairn. McLean noticed the twitch of a smirk around the corners of her mouth. He'd played this game with plenty of interviewees down the years. Ritchie presumably less so. Either that or she'd let Jenny get the upper hand on purpose. It wasn't a bad strategy to take with a hostile witness.

'OK. One thing. He never made a pass at me. He was too busy ogling Maeve's chest for that.'

'Did he ever make a pass at her, then?'

'Wouldn't have known how to. Poor wee thing. He wasn't good at talking to people, specially not women. He used to blush every time he asked to borrow my stapler. It was sweet, in a way. But creepy, too.'

'So it's possible he was badly affected when Maeve left. You'd already been gone what, a month by then?'

'Something like that. Said they were all going out for

drinks and did I want to come. I was surprised as the next one when Paddy was there too.'

'Did the evening go well?'

'What do you mean? Did I get off with anyone?'

'Did Sands?'

'Ha! As if. No, of course not.' Jenny paused, then added, 'least not while I was there. He might've done later. Or he might've passed out from all the Dutch courage he was drinking. Here, maybe he was going to propose to Maeve or something. I don't know, declare his undying love to her. She'd've laughed like a drain at him if he had, drunk or no'. That might be what tipped him over the edge.'

Ritchie paused a moment before speaking again, as if she found the thought objectionable. 'This Maeve. You have a contact number for her?'

'Somewhere, aye. Won't do you much good though. She went home to Canada the day after the party. Far as I know she's still there.'

'Far as you know? You don't keep in touch then?'

'Not like we were best buddies or anything. I worked with her in that shithole call centre a couple of months. She's hardly been gone that long. Don't think I even spoke to her that much the last time I saw her. Like I say, Paddy was drinking, so he might've tried something on with her. I left early, no idea what happened later.'

'Why?' Ritchie asked. 'Why'd you leave early?'

'Job interview.' Jenny pointed a finger straight at McLean's chest. 'Had to have a clear head so's I could make a good impression on the boss.'

*

A heavy silence filled the car as McLean drove across town, headed for home. Beside him in the passenger seat, Jenny Nairn stared ahead. He'd glanced at her a couple of times, under the guise of checking his mirrors, but her expression was unreadable. He hoped for Emma's sake that she wasn't going to hand in her notice as soon as they arrived.

The interview hadn't been a complete failure, but neither had it yielded much in the way of useful information about Patrick Sands. Maybe he'd be able to get some more out of her, away from the station and its unmistakable reek of police authority.

'Look, I'm really sorry about all that back there.' McLean nodded his head backwards, as if the station were still directly behind them. Jenny said nothing, continued her stare into the middle distance. McLean knew that she was leaving a silence for him to fill; he wasn't exactly a novice at this game himself.

'I'd have talked to you at home, informally, if I could have done. Soon as your name came up though, I had to do it all by the book.'

'Why?' Jenny hadn't moved, hadn't turned to face him, but the question was a good sign.

'I'm your employer right now. That's a relationship, a connection between me and Patrick Sands beyond the fact that I'm investigating his death. My boss is . . . Well, he insists on everything being done by the book, and lately he's been double-checking everything I do. Making sure it's all above board.'

'You cock up somewhere?'

'That depends on your definition of cock up. If you mean did I solve his case for him and not make a fuss when he took all the credit, then yes, I cocked up.'

That brought a ghost of a smile. It didn't last long though.

'I don't like police stations. Don't trust you lot.'

'I know. I read your file.' Arrested during the G8 protests. No charges pressed. A couple of minor altercations at other rallies, lots of cautions but always managing to stay out of court and jail. Clever, but angry.

'And you still hired me?'

'Well, I should probably have read it before taking you on. That would've been an inappropriate use of my privileged access though. I've bent a few rules in my time, but that's not somewhere I'd be all that happy going.'

'Why'd you read it now, then?'

'Because your name came up in connection to my investigations.'

Jenny didn't respond at first, just carried on staring out the window as they neared their destination. Finally the wheels scrunched on the gravel drive and McLean pulled the car to a halt outside the house. Only then did she turn to him and speak.

'So are you going to fire me?'

'I don't think Emma would let me, even if I wanted to.'

'You don't mind about all the . . . stuff?'

'Far as I can see you've not committed any actual offence. You might find it hard to believe, what with this house and everything, but I'm not a huge fan of the one per cent either. You do a good job, Jenny. Emma likes you, and that's all I care about. I really am sorry that I had to drag you down to the station. If I could've done it any other way, I would have.'

McLean pushed open the car door and climbed out. That was the other thing about old sports cars; they were low to the ground, and he wasn't getting any younger. His back creaked in protest as he straightened up. Perhaps he should get a Saab. He'd read somewhere they had the best seats of all modern cars. But they'd gone bust, hadn't they?

Shaking his head at the random thought, he trudged across the gravel towards the back door. Only then did he realize that something had been bothering him. A step back and a quick look. The front door was wide open.

A horrible cold sensation settled in the pit of his stomach. The front door was never opened these days. Everyone came around the back, through the little utility room and straight into the kitchen. Standing on the other side of the car, Jenny had noticed too.

'Em wouldn't have gone out into the garden on her own.' It wasn't a question.

Both of them hurried to the front door. Jenny was about to dash in, but McLean stopped her, held up a finger to his lips. He went in first, listening for any sounds that shouldn't have been there, hearing none. No noise from the television either. Across the hall, the library door hung open like the front door, as if Emma had just got up and walked out in a daze. McLean looked inside, but she wasn't there. When he turned back, Jenny was at the doorway that opened onto the narrow corridor past the scullery and butler's pantry to the kitchen. She shook her head.

Together they checked the other ground floor rooms, then the upstairs and finally the attic. The garden was empty, as was the coach house, except for Emma's light blue and rust Peugeot 106 which had been put into storage there months before. There was no getting away from the fact. She was gone.

25

'About five two. Black hair with a life of its own. Skinny as a rake. Kinda scruffy, aye?'

McLean sat at the kitchen table, watching as Jenny Nairn spoke on the phone. He'd already called everyone he could think of; now she was putting the word out among a different stratum of Edinburgh society. He stared down at his mug of tea. It had gone cold, a surface scum congealed on the milky top. Up to the clock on the wall; half past four. Two hours since they'd found Emma gone; four since she'd been left happily watching telly, maybe five.

'I should have got someone in to look after her,' he said as she hung up. 'Shit. I should've just talked to you here, not taken you down the station.'

'Em was fine when I left. She said she was OK being on her own in the house for a few hours. You know that, I know that. If anyone should be kicking themselves, it's me, right? I'm the one being paid to be her carer.'

McLean didn't answer that, didn't want to suggest it was true when he'd been the one who'd dragged her away from her job. All so he could cover his own arse.

'Look, she can't have gone far. She's on foot, doesn't much like being out in open spaces. Chances are she's at one of your neighbours drinking tea and chatting about flowers.'

Jenny didn't look like she believed what she was saying.

McLean almost laughed. 'That's my line, you know. Reassuring the worried parent, other half, whatever.'

'Maybe I should have been a copper then.'

'You'd make a good one. Family liaison, that kind of thing.'

'Not finding missing scatterbrains though.' She twirled her phone around on the kitchen table for a moment, then snatched it up. 'Sod this, I'm going to look around the garden again. There's a gate through to the dell. Over in the far corner, right?'

'It's padlocked tight, rusted up. Hasn't been opened since I was a boy.' McLean knew that he'd checked it, but felt the pull all the same. It was always possible, just, that Emma had found a way to open it and wandered off into the woodland, down to the river maybe. Except that he had checked it, not half an hour ago. It was unlikely to have changed in the interim. He let Jenny go anyway. Better to do something, even if it was a waste of time, than to sit around and wait.

'I'll have a look up in the attic again. She's had a fascination with the place for weeks now. Probably crawled into an old trunk and fallen asleep.'

They set off in their different directions, Jenny out the back door, McLean up the main stairs and then the echoing, wooden servants' staircase to the attic. The door creaked theatrically as he pushed it open onto the void under the rafters. Afternoon light speared in through the window at the end, shadows moving as the wind outside played with the branches of nearby trees. Dust hung in the warm air, gravity and thermodynamics in perfect balance. He remembered the pictures Emma had shown him, just a few nights earlier. Those ghostly figures sitting on the empty sofa, standing around the wardrobe. In his mind's eye they reminded him of Victorian spiritualist photographs, simple double-exposure fakes from a time when photography was new and anything was possible. Conan Doyle had been a true believer, hadn't he? Taken in by the hoaxers in his later years. Sad to see the mind that had invented Sherlock Holmes believing in faeries like a little child.

For a moment McLean stood still, wondered where the thought had come from. Then he noticed something lying on the floor beside the old sofa. A book. The book he'd paid a king's ransom for at auction. The book that had once belonged to Donald Anderson, and possibly before that to Sir Arthur Conan Doyle. His feet echoed on the floorboards as he walked over and picked it up. The note from Madame Rose had been folded in half and used as a bookmark. An indentation in the sofa cushion showed where someone had sat whilst reading, but when he put his hand to it, there was no warmth. Emma had been here, yes. Not recently though.

With the book tucked under his arm, he worked his way around the space methodically, checking trunks, the old wardrobe, and even the half-height cupboard doors that opened up onto the roof eave space. There was ancient wiring in there, and no loft insulation worth talking about, but no missing women.

He stopped by the window in the gable wall, stared out through the dust and cobwebs at the tiny form of Jenny Nairn stalking back across the garden. Hers had been a futile search as well, it would seem. In the light from the window, he opened up the book again, flicked idly through the pages as if he might find Emma in there. Looking up, he realized he was standing in the exact spot she must have taken the first of her photographs from. There weren't any ghosts to be seen.

'Where are you, Emma?' It wasn't a question he expected to have answered, but as he spoke, the bookmark slipped from the pages and fell to the floor. He stooped, picked it up and unfolded it, seeing the neatly inked handwriting of Madame Rose's letter again. And as he read the first line, he heard a voice call faintly from below.

'Halloo! Is there anyone home?'

Shoving the note back in the book, McLean rushed out of the attic, taking the stairs two at a time. From the first floor landing he couldn't see into the hall, but halfway down the stairs it hit him. He knew that voice, had heard it in his head as he read the letter. And sure enough, there she was. There he was. Whatever. Standing in the little porch that separated the main hallway from the outside. Madame Rose in all her Jenner's Tea Room finery. And beside him, her, dwarfed by the transvestite's bulk, the tiny, frail form of Emma.

'Oh my god! Where have you been?' McLean rushed down the stairs and was halfway across the hall before he stopped. Emma was a state, her hair even less kempt than ever, her face muddy. The clothes she had been wearing that morning hung from her as if she'd been on a diet for months, and her feet, good Christ, her feet. He stared at the blood-stained mess poking from the bottom of her sweatpants. 'You went out without shoes?'

'Calm yourself, Inspector.' Madame Rose put a gentle

arm around Emma's shoulder and steered her into the house. At the same moment, Jenny Nairn appeared from the kitchen clutching a familiar-looking pair of trainers. Her eyes widened at the sight, the shoes tumbling from her hands as she ran across the hall and gathered Emma into a large embrace.

'Where did you go? I thought you were lost.' She pulled back, briefly looking Emma up and down and then added: 'Why'd you not put on some shoes? Why'd you not –'

'I think a cup of tea is in order, don't you?' Madame Rose looked around the hallway, eyes finally alighting on the door through which Jenny had just come. 'Kitchen this way, is it?'

McLean leaned against the Aga, unsure what to say as he waited for the kettle to boil. Madame Rose had taken a seat at the large wooden table and was leafing with great interest through the copy of Gray's *Anatomy*. Emma sat beside her, him, dammit. Clingy like a child while Jenny fetched a basin and filled it with warm water. Soon the air was filled with that school-familiar smell of antiseptic.

'Here, Em. Let's have a look at your feet.' Jenny knelt down and lifted one of Emma's legs, gently resting it on another chair so that her foot was taking no weight. Then she set about the task of cleaning away the blood and grit, tutting all the while as she worked.

'Where did you find her?' McLean pulled the boiling kettle off the hotplate and poured water into the teapot. He placed the pot on the table and took a seat opposite the large medium.

'Well there's the strangest thing.' Madame Rose carefully closed the book and put it down in front of her before continuing. 'I was doing a card reading for a client. Lovely chap, comes in once a week. Every time his tarot's the same, but he insists it will change.'

'And Emma?' McLean interrupted before Madame Rose could get into full flow.

'I was coming to that, Inspector. Anyway, I was reading the cards and all of a sudden, out of nowhere, I found myself thinking about Donald Anderson's shop.'

'Anderson?' A lump of ice began to form in McLean's guts.

'We'll get there much quicker if you don't keep interrupting me. Tea?' Madame Rose nodded at the teapot. Instinct kicked in, and McLean began the ritual of pouring. Milk. Two sugars. He should probably have offered biscuits.

'Thank you.' Madame Rose accepted a mug. 'As I was saying, I found myself thinking about Donald's shop. Not just an idle "I wonder what's happened to the old place" kind of thing, you understand. This was a portent. Something had thrust the idea into my head. Well, I couldn't ignore such a thing, so I finished with Mr Mortimer and then closed up for the afternoon. Took a taxi to the Canongate. You know, people still step off the pavement as they pass that place, without noticing they're doing it. But she was there.'

McLean's gaze slid from the medium to the skinny woman sitting beside her. 'Emma? At Anderson's shop?'

'Apparently she'd been there almost an hour. Just standing by the door, staring at it.'

'How do you know that?'

'Am I being interrogated, Inspector?' Madame Rose placed a theatrical hand over her fake bosom. 'How exciting.'

'I'm sorry. I should be thanking you for finding her. For bringing her here.'

'You were worried sick, Inspector. You and Miss Nairn both. I can see that plain as my hands.' Madame Rose put down her mug and waved them about, just in case McLean didn't know what a man's hands looked like. 'I know the old fellow runs the coffee shop just across the road from Anderson's place. He told me he'd seen Emma standing there. He'd been about to call the police.'

'But what was she doing there?' McLean turned to Emma, realized as he did so that she hadn't said a word since she had been brought back. 'What were you doing there, Emma?'

Slowly, as if half asleep, Emma raised her head, stared at him with deep, black eyes. It was like being gazed upon by the abyss.

'I lost something. Looked everywhere for it. I thought maybe it was there.'

'You lost something? What did you lose, Emma?'

A frown creased her forehead and those eyes shifted focus, took in his face rather than his soul. 'I don't know.'

Madame Rose placed a hand on Emma's shoulder. 'Don't you worry dear. Your Auntie Rose will help you find it.' Then: 'Jenny, why don't you take Emma upstairs. I'm sure she could do with a long hot soak after her ordeal, don't you think?'

Jenny Nairn looked across to McLean for confirmation. He nodded, wondering how it was that Madame

Rose knew her. Something to do with Ouija boards and séances, no doubt. He watched silently as Emma allowed herself to be led from the room, more childlike now than she had been since first waking. Only when she was gone, and the door was closed behind her, did he speak.

'Why do I get the impression you know more about this than you're telling me?'

'Because you're a detective inspector?' Madame Rose took a long, unladylike slurp of tea. 'Or maybe because you know what this is about but just don't want to accept it.'

'What are you talking about? Emma? She had a nasty blow to the head.'

'Her brain has recovered. That's not what's wrong with her.'

'If it's not her brain, then what?'

'Think, Inspector. Use that mind your grandmother was so proud of.'

That set him back a step. First Emma, then Jenny Nairn. Now his grandmother. Was there anyone in his life this strange transvestite medium didn't know? McLean suppressed the urge to ask. Kept his mind focused on the task at hand.

'Why was she at Anderson's shop?'

'Ah. Now we're getting somewhere. Why do you think?'

'She had nothing to do with that place. Apart from being part of the SOC team that went over it after we found it had been used again.'

'And you think that might be it? That maybe it was one of her last memories before she had her blow to the head?'

Damn, this was worse than a session with Grumpy Bob. 'It's a possibility.'

'Possible, yes. But it's not why she went there.' Madame Rose put down her mug and picked up the medical textbook. 'Why did Anderson kill those women? Why did Needham?'

'Anderson was a sick bastard who got off on pain. Needy went mad when his dad died leaving him with a million quid in death duties to pay.'

'OK. Let's try that again. Why did they both claim they killed those women?' Madame Rose dropped the book back on the table. McLean knew damned well what he, she, whatever, was doing. That didn't mean he had to like it.

'The *Book*. The bloody *Book of Souls*. It doesn't exist. Never did. It was just Anderson trying to get off with an insanity plea. It didn't convince the jury and it didn't convince me.'

'Even after what you saw in the fire?'

'How do you know what I saw in the fire? How do you even know about the fire at all?'

'I make it my business to know what's going on at the fringes, Inspector. You might not be ready to accept it, but you are part of that world. I know what you saw in the fire. I know what happened when the book burned. The souls trapped inside it were released. There isn't a medium in Europe can call themselves that who didn't feel it when those souls were freed.'

McLean used the excuse of taking a sip of tea to study Madame Rose more closely. The man was a fraud, of that he was sure. For a start, he was a man dressed as a woman. That was a deception up front. She, he, whatever, peddled fortunes to the gullible, no doubt held séances too. That was probably how Jenny Nairn fitted into the picture, and no doubt how Madame Rose knew so much about him.

At least, that was what the rational, trained detective in him said. That was the simplest of explanations, the truth revealed after everything else had been pared away. On the other hand, there was a seductive quality to the argument. It fitted so well with the things he had seen and done. And there was no denying that Madame Rose believed in it completely. Even heavily made up as he was, you could see it in his face. And the way he held himself, the way one hand absent-mindedly stroked the cover of the copy of Gray's *Anatomy*.

And, of course, he had found Emma. Brought her home.

'Needy did have a book,' McLean said after a long pause. 'But it wasn't anything special. Just a prop. An old ledger or something he'd got from the evidence stores. It burned in the fire, but to be honest I don't remember much about what happened back then. I was concussed for one thing, and there wasn't much air.'

'Well, let me spell it out for you then.' Madame Rose gathered her hands together, leaned forwards with her elbows on the table, eyes boring into McLean's. 'The *Book of Souls* existed. Donald Anderson stole it from the monastery where he was librarian for many years. He tried to read it and failed. It consumed his soul and you know what happened next. When you caught him, the book went into hiding. It ended up in your evidence stores, where Sergeant John Needham found it. He tried to read it, and you know what happened to him.'

'You're saying Needy did what he did to those women – to Emma – because he had no soul?'

'The book did those things. It just used the man as its vessel.'

'And the women? Emma? Kirsty?'

'The book traps the souls of the victims as they die. You cannot destroy a soul, Inspector, but you can capture it and feed off it.' Now Madame Rose was staring straight at him, her eyes wide and intense. 'Or at least so I am told.'

'But Emma didn't die.'

'No, Inspector. She didn't. But I fear your Sergeant Needham made her read the book. I fear it took a part of her, and that missing part is what she was looking for today, why she can't remember anything from her adult life and why she's becoming more childlike day by day. She has lost a piece of her soul. There is really no hope of recovery until she gets it back.'

The sound of Madame Rose's taxi disappearing down the drive on its way back to Leith had long since echoed away into the background hum of the city. McLean sat at the kitchen table, a mug of cold tea in his hands, staring at nothing as he played the conversation back in his head. Half-remembered snippets flickered through his mind, suppressed memories of the fire that had claimed Sergeant John Needham, the strange underground chapel beneath the house, the factory bursting into flames spontaneously.

No, it hadn't been spontaneous. He'd taken a candle in there with him, dropped it when Needy hit him with that bit of two by four. Old, dry timber. A factory that hadn't been used in years, methane gas seeping up from ancient coal mines. No wonder it had gone up like a bonfire on Guy Fawkes night.

But there had been a book, hadn't there? Needy wouldn't give it up even when the flames took him, caught that ridiculous cloak he'd been wearing, went through his hair like a knacker-man singeing a pig. McLean put down his tea, scrunched his hands into his eyes as hard as he could stand in an attempt to erase that image. A man on fire, screaming as much in frustration and rage as in pain. Or was that his imagination, his brain filling in the gaps where memory had been erased by the heat, the smoke, not enough oxygen?

Pulling his hands away from his eyes left ghost images dancing in the dim kitchen light in front of him. Spirits rising up from the ashes of a book, burned by a mystical flame. The souls of countless victims, trapped down the years. Victims and murderers both; the innocent and those who had sought to test themselves against evil and found themselves wanting. Needy had been there, a man broken by the weight of expectations laid upon him. Anderson too, small and frightened, a little boy abandoned by his parents and never understanding why. And then the women they had abducted, tortured, raped, killed. All because a book told them to? Well, was that so hard to believe, after all that had been done in the name of the Bible, the Koran?

They were naked. Does he remember that? Or is it the memory of the post-mortem slab, the endless photographs of dead bodies he has seen. No, they were there. Surrounding him, keeping the flames away until rescue came. Kirsty.

A noise and flurry of movement. At the same moment he registered that he'd heard the cat flap clatter in the back door, Mrs McCutcheon's cat was on the table in front of him. The normally unflappable beast looked wild, its fur straggled and unkempt, mud spatters all along one side.

'Jesus, you gave me a shock.' McLean rocked back in his chair, feeling his heart bashing away in his chest like a cheap horror movie. The cat just looked at him, sat down and started to clean itself.

'Where've you been anyway?' He didn't expect an answer and wasn't disappointed. It occurred to him that Mrs McCutcheon's cat had not been there when he and Jenny had returned from the station. Normally it would present itself at some point soon after he came home; ever since Emma had come from the hospital it had been her shadow. And then he knew exactly where it had been. Halfway across town and back. Following Emma all the way to the Canongate and Donald Anderson's shop. Only when Madame Rose had brought Emma home in a taxi, she hadn't noticed the familiar. Poor bloody thing must have run the whole way back.

'Let's get you something to eat then.' McLean pushed himself up from his chair, ignoring the creaks and groans from his knees as he did so. The cat stopped its cleaning, watched him with glass-black eyes as he went to the cupboard where the cat food lived. It stayed where it was, sitting in the middle of the kitchen table, until he'd bent down and brought out the box. Then with a disdainful flick of the tail it jumped down to the floor and trotted off into the hall.

26

He must have been a drummer, once. He has one of those little round stools with the padded top that rises on a screw thread. The drum kit has long gone, no doubt to pay off debts, or the rent, or just to eat; he looks like he hasn't been doing enough of that. But he kept the stool. I like that. A reminder perhaps of a better time, when life was full of possibilities.

Now the possibilities are all gone, and there is just the stool. Unwound to its fullest extent, he teeters on the edge, wobbling slightly, toes flexing as he tries to maintain his balance. He really is a skinny thing. Not an inch of fat on him. There's muscle in his legs but it's wasting away now, and his arms, his torso, are weedy. Naked, I can see the scars all around his middle and yes, there across his buttocks. Dark purple stains in the skin, slashed with shiny, white tissue. He looks like some mad headmaster has flayed him to within an inch of his life. Some malevolent first mate gone at him with the cat-o'-nine-tails, but kept the strokes low. Even if I couldn't taste the despair in his soul, I could see it written all across his ruined body. Once he was alive, fit, strong. Now he is reduced to a hobbling, pain-wracked mess of a boy. No future at all. The spirit sings in me to end him.

'You are in your safe place now. Nothing can harm you here.' My voice fills the room like smoke, spreading into every corner, pushing its way deep into the boy's mind. It is always like this when the spirit is with me. The power sends shivers deep into my core. I take the rope from my bag. Not much left now; I will have to send the next one out for some more. Heavy, rough hemp, my hands work it as if I had done this all my life, the knot appearing without any thought, perfect, deadly. I pull a chair over from the nearby table, climb up and throw the other end of the rope over the ceiling beam. I have no idea what I am doing, and yet I know exactly how long the rope must be, how far the drop. I have done since I first saw this boy, first shook him by the hand and sized him up, first knew that his struggle would soon be over. The spirit guides me in this, as it has always guided me. Since we first came together in our perfect union.

'We are close, you and I. Much closer than lovers could ever be.' I whisper the words into his ear as I lower the noose over his neck. His eyes are closed, little fluttering movements under the lids. He breathes lightly, slowly, his hands hanging loose beside him like branches swaying in the gentlest of breezes. This close, I can smell his musk, an intoxicating mixture of sweat and hormones, soap and shampoo. His mouth is shut, but his lips are pursed, dark red, full like a girl's. I have to suppress the urge to kiss them, though I feel no attraction to him. The spirit would not want me to sully myself, not when it can offer me so much more.

'Not long now and we shall be joined so perfectly you cannot begin to imagine it.' I step lightly from the chair, put it back where it came from. A quick look around the room, the shelves of bric-a-brac, the boxes strewn here and there, the thin glass panes set into the top of the old garage doors. So much bigger than the hovels the last two lived in, and this is a house, not some dingy bedsit squashed into the back of a tiny terrace. Once he had a future, this poor, poor boy. Once he might have been something. All that was taken from him in a squeal of brakes, a moment of lost attention, a terrible accident. The van that broke his bones might not have killed him straight away, but it killed him nonetheless.

I feel the spirit rising up in me now. Its power is overwhelming and pure. I give myself to it without pause or regret. The world expands in my sight and I can see every tiny detail laid out before me. The note pinned to the corkboard over the workbench. The door, slightly ajar, leading through to the kitchen where this beautiful, damaged boy took off his clothes and folded them neatly over a chair. The pores on his skin, glistening as the effort of keeping his balance brings a sheen of sweat to his cheeks and forehead. The slow, relaxed beat of his heart and the steady rhythm of his breathing.

'Come to me, now.' And my voice is a command so strong even I take a step. The boy responds without hesitation, without fear. Forward, forward.

And down.

27

'I want you to close your eyes, Emma. Take a breath. Hold it. Now let it out slowly.'

The office of Doctor Eleanor Austin, early morning. McLean sat on the low, comfortable sofa, cradling a cup of coffee. As ways to start the day went, it wasn't too bad. Just a pity he'd been awake since half past four, when Emma had crawled into his bed, sobbing and shivering in her sleep.

'That's good. Concentrate on my voice. Take a breath. Hold it.' A pause, and McLean found himself struggling to breathe out. 'And let it out slowly. Good.'

Emma's nocturnal visits had become regular as clock-work in the days since her disappearance. She'd started talking in her sleep, too. Low whispers that he could never quite understand. There was no mistaking the distress in her voice. Or the fact that it often didn't actually sound like her voice at all.

'Now, concentrate on your breathing. In. Hold. Out. Good. I want you to keep that rhythm.'

McLean struggled to keep his eyes open, took a long sip of coffee and looked around the room. There wasn't all that much to it. His sofa, the two high-backed arm-chairs one facing the other, a bureau under the window at the far side of the room. There were no pictures on the walls, just a pair of antique mirrors, candle holders set into the frame dripped with wax. A similar pair hung in the living room in his grandmother's house. He couldn't remember them ever having held candles, but presumably they must have done once. Back in the days before electric light. Before he was born. Before even his grandmother was born.

'Now I want you to think back to your earliest memory. Keep breathing. In. Hold. Out.'

His hand in someone else's. His mother's, perhaps. An adult's, certainly. He has to reach up almost above his head. He is standing alongside a car, staring into fog that swirls about the trees. Everything is white, and yet at the same time dark. The car's headlights spear through the fog, making it seem like the road is a tunnel leading to who knows where?

'And breathe – Inspector, really!' The tinny warbling of his mobile phone cut through McLean's dream. He scrabbled around, trying to get the damned thing out of his pocket, succeeding only in pouring lukewarm coffee all over his trousers.

'I'm sorry. I could have sworn I'd turned the thing off.' Finally McLean pulled the phone out, just as it rung off. Caller ID told him it had been DC MacBride. He stood up, the room swaying gently as he shook away the last vestiges of sleep. 'I'd better phone this in. Sorry.'

'I think we've probably got as far as we're going to today anyway.' Doctor Austin turned her attention back to Emma, who was trying hard to suppress a smirk but not really succeeding. 'Now I need you to practise that breathing exercise every day. Jenny will help you. It's important to learn to relax.'

McLean left them to it, heading out the door and into the small reception area as he tapped the recall button on the screen. Dave looked up at him with a slightly startled expression, but said nothing. The phone rang twice before it was answered.

'What's up, Constable? I said I'd not be in until later.'

'I know that, sir. And sorry to phone, but I thought you'd want to know as soon as. We've got another hanging.'

'You have got to be fucking joking.'

McLean stood in the small yard outside a nondescript fifties detached house in Colinton, looking in through the opened doors to a garage that like most of its ilk was not actually used for the housing of cars. This one had been pressed into the inevitable storage role, with a distinct theme of bicycle about the place. There were also a workbench, table, some chairs. And a naked man hanging by a rope, his toes just a few inches off the ground.

'Why do they always take their clothes off?' Detective Constable MacBride slammed the door of the pool car and came to join him, unwilling to go any further into the crime scene. Probably best to leave it to the SOC officers who were even now swarming over the place like well-trained, white boiler-suited ants.

'That, Constable, is a very good question. Would you like to hazard an answer?'

MacBride said nothing, which was probably a good thing. McLean looked around the street, a long line of identikit dormer bungalows each with its pitched-roof garage alongside. Homes for Edinburgh's swelling middle class at a time when the motor car was every man's dream and global warming hadn't been invented yet.

'Maybe there's a sexual element to it?'

'What?'

'The nakedness, sir. Maybe it's a . . . I don't know, a fetish or something.'

'What, like auto-erotic asphyxiation? Aren't we missing a couple of items here? A broom handle and an orange?'

It was difficult to tell whether the young detective constable was blushing or not, his face was always pink. The way MacBride turned away from the dangling man, full-frontal but not exactly stimulated, suggested he was. McLean looked back too, distracted by a car as it drove slowly along the street, almost stopping as the driver tried to get a look at what was going on.

'Why's this street not been cordoned off? Jesus, who's the officer in charge?'

'Umm . . . I just got here, sir. With you?'

'Well go and find out, won't you? And while you're at it get someone to tape off this road, at least fifty yards each way. See if the SOC boys have got a screen they can put up to stop the gawkers seeing your man there in all his glory.'

MacBride scurried off on his errands. McLean shoved his hands in his pockets and approached the nearest SOC officer. She looked at him with a scowl, her eyes dropping to his feet in a deliberate, slow motion. He stopped, backed away from the scene.

'I just need to know who's in charge, OK? I won't come inside and spoil anything.'

'Speak to him. And don't come in here without a suit. Better yet don't come in at all till we're done, aye?' The

SOC officer pointed towards the front door to the house. The porch was open, little more than a slim shelter to keep the rain off as you entered. A thin haze of blue-grey smoke hung around it, the telltale sign of someone sneaking a crafty smoke. Sure enough, as he rounded the corner, McLean was confronted with the sight of two uniform constables and one plain clothes detective sergeant keeping well out of the way.

'Everything under control is it, Sergeant?'

'I . . . Sir . . . No one told me . . .' Detective Sergeant Carter hurriedly dropped his half-smoked cigarette and scrunched it under his foot. The two constables with him hid theirs behind their backs, shuffling in the tight porch to put the DS between them and McLean.

'You two. Go see DC MacBride. We need to secure this crime scene. I want someone at each end of the street, too. Only let people in who live here, and take their names. Get started on a list so we can go house to house and speak to people.'

'Sir, is that really necessary? Silly bugger topped himself. It's not as if –'

'A man's dead, sergeant. I don't consider that silly in any way.' McLean had a head's height on Carter, and the advantage that the DS was backed into the porch.

'I was waiting for the pathologist, sir. I didn't think there was any rush. Suicides don't normally get high priority.'

'Were you aware that two other people have hanged themselves in this city in the past fortnight?'

'Ah. Way I hear it we get about two hangings a week, sir. No' that unusual a way fer folk to top themselves.'

'Like that?' McLean nodded in the direction of the

dead man, hidden round the corner of the building, and now, finally, by a hastily erected screen. Carter didn't answer, instead shifted his weight from foot to foot like a schoolboy needing to be excused.

'And no doubt you were aware that I was investigating whether they were in fact suicides at all. I seem to recall DCI Brooks making some derogatory comments about it during his briefing yesterday morning.'

'Sir, I'm sorry. I . . .'

'Forget it. Just bring me up to speed, OK?' McLean itched to tear him off a strip, preferably in front of as many junior officers as he could find, but that had happened more than enough to him in the past, and he knew just how counterproductive it was. Carter paused a while, as if considering whether to apologize or just get on with his job. He wasn't a bad detective, McLean knew, just a touch on the lazy side. And he'd been cosying up to Spence, Brooks and the rest of the cabal whose mission these days seemed to be to make life as difficult as possible. As if the job wasn't hard enough already.

'Suicide . . . That's to say the victim's name is John Fenton. Local boy as far as I can tell. Lived here all his life.'

'How was he found?'

'Neighbour.' Carter nodded towards the house on the other side of the garage. 'Said he dropped round for his bike. Fenton was the local repair man. Mad keen cyclist. Worked as a cycle courier until about six months ago when he had an argument with a Transit van and came second.'

McLean looked back at the body, still dangling from its rope. Was that stout hemp? The same as the other two?

'He didn't try to get him down, this neighbour. Most people would do that, wouldn't they?'

'He's one of ours, sir. Constable Stephen. Works with traffic and knows his way round a crime scene. He could tell Fenton was dead, thought it best not to disturb anything.'

'That's something at least. He at home now?'

'Had to go for his shift. We can get in touch with him easily enough.' Carter pulled a hefty Airwave set from his jacket pocket.

'Jesus. You actually carry one of those things around?'

'We all have to now, sir. And they're not so bad, really. Not the new ones, anyway. Save a fortune on the mobile, too.'

'Well, set up an interview for the end of his shift. His clock, not ours. I'll square it with his sergeant if there's any kickback. Now grab us a couple of monkey suits and let's go look at poor old John Fenton.'

'PC Stephen, sir. I was told you wanted to see me.'

McLean looked up at the noise, seeing an officer standing at the open door to his office, one hand held up high where he had knocked quietly on the door jamb. Police Constable Kenneth Stephen was not what he had been expecting. Truth be told, he'd not really been expecting anything at all, but if he had been, this surely wasn't it. He was young, for one thing; mid-twenties at the most. And he was dressed in police-issue cycling gear, a helmet stowed under one arm. Traffic, that's what DS Carter had said. Well, traffic cops rode bikes, especially in the city centre. He knew that but had somehow failed to consider exactly what it meant. Sweat, mostly, it would seem. Had the man just cycled here at full speed?

'Yes. Thank you. Ummm. Have a seat, if you can find one.' McLean nodded in the direction of where a seat might be, were it not covered in a mound of boxes and paperwork.

'I'm OK standing, sir. I take it this is about John.'

'Fenton, aye. You knew him, I understand.'

Stephen shook his head. 'Thought I knew him. Never thought he'd be the type to . . . well . . . you know.'

'So he wasn't depressed then?'

Stephen paused before answering, a frown wrinkling his damp brow. 'Actually, now you mention it, he had every reason to be depressed, just didn't seem to show it.'

'How d'you mean?'

'Well, sir. See, John's a bicycle nut. That's why I was away round his place this morning, to fetch my road bike. He'd been fixing the brakes and making me a new wheel.'

'Yes, I saw the bikes in his garage.'

'He was an off-road racer. Semi-pro. Endurance stuff mostly. Don't think I've ever met anyone as fit. Used to work for a cycle courier firm in the city. Wheel Deliver, I think they're called. Told me it was his ideal job. He kept race fit, and they gave him time off to compete. Sponsored him for a while too, I think.'

'Sounds like a man with every reason to be happy.' McLean leaned back in his seat until his back hit the wall. He still had to crane his neck rather more than was comfortable to look the standing PC in the eye.

'Well, he was. I mean it was sad when his mum died, but

that was a few years back. Told me he'd never known his dad, but he and his mum were close. I guess that's why he kept the house. Could've sold it for a fortune if my rent's anything to go by.'

'So if he was happy enough in his job and he'd got over his mum's death, why was he depressed? Sorry, that's not what you said. Why did he have every reason to be depressed?'

'He was in an accident, sir. About six months ago I think. No, more like eight. Got hit by a Transit van that pulled out of a side street without looking. We got the bastard, lost his licence for two years. You ask me, they should've locked him up and thrown away the key.'

'Fenton was badly injured, I take it.'

'Broke his pelvis in three places. Right femur too. Doctor reckoned he was about a millimetre away from severing the artery. Would've killed him in seconds. He'd've bled out.'

McLean made a mental note to tell Cadwallader, then realized that the pathologist would look up Fenton's medical file long before he started examining the dead body.

'How long did he take to recover?'

'He wasn't really back to full mobility yet, to be honest, sir. He was in hospital for three months, then a wheelchair and crutches for a couple more. But I saw him out on his bike recently. Going slow, but steady. Thought he was doing OK. And he was always cheerful when you talked to him.'

McLean scratched a little question mark in his notebook underneath the line where he'd written 'John Fenton'. He hadn't actually taken any notes. He hastily added 'Wheel Deliver. Cycle Couriers'.

'Thank you, Constable. You've been very helpful.' He snapped the notebook shut and stood up. 'We'll need a proper written statement, too. Let's see if we can find DC MacBride and get that done before your shift's over.'

Stephen nodded, then stepped aside to let McLean out of the office. He fell into step alongside as they walked up the corridor towards the CID room.

'Can I ask a question, sir?' Stephen asked after a few seconds.

'Of course.'

'John hanged himself. I could see that clear enough when I found him this morning.'

'That's not a question, Constable.'

'No. I mean, well, it is. Sort of. Only I called it in, soon as I found him. SEB were on the scene pretty sharpish, and that DS Carter arrived with a couple of constables to check everything over. But they didn't seem all that interested.'

'Still not an actual question.'

'No. Sorry. What I'm trying to say is, if this is just another suicide, then why's a DI looking into it? I mean, I'd expect a report to go across your desk. You might even read it before signing off the investigation costs. But asking questions? Getting involved?'

They had reached the door to the CID room, and McLean pushed it open, ushering PC Stephen inside. MacBride looked up from his desk in the far corner, saw them and picked up his notebook in readiness.

'You go speak to Detective Constable MacBride there.' McLean pointed him out. 'And if you ever fancy a change to plain clothes, give us a shout. I'm always on the lookout for officers not afraid to ask questions.'

He was on his way back to his office and the ever-renewing stack of paperwork when his phone vibrated in his pocket. He managed to get it out before it switched to voicemail.

'McLean.'

'Ah, Detective Inspector. Good. Jemima Cairns. From the forensic labs. We met briefly at the hanging crime scene in Colinton. John Fenton.'

McLean tried to remember who he'd spoken to that morning. Failed.

'What can I do for you, Miss Cairns?'

'You asked for someone to look at the rope used in the earlier two hangings. I've been comparing them with the one we found this morning.'

'Are they all from the same length?' He paused mid-stride, all too aware how much hinged on the answer.

'It's . . . complicated. I really think you should see for yourself.'

'So this is what you wanted me to see then? Would it not have been easier just to send me some photos?'

McLean stood in the middle of the Scene Evaluation Branch main lab, trying not to touch anything in case it brought yet another scowl from the short, round woman beside him. She had introduced herself as Jemima Cairns, but he had a feeling she was always going to be Miss Cairns to him. Either that or Ma'am. She didn't have the look of a Jemima.

'Photographs can only show so much, Inspector. Much easier if you can actually handle the objects. Here.' Miss Cairns handed him a pair of latex gloves, which he dutifully pulled on. She was already wearing a pair, and bent down over the bench to pick up the first of the three objects that had brought him all the way across town at her summons.

It was a noose, expertly tied. Good hemp rope. Three-quarter-inch stock, but then that much he already knew. The knot was still intact, a neat cut through the loop showing how it had been removed from its last user. This one had come from either Mikhailevic or Fenton, as it wasn't stained with the juices of decomposition.

'It's a noose,' he said, aware that he was stating the obvious but needing something to say.

'It's not just a noose, Inspector. This is a hangman's knot. Thirteen loops, see. Makes sure it doesn't slip, and it's unlucky.' Miss Cairns carefully twisted the rope around until the intricate loops could be seen in the best light. 'It's been tied by an expert. Someone who's done it many, many times before.'

'I can barely tie my shoelaces, so I'll take your word for it. These are all from the same piece of rope?' McLean pointed at the other two knots on the bench. Miss Cairns carefully put down the one she was holding and picked up the next, again angled it so that the knot itself was easy to see.

'As far as we can tell, yes. Which is to say the chances of them not being the same piece of rope are vanishingly small. A lawyer might try reasonable doubt if a trial hinged on it, but I'd be happy to square up to him if he did.'

I bet you would. McLean stopped himself from taking a step back. Miss Cairns might have been short, but she made up for it with girth and an indefinable presence that set his self-preservation alarms ringing.

'That's not the interesting part though. See?' She held up the second rope for a closer inspection. Judging by the reek coming off it, this had been the one that had seen Patrick Sands through into the next world.

'Like I said, not an expert in knots.' McLean backed off this time. Miss Cairns gave him a look that was a mixture of disappointment and pity, then shook her head and put the noose back down again. She didn't bother picking up the third, but as far as he could tell it was exactly the same as the other two.

'Well, as it happens, I am. Member of the International Guild of Knot Tyers and a registered forensic expert in knots and ropes. Dad was a trawlerman, worked out of Crail. He taught me a thing or two about tying rope. They're a bit like signatures, you know. Knots. Sure, the knot might be the same, but everyone ties it differently. A twist here, a bit tighter there. I could always tell when I was mending the nets who'd tied them before. And I can say with absolute certainty that these three knots weren't tied by three different people.'

'You're sure of that?' McLean saw the scowl, raised his hands in defence. 'I mean, of course you're sure of that. But is there any, I don't know, objective way of measuring this? I don't mean to be sceptical, but I've never heard of the science of knots before.'

'I'm sure of it, and, yes, I have done an objective analysis. And that's where it gets complicated.' Miss Cairns turned her attention to a computer nearby, clicking away until three photographs of the three nooses were lined up.

'This works better if you've got the 3D goggles on, but you'll get the picture.' She clicked again and the first noose shifted on top of the second. It wasn't a perfect fit, but it was damned close. Another click and the third noose shifted onto the other two. If it weren't for the discolouration on one of the ropes, courtesy of the late Paddy Sands' decomposition fluids, McLean might have thought he was looking at the same rope photographed three different times.

'I've never seen anything quite like it before, Inspector. In all three dimensions these knots are virtually identical. That's after they've been tied and then used to standard-drop hang three very different people.'

'That's pretty impressive,' McLean said, not really knowing what Miss Cairns was getting at. The SOC officer glared at him as if he were an imbecile, which given the circumstances was perhaps fair enough.

'No, it's not. Not impressive at all. What it is is impossible.'

28

'So we've got three deaths by hanging. All very similar MO. Two I could put down to coincidence, but three's just too much. And besides, I don't believe in coincidences anyway. This could be some kind of suicide pact, but if it is, it's a very odd one. Looks like all three nooses have all been tied by one person, probably using one length of rope. To my mind that makes this at the very least manslaughter.'

The CID room, early, for an impromptu briefing and catch-up. McLean looked upon his gathered team with a mixture of relief and despair. True, they were all people he'd worked with in the past and all people he trusted to bring something to the investigation. But they were also very few in number. Grumpy Bob lurked at the back, his feet up on his desk, cradling a mug of coffee that quite plainly hadn't come from the vending machine in the canteen. DC MacBride perched on the edge of the neighbouring desk, pink and scrubbed and eager. DS Ritchie had somehow managed to avoid being sent up to Tulliallan for more Police Scotland workshops and was gracing them with her presence, along with a delicate whiff of some perfume McLean couldn't immediately identify. Unless that was coming from PC Sandy Gregg, on secondment and fair quivering with the excitement of being in plain clothes for a change. DS Carter had put in an appearance a few minutes before the start of the briefing, and for a moment McLean thought he might have defected. As soon as he'd realized what was going on, he'd grabbed a folder from his desk and darted out of the room. No doubt to report back to Spence and Brooks that the upstart McLean was conducting investigations and what were they going to do about it?

'They knew each other?' This from Sandy Gregg. No one else would try to state the obvious so, well, obviously.

'That's our working hypothesis. We've not managed to find any solid links between them yet, other than the rope and the knots.' McLean turned back to the whiteboard where he had taped up photographs of Patrick Sands, Grigori Mikhailevic and John Fenton.

'The deaths are approximately three weeks apart. All left suicide notes. You should have copies of them in the packs MacBride handed out earlier. I think you'll be as struck by the similarities between them as I was.'

Cue a rustling of sheets as everyone leafed through their paperwork. Except Grumpy Bob, who just took a slow drink of his coffee.

'All three of them were naked when they hanged themselves, and all three used the standard-drop method to do it.'

'Standard drop?' This from Ritchie, sitting at the front like teacher's pet.

'Standard drop is between four and six feet, though these were all at the lower end of that. As opposed to long drop, where the optimum drop is calculated for each individual to be hanged. The idea's to snap the neck cleanly and swiftly so the hanged man is dead before he starts swinging. Problem is, it's not very reliable. How far you need to drop depends on your weight, height, body type. There's a whole load of calculations. You just string someone up and let them fall three or four feet, chances are it's not enough to break their neck and they suffocate to death. Or if it's too much, their head pops off, which is messy.'

The whole group turned as one to DC MacBride, the font of this unusual wisdom. His pink face turned even redder under the combined scrutiny.

'Is that usual?' Sandy Gregg asked. 'The standard thingy?'

'Actually, no. Hanging's one of the most common methods of suicide; about half of the annual total. But it's usually just a form of self-strangulation. It's not easy to engineer a drop, and even if you do, most people underestimate, choke themselves to death. All three of these men put a chair on something, or over a drop, so they knew what they were doing.' MacBride shrugged at the collection of dropped jaws staring at him. 'What? I looked it up. OK?'

'Just as well someone did. Thank you, Constable.' McLean turned his attention back to the whiteboard and its three photographs. 'These three not only opted for a very complicated way of killing themselves, they also all succeeded. PM results show three clean breaks. Only Sands possibly overdid it a bit, which is why . . . well, you've seen the photos. They died instantly and painlessly, not slowly strangling to death, which I'm told is a nasty, protracted and agonising way to go. They also all used nooses that were tied by one person. Could have been one of them, could have been someone else entirely.'

'So they all used the same rope. One of them tied the nooses. And Grigori Mikhailevic bought the rope from The Captain's Rest in Newhaven?' Acting DC Gregg ran her finger down the page of the report as she asked the question.

'That's how it looks,' McLean said.

'But Patrick Sands died a fortnight before Mikhailevic. Isn't that right?'

McLean stared at the constable in consternation. He'd forgotten that the sequence of deaths wasn't the same as the discovery of the bodies.

'That's a bloody good point,' Grumpy Bob said. 'What's the timeline for these suicides? How's it all fit in with when the rope was bought?'

All eyes turned to DC MacBride again. He shrugged, then dug out his notebook, flicked through the pages.

'According to the pathology report, Patrick Sands died sometime in the first week of July. Grigori Mikhailevic hanged himself on the twenty-second and Jonathan Fenton was found yesterday, seen alive the day before, so died sometime on the night of the thirteenth.'

'Oh bugger.' Grumpy Bob had his own notebook out, but McLean didn't need to see what was written in it to know what was upsetting him. If the shopkeeper was right both in his identification of Mikhailevic and his book-keeping, then the rope hadn't been purchased until the second week of July, when Paddy Sands was already hanging from the skylight in his tiny Colonies flat. He might have used the same type of rope, but it hadn't been cut from the same length.

'What? Did I say something wrong?' PC Gregg looked

backwards and forwards between the two senior detectives, a horrified look on her face.

'Far from it, Constable. You stopped us making complete tits of ourselves.' McLean slumped into a nearby chair. It wasn't like him to miss something as obvious as that, but then he wasn't normally working for two different teams.

'OK then, people. Where does this leave us?'

DC MacBride looked like he was about to answer, but then the door to the CID room swung open and Detective Sergeant Carter poked his head through.

'You come to join us?' McLean asked. 'Only we could use some intelligent input.'

Carter made a quizzical face, which wasn't far off his normal one. 'No. I mean . . . Sorry, sir. It's Dag– . . . Acting Superintendent Duguid, sir. He wants to see you in his office.'

'I'm kind of in the middle of something here.'

'He knows, sir. Think that's why he wants to see you.' Carter had the decency to look embarrassed.

'OK. I'll go and see what he wants.' McLean hauled himself out of the chair, paused at the door to address what he hoped would still be his team in an hour. 'Let's start from scratch here. Set up a timeline, go over the interviews with friends. These three people are linked. Find out how.'

'You know your problem, McLean? You make everything more complicated than it needs to be.'

Jayne McIntyre's office. Well, technically Acting Superintendent Charles Duguid's office, but he was damned if he was going to give in and start calling it that. McLean stood in front of the wide desk like a persistent trouble-maker called up in front of the beak. On the other side, Duguid flicked through the latest in a long line of tedious and time-consuming daily reports with the air of a man who really couldn't be arsed reading the thing.

'The way I see it, you've got it in your head these deaths are suspicious, and now you're going looking for the evidence to back up your theory. Feel free to correct me, but that's not how I was taught to conduct an investigation.'

Deep breath. Try to keep a lid on the anger. That's what he's trying to do, after all. Goad. 'With respect, sir. Three very similar deaths by hanging in the space of just over a month is suspicious enough to warrant a second look, wouldn't you say?'

'We went over this already. People commit suicide every day, McLean.' Duguid stopped a moment as what he'd said sunk in. 'I'm not saying that's good or inevitable or whatever. It's just that we can't go treating every single one as if it's a potential murder.'

'Seven hundred and seventy-two in 2011, sir. In Scot-land as a whole that is. So yes, about two people a day take their own lives. And about half of that total hanged them-selves in one way or another. I know the stats.'

'Like I told you before. Someone hangs themselves in this country every bloody day. And yet you think these ones are so important you've got two sergeants working them, three if you count Carter on this latest case. God only knows how many constables running around after you. And that's just CID. I dread to think what the uniform count is. All just for a couple of suicides. Have you any idea how much this is costing?'

More than you, in all probability. 'It's three deaths actually, sir. And I don't think they're suicides. At least not just suicides.'

'I don't care what you think. You were only meant to be using DS Ritchie for this investigation. Not half the bloody station.' Duguid threw the report down on his desk. It missed the edge and tumbled to the floor.

'Ritchie's on the local liaison group for the new Police Scotland, sir.' Which you know perfectly well, since you were the one who ordered her to do it. 'She's not here most of the time. And DS Carter's back working with Spence and Brooks, which is frankly the best place for him. I've got Grumpy Bob co-ordinating the investigation with MacBride and Gregg helping him out. I'd hardly call that half the station.'

'Gregg?' Duguid's confusion spoke eloquently of his skill at personnel management. Christ, this man was supposed to be in charge. Of the whole station.

'PC Gregg, sir. She's on probation with CID. You know. You suggested her for my team earlier.'

'Oh, that Gregg.' Duguid shook his head as he spoke, suggesting he didn't really have a clue who McLean was talking about. He looked around for the report, made a show of bending down to pick it up and place it on the desk between the two of them. 'It's still too much manpower. This PC Gregg could collate the forensic, pathology and background reports on her own. Deliver the whole lot to the Procurator Fiscal's office and the job's done.'

Gods, it's like dealing with a four-year-old. 'I could ask

her to do that, sir. Or DC MacBride, since he was the officer initially investigating the first one. But he thought there was something odd even then, and everything that's happened since has only confirmed that for me. These three hangings are all linked.'

'And yet for all the manpower you've thrown at the investigation so far, you can't find anything except circumstance and supposition. Dammit, McLean, you had a hunch and it didn't pay off. Happens to all of us. Let it go and move one.'

'Is that an order, sir?'

'If it has to be. Wrap it up, and get back to the SCU. I've had Jo Dexter bending my ear all day about your beaten-up whore and her dead pimp, not to mention the Port Authority calling me about a freighter that's still impounded and clogging up their docks. Get on top of things, man. Or move aside for someone who can cope.'

Time was he'd been able to take a meeting with Duguid in his stride. Brush it off in the full and frank knowledge that the man was a complete arse and anything he said was deserving of as much attention as a tabloid headline. But recently McLean had been finding it hard to shrug off the man's incompetence, and his latest meeting had been a particularly bruising one. Bad enough Duguid was fixated more on keeping costs down than on finding out what had happened, but that last jibe had cut deep.

He couldn't face going back to his office and the inevitable stack of paperwork to deal with. Neither was he in any great hurry to get back to Jo Dexter and her team, although he'd have to check in on Magda sooner or later.

No, what he needed was to sit down with Grumpy Bob and thrash out this case that Dagwood wanted closed.

But first he needed coffee, and possibly a bacon buttie if there were any left.

The canteen was in mid-shift quiet mode, just a few uniforms catching a breather and a couple of admin staff huddled in the corner with a stack of papers. McLean grabbed his booty and was almost out the door when a low voice stopped him short.

'The streets must be safe if the great Detective Inspector McLean feels there's time to get himself a coffee.'

He could have ignored it, could have pretended he'd not heard, walked out the door, but it had been a shit day, really. He turned to face his accuser, unsurprised to see DI Spence was not alone. On his own, little Mike Spence would never have had the temerity, but the presence and bulk of his fat superior emboldened him. Or perhaps made him more rash.

'I'm guessing all the really bad criminals are tucked away in jail if the two of you can spare the time to sit and hold hands.' Not his most brilliant riposte, but hey, he was busy. Mike Spence's face crumpled at the words, but alongside him, DCI Brooks flushed an angry red. His hands were on the table, cupped around a gently steaming mug. A plate that had once held a large portion of lasagne and chips sat on the table between the two men, but it wasn't hard to work out which one had eaten it.

'Heard you'd been hauled up in front of Dagwood again. What you do this time, lose your girlfriend in the park?'

Had he not been carrying a Styrofoam cup and a bacon

roll, McLean would have clenched his fists, might well have swung for the DCI. As it was he slopped hot coffee on his hand, the splash of pain diverting his attention just long enough to stop him from doing anything rash.

'Actually, sir' – he emphasized the title by clenching his teeth as he said it – 'the acting superintendent is very concerned about budgets and wanted to know where all the manpower was being directed. I showed him my team roster, think he was just about satisfied there was no wastage. No doubt he'll be wanting to see yours soon.'

Brooks scowled, which just made the rolls of flesh on his face wobble. 'Why are you still here, McLean?'

The question took him by surprise. McLean looked around the canteen, then hefted his booty. 'A man's got to eat. You of all people should know that. Sir.'

The scowl deepened, folds of skin rippling across Brooks' damp, ruddy forehead. 'Don't get cocky with me. You know damn well what I meant.'

'I do? Come on then. Say it out loud. Everyone's been dropping enough hints to start a war. About time someone said it to my face.'

'You don't need to do this job, man. Way I heard it you inherited big time when your grandmother died. So why are you still here? Why don't you fuck off to the country or something? Let us get on with our jobs.'

McLean let out a long slow breath he hadn't realized he'd been holding. Finally, someone getting to the bloody point. A shame it had to be a senior officer he'd get into trouble for being insubordinate to. He put his coffee cup and bacon buttie down on the table, pulled a handkerchief out of his pocket and dabbed at the damp spot on his hand. Taking his time and keeping his eyes on Little and Large while he did so. Normally he'd have just shoved the hanky back in his pocket when he was done, but this time he folded it neatly before tucking it away. Finally he picked up his cup and roll again. Maybe thirty seconds of silence had elapsed, but it felt like a week.

'You're a detective, sir. Why don't you see if you can work it out, eh?'

29

'Your man Fenton. Now there's an interesting case.'

Angus Cadwallader sat at his untidy desk in the little office off the main examination theatre of the City Mortuary. For so late in the day, his green scrubs were very clean, which probably meant he'd had to change. McLean leaned against a long workbench by the door, happy to be out of the station and the idiot politics of the place for a change.

'Interesting for you, or for me?'

Cadwallader smiled. 'Oh both, I hope. But mostly me. It's not often I get to see reconstructive surgery so soon after it's been done. The work on rebuilding his pelvis is masterful. Just a shame they couldn't do much about his femur. Poor bugger would always have walked with a limp, and I doubt he'd have ever been completely free of pain.'

'So what's interesting for me then?'

'You mean apart from the warm glow of knowing you've rescued what was otherwise a particularly rubbish day for me?' Cadwallader grabbed a pair of latex gloves from the desk beside him, stood up. 'Come.'

McLean followed his old friend out into the examination theatre and over to the banks of chill stores. It was a route he'd trodden far too many times before. Cadwallader opened a door that wouldn't have looked out of place on a commercial catering refrigerator, slid out a drawer holding a corpse covered in a heavy rubberized sheet. Pulled aside, it revealed John Fenton as naked as he'd been the day before, dangling from his rope.

'Don't need to get him up onto the table, really.' Cadwallader pulled on the gloves, then picked up one of Fenton's hands. 'The other two suicides you're looking into had no traces of hemp fibre under their nails, you'll recall. Well, this one's just the same.'

'He never touched the rope?'

'I'm not saying that. Not never touched it. But certainly not any time soon before he died. It's possible he strung up the rope, then went away and had a thorough scrub, but he'd still have had to touch the bloody thing to get it over his head and tighten it up.'

McLean looked down at the young man's face, pale in death. His hair was short, recently cut, and he was clean shaven. Were those the actions of a man in the pit of despair? He didn't know. Time was he'd been close himself, but he'd still managed to keep clean and tidy, so maybe there wasn't anything suspicious about that.

'The lack of fibres is interesting enough,' Cadwallader continued. 'It suggests a similarity between the three that goes beyond chance. And it's a puzzle of course. But there's something else I thought you might like to see. Here.'

The pathologist covered up the mortal remains of John Fenton and pushed him back into his chill rest, then led McLean back to the examination theatre. Where the old x-ray examination light boards had once been, now a sleek set of flat panel screens hung from the wall. Cadwallader flicked these on and fiddled around with the controls a bit until he had three images side by side.

'It's much easier when Tracy's here. She's brilliant with all this modern stuff.'

'I was going to ask where she was, actually. You've not done away with her and buried her under the patio have you?'

'No. She's off on some orientation workshop to do with all this new single body bollocks. Police Scotland, what a waste of time and money.'

'I keep on losing DS Ritchie to the same thing. Bloody nuisance if you ask me. I'm still not sure what problem it's meant to be solving.'

They fell silent for a while, staring at the images on the screen. McLean had seen enough x-rays in his time to recognize neck vertebrae and the signs of a clean break.

'These are the three hangings, I take it,' he said eventually.

'Indeed, yes. Sands, Mikhailevic and here the new boy, Fenton.' Cadwallader prodded the screen with a finger, causing it to change to a menu of options. A little cursing and poking brought the original images back.

'They all died quickly then.'

'Oh yes. Instant for all of them. And that's the problem, really.'

'It is?'

Cadwallader fixed McLean with one of his best teacher stares. 'How much do you know about the science of hanging, Tony?'

He thought back to the morning's briefing. Something about short drops and long drops that had made his neck hurt in sympathy. 'Not as much as Detective Constable MacBride.'

'Ah yes. Stuart. A quick learner. Well, I'll give you a brief summary.' Cadwallader pointed at the first fracture, careful not to touch the screen this time. 'The idea of hanging, at least in semi-civilized countries, is to swiftly dispatch the condemned. A broken neck is ideal, but it's not as easy to achieve as you might think.'

McLean remembered now. 'You need to get the drop right, that's what I was told. Too short and you choke to death, too long and your head comes off.'

'Something like that, yes. But there's more to it than just velocity. You need to jerk the head in a particular way to get a clean break. That's why the knot of the noose is usually placed here, under the left ear.' Cadwallader laid his hand on McLean's left shoulder to demonstrate.

'Sometimes it's put under the chin in an attempt to get the head to snap backwards. Putting it to the back is almost guaranteed to cause death by asphyxiation, and none of these victims showed signs of that. Most suicides will put the knot directly behind their head, straight up.' Cadwallader made the universal 'being hanged' motion, sticking his tongue out and scrunching his eyes up as he did so. 'That doesn't work. Just strangles you.'

'I'm still not sure why you're getting so excited about it though. This was supposed to happen, right?' McLean pointed at the three snapped necks. 'So what's the problem?'

'Two things, Tony. Since you're determined to be slow on the uptake today.' Cadwallader shook his head in disappointment. 'First, whilst this is the desired outcome, it's extremely difficult to achieve. I was impressed at the first one, surprised at the second. A third is unprecedented.

Law of averages says at least one of these three would have botched it.'

'I thought Sands did. That's why his head came off.'

'Only after he'd been rotting for the best part of a month. Would likely have happened to the other two if they'd been left long enough.'

'So what's the other thing, then?'

'Here. Here. Here.' Cadwallader pointed out the three fractures. 'The hangman's fracture. Subluxation of the C_2 and C_3 vertebrae if you want me to get technical. These injuries are almost identical in all three cases. All caused by the noose being placed under the left ear, as per the hangman's manual.'

'There is such a thing?' It would certainly make life easier if they could find evidence the three men had read it.

'I was being facetious, Tony. No doubt there's endless stuff on the internet about hanging. That's how young MacBride found out, I'd guess. But the point is most suicides don't know this stuff.'

'So you're saying these three didn't kill themselves.'

'I can't be as definite as that, Tony, no. None of them struggled at all before they dropped, which would suggest they at least partly wanted to kill themselves. But I can tell you they all had help. Either they all got their information from the same place, or one of them found it and then shared it with the others. It's possible they even helped each other, which would explain the lack of fibres.'

'Are you suggesting there's someone else out there?'

'That's your department, Tony. All I'm saying is that none of these three died alone.'

*

It wasn't until he'd climbed into his car and started the engine that McLean noticed the brown paper envelope wedged under the windscreen wiper. Climbing wearily out, he snatched it up before sinking back into the seat. A4 size, not very thick. There was nothing written on the front of it, and just the manufacturer's logo and part number stencilled on the back. It had been sealed, and for a moment he considered taking it straight to forensics for examination. Only for a moment though. He knew exactly what it was, and from whom.

He still put a pair of latex gloves on before switching off the engine and using his car keys to open the envelope from the wrong end. Inside was a very slim report, printed on anonymous office laser paper. The title on the front page read 'Magda Evans/Ivan ? (Russian)'. Beneath it, the cheap printer had done a poor job of reproducing a pair of mug shot photos of Magda.

McLean skim-read the text, then went back and read it again properly. It was mostly snippets of information taken from other reports; mentions of Magda in connection with ongoing or completed investigations. There were a few redacted black lines, but it didn't take a genius to work out that she'd just been a pawn in the games of bigger players for most of her working life, and that had started painfully early. At the back was a copy of the hospital report detailing her injuries, which at least meant the SCDEA were up to date with their information gathering. He flipped over the last page, noting that the surgeon expected his patient to need at least eighteen months of reconstructive surgery and rehabilitation. Flipped back again when he realized there was nothing more. Bloody typical of them to leave the job half done, much like it was bloody typical of them to hand over the information to him in such a stupid, faux-spy manner. Anyone could have seen the envelope there and helped themselves to it. Unless someone was watching him even now, waiting to see what he did so that they could report back to their ringmaster. And Duguid thought he was wasting time and money.

'Bloody idiots.' McLean slid the report back into its envelope and dropped it onto the passenger seat. Peeled off his latex gloves before starting the car. Of course, it could always be that Buchanan was right and there was no Russian called Ivan. Which begged the question: who had beaten Magda to within an inch of her life?

30

McLean wasn't sure what he'd been expecting. Perhaps something a bit more Bedlam. After all, cranial electric therapy brought to mind Victorian asylums, high-ceilinged rooms tiled in white porcelain and with the windows set too far up the wall to see anything but the sky. Or for anyone to see in from the outside and realize what was going on. There should have been a dreadful contraption of a bed, with heavy leather restraints for head, arms and legs, and alongside it something that looked like the control system for a city-scale power station. There should, in short, have been more wires.

Instead, the room into which Doctor Wheeler had brought him and Emma was pleasantly bright, with a long window showing views out onto city rooftops and the far-distant castle. There was a reclining chair, and it had restraints, but they were slim and padded with what looked like sheepskin but was presumably more hypoallergenic than that. The machinery that would do the actual shocking was disappointingly small. It looked a bit like a transistor radio designed by someone with a knob fetish.

'You sure you want to go through with this?'

Emma was standing very close, hand clasping onto his as if it were her only lifeline. Her eyes were wide as she took in the room, perhaps seeing it very differently to him.

She was the one who was going to have a million volts zapped through her head, after all.

'I don't have much choice, do I.' She squeezed his hand and then let it go.

'OK, Emma. If you'd like to take a seat.' Doctor Wheeler pointed at the chair. 'Tony, you can sit over there if you want. This won't take long.'

McLean reluctantly retreated to the far side of the room, where a couple of uncomfortable armchairs had been pushed against the wall. As he sat down, Doctor Wheeler pulled some thin wires from the small machine on its trolley beside Emma's chair.

'Right then. We just attach these here.' She reached around, clipping something to Emma's earlobe. 'And here. That's not uncomfortable, is it?'

Emma shook her head very slightly, but McLean could see her hands clenched tight to the arms of the chair, knuckles white as if she were on a rollercoaster. He couldn't begin to imagine what was going through her head just now, and that was before the voltage was applied.

'Now, this isn't electro-convulsive therapy, so we don't need restraints or muscle relaxants. The machine takes a little time to power up, but don't worry. You won't feel anything.' Doctor Wheeler flicked a couple of switches on the box, which began to emit a high-pitched whine, like a terrier left on the wrong side of a door. From the corner of his eye, McLean thought he saw movement at the door, but when he turned to look there was nothing. When he dragged his eyes back to Emma and the machine, Doctor Wheeler had placed a hand on Emma's for reassurance.

'Don't worry. I've done this hundreds of times. It's perfectly –'

Emma froze. She had been staring at McLean, but her eyes rolled up in their sockets so completely all he could see was whites. Then she started to shake, so fast it was almost a vibration running through her whole body. Her mouth opened and a sound came out like nothing he had ever heard before. It went straight through his head without passing his ears. A million voices clamouring to be heard, a thousand thousand different tongues.

In an instant, Doctor Wheeler had flicked off the power. Emma continued to wail for a second that seemed like an hour, then relaxed like a puppet that has lost its master, flopping forward in the chair. The silence left an echo ringing in McLean's ears, doubt already creeping over the memory of what he thought he'd just seen.

'Is she all right?' He pulled himself out of the seat, feeling an ache as if he'd been sitting for days. Doctor Wheeler was at Emma's side, checking her pulse, shining a tiny pen torch into a forced-open eye.

'I think so. She seems to have fainted. Never seen that happen before.'

McLean crossed the room, knelt down and took Emma's hand. She stirred gently at his touch, but didn't wake. After a moment he turned his attention to the control box, pulled at one of the thin cables. A thin wisp of smoke rose up from it in a single tendril.

'What . . . What just happened?' McLean pulled himself up, his whole body aching as if he'd been the one being shocked, and at a much higher voltage.

'I really don't know.' Doctor Wheeler stared at the cable

he'd pulled out. One end was still attached to the electrodes taped to Emma's head, the other was a lump of molten plastic and wire.

Mid-morning after a late start. Emma hadn't woken from the failed electro-cranial stimulation therapy for an hour, and had gone straight to bed after he'd finally brought her home from the hospital the previous evening. McLean had hoped for a good night's sleep himself, but she'd climbed into his bed at half four again and he'd not slept a wink after that. He felt dog-tired, and a dog that had been kept awake for weeks by howling cats at that.

For once, the CID room was a hive of industry as he entered; all the desks occupied by sergeants and constables quietly going about their tasks uninterrupted by the demands of senior officers for a change. It couldn't last, not least because he was about to ruin the moment, but it was nice to see.

DS Ritchie noticed him first as he stood in the open doorway. She tapped a couple of keys on her computer as if to make a point before standing, grabbed her notebook and wound her way through the desks towards him.

'You after something, sir?' There was a hint of desperation in the question. As if anything was better than being sent off to Tulliallan again. McLean could only sympathize.

'Updates, mostly. Grumpy Bob about?'

'He sloped off with his paper about fifteen minutes ago. Find an empty meeting room and that's probably where he'll be.'

'What about MacBride?'

At the question, a round face poked up from behind a nearby screen, freshly scrubbed and pink. 'Here, sir.'

'You got a moment?'

By way of an answer, MacBride leapt to his feet, note-book at the ready.

'OK then. Round up Gregg and let's see if we can find Grumpy Bob's meeting room. We need to go over these hangings again.' McLean turned back to the door, only to find a rather frightened-looking young PC standing in the doorway, struggling with an enormous wicker hamper.

'Package for Detective Inspector McLean. I was told I'd find him in here?' The PC almost tripped forward, and McLean had to grab the hamper to stop her from dropping it.

'Steady, Constable. Here, let me take that off you.'

'Thank you, sir. Thought I was going to drop it. Weighs a ton.'

McLean could only nod in agreement as he took the full weight of the hamper. It was about the size of a trunk and if he was any judge was full of expensive delicacies. He staggered over to the nearest clear table and set it down as carefully as he could.

'Any idea who this is from, Constable?' he asked.

'Van had Valvona and Crolla written on the side, sir. Oh, and I've to give you this as well.' The constable pulled an envelope out of her jacket pocket and handed it over. McLean thanked her and she scurried off with obvious relief. Confused as to who might be sending him gifts, he slid open the envelope and pulled out the note. The last time it had been a bottle of very expensive single malt whisky from one of Glasgow's more notorious thugs.

This looked even more expensive, and he wasn't aware of having helped out anyone recently.

'You've got an admirer, sir.' DS Ritchie was trying not to peer over his shoulder at the note as he unfolded it. Not a note at all, but an invoice for almost two grand still outstanding, addressed to him care off the station.

'What the . . . ?' McLean handed the invoice to Ritchie. He looked at the hamper, noticed for the first time that it had already been opened. No doubt some key item had been removed by whichever smartarse had ordered the thing in his name in the first place.

'I don't get it. You ordered this, sir?'

'Does it look like Christmas to you, Ritchie?' He immediately regretted snapping at her. 'Sorry. No, I didn't order this. Someone pretending to be me ordered this, and I'll bet you a fiver it's the same person who opened it and removed the most valuable item.'

He unlatched the clasps holding the hamper closed and lifted the lid. As might be expected, it was full of extremely expensive delicacies. There was even a helpful printed sheet detailing everything. Sure enough, the bottle of VSOP Brandy was missing. Hard not to notice given the large gap right there in the middle, between the Colston Bassett Stilton and the Royal Beluga Caviar.

'What kind of outfit sends out something like this without payment up front?' It was DC MacBride who asked the obvious question. His eyes were wide as he looked at the invoice. Not surprising given it was probably more than he earned in a month.

'Well, if you can't trust a policeman, who can you trust?' McLean appreciated the cunning of the prank as he said it, if not the outcome. And the final touch, making sure the CID room was full when his extravagant purchase was delivered. That was a touch of genius. By the end of the shift, every officer in Lothian and Borders would know of it.

After such a good start, the day could hardly fail to get better. McLean hid the hamper in his office, covering it with paperwork where no one would think to look. He cadged a ride over to HQ and the offices of the SCU, mindful of Duguid's words the day before and all too aware of how little time he was spending there. Not that he was spending much in CID either. Split between both meant not really being able to do anything properly.

DS Buchanan was sitting at his desk in the SCU main office, peering myopically at his computer screen when McLean arrived. The sergeant looked up with something close to a sneer on his face as he saw who it was.

'You back then?'

McLean fought down the urge to call him out on his insolence. It was, after all, exactly the sort of thing Duguid would do. Better just to let it slide.

'Where are we with the Malky Jennings murder?'

'Report's over there.' Buchanan nodded in the direction of the desk McLean had been allocated when he'd first arrived. It was almost as deeply covered in paperwork as his desk back at CID, much of it of no relevance to him whatsoever. The Malky Jennings file was at least on the top, and easily identified. It was also very slim. Transcripts of the door-to-door interviews filled the bulk of the file, and they were almost all identical. 'Din't see nothing, aye.'

Or words to that effect. Scanning through, McLean could see that they had got precisely nowhere since Magda Evans had positively identified the body. He could sort of understand why. Nobody much cared if a drug dealer and pimp was beaten to death and left for the foxes to eat. There'd be more effort going into finding out who was taking over his patch, working out how best to contain them. If forensics couldn't come up with anything, then a conviction was about as likely as Duguid taking early retirement.

'We ever find a murder weapon?' McLean flicked through the front pages of the report, barely taking in the words.

'Nah.' Buchanan shook his head once, went back to his screen. Sod you then.

'How'd you get on with your kiddie fiddler?'

'You what?' Buchanan looked up again, a puzzled frown on his face.

'Playground stalker over in Sighthill? You know.'

For a moment it looked like he genuinely didn't. Then realization dawned across the detective sergeant's face. 'Oh, aye. The kiddie fiddler in Sighthill. Aye. One of the Sex Offenders Register boys. He's not meant to go anywhere near the primary school. Local plod got a call saying they'd seen him hanging around during playtime. Wanted me to go have a word. He's harmless, really, but. You know.' He shook his head again, went back to whatever it was he was doing. Conversation over.

McLean flicked through the report again, looked down at the desk to see a thicker one for the prostitute-trafficking case. There was a stack of the all-too familiar overtime sheets attached to it, and a pile of requisition orders to sign off. Home from home. He shuffled around to the business side of the desk, dropped into the seat and realized it wasn't the comfortable one he'd nicked back from DS Buchanan's desk the day before. Sod it, the sooner he got started, the sooner he could go home, and starting an argument with a stroppy sergeant was just going to waste precious time. With a sigh, he reached for the first in an impossibly large pile of forms.

31

He was driving home when the call came through. No hands-free in his little Alfa, so normally McLean would ignore his phone on a short trip, pick up the message when he got wherever he was going. Maybe it was the slow-moving traffic, maybe just chance, but something made him pull the phone out of his jacket pocket this time, glance at the screen. Jenny Nairn.

To a chorus of irate horns, he indicated and swerved over to the kerb, hit the hazard lights whilst accepting the call and clamping the phone to his ear. There was only one reason why the young carer would phone him at work.

'Thank fuck for that. Where've you been for the last three hours?'

'Umm. Jenny?' McLean frowned, even though there was no one there to see him.

'Too bloody right, Jenny. I've been trying your phone for ages. Check your messages why don't you.'

McLean looked at his phone, but in call mode he couldn't see if there were messages waiting or not. He didn't remember there being any, and, anyway, the thing had been in his pocket all day. He'd have heard if it rang.

'I'm sorry, OK? I'm here now. What's the problem?'

'It's Emma. She walked out again. Ran, more like.' Jenny sounded winded, breathing heavily as if she were running.

'I thought you were with her.' McLean stared in the rear-view mirror as the traffic snarled up behind him even worse than it had been before.

'I am with her. Now. Can barely keep up.' More heavy breathing and the sound of cars in the background.

'Did you not try to stop her?' He knew it was a stupid question even as he asked it.

'Yes, and if she's broken my nose you're paying for the plastic surgery. She's a lot stronger than she looks, you know.'

Now he listened carefully, there was something of a more nasal quality about Jenny's voice.

'Look, where are you. I'll come and get you. OK?'

'Just past IKEA at Loanhead, walking towards Bilston.' Jenny wheezed and coughed. 'More like jogging. Jesus, she's going like a train.'

McLean flicked his indicator, saw the narrowest of gaps in his mirror and pulled out into the traffic, only then remembering that the hazard lights were on. He floored the throttle and shot forward to another chorus of horns. With the phone still clamped to his ear, he couldn't change gear, so he red-lined the engine, spinning the back wheels around as he did a U-turn. 'I'm on my way. Just don't lose her.'

He hung up before Jenny could come up with a witty rejoinder, chucked the phone onto the passenger seat and grabbed second gear. Loanhead. Bilston. He knew exactly where Emma was going.

Needham House was no longer the fine mansion it had once been. Truth be told, it had been falling down from neglect for over a generation. Too expensive for the two career policemen who had been its last owners to keep up, but too much family history for either of them to sell. Old man Needham had flogged the paintings and family silver to pay death duties when his father died, which had left only a rattling, empty shell for his son to take over. That hadn't stopped the man from the revenue from valuing the place high enough to demand a seven-figure sum in inheritance tax, which had probably been the final straw that broke poor Needy's mind.

Poor Needy. The words hung in McLean's mind as he approached, driving carefully now he was off smooth tarmac and onto rutted, pot-holed driveway. Sergeant John Needham had murdered three women in his madness, abducted Emma and very nearly killed McLean himself. And yet for all that McLean couldn't bring himself to blame him. Not now, and not seeing what had become of the once grand house.

It was a ruin now, the roof gone, the insides burned away. Behind it the bulk of the McMerry Ironworks, the source of the Needham family's wealth in an earlier century, was being bulldozed away. Plans submitted for a development for four hundred starter homes, if McLean remembered rightly. So far the legal wheels were still turning over exactly who owned the remains of the house and its grounds.

McLean had made good time from the city centre, mostly by flouting all the traffic regulations and speed limits that he could. The gods were obviously on his side, as there were no patrol cars on the route. He'd still had a few heart-stopping moments, and no doubt the switchboard would be buzzing with calls about the nutter in the old sports car burning up Liberton Brae. He'd just have to square it with Traffic later.

Jenny appeared from around a half-demolished wall as he arrived, hugging herself against the chill wind dropping down off the Pentland Hills. She'd come out without a coat, which was fair enough given that she'd probably not counted on walking the best part of five miles. As soon as she saw the car, she trotted over and had clambered in before McLean had switched off the engine.

'Took your time.' She stared at the minimalist dashboard before working out how to switch the heat on. Cranked it up full.

'I was in the middle of the city. Got here as quick as I could.'

'I meant three hours ago, when Em first got it in her mind to take off on a little jaunt. Why didn't you answer?'

'Give me my phone and I'll tell you.'

'Eh?' Jenny looked at him as if he were mad.

'My phone. You're sitting on it.'

'Oh.' She shuffled her bottom, reached underneath and pulled out the phone. McLean was relieved to see the screen unbroken. He clicked the menu for missed calls, held it up for Jenny to see. Nothing.

'Where's Emma now?'

'Round the back, in the rubble.' Jenny scowled at the phone as if that would make it change its mind. 'I told her not to go up there, but she's . . . well, you'll see.'

The front of the house, with its ornate fascia and grand hallway, had largely survived the explosion and fire. The back of the building hadn't fared nearly so well. Someone from the council had put up metal barriers and a notice that read 'Danger of Death. Unsafe Building.' As if that was going to stop the local youth from coming here to play. As he walked around to the back, McLean saw the empty lager cans and cider bottles, dog-ends and used condoms, the graffiti that marked it as turf for one gang or another. At least there didn't seem to be any syringes or needles. Not yet.

He found Emma crouched down on the top of a pile of rubble, pulling at the rocks with bloody hands. She was wearing trainers this time, but still only dressed in a T-shirt and sweatpants. Unlike Jenny, she didn't seem to have noticed the cold. Mrs McCutcheon's cat sat just behind her, cleaning a paw as if this was the most natural place for it to be. McLean climbed slowly and carefully up the pile until he was standing beside them both.

'Down under all the rocks. Can't reach it. Sure it's here.' Emma muttered under her breath as she pulled first at one rock, then another. She was reaching out for a point too far away, would surely overbalance and tumble over the edge, when McLean touched her on the shoulder.

The contact sent a shock up his arm like static from a cheap rug, set up a ringing in his ears that sounded almost like a clamour of high-pitched voices far in the distance. Then with a pop, it was gone. Emma stiffened at the contact, fell back onto her heels, leaning hard against him. She looked around like a person who has just woken up somewhere very different to the place they went to sleep. Then she saw her hands, bloodied and torn, fingernails ragged where she'd been digging at the rubble. She held them in front of her face for long moments, turning them this way and that as if they were someone else's. Finally she held them up for him to see, like a child suddenly realizing they aren't alone in the world. Mouthed a single word.

'Tony?'

And then she collapsed.

'I've really never seen anything like it. Frankly I'm baffled.'

Doctor Wheeler stood beside the hospital bed as a nurse tended to one of Emma's hands. The other had already been cleaned and bandaged and lay across her chest. She hadn't woken since collapsing at Needham House and was now hooked up to a drip and an EEG monitor.

'Is she in a coma? Is this some kind of relapse?' McLean really didn't want to ask the question, didn't want to face the possibilities an answer would bring.

'Not in a strict medical sense, no.' Doctor Wheeler bent down to peer at the monitor, adjusting a dial that seemed to have no effect on the jagged lines plotting themselves across the tiny screen. 'It's almost like she's asleep and dreaming. But the patterns are too chaotic for that. How long's she been out?'

'About an hour, I'd say. Maybe a little less.' The journey to the hospital had been slower than the drive out, McLean unwilling to chance his luck with the traffic gods any further. Emma had been comatose on the rear seat all the way, covered by his jacket but shivering anyway. Mrs McCutcheon's cat had, perhaps predictably, jumped into the car as soon as McLean had put Emma inside. It hadn't done anything useful like lie on her lap to keep her warm though. Jenny had said nothing beyond a grunt to keep the heat turned up and a moan that her feet hurt. She was off parking the car now; at least that was what McLean hoped she was doing. She'd been gone a long time. Hopefully the cat wouldn't try to find Emma here in the depths of the hospital.

Doctor Wheeler put a hand to Emma's forehead, forced open one of her eyes and shone a tiny pen torch into it, took a pulse. All things she'd done twice already in the last half hour. McLean knew displacement activity when he saw it.

'You're worried this is a side-effect of the electrotherapy treatment.'

She turned to face him. 'Am I that obvious?'

'Detective Inspector, remember.' McLean watched as the nurse tidied up her tray of bandages and bustled out of the room before continuing. 'To be honest, I'm worried too. She seems to be regressing ever further back. When she woke up it was like she was, I don't know, twenty-one or something. Lately she's been acting like an eight-year-old.'

'Like I said, it's got me baffled and believe me, I've read up everything I can find, put the word out to everyone I can think of. The CAT scans don't show any sign of further damage, far from it. Her brain's as good as it ever was, so there's no reason she should be getting worse. If anything, memories should be starting to come back by now.'

McLean walked around to the other side of the bed and slumped into a chair. He should really have been getting back to the SCU and the ongoing investigations there, but he was dog-tired. Maybe he could get away with sitting here for an hour or so. He could always drop in on Magda on the way out. That counted as work, surely?

'How's she been getting on with Doctor Austin?' Doctor Wheeler asked the question almost too casually.

'Early days. Emma seems to like going there. Me, I just fall asleep as soon as the session starts.'

'Yes, Eleanor can have that effect on people.' Doctor Wheeler looked at her watch, the universal sign that she needed to be somewhere else. 'I'll leave you here with her then. The monitor will let the nurses know if she's waking up.'

'I can't stay long. Just a little while.'

'You look like you need a good sleep, Inspector. I could arrange a camp bed if you'd like.'

'Don't tempt me.' McLean scratched at his chin, feeling the need for a shave.

'Well, just get a nurse to page me if you need anything, OK?' Doctor Wheeler gave him a smile that was warm but as tired as he felt, and then she was gone.

32

A bored PC sat on an uncomfortable-looking plastic chair outside the room where Magda Evans was recovering. He saw McLean approaching and scrambled to attention, dropping what looked suspiciously like a copy of a Mills and Boon romance.

'Sorry, sir. No one told me you were coming.'

'Don't worry, Reg. You know if she's awake?'

'Couldn't say, sir. Nurse was in about a half-hour ago, so she might be.'

'Well, I won't be long anyway.' McLean knocked gently on the door, listened for a reply. He could hear the soft noises of a television playing, so he let himself in.

Magda was lying on her back much like Emma on the other side of the hospital. Only where Emma was now sleeping peacefully, and encumbered only by the bandages on her hands, Magda was surrounded by stands and apparatus supporting her legs and one arm. Her toes, poking out of the ends of the heavy casts, were blue, though whether that was from bruising or lack of circulation, McLean couldn't be sure. The cast that encased her hand ended in a curious arrangement of metal spikes that held her fingers in place. Her attackers had broken them methodically, at least that's what the surgeon had told him. It was doubtful she'd ever regain more than very rudimentary use of them, and they'd had to amputate the crushed remains of her thumb.

But it was her face that was the worst. McLean remembered the young woman he'd first encountered when they'd raided the boat. Was it really just a month ago? She'd been rake thin then, and hardly what you'd call a looker. But she'd had a certain elegance to her features. Now the bandages hid most of the damage, but she would need a lot of reconstructive surgery if she was ever going to have a nose again. The razor cuts to her cheeks would always be scars, twisting her mouth into a Joker's rictus grin.

She was barely awake, drowsy with morphine and watching the television that had been thoughtfully hung on the wall. Whatever was on was not so engrossing that she was unable to drag her attention away from it as he entered. She squinted at him through eyes still puffed almost closed, reflexively tried a smile and then winced in pain.

'Just thought I'd pop in and see how you were doing.' Now he was here, McLean realized it wasn't the most brilliant idea he'd ever had. Magda couldn't talk. She struggled with her one good arm to reach something on the table beside the bed. Good being a relative term, as her hand was stitched and taped up, two fingers spliced together. Her hand connected with a small spiral bound notebook, and she grimaced as she knocked it to the floor, letting out a little squeak of pain. McLean bent down and picked it up, flipped it open to find only blank pages. Hardly surprising given her injuries. The woman couldn't feed herself, let alone hold a pen.

'What are you doing in here? You mustn't disturb her.'

McLean was startled by the arrival of a nurse, cowed by the withering look she gave him. She bustled around Magda's bed, checked the monitors and finally squeezed the morphine drip to send the patient back into sedation.

'I was just seeing how she was.' Even as he said it, he realized it was a lie. He'd wanted to talk to Magda, ask her questions. As she slipped away, he realized that had been a forlorn hope. She wasn't going to be in any position to talk for days, possibly weeks.

'You really shouldn't have gone to see her alone, Tony.'

Jo Dexter leaned back in her chair, stifled a yawn. She looked like she'd been up for days, her face lined and ashen, her hair even less kempt than normal. McLean shuffled uncomfortably, trying to ignore the leering presence of Detective Sergeant Buchanan. He'd been offered a seat but seemed determined to stand.

'I was just checking she was OK. Reg was outside the whole time.'

'Yes, but he should have been inside, shouldn't he. I should tan his hide for letting you in anyway.'

'For what it's worth, she didn't say anything. Couldn't say anything to be honest. Whoever attacked her did a real job of work. They're keeping her heavily sedated.'

'I know. I've read the medical report.' Dexter flicked a sheaf of papers that was perched atop the mess of reports and general detritus strewn across her desk. McLean thought his office was a study in chaos, but maybe he was just an apprentice.

'Probably had it coming to her, right enough.'

McLean and Dexter both stared at the detective sergeant, who looked slightly surprised himself at the words that had come out of his mouth.

'I'll pretend I didn't hear that, Pete,' Dexter said.

'Well, I won't.' McLean was on his feet in an instant. 'What do you mean by that, Sergeant?'

Buchanan stared at him with that all too familiar mixture of disdain and loathing. 'Nuthin. Just saying. She's a whore. Getting beat up comes with the territory.'

'No. It's more than that. You've seen the photos. That's not a pimp knocking one of his girls around. That's someone making a statement. You know anything about that, Sergeant?'

'What the hell d'you mean by that?' Buchanan pushed himself away from the wall, his face flushed red, eyes threatening. McLean stood his ground, squared up for the fight. He'd had enough of Buchanan's attitude to last him a lifetime. Quite looked forward to taking the man down a peg or two.

'Enough. Both of you.' Of course, Jo Dexter was never going to allow it to come to blows. Then there'd be paperwork and she obviously had quite enough of that already.

'Let's get back to the point, shall we? Tony, sit down. And you too, Pete. Stop lowering over us like some great ogre.'

McLean caught himself waiting until Buchanan had sat before doing so himself. How swiftly the pettiness came. But lately even the smallest of things had been getting his back up. There wasn't really any reason to react to the detective sergeant the way he had done. Maybe he was as tired as Jo Dexter looked.

'Right then. I've had another demand from the Port Authority to release the freighter. What d'you reckon, we let it go?'

'Forensics came up with nothing,' McLean said. 'Captain's story checks out. He really didn't know anything about it. Don't think there's anything to be gained from holding on to it any longer.'

'OK, I'll let them know.' Dexter leaned forward and placed a tick against a paragraph scrawled on a piece of paper at the top of her piling system. 'So where does that leave us with the investigation, then?'

McLean looked over at Buchanan, who shrugged and said nothing.

'None of the girls will say anything. They wouldn't before, and once they hear what happened to Magda they'll be even less helpful. Most of them just want to get away. We've been working with Clarice Saunders and her charity on that.'

'What about the van driver?' Dexter ticked another paragraph.

'Just a delivery boy. Paid a chunk of cash, no questions asked. He'll do a bit of time, but I've seen his type before. He won't say who paid him. Even if he knows.'

'Pete? You got anything to add?'

'What he said.' Buchanan nodded in McLean's direction. 'It's a waste of bloody time. We put away the driver and the second mate on the ship. Case dies there. Meanwhile the gangs keep moving these whores around under our noses.'

'Thanks for that upbeat appraisal, detective sergeant.' Dexter ticked another paragraph, then drew a line through it. 'So what about Malky Jennings then? We any closer to finding out who put him out of our misery?'

'Dead end.' Buchanan seemed to have warmed to his theme now. 'No one saw anything. Forensics can't find anything useful. There's plenty folk wanted him dead, but we can't arrest them for that. If we had the murder weapon, we might get somewhere, but we don't even know where he was killed. Let alone what with.'

McLean was about to say something, but the way Dexter scored out the next paragraph on her list stopped him. No one was going to spend too much time and effort trying to find the killer of a scumbag, it would seem.

'Which just leaves us Magda Evans.' Dexter lifted the medical report off her desk, then dropped it back down again. 'What's the low-down there?'

McLean looked at Buchanan, who was slouching in his seat as if he hadn't a care in the world. He caught the gaze, sneered.

'What? Not my case, is it.'

'You've done nothing about it?' McLean asked.

'Why should I? You're SIO, right?' Buchanan's sneer turned into a cheeky grin.

'I told you to take over when I went with her to the hospital. What the hell have you been doing since then?'

'My job, of course. Not yours.'

'Your job is to do what I bloody well tell you to do, Sergeant, and I told you to take over the Magda Evans crime scene. Are you telling me you've done nothing about it at all?'

Buchanan shrugged, as if that were enough of an answer. 'I set a couple of constables on door-to-door.

SOC came and dusted for prints, took some photos. Wasn't a lot more we could do.'

'So where's your report? What's the situation with the crime scene now?'

'DC Watson was typing up the report. Far as I know the crime scene's secure. Council were sending someone round to fix the door and board up the window. Local toerags'll break in soon as they know the place is empty otherwise.'

McLean realized he had clenched his hands into fists, willed himself to relax. How many days had passed since Magda Evans had been attacked? He'd been so busy he'd lost count. And he was partly to blame, too. If he'd been on top of things he'd have checked what Buchanan was up to more regularly.

'So I think it's fair to say we're nowhere with the investigation, then.' Jo Dexter summed things up with a shrug.

'I'll get on it right away.' McLean stood, ready to leave. Beside him, Buchanan still slouched in his seat.

'You do that, Tony.' Dexter gave him a weary smile, which disappeared as she turned on the detective sergeant. 'And as for you, Pete, consider this a formal warning. If you can't run an investigation without constant supervision, then you're not fit to be a sergeant. There's plenty of young constables looking for promotion.'

Something finally seemed to get through to Buchanan. He struggled to his feet, straightened his jacket and nodded at Dexter, adding a gruff 'Aye, ma'am.' Then he turned and left without another word.

*

'What the hell's your problem, Buchanan? You looking to be reported to Professional Standards or something?'

Out in the corridor. McLean had barely shut the door to Jo Dexter's office and Buchanan was heading off in the direction of the canteen. He'd picked up a slight limp somewhere along the line, McLean noticed. Maybe that was why he'd not wanted to sit down. Didn't explain the general surliness though.

'You want to know what my problem is, sir?' Buchanan emphasized the title in a manner McLean couldn't help recognizing. It was exactly how he addressed Duguid, DCI Brooks and pretty much any other senior officer who was pissing him off. The detective sergeant came back up the corridor towards him, trying hard to hide the limp, but grimacing every so often when something twinged in his leg. Serve the bugger right, really.

'You're my problem. That's what. Swan in here with your high and mighty ideals. Stick your nose in an investigation then bugger off back to your own station for days, leaving me to do all the legwork.' Buchanan shifted his weight as he said this, leaning on his left side. So it was his right leg giving him gyp. McLean wondered what he'd done to hurt it. Fallen down the stairs drunk, most likely. He kept silent on the matter though. Buchanan was in a mood to talk, and a wise man took the opportunity to listen.

'And then you go visit a witness without anyone to corroborate what you've said. A witness in secure custody, for Christ's sake. What if we need her testimony in court and some smart-arse lawyer finds out you've been coaching her?' Buchanan shook his head. 'Duguid's bloody well right. You're the liability. Should be you in front of Professional Standards, not me.'

Buchanan turned away again, stalked off towards the stairs. McLean let him go, stung by his words. It wasn't a fair appraisal, of course, and the detective sergeant was ten times worse. But there was a nugget of truth in what he'd said, and the truth always hurt.

33

The rumbling echo of an expensive V8 engine burbled in through the open window of his office, but McLean barely paid it any attention. A couple of the detective chief inspectors drove cars way above their pay grade, and it was almost a job requirement if you were a superintendent to have a Range Rover, even if your area was entirely urban. Something about this rumble suggested exotic and pricey; no doubt there'd be a gaggle of young constables ogling whatever it was when it parked up in the visitor space in the yard behind the station. Shaking his head, he focused back on the report that was failing to come to any meaningful point.

Something of the noise was still in his head five minutes later, when the phone rang. He knew as soon as he saw the light that indicated it was the front desk, the arrival had to be connected. Either someone high up in the organization wanted to give him a bollocking in person or another in a seemingly endless line of tiresome pranks was afoot.

'McLean.'

'Ah, I thought you'd be in, sir. There's a gentleman in reception to see you.' Reg on duty this time. Usually not one to muck people about, so maybe he wasn't in on it this time.

'Did he say what it was about? Only I'm up to my ears here, Reg.'

'Something about a car, sir. Was yours being fixed?'

'I'll be right down.' McLean hung up, secretly glad to be shot of the report, even though he knew it would still be waiting for him when he got back.

The reception area was busy this afternoon, but it was easy enough to spot the man waiting for him. He might have been wearing a designer suit, but he had car salesman written all over him. Something about the shiny face, slicked-back hair and bad skin.

'Inspector McLean?' He took a couple of steps forward, holding out a hand.

'It's Detective Inspector, actually. What can I do for you?'

A flicker of uncertainty in the man's eyes, quickly recovered. 'A man like you, must be always busy, I'm sure. That's why it's no problem at all to bring her out for you to see.'

'Her? I'm sorry. Who are you?'

'Johnny Fairbairn? Northern Motors? You booked a test drive?' That flicker was back, growing into a full puzzled frown. Johnny Fairbairn glanced around the reception area as if searching for another Inspector McLean.

'I did?' McLean held in the sigh he so desperately wanted to release. Of course he had, although if the call had been recorded, the voice he used to make it would sound very different to the one he normally used. 'Oh well, you're here now. Might as well show me.'

Escorting Johnny Fairbairn through the station to the parking yard at the back, McLean couldn't help but wonder what it was that his colleagues had set him up with this time. Something flash, for sure. And expensive. He'd accepted the other pranks with as good grace as he could muster, but somehow he didn't think this time he'd be getting out his wallet.

'Sergeant at the desk tells me you drive a classic Alfa. Always been a great fan of the marque myself. Had a Sud when I was at college. Great little car for chucking round the corners, and that lovely growl off the boxer engine. But the rust? Bloody thing had more holes than a tea bag.' It wasn't hard to have a conversation with the salesman; all you had to do was listen. McLean had tried the occasional nod and 'yes', but they really weren't necessary. It didn't take long to get through the station, but by the time they emerged into the sunshine he knew considerably more about the man than he really needed to, whilst also knowing almost nothing at all.

'And there she is. Conti V8. A good bit cheaper than the twelve, but a nicer car if you ask me.'

McLean stared. Much like the dozen or so constables who had gathered around, some with their camera phones out. The car was red, very red. He'd not really been keeping up with things as much as in his misspent youth, but even he could recognize the Bentley logo on the back. Conti, Johnny Fairbairn had said, so this must be the new Continental GT. It had to be well over a hundred grand's worth of car, easy. And for something with just two doors, it was huge.

'Shall we take her out? See what she can do away from all these . . . ahem . . . Policemen?' Johnny Fairbairn pulled something that didn't look much like a key out of his jacket pocket and handed it over. Solid, weighty and with the Bentley logo in shiny enamel, it had a button set into it exactly where your thumb fell whilst cradling it in your palm. McLean pressed it and was rewarded with a flash of the indicator lights and a solid thunk as the car unlocked itself. At least two of the constables jumped, turned around with guilty faces. They all knew who he was, of course, even if he could probably only name about four of them. Soon they'd be telling their fellow officers all about the brand new car DI McLean had bought.

Not that he was going to buy it, of course. Although sinking into the comfortable and supportive leather seat and seeing the obvious craftsmanship that had gone into making the thing, he was tempted. The thunk of the door closing was echoed by the salesman as he climbed in on the other side. McLean hadn't really been aware of the noise outside but, sealed in, he was aware of the silence. It was a release of a pressure he hadn't realized was there. He would have been happy to have just sat back and breathed in the smell of leather and walnut veneer for a while; forget that he was a detective with a heavy caseload and a bunch of colleagues he wouldn't piss on if they were on fire.

'It gets me like that every time.' Johnny Fairbairn managed to ruin the moment by speaking. 'It's like a little oasis away from life's worries and stress.'

McLean looked at the salesman. How much of a line had he been spun to believe that a DI could afford a car like this? OK, so technically he could afford a car like this, and he was a DI, but that wasn't the point. 'Mr Fairbairn . . .'

'Please, call me Johnny.'

'Mr Fairbairn. I feel I need to get something straight

here before I even start the engine. I have no intention of buying this car.'

'Ah, you say that, sir, but just wait until you start her up.'

Well, he'd tried. McLean studied the fob, finding out how to extract the key from it. The engine fired up with a satisfyingly deep rumble, accompanied by a complicated sequence of lights flashing across the dashboard. There were controls and levers everywhere, unlike the nice and simple gear stick and indicator stalk in his Alfa. He'd driven plenty of cars in his time, though. This couldn't be all that difficult. It was an automatic, after all.

The Bentley garage was out on the Niddrie road, heading towards Musselburgh. He'd noted the address on the discreet dealer badge in the rear window. McLean thought it best to take the car straight back, rather than waste too much of Johnny Fairbairn's time. Or his, for that matter. It was true, this was a most pleasant distraction from a particularly boring report, but this wasn't really something he should be doing during working hours. Wasn't really something he should be doing at all, if he was being honest.

'You might want to head for the bypass. Open her up a bit.'

McLean ignored the suggestion. 'Like I said, Mr Fairbairn. I'm not going to buy this car.'

'If you're worried about the finances, we have some very good offers on.'

'I could write you a cheque for the full amount right now. The money's not the problem, and the car is superb.' McLean snatched a sideways glance at his passenger, seeing the ever-cheerful face form into a confused frown.

'I don't understand, Inspector. Why did you ask me to bring her out for you to see if you weren't interested in buying her?'

'I have to apologize to you, Mr Fairbairn. And frankly that makes me quite angry. I never called you, never asked about a test drive. My colleagues at the station have recently taken to playing pranks on me, and like all pranksters they see only the amusement of making a fool of me, not the inconvenience they cause to everyone else involved.' McLean suddenly noticed the little flappy paddles behind the steering wheel. He flipped one, and the car magically changed down a gear, the engine note deepening to a fruity bellow as they shot forward. Fortunately the road was clear.

'I'm sorry,' he continued. 'You were never the brunt of this joke, but you're the one who's lost a couple of hours work. I'm happy to pay for your time, and for the chance to have a go in this car. It's great. Better than anything I've driven before. I do need a car, can't keep using the old Alfa. But this isn't exactly inconspicuous. Not the sort of thing I could park up at the side of the road and watch a suspect from.' McLean blipped the throttle again, feeling a bit like a schoolboy. 'Dare say if he did a runner I'd be able to catch him though.'

Johnny Fairbairn smiled. 'That you would. Nought to sixty in four point eight. Ah well. We don't sell them every day anyway. No harm done, and I maybe should've done a few more checks before hurrying out. But like you say, she's great. Any excuse to get out, really.' He patted the dashboard with a light hand, fell silent for a while. McLean piloted the car down the narrow lanes that were a feature of this part of Edinburgh, where the city gave reluctant way to the countryside. They were almost at the garage before the salesman spoke again.

'So you need something a bit less conspicuous, considerably less expensive, I'm guessing. And you're an Alfa fan.' He had a schoolboy grin on his face, back in full salesman mode. 'You know I might just have something you'd be interested in. And as it happens, it's also a GT.'

Six grand lighter of pocket, but with a nearly new car being given a service before delivery, McLean was hurrying back to his office when a voice he really didn't want to hear bellowed out down the corridor.

'Where the fuck have you been? I've been trying to find you all bloody afternoon.'

Constables scattered like extras in a war movie as Acting Superintendent Duguid advanced. His face was its usual florid red, blotchy around his forehead where no doubt he'd been kneading it with his thumbs to try and force out a coherent thought. McLean pulled out his phone, checked the time. He'd not been out of the station more than two hours.

'I had to go out, sir. You could have called.'

'Aye, road testing some flash sports car. That's what I heard. Exactly how does that fit in with the working day?'

'I wasn't road testing anything, sir.'

'No? And what about arranging for a tailor to come and measure you up for a suit? That didn't happen either, I suppose. And you know you're not supposed to have personal items delivered here. We don't let the constables do it, so what the hell makes you think it's OK for inspectors?'

Duguid's head looked like it might explode any minute, which would at least have made life a bit easier for everyone. McLean glanced past him at the surprisingly large number of officers, uniform and plain clothes, who just happened to be passing that very spot at that very moment. Well, if they wanted a show, who was he to deny them?

'About that delivery, sir. I wasn't going to mention it, but since you brought up the subject, here in this rather public place, were you aware that there's a thief here in the station?'

You could almost see the cogs whirling in Duguid's brain. 'What are you talking about?'

'That delivery, sir. The one that shouldn't have come here?' McLean pitched his voice just a little too loud not to be overheard. 'You're right. I know the rules as well as the next man. Which is why I never made the order in the first place.'

'Don't be ridiculous, McLean. It was a delivery for you. Bloody great luxury hamper. Sergeant Murray signed for it at reception. It was logged in.'

'I'm aware of that, sir. What I don't know is why it then took three hours for someone to bring it to me. I don't know why it was given to a constable, who found me in the CID room. I don't know who pretended to be me and ordered the bloody thing in the first place. And most of all, I don't know who opened it and took out a very expensive bottle of brandy, thus ensuring that I couldn't return the whole package. Strange that, the way everything's logged and noted and checked through the system, and yet nobody knows who opened up a parcel that wasn't addressed to them and took something out of it.'

A puzzled frown wrote itself across Duguid's brow. 'I don't –'

'It was a prank, sir. An expensive one at that. Someone phoned in that order, persuaded a very reputable city business to deliver two grand's worth of goods here on invoice rather than demanding payment up front, then made sure I wouldn't be able to return the goods once I received them. I paid up because I didn't want to tarnish the reputation of the police.'

'Don't you dare suggest –'

'I'm also getting a pair of new suits, thanks to whoever it was phoned up Garibaldi and Sons pretending to be me. And yes, I've been out for the last two hours placating a car salesman who thought he might make a one hundred and twenty-five thousand pound sale. That one I wasn't prepared to take on the chin. Sir.'

Duguid was sweating now, his anger mixed with confusion and not a little worry. He glanced around at the collected officers as if unsure whether to shout at them or not. McLean had thought he was complicit in the pranks, but now he wasn't so sure. It was a shame; a blustering Duguid who nevertheless knew he was really in the wrong was easy enough to deal with, but a Duguid realizing that serious misconduct had happened without his knowledge was another matter entirely.

'So you're telling me you're not responsible for any of these . . . things?'

'No, sir.'

'Then why the fuck didn't you come to me?'

Really? 'I didn't think it was important, sir. Figured if I

acted like it wasn't happening, then whoever was doing it would get bored and stop soon enough.'

Wrong thing to say. Duguid advanced on him, visibly shaking as he tried to control his rage. He stabbed McLean repeatedly in the chest with a finger as he spoke. 'That's precisely why you'll never be more than an inspector, McLean. Christ, it's amazing you even made it this far. You don't cover up this sort of thing and hope it goes away. These miscreants are wasting police time. We arrest people for that.'

'Sir, I hardly think –'

'My point precisely. Think, McLean. That's what you're paid to do. Even if you don't actually need the money. I want a list of all of these so-called little incidents on my desk by the end of the day. OK? And if you've any suspicion who might be behind them, then don't be shy about saying so. We're professionals, not fucking schoolboys. I expect my senior officers to behave as such.' And with that, Duguid turned and marched off in the direction of his office.

McLean let out a sigh of relief, then realized that the corridor was still half full of constables and sergeants. He caught the eye of one in particular. DS Carter, favoured lackey of DCI Brooks and DI Spence, Little and Large. He had a haunted, guilty look on his face, and quite probably a bottle of expensive brandy in his locker.

'It ends. Now.' McLean waited for the sergeant to respond, took the tiniest of nods as all the confirmation he needed.

34

No one paid him much attention as he climbed the stairs to the fourth-storey walkway, although McLean noticed one or two sideways glances. It was an open secret that prostitutes worked out of some of these flats; no doubt they thought he was just another John, here for a bit of executive relief.

The window to Magda's flat was broken, a torn flutter of blue and white police tape the only thing stopping the locals from climbing in and helping themselves to anything they wanted. Tape also covered the door, and this at least didn't look like it had been disturbed. McLean tried the handle, unsurprised but nonetheless angry to find that the door pushed open to his touch. Buchanan said the council had been round to seal the flat up, so either he was lying or someone had cocked up big time.

Inside, it was obvious that Scene Evaluation Branch had been and gone. Every surface that might have held a fingerprint had been dusted, faint grey powder everywhere, at least in the hallway. Through into the living room and it was less clear that anything had been touched. The place still looked like a small explosion had ripped through it. The window wall opposite was still cracked, that horrible smear of blood now turned black as it dried. A stench hung in the air, part rot, part something more human. McLean pulled a pair of latex gloves out of his jacket pocket and snapped them on. More concerned with inadvertently touching something unpleasant than with contaminating a crime scene. If SEB had decided there was nothing more to be found here, then moving things around was hardly going to be a problem.

He'd been the first on the scene, and as he stood in the middle of the living room he tried to picture it as he'd seen it then. The sofa and armchairs had been turned the right way up, pushed against one wall with the broken television piled on top of them. The coffee table's glass top had been cleared away completely; fragments taken back to the lab to test for fibres and fingerprints no doubt.

The floor had been swept too, some poor bugger would have had to go through that lot with a magnifying glass. Cleared of debris, it was possible to see the blood stains though. McLean crouched down, imagining the scene played out. The door had been kicked hard enough to break the security chain, but the latch wasn't broken. That meant Magda must have answered a knock at the door. He glanced back from the living room. Yes, there was a security spy hole, and the window, of course. So she would have known who was outside. Someone she knew well enough to open the door and talk, but not trust to let in? Or someone she didn't know at all, but had no reason to feel threatened by? Impossible to tell, but either way they'd kicked the door down anyway. Hauled her across the hall to the living room. Picked her up and thrown her across the table, shattering it. Dragged her up and smashed her against the window, her head cracking the glass and leaving that bloody smear. Thrown her back down onto the floor, catching the television as she went. Two parallel smears of blood showed where she'd tried to break her fall. And then, what?

And at what point had she phoned him? When whoever it was had come to the door? That would suggest it was someone she was wary of. Someone she both knew and knew not to trust.

He turned slowly on the spot. Something was bothering him, but he couldn't put his finger on it. He should really have done this before the forensic team started moving things. Sure, they'd have photographs, but that wasn't the same.

His eyes came to a rest on the sofa and chairs. They had been upside down when he'd first arrived, stuffing ripped out of the cushions. Peering close now, he could see no blood on them, so the damage at least had been inflicted directly on the furniture, but why?

McLean pulled out one of the cushions, surprised that it hadn't been bagged and taken away for further analysis. The cuts to the cheap leatherette had been done by something sharp. A Stanley knife, most likely. The same one that had been used on Magda's face? Or had someone come in afterwards and done this with a different knife? At the time he'd not given too much thought to the damage. It was just the result of a frenzied attack. But now he could see the pattern to the cuts. Not random slashes, but a cross, opening up the cushion to get at something hidden inside. He looked carefully at the cuts, the wad of foam left inside. Then at the other cushions, one by one. They'd all been done the same way. Impossible to tell which had been done first, but to the naked eye there was no sign of blood on any of them.

McLean put the final cushion carefully down and looked over the scene again. This time the scenario painted itself differently. The assailants had still broken in when Magda hadn't been expecting anyone, but this hadn't been a simple case of beating her up as a warning to the other prostitutes in the area to keep in line. No, they'd been looking for something, even knew where it was hidden. But his best guess was that they'd not found it, hence Magda's injuries.

He stepped carefully over to the window, realizing for the first time just how high up the central point of the fracture in the glass was. Higher than his eye line by a good couple of inches. Magda wasn't small, but she was shorter than him, which meant whoever had smashed her against the glass had lifted her off her feet. Strong, then, throwing her around like a rag doll.

Through in the kitchen, McLean found the source of at least one of the odours. Someone had taken the bin out from under the sink and placed it on the counter. Several warm days and no open window, it was buzzing with flies. Trying not to breathe in, he went through to the corridor beyond and the bathroom where he'd found Magda. He'd assumed she had half staggered, half crawled here after her attackers had gone, but if they were looking for something and she wouldn't tell them where it was, then the bathroom became a torture chamber, an interrogation room.

The shower curtain was gone, wrapped around her as she lay on the trolley the paramedics had used to get her out of the flat. Dry black blood caked the walls, but in the sink hole it had retained enough moisture to clog the air with a foetid smell. More flies buzzed lazily around, fat on the stench. It was all McLean could manage to stay in the small bathroom for thirty seconds. He backed out into the corridor, taking shallow breaths of the slightly less foul air, debating whether to go back in for another look. Again, there was that niggling thought in the back of his mind, that he had missed something.

McLean picked his way back through the flat and out onto the walkway, climbed carefully through the unbroken police tape and pulled the door closed. He'd have to get on to the council to come out and fix the lock and window. And then it hit him. The first thing he'd noticed when he'd arrived after Magda's call. The door had been kicked in, the security chain splintered off and a dirty great boot print in the wood. But now there was nothing showing on the paintwork at all.

He stared at the door for long minutes, searching his memory, trying to convince himself he hadn't just imagined the boot print. He leaned in close, inspecting the surface for any telltale signs that it had been cleaned. He thought there might have been something, but it was impossible to see in the half-shade from the walkway overhead. Then a slight noise to one side distracted him.

The little girl's face was still dirty, and her doll still had no clothes and no arms. She stared at him with wary eyes and said nothing. He was useless when it came to children, but McLean guessed she must have been five or so. Maybe older if she didn't get enough to eat; something all too common in this part of town. No doubt there'd be a huge telly in the flat, and the girl's mum would have the latest model of mobile phone though. Probably spent a tenner a day on cigarettes, too.

'Do you know the lady who lives here?' He crouched down until he was almost at her level, but didn't come any closer. In response, she clutched the doll to her grubby chest and leaned away. She reminded him of nothing so much as a cat, wary of something strange but unwilling to cede any territory too easily.

'I'm a policeman.' McLean put his hand in his pocket, brought out his warrant card. It had his photograph on it, which was probably the only thing that would make any sense to the little girl. She still didn't respond.

'She was attacked a few days ago. Some people came here, broke in. Did you see them?' He shouldn't have been doing this, Jo Dexter would tan his hide, and DS Buchanan would sneer at him about protocol. You couldn't question a child without a parent or guardian present. On the other hand, no one else was going to help him.

The little girl shook her head, but something about the way she clamped her mouth shut made McLean think that maybe she was just unwilling to say. He wondered whether it would be possible to get someone from Child Support in to question her. Perhaps in the right environment she might open up.

'Senga. Stop playing with that fucking doll and get your arse in here.' An expression of pure terror swept over the little girl's face and she looked away from McLean towards the door. He was halfway to standing when a woman appeared in the opening.

'Who the fuck are you? You a fucking nonce?'

The woman took her eyes off McLean for a moment

and barked: 'Get inside and clean up the kitchen.' The little girl darted past, narrowly avoiding a skelp to the back of the head in what was obviously a practised move.

'I'm a police officer.' McLean held up his warrant card, still in his hand. 'That your daughter?'

'What the fuck is it to youse?'

She took a step out onto the walkway, and McLean could see the woman properly. His first impression was of fat, in stark contrast to the tiny, skinny girl. Probably her who ate all the pies. She was dressed in sweatpants that had probably once been black but were now faded to grey, stained and pock-marked with burn holes. Her T-shirt was no doubt the largest you could buy from Primark, but still too small by an order of magnitude. It clung to her in all the wrong ways, emphasizing the rolls of fat around her middle, her sagging lumpy breasts. Fat hung in pendulous loops from her arms, wobbling as she lifted a cigarette to her mouth. She barely looked at his card, sized him up and down in a brief glance as if wondering whether he was worth eating or not.

'Fuck you looking at anyway?'

'You know your neighbour was badly beaten a few days ago?'

'Fucking whore. Deserved it, din't she. Men coming and going all hours of the day. Screaming all fucking night. You know they made these fucking buildings out of paper, aye?'

'Did you see anything? Anyone coming you might recognize again?'

'Do I look like I give a fuck?'

'A woman was beaten near to death. Her face has been

cut open, her arms and legs broken. Her assailant smashed her so hard against the window it nearly shattered. This happened here, in the middle of the afternoon. You happy with that sort of thing going on around your daughter?'

The fat woman gave him an angry stare. 'She coming back?'

'I've no idea. For a while, maybe. Once they let her out of hospital. Won't be for at least a month, the way she is at the moment.'

'Then I get a month's fucking peace. Might as well enjoy it.' The fat woman flicked her dog-end over the parapet, turned her back on him and waddled inside, slamming the door behind her. McLean heard her voice shouting obscenities at the little girl from inside. He took out his notebook, scribbled down the address. He'd put a call in to social services in the morning.

35

The Scene Evaluation Branch labs were busy when McLean stuck his head round the door later that afternoon. He'd thought of phoning, but coming here in person meant he'd most likely get a response to his questions quickly; they were always keen to get rid of visitors. And it meant he could stay away from the station for a while too. There was an office-shaped stack of paperwork waiting for him, and no doubt an irate acting superintendent.

'Is Miss Cairns in today?' he asked the first passing lab tech who was foolish enough to let him catch his eye. The young fellow looked alarmed, but indicated another door before scuttling off about whatever task he had been assigned.

The door led through to an office, which was a relief. McLean had visions of wandering into some clean room and being shouted at for destroying a day's work. Miss Cairns had her back to him as he entered, working at a large flat-screen monitor that displayed an image he wouldn't be able to un-see in a long while. She turned as he knocked on the doorframe, scowled when she realized who it was.

'You know this is a restricted area, right?' As friendly greetings go, it was almost as welcoming as the fat woman back at the tower block in Restalrig

'I was told you were here. No one said I couldn't come in. Sorry.'

Miss Cairns tapped a keyboard and the image disappeared, replaced by a wallpaper picture of sunny skies and clouds over a hilltop. 'Well, you're here now. What can I do for you, Inspector?'

'The Magda Evans case.' This drew a blank. 'You know. Tower block over in Restalrig, woman beaten near to death. You were the crime scene manager for that one, weren't you?'

Miss Cairns frowned some more. 'I guess. We've not really done more than a preliminary sweep so far.'

It was McLean's turn to frown. 'A preliminary sweep? I thought you were finished.'

Miss Cairns actually laughed. 'You'd be lucky. You any idea how backlogged we are? Case like that we only do the stuff that has to be done, then seal the place off. No point treating it as a murder scene if your wifey gets better and tells us who did it.' A fresh frown wrinkled her forehead. 'She's no dead, is she?'

'I . . . No. She's in intensive care, but she should pull through.' McLean struggled to make sense of what he was being told. 'You sealed off the crime scene then?'

'Well, not me personally, no. Bloke from Housing was coming round to board up the window and the SIO should have the key for the front door.'

'I'm the SIO.'

'Well, there you are then.'

'But I don't have the key. I've just been at the scene and it's far from secure. Door unlocked, broken window. Chances are every Ned in the scheme's been in there for a nosey.'

'You are joking, aren't you?' Miss Cairns was wearing the frown again.

'I wish I was.' Christ, he was going to get a bollocking for this. 'Don't suppose you remember who was actually there when you left? I had to go the hospital with the victim.'

'Pete Buchanan was swanning around the car park. Don't think I saw him up on the fourth floor though. There were a couple of new constables I had to tell not to come inside. One of them would have been waiting for the chippy to come and board up the window.'

'Oh bloody hell.' McLean withered under a disapproving glare from the SOC officer. 'Sorry. It's just I get told off for not delegating stuff, then when I take my eye off the ball it all goes ti–... wrong.'

'Welcome to senior management. You should see what this lot get up to when my back's turned.'

McLean looked for any sign of a smile on Miss Cairns' face, but found none. The silence hung heavy for a while as he tried to find anything that might even partially salvage the situation.

'You've got crime scene photos?' he asked finally.

'One or two, aye. You want to see them?' Miss Cairns turned back to her keyboard and mouse, clicked away until a page of photo thumbnails appeared on the large monitor. It reminded McLean of Emma, how she'd manipulated the images so quickly he couldn't begin to keep up. This was where he'd first met her, not much more than a year ago, wasn't it? And it was her skill with the image software that had made him suspect her of posting crime scene photos to dodgy internet forums. That as much as anything was what had brought them together, and look how much good that had done her. He really would be better off alone.

'Here you are.' Miss Cairns' voice snapped him back into the present, and McLean's eyes focused on the screen. It was like a hundred other sets of crime scene photographs he'd stared at, a dozen or more pictures all showing the same thing, then a dozen showing something else, or the same thing but from a different angle. Digital cameras were great, but a modern day crime scene photographer could take hundreds if not thousands and some poor bugger then had to go through the lot of them.

'Have you got any of the front door?'

'Should have.' Click, click, click. 'Here you go.'

And there it was, the front door. A dirty great boot print just by the handle.

'Do you know if anyone took any samples from this?' McLean pointed at the photo.

'I'd've thought so. That's outside. More difficult to secure for later examination. I can check for you, but it'll take a while.'

'Thanks. You're a star.' McLean would have kissed her, but that might have given her ideas.

'I'm doing it for Emma, OK? Not you.'

'Well, I'll be sure and tell her. And thanks anyway.' McLean left her to her work, headed back to the door, then stopped.

'Actually, could I ask one more favour?'

'You can ask.' Miss Cairns didn't turn to face him, just spoke to her monitor.

'Can you send a copy of all the photos to Grumpy . . . Sorry, DS Laird. Not the SCU. The analysis on that boot print, too. When you've time.'

Miss Cairns turned this time, raised a quizzical eyebrow

and then smiled. It suited her better than the scowl or the frown. 'Aye, I'll send it all to Grumpy Bob.'

'Thanks. I owe you.' McLean ducked out of the room and headed back towards his car, pulled out his phone to call Grumpy Bob. It was just possible that this was all a giant cock-up, but it felt like something a lot more deliberate to him. It would be hard enough to prove, though And as SIO, he was going to have a hell of a job convincing anyone he wasn't just trying to cover his arse.

'My office, Tony. Now.'

McLean had barely walked in through the SCU door and Jo Dexter was shouting at him. He knew what it was about, took a quick look around to see if his chief suspect was in. A small gaggle of constables sat in the far corner, heads down and nattering about something. No sign of DS Buchanan though.

'Now, Tony.'

It wasn't wise to make Jo Dexter ask for something twice. He followed her along the corridor and into her office. The mess on her desk hadn't improved much since their morning meeting.

'I've just had a call from SEB about the Magda Evans crime scene. Seems someone forgot to make sure it was secure before everyone left.'

'I . . .' McLean started, but Dexter waved him silent.

'I know it wasn't you, Tony. How the fuck could you have? You were at the hospital, not running the crime scene. Who was SIO?'

'That's the whole point, Jo. I was. I am. I should have made sure everyone was doing their jobs properly.'

'That's bollocks, Tony, and you know it. You delegate, that's how it works. You must have left someone in charge when you went to the hospital.'

'Aye, I did. DS Buchanan. Remember? I told you.'

Dexter must have read his expression. Certainly McLean didn't make any effort to hide it. 'What, you think he did this on purpose? Why the fuck would he do that?'

McLean told her about his visit to Magda's flat, the slashed cushions, the missing boot print. He didn't tell her he'd asked for what little forensic evidence there was to be sent to Grumpy Bob for safe keeping.

'I rang Buchanan when I got Magda's call. Said he was over in Sighthill, but he confirmed it was her number. I asked him to put a request in to control, get a squad car over ASAP, but it didn't turn up until I'd been there twenty minutes myself.'

'That's hardly damning. You know what patrols can be like.'

'Pretty much what I thought. But Buchanan told me on the phone the Sighthill call-out was a false alarm. When I asked him about it this morning, he spun me a completely different story.'

'You don't think he was there at all.' Jo Dexter slumped back into her seat.

'No, I don't. I think he was at Magda's flat beating the shit out of her.' McLean recalled the conversation, how Buchanan had sounded out of breath. Like he'd been walking uphill. Or smashing up someone's flat. 'He got out of there sharpish, called control when he was far enough away.'

Dexter said nothing for a while, the thoughts flickering

across her face in a series of frowns. 'I still think it's a hell of an assumption. I mean, why? What possible reason could he have?'

'I don't know, but whoever beat Magda up was looking for something. Drugs, money, who knows? They turned the place upside down, cut open all the cushions. It wasn't just random.'

'Still. I mean, Pete's methods aren't always strictly legit, but that's a hell of a leap to make. We're talking attempted murder here, not GBH. It's a miracle she survived at all.'

A horrible thought crept into McLean's mind. 'Where's Buchanan now?'

'I've no idea.' Dexter pushed herself out of her chair, swept past McLean on her way to the door. He had to rush to catch up as she went back to the main SCU room and its cluster of constables.

'You lot, any idea where Pete is?'

They looked at each other, then around. One or two of them even got up. Eventually a spokesman was elected by silent consensus. 'Not sure, ma'am. He went out about an hour ago. Said something about the hospital?'

'Shit.' Dexter stopped a moment. 'Find him. Call him. Track his Airwave. I want him in my office right away.'

With a scraping of chairs, the constables hurried about their new task. McLean already had his phone out. 'Who's guarding Magda right now?'

Dexter looked at him with horror. 'You can't think . . .'

'I'm not taking any chances.' He spooled through the contacts list on his phone, looking for the hospital switch-board. Magda was in intensive care, and you couldn't have mobile phones or Airwave sets anywhere near. 'Bollocks. It'll be quicker if I go there myself.'

He sped down the corridors, skirting around startled nurses and slow-moving patients. In the back of his head he could hear his headmistress shouting at him to stop running, but she was long dead and he never much cared about those rules anyway. At least enough of the staff here knew who he was and had the sense not to try and stop him.

Through the final set of double doors, McLean saw the reassuring sight of PC Jones sitting on his uncomfortable plastic chair by the door to Magda's room. The constable looked up at the noise, folding his paper and setting it down on the floor when he saw who it was, then standing when he realized that McLean was running.

'You all right, sir?'

'Magda. She OK?' McLean sucked in air in big gulps, wondering when it was he had become so unfit.

'Fine, I think.' PC Jones shrugged. 'Pete Buchanan was in a half hour or so ago. No one else been since.'

McLean said nothing, just pushed past the constable and through the door. He already knew it was too late.

Magda stirred as he entered, but didn't wake. Someone had put a vase of flowers on the bedside table. Otherwise the scene was pretty much the same as the last time he'd been in. It might even have been the same television programme playing.

'She's OK.' McLean shifted uncomfortably, not sure what to do with his hands. Constable Jones poked his head through the doorway.

'Is there a problem, sir? Only I was told no one on their own.' PC Jones hovered in the doorway.

'You said Sergeant Buchanan was here. He see her alone?'

'No, sir. I know the rules. I was in here with him at all times.'

'Was she awake then?'

'I think so, maybe. Difficult to tell with the amount of morphine they keep pumping into her. He didn't say anything, mind. Just stood there, where you are. Looked at her for a couple minutes and then went.'

'He bring the flowers?' McLean pointed at the vase and its gaudy contents.

'That was Ms Saunders, sir. She came not long after you were here. One of the SCU detective constables was with her. Patterson, I think. They come and go so quickly I find it hard to keep track of their names.'

'I know what you mean, Reg.' McLean took one last look at Magda as a nurse came in. She gave them both a disapproving scowl, then went to check the monitors. A couple of clicks to a button just out of the patient's reach and Magda relaxed back into her pillows. Intravenous morphine could cure a multitude of ills.

'What are you doing in here disturbing the patient?' The nurse rounded on McLean as soon as she had finished. For once, he didn't know her name, but he could tell she wasn't one to be messed with.

'Sorry. Emergency. We thought someone was trying to kill her.' McLean backed out of the room as the nurse held up a finger to her mouth.

'Quiet. She may be drugged, but she can still hear you.'

*

Outside, with the door firmly closed, McLean let out a long breath and collapsed against the wall. Had he been wrong about Buchanan?

'You all right, sir?' PC Jones asked. McLean turned to face the old constable. Solid Copper, one of the old school. But then so was DS Buchanan.

'Fine, Reg. Thanks.' He pushed himself off the wall. 'I think I may have made a huge cock-up though.'

As if to underline the point, his mobile phone started to ring. He pulled it out of his pocket, looking for the off switch. The 'no mobile phones' posters taped at ten-foot intervals all along the corridor left little to the imagination. And for those who couldn't take a hint, the scowl he received from the nurse, who had stopped mid-stride halfway to the swing doors, should have hammered the point home. The screen told him it was DCI Dexter calling, though.

'Just don't let anyone in there unsupervised until I get back to you, OK, Reg?' McLean pointed back at the door to Magda's room as he hit 'answer' and hefted the phone to his ear, jogging away from the ICU as fast as he could.

'. . . fucking right I'll shout. Accuse me of deliberately sabotaging an investigation . . .' McLean pulled the phone from his ear, checked the number and name on the screen. Definitely Jo Dexter. Not her voice he was hearing. He put the phone back to his ear again.

'Jo? You there?'

'Ah, Tony. Sorry about that.' The sound muffled, but McLean thought he heard Dexter shout: 'Just get out. If you can't act like a police officer, then don't expect me to treat you like one.' Then the voice came back clear. 'Where are you now?' In the background he heard a door slam.

'The hospital. Magda's OK. Buchanan was here seeing her though.'

'I know. That was him just now. Seems he's got wind of your accusations and isn't all that happy about them.'

'Well, tough shit. If he wasn't such a prize arse then people might give him the benefit of the doubt. I seem to recall you thought he was our man too.'

'Yes, well. That was before he had a decent excuse for pretty much everything you accused him of. He may be a prize arse, Tony, but he's a well-connected prize arse. You need to tread carefully.'

'With respect, Jo, fuck that. If I suspect an officer of misconduct I'll bloody well investigate it. And if I find anything suspicious I'll have Professional Standards on it like a ton of bricks.'

'Even after what they did to you last year?'

That gave him pause, but only for a while. 'They did what they had to given the circumstances.'

'Oh don't sound so fucking pompous. They fucked you over, Tony. Rab Callard and his cronies. If it hadn't been for that forensics girlfriend of yours you'd be in Saughton right now.'

'I was innocent. I have to believe that would have come out eventually.'

'Aye, in eight to ten years. Look, I know you don't get on with Pete, but a lot of the senior detectives like him. He's one of them, came up through the ranks with them, except he got stuck at sergeant. And he gets results. The high heidyins see that and turn a blind eye to everything else.'

McLean had been pacing all the while and was now in

the public waiting area at reception. The walking had calmed him down a little, but his nerves were still fizzing.

'I still think it's him, Jo. Or there's something in it for him. It's too bloody convenient to put it down to incompetence.'

'Yeah, well. You'd better be damned sure about that before you start making accusations again. And don't be at all surprised if Duguid tries to rip you a new one when he hears about this.'

Duguid. Of course. Brilliant.

'I've coped with worse.'

'Of course you have, but you can cope with it tomorrow. It's been a long day. Go home, get some rest and we'll pick up the pieces in the morning.'

Mrs McCutcheon's cat paused, halfway through the routine of cleaning its arse, and gave him an old-fashioned stare that would have done his grandmother proud. McLean sighed as he closed the back door and dropped the bundle of papers he'd brought home with him onto a chair. He could have put them on the kitchen table, except for that look from the cat, sitting there right in the middle, next to the uncovered sugar bowl and the salt and pepper pots.

'I ought to tell you to bugger off, but what would be the point?' He pulled off his jacket and draped it over the chair back. The constant heat from the Aga made the kitchen by far the most welcoming and warm place in the house. At this time of year it could even get a bit stifling. He knew people who let their ranges go out over the summer months, but that felt wrong. There was something dead about a kitchen with a cold Aga in it.

Bored of him, or perhaps of cleaning its back end, Mrs McCutcheon's cat stood up, stretched and then leapt off the table, walking swiftly towards the door that led to the rest of the house. As it passed through, McLean noticed the sound of music. He glanced at the clock, wondering if Emma was still up. He'd left her asleep in his bed, curled up in her fleecy pyjamas with the cow print on, far too early in the morning and only scant hours after she'd woken him by crawling in. He headed through to see, hoping for a glimpse of her cheerful smile to lift his mood after a weary day. The papers could wait another hour, surely.

Wafts of smoky scent hung in the hallway air, the half-open door to the library spilling out the muted tones of Liz Fraser as she wailed her way through 'Pearly-Dewdrops' Drops'. He'd not replaced very many of his old records yet, turned to so much vinyl slag by the fire that had destroyed his Newington tenement flat, but McLean had managed to find a set of early Cocteau Twins albums in a charity shop on Clerk Street one rare afternoon off. They crackled a bit, but the music still held its magic, even thirty years on. Thirty years. Christ, but that made him feel old.

Jenny Nairn was sitting cross-legged on the sofa. She'd pulled the table close and spread open some reference books, bending low to see the text in the soft light from a standard lamp and scribbling notes on a cheap, lined A4 pad. The source of the scent was smoking away merrily in a little holder, filling the room with an aroma that the detective inspector in him immediately thought was there to mask something else. McLean could see no evidence of illicit substances though. Nor of Emma. The first was a relief. The second, he was surprised to find, something of a disappointment. It put him strangely in mind of being a teenager, hanging around the Victoria Street boutiques in the hope that a girl he fancied might show up. More often than not she didn't, and even if she did he'd not have had the courage to go and talk to her. Not when he was on his own. But on those days when she was there, he'd felt, well, happy. And when she wasn't, then the world was a little more grey.

McLean rubbed at his forehead self-consciously, trying to scrub away the adolescent memory. Maybe it was the music, taking him back all those years. He couldn't even remember the girl's name, for heaven's sake. But she had flame-red hair and freckles all over her nose. He remembered that.

'Oh, you're back.' Jenny unfolded herself from the sofa, flipping the books closed and coming to her feet in one fluid, catlike movement. McLean envied her, for a moment. His bones ached even at the thought of sitting cross-legged, let alone being able to stand again afterwards.

'Oh my god. Sorry.' Jenny noticed the joss stick smoking away merrily, lunged forward and pinched out the end. 'I should have asked if it was OK.'

'No, it's fine.' McLean waved in the general direction of the table and the dresser beyond, where his fabulously expensive turntable was clunk-hissing its way around the end of the record. 'Emma gone to bed?'

Jenny gave him an odd look, almost as if she couldn't believe he was asking. Fair enough, it was a pretty stupid question. But maybe it was more that she hadn't been expecting him to care. He'd been so busy these past few weeks he'd barely been in the house, let alone had time to sit and chat.

''Bout an hour ago. Yeah. Why?'

'Just wondered what she'd been up to. Sometimes I worry she might think I'm avoiding her on purpose.' He went over to the drinks cabinet, poured himself a small measure of whisky and topped it up with some water. Turned back to Jenny. 'You want one?'

'Bit late for me, thanks. I probably ought to be heading up myself.' She yawned, paused long enough for McLean to savour a taste of his dram. 'She doesn't, though. Think you're avoiding her. Not exactly.'

'Not exactly how?'

'Well, she knows you're busy with work, but she misses you. What she's going through, it's not easy. Her memory's not so much gone as shattered. Bits come and go, disjointed, things shoved together that shouldn't be, big holes where she can do stuff but doesn't know how she knows how. If that makes sense. I see it all the time I'm working with her. The conflict inside.'

McLean said nothing, just nodded. Took another sip of his whisky even though the flavour had gone out of it.

'But you're something she can latch on to. She remembers . . . Well, not you exactly. Not the life you had together before. But part of her deep down trusts you, and it's more than just because you've taken her in, put a roof over her head and not taken advantage of her.'

Jenny bent down and gathered up her books, took the joss stick and shoved it and its little ceramic pot-stand into the pocket of her hoodie.

'I miss her too, you know.' McLean surprised himself by saying the words he was thinking. Jenny just looked at him, head slightly cocked to one side like a dog trying to work out what the idiot human was doing.

'Well, she's here,' she said finally, then left him alone with his dram.

36

McLean sat at his desk, staring sightlessly at the stack of reports, overtime sheets, memos and other junk that had somehow grown in his absence. He was fairly certain he'd squared everything away just a couple of days past, so this new load was yet one more play in the tiresome game. Like Duguid's constant demands, the secondment to the SCU and the dispersal of his team to the four corners of Lothian and Borders, it was all part of a concerted attempt to get him down. And it was all just spiteful jealousy.

He could take it in reasonable spirit from the junior ranks. There wasn't a day went by when some cocky sergeant or constable didn't ask him if they could borrow a hundred quid. Everyone knew he was loaded, didn't really need to work, and that pissed off the senior ranks for reasons he couldn't quite fathom. OK, so they might think him a jammy sod, but it wasn't as if he'd always been wealthy enough not to have to worry about working. He'd struggled up through the ranks like the rest of them, proven his worth time after time, and yet now they treated him like some kind of dilettante. Or worse, the station pariah.

There were those who blamed him for Needy's death too, mad though that was. If anything they should have been thanking him for saving their old friend from the shame of a trial, or worse being sectioned and sent to a secure mental hospital. But that wasn't the logic of coppers. No, McLean had been there when Needy had died, so it was somehow McLean's fault. Brilliant. And this lot were meant to solve crimes.

With a sigh, he reached out and pulled the first item on the pile towards him, praying as he did so for some form of distraction. It arrived in the form of a round-faced young detective constable knocking on the frame of the open door.

'Morning, Stuart. What can I do for you?'

'I was putting together the final report for the Mikhailevic and Sands suicides, sir. Wondered if you'd had a chance to look over the case notes I left you.'

McLean stared at the pile on his desk. It was news to him that either investigation had been concluded. 'In here somewhere, are they?'

MacBride took two steps into the room, reached towards the precarious stack of papers and whipped out a slim folder with commendable dexterity. The pile rocked slightly, but didn't fall. 'No one else uses the right folders. It drives Elsie in filing mad.'

McLean took the report, noticed the official stamp and file number on the cover. He opened it up and looked at the neatly typed notes inside. Closed it and handed it back. 'You couldn't give me the executive summary, could you?'

'Both men died from snapped vertebrae as a result of hanging. There's no direct evidence to suggest anything other than that they did it to themselves. They appear to have used rope from the same manufacturer, possibly bought from the same store, but forensics can't say that with a hundred per cent certainty. Likewise, the knots appear to be identical, but there's a million and one sites on the internet that tell you how to tie the things. The blood profiles of both men are similar, unusually elevated levels of dopamine and serotonin, but Doctor Cadwallader couldn't find any evidence this was due to outside agency. It could just be that you need to be in that state of mind to want to kill yourself.'

'No luck finding any links between them, then.'

'We've looked, but they don't seem to have any friends in common. Don't think we've been as thorough as we could've been there though. Could've done with a bit more manpower.'

But there was no way Duguid, or Brooks, would sanction that. Not for a couple of unimportant young men with no immediate family clamouring for answers and no press interest bringing pressure to bear. 'What about the suicide notes? You look into those?'

'I ran a textual analysis, sir. They were different enough that it seems unlikely they were written by the same person. Mikhailevic's was odd. Full of spelling mistakes and grammatical errors where his other writing was meticulously correct. Again, that could just be a result of his state of mind.'

'No one thinking straight would put a rope around their neck and jump. Right enough. So the conclusion is suicide in both cases, similarities notwithstanding.'

'That's what the report says, sir.' MacBride tapped the offending article against his arm. 'Also I checked the TV schedules. There's been a documentary about Albert Pierrepoint on BBC4 recently. It got repeated half a dozen times. Last showing was six weeks ago, just before

Patrick Sands hanged himself. Add it all up and suicide's the obvious conclusion.'

'I sense a but in there, Constable.'

'Well, it's bollocks isn't it. A blind man could see the two are hooky, and connected. This latest one too.'

'So why the final report then?' McLean nodded at the folder clasped in the young detective constable's sweaty hands. 'I don't remember asking for one.'

'Lar–... DCI Brooks wants it all squared away, sir. "If there's no obvious sign of foul play, then we can't keep digging until we find some" were his exact words.'

That sounded about right for Brooks, especially if Dagwood was breathing down his neck. 'What about John Fenton?'

'That one's still open, sir. But only because we're waiting on the forensic report. Chances are it's going to be the same as the other two.'

'You want to do some more digging? See if you can come up with anything to link the three together?'

MacBride wore his worried expression openly, like all his other expressions. Guile wasn't a part of his nature. Not a brilliant trait in a detective.

'It's all right. You can make calls from here if needs be, and if anyone asks, I told you to do a bit more background on Fenton, OK? I can sit on those case notes for weeks if you want.' McLean swept an arm across the air above his desk, taking in the expanse of paperwork awaiting his attention. 'It's not as if I've nothing else to do, and there's another desk just like this one waiting for me over at the SCU.'

A knock at the door stopped MacBride from answering.

DS Ritchie stood in the doorway, a thick padded envelope in one hand.

'SOC sent this lot to Grumpy Bob, sir. He's out with DCI Brooks. Asked me if I could pass them on to you.'

'Thanks.' McLean took the package. 'You back with us then?'

'For now. God only knows when they'll want me back up at Tulliallan though. Still, it beats being stuck down in the cellars. At least I get to see the sun.'

Opened, the package revealed a thick sheaf of photographs, printed on a better-quality colour printer than the one up the corridor. Proper glossy paper, too. There was a note with it, but McLean didn't need to read it to recognize Magda's smashed-up flat.

'Anyone fancy a trip down to Restalrig?'

MacBride looked crestfallen. 'Sorry, sir. I've got to report to DCI Brooks in half an hour. Wrap-up briefing on the post office robberies.'

'I'll come along, sir.' DS Ritchie smiled. 'It's been a while since I did any actual detective work.'

McLean shuffled the photographs back together and slid them into their envelope. He wanted to compare them with the scene now, if it hadn't been even further contaminated. 'Excellent. You can sort us out a car then.'

McLean piloted his old Alfa down Leith Walk, heading for Lochend and Restalrig. He wasn't too happy using it in heavy traffic in the heat of late summer, but DS Ritchie had sworn blind there were no pool cars to be had anywhere in the entire Lothian and Borders area. McLean could well believe it, though there was always the possibility she just wanted another drive in the classic car.

'What's the score here?' she asked as they crawled through the permanent traffic nightmare caused by the tram works.

'Ex-prostitute. One we picked up off that boat a month or so back, you remember? Someone gave her a punishment beating. Left her almost dead.' McLean brought Ritchie up to speed. By the time they reached the tower block, she knew as much about it as he did.

The car park in front of the block was surprisingly full. McLean parked directly beneath the front of the building, too close to the concrete walkways and the scaffolding for comfort.

'I can see why you wanted a pool car,' Ritchie said as she looked up and around. A couple of smashed breeze blocks just a few paces away had obviously been heaved over the parapet several storeys up. Probably for shits and giggles, but there may have been more malicious intent.

'Yeah, well I should be getting something a bit less conspicuous in a day or two.' McLean made a mental note to give Johnny Fairbairn a call. 'Let's just get this over with as quickly as possible, aye? Sooner we're gone, the less likely someone'll notice.'

They took the stairs to the fourth floor, not trusting the elevator to work and sure that it would smell worse than the stairwell. Glancing along the concrete walkway at each floor as they passed, McLean saw only one person; an old lady who scowled at him from her doorway, flicked her cigarette butt over the parapet and went back into her flat. He winced at the thought of the dog-end bouncing over his shiny red paintwork, but it was too late to do anything about it.

The window beside Magda's front door had been boarded up, so the message had finally got through to Housing. Stable door and horses bolting sprang to mind. The door itself appeared to have had a new lock fitted, as well. Beyond it, the little girl was in her favourite spot, with her armless, naked doll. She looked at him wide-eyed, but said nothing. Another mental note he needed to do something about.

'I don't suppose you've got the key, sir?' Ritchie reached for the door handle. It clicked as it turned and the door swung open. 'Ah, we don't need one, it would seem.'

She was about to step inside, but McLean stopped her. Something about this didn't feel right. No, everything about this didn't feel right. He raised a finger to his lips for quiet, then motioned for Ritchie to step back. When they were both clear of the doorway, he nudged it wide with his foot and peered inside.

It was empty, and just as messy as when last he had been here. The council services department had only boarded up the window and repaired the lock, thankfully. He took a step into the hallway, which was when he heard a voice coming from the living room.

Backing silently out onto the walkway, McLean closed the door and pulled Ritchie back towards the stairs before speaking. 'Get onto control. I want backup here as soon as possible.'

Ritchie made the call while McLean kept an eye on the door in case whoever was in there decided to come out. The little girl watched him with large, round eyes; he was obviously providing far better entertainment than her doll. Really he should have sent her back inside, but the thought of another confrontation with her mother filled him with dread. And there was no way it could be done quietly, either.

'What do you suppose they're doing in there?' Ritchie asked in a low whisper.

'Destroying evidence? Looking for something? Could just be local kids being nosey, for all I know.' McLean took a couple of steps towards the door. Stopped. Came back to where Ritchie was standing by the stairwell.

'You got your pepper spray?'

Ritchie opened up her shoulder bag and guddled around inside. Brought out the small canister and held it up.

'Right then. Stay here and wait for backup. If anyone comes out and tries to get away, let them have it.'

He didn't wait for her to argue, instead went straight back to the front door. No point in being subtle, and perhaps he'd be able to catch whoever was inside off guard. Surprise was always an advantage. McLean reached forward for the handle.

The door swung open before he could touch it, revealing the startled figure of Detective Sergeant Buchanan.

'What the fuck are you doing here?' McLean thought the words, but it was Buchanan who spoke them.

'What the –? How dare you speak to a senior officer like that?'

'I'm sorry, sir.' Buchanan emphasized the title with little effort to hide his sarcasm. So that was what it sounded like. 'You took me by surprise. I was just checking over the crime scene. Bit of a cock-up with housing not turning up to board up the window. But they've done it now.'

Far too rehearsed to be the truth. McLean looked back to where Ritchie was standing. She had her phone in one hand, the other holding the slim can of pepper spray. She had seen them both, started to approach, but McLean waved for her to stay where she was.

'OK then.' He turned to Buchanan, fumbled in his pocket for his own phone. 'Let's go in and see what you found.' As they stepped through the doorway, McLean saw the little girl clasp her doll to her chest with one hand, and with the other point straight at Buchanan. He pointed at the detective sergeant's back and mouthed 'him?' at her. She nodded, her face very serious, then got up, crossed the walkway and went into her own flat.

Buchanan wasn't hanging around, which gave McLean enough time to find the record button on his phone. He slipped it into the breast pocket on his jacket as he walked into the living room.

'About that little cock-up' he said. 'Why'd you not wait for them to turn up? Housing, that is.'

Buchanan scowled at the question. 'It was your bloody crime scene. Besides, it's usually forensics who arrange that sort of thing.'

'You mean you didn't even call Housing? You didn't even check to see if someone else had done?'

'Like I said. Not my crime scene.'

'Actually it was. Right from the moment I stepped into the ambulance. But I don't really give a fuck whose crime scene it was. Even if Charles bloody Duguid was supervising in person, it would still have been your responsibility to make sure the scene was secure. You and every other bloody officer on site, plain clothes or uniform. You don't leave the scene without making sure it's being processed properly and someone is in charge.'

Buchanan snorted a humourless laugh. 'Don't quote procedure at me like you're some kind of perfect copper. Everyone knows you take short cuts, McLean. Get people killed, too.'

McLean stared at the sergeant, let the insubordination slide this time. Buchanan was angry and on the defensive; hardly surprising if the little girl outside was telling the truth. Pushing him now might reveal even more nasty little secrets.

'You know she phoned me, when her attacker arrived?' McLean looked around the living room as he talked. It was still a mess, but a different mess to the one he'd seen previously. The chairs that had been stacked on top of the sofa were now lying on the floor, their cushions scattered about. Someone had been poking around for sure, none too carefully either. It didn't take a genius to guess who.

'I found her phone under that chair when I got here.' He pointed at the metal and velour monstrosity that was the only piece of furniture not broken or upside down. 'She must've dropped it when her attacker came in. Heard the whole thing as I was driving over here.'

'Oh aye? Why've you not arrested the bastard then?' Buchanan stood with his back to the window. McLean couldn't help but notice that the blood stain at the point where the glass had cracked, where Magda's head had been smashed against it, was almost exactly the same height above the ground as Buchanan's shoulders. Maybe a bit higher. A head higher.

'All I could hear was screaming, and the noise of things being broken. Sounded like an army.'

'Must've been a gang of them, the damage they did.' Buchanan kicked lightly at the edge of the upturned sofa. 'To this place and the prozzy.'

'You were over in Sighthill when it happened, weren't you.'

Buchanan twitched at the question, thrown by the change of subject.

'That's right, aye. What of it?'

'Nothing, really. Just that you told me at the time it was a crank call. Then you said it was a kiddie fiddler hanging around the school playground.' McLean crossed the room as he spoke, picking his way through the debris over towards the destroyed sofa. Someone had definitely been through the pile of cushions.

'Nah. You're imagining things. It was just a hoax call in the end. Had to check it out mind. You know what it's like with the register.'

McLean picked up one of the cushions and made a play of inspecting the slashes across it. Put a hand inside and felt around as if looking for something. 'Yes, of course. Can't take a chance where children are concerned. You have children, Pete?'

'What?' Buchanan's gaze had been fixed firmly on the cushion. Now it swung back to McLean's face. 'No. Never married.'

'The two are no longer mutually exclusive. I bet ninety per cent of the kids living in these blocks have parents who never married. But still, I'd've thought a detective of your long standing and experience would have known

328

that it's the school holidays right now. Kids won't be back in the playground for a couple of weeks yet.'

'Ha. That the best you can come up with? School's out? Come on, McLean. A playground's a playground whether it's got kids in it or no. You're on the register, you're not allowed anywhere near. We get a call saying someone's been seen in the wrong place, we investigate. Plain and simple.'

'Why'd you go alone, then? Why not take a constable with you?'

'That, coming from the great Detective Inspector McLean, just makes my day.'

It was a fair point, even if it didn't answer the question. McLean dropped the cushion back onto the pile and took a good look at Buchanan's shoes. Heavy-duty, thick soles. Built more for the beat than plain clothes, but a lot of coppers wore them. He opened up the envelope Ritchie had given him, pulled out the sheaf of crime scene photographs and leafed through them until he found the one he was looking for. The living room, as seen by SOC when they first arrived, looked much as McLean recalled it himself. He paced around the room until he found the spot where the photographer had stood, lifted up the picture for comparison. It was still a bomb site, but whereas before the furniture had been scattered around more or less at random, now it was arranged in piles, as if someone had been systematically going through the place. Looking for something.

'You use an Airwave set, sergeant?' McLean didn't look directly at Buchanan, instead shuffling through the photographs until he found another interesting one.

'I did. Had it nicked out of a squad car a couple of days back. Thieving bastards. What of it?'

'Aye, I heard that. Unfortunate, but they'll give you another, I guess. Just wondered if there'd be a record of our conversation. You know, when I called you and asked about Magda's number? Why do you suppose they did this?' He turned on the spot to encompass the whole room. Buchanan seemed reluctant to respond to the question. He hadn't moved from the spot near the cracked window since they'd entered the room, as if he was defending it. Now his gaze was firmly on the stack of photographs.

'Nothing? No? Well, here's my theory. I think he was looking for something. Money, probably, or some money equivalent. Could be drugs, but that doesn't seem like Magda's style. She wouldn't tell him where it was, so he threw her around here a bit. She still wouldn't tell him where it was, even after he'd cut her up in the shower.' McLean noticed that Buchanan's eyes shifted to the door that led through to the corridor and bathroom. 'He kept on looking though. Can't have been anything too large. Otherwise why bother cutting these cushions open?' McLean picked one up again, then dropped it back onto the remains of the sofa. 'Something tipped him off though. Either that or he found what he was looking for. He was long gone by the time I got here.'

'It's all very interesting conjecture, sir. But why do we care, exactly? I mean, she's just another whore got herself beaten up as a warning to the others. I tried to explain it to you when you first came into the SCU. We tolerated Malky Jennings because he was a known quantity. We could control him, more or less. Soon as he's gone, someone else decides to make this their turf. Best way to do that's to make an example of one of them. You saw what they did to this one. She'll never work again. The rest of 'em will be handing over their takings like good little girls now.'

McLean shuffled the photographs again until he found the one he wanted. The front door with its boot print. The next picture in the pile showed a detail of the locks. The deadbolt was unlocked, as you'd expect with Magda at home. The snub lock was in place, but there was no sign of it having been forced. Only the security chain was damaged, hanging from the door, its anchor in the frame ripped out. A picture began to form.

'I reckon Magda knew her attacker. She opened the door to him but was wary enough to keep the chain on.' He turned his back on Buchanan, felt a chill run down his exposed neck as he walked slowly to the hallway.

'Didn't do her much good though.' He peered through the spyhole as he spoke, seeing the distorted image of Ritchie on the walkway outside, before turning back again. Buchanan was very close behind him. Too close for comfort, really.

'I don't think you were in Sighthill at all, Sergeant. I think you were here. You do realize that it's the control centre that logs the location of the Airwave sets, not the sets themselves? Conversations too.' McLean opened the door wide, took a step out onto the walkway, then held up the photograph for comparison. The one was suspiciously clean given the grime all around; the other showed a neat boot print. 'What do you reckon, Ritchie? This Buchanan's size?'

Buchanan let out a low snarl and launched himself at

McLean, hands reaching for his throat. McLean lurched backwards, tripping over his own feet in his rush to get away. He was dimly aware of movement further along the walkway as Ritchie started towards them, and then Buchanan screamed as he lost his balance, swept past in a lunge towards the parapet. McLean could see what was going to happen with a horrible certainty. He pushed himself up, grabbing at the detective sergeant's jacket, fingers gripping the fabric of one arm as Buchanan hit the crumbling blockwork, which broke away and disappeared. A split second later the sound of breaking glass and crushed metal underscored Buchanan's scream as he toppled over. McLean thought he had him by the wrist, but Buchanan's hand slipped past his own until he was holding only the sleeve. The weight almost pulled his arm out its socket, and he slammed up against the remaining brickwork with a force that winded him. He could see the mortar failing, harling cracked and bowing as his weight combined with Buchanan's threatened to pull them both over.

'Hold still, dammit.' McLean grunted the words as Buchanan flailed about. They were close to the scaffolding, but just too far to reach the rope that hung from a pulley up above. Each swing bowed the weak wall of bricks a little more, and McLean could feel himself being dragged across the concrete towards the drop. His fingers ached and his arm felt like it was going to pop off at any moment. Then Ritchie was there, kneeling by his side. She grabbed McLean by the waist so he could lean further over the parapet, try to get a hold with his other hand. Buchanan looked down, then raised his head up, staring straight into McLean's eyes.

'Don't you fucking dare let go.'

'Well, stop swinging around like a fucking monkey then, you idiot.' McLean spoke through gritted teeth, barely able to breathe with the effort. Ignoring him, Buchanan made another swing for the rope, his outstretched fingers just reaching. At the same moment, there was a terrible ripping sound. McLean fell backwards onto the walkway, the sleeve of Buchanan's jacket still in his hand as the weight suddenly disappeared from his arm. Struggling to extract himself from Ritchie's embrace, he could see the rope snaking up to the pulley high overhead. It swung wildly, then started to run through the wheel as a heavy weight pulled it down. It stopped suddenly as a knot jammed in the pulley, then hung straight and taut.

McLean scrabbled to the edge, trying to make sense of what he was seeing. Buchanan had reached the rope, but somehow in his fall it had tangled around his head. He hung there, four storeys up, neck quite clearly snapped, body swaying gently from side to side.

'Oh fuck.' Ritchie crawled to the edge beside him on all fours. Peered down with wide eyes. She shuffled away from the drop and slumped against the doorframe of Magda's flat. McLean leaned back against solid parapet, drinking the air in deep gulps and staring at the sleeve in his hands. He shook his head once, then looked down at the walkway. Lying in the middle, exactly where a man attacking another man might place his foot and slip, lay the crushed remains of a doll, naked and with no arms.

37

It was probably delayed shock. That at least was what he kept on telling himself as he walked slowly around the car park, staring at things but not really seeing them. The place was full of uniforms, scurrying around securing the scene, attaching tape to anything that didn't move, interviewing anything that did. The irony of it all wasn't lost on him: when Malky Jennings had been found dead around the back of the tower block, there'd been a cursory investigation but nothing serious. When Magda had been beaten within an inch of her life, the investigation had been a cock-up from the start. Now that a detective sergeant was dead though, the whole of Lothian and Borders were crawling over the scene.

McLean stopped pacing, vaguely aware that someone had spoken, possibly to him. His feet had brought him back to his Alfa, its windscreen smashed, roof and bonnet dented by falling brickwork. High up above, a team of firemen were working to get DS Buchanan's body down.

'You OK, Inspector?'

The voice finally broke through his musings. McLean looked around to see the SOC officer, Jemima Cairns, standing beside him. He couldn't immediately work out how she had got there.

'Miss Cairns,' he said.

'Well, at least that much is working.' The SOC officer

peered at him in an all too familiar manner. 'You really shouldn't be here. You're in shock.'

'I'm fine. Really.'

'No, actually. You're not. And you're messing up my crime scene. Why don't you go see Wally over at the van. He'll give you a cup of tea.'

Miss Cairns put a hand on his shoulder and steered him away from the cars. There was enough truth in her words for McLean to allow himself to be led. And, besides, it was never wise to turn down a cup of tea. Who knew when the next one would come along?

DS Ritchie was already at the van, cradling a mug between her hands. She always looked pale, her north-eastern complexion never that well attuned to the sun. But now her eyes matched the whiteness of her skin, the freckles across her cheeks dark spots across a bloodless canvas.

'This is so fucked up,' she said as McLean sat down next to her. The SOC officer called Wally handed him a mug of hot tea and he drank, noticed the sweetness and didn't care.

'Ever the master of understatement.'

'I keep seeing it in my head, but it makes no sense. How did it . . . ? How did he . . . ?'

McLean saw an image in his mind. DS Buchanan staring up at him with more anger in his eyes than fear.

'You saw what happened, right?'

'I saw something happen. Not quite sure what. You came out of the doorway, said something I couldn't hear. Next thing there was a shout and Buchanan came charging out through the door. He didn't even scream. Just went over and –'

'He was trying to get to the rope, stupid bugger. If he'd stayed still I could have got a better grip on his arm instead of . . .' McLean shuddered, suppressed the urge to look up and see if the body was still there. For some reason he couldn't immediately process, it wasn't a simple case of putting up a ladder and bringing Pete Buchanan down.

'But he was shouting – no, screaming – at you when he came out. Looked like he was going to throttle you.'

'Actually I think he wanted to push me over the edge.'

'Christ. Why?'

'I'm hoping Magda Evans might be able to shed some light on that, just as soon as she can talk.' McLean took a sip of his tea. It really was disgustingly sweet. 'I'm fairly sure it was Buchanan who beat her up. I'm just not sure why.'

'Oh God. Here we go.'

McLean looked at Ritchie. She had been staring into her mug, but something had attracted her attention. He followed her gaze past the SOC van towards the road. A shiny silver Range Rover had pulled up and was even now disgorging Detective Chief Inspector John Brooks. A second figure climbed out behind him. McLean expected little DI Spence, but instead the balding ginger and grey head of Acting Superintendent Duguid emerged. Just what he needed.

'You reckon Wally'll let us hide in the SOC van?' But it was too late. Duguid had scanned the scene and spotted them.

'What the fuck's going on, McLean? A man's dead and you're sitting around drinking tea?' Ever the master of observation. DS Ritchie struggled to stand as Duguid marched up to them. McLean put a hand on her arm to stop her.

'It was an accident, sir. DS Buchanan came out of one of the fourth floor flats at speed, tripped on something lying in the walkway and went through the parapet. Bloody thing should have been repaired by now. That's why the scaffold's there. And the rope.' He looked up now, as did Duguid. The view was partially obscured by a high access platform that had backed into the car park, blocking everything else in. You could still see the body hanging there though.

'Dammit, man, what were you even doing here?'

'Would you believe conducting my investigation?'

'Don't get smart with me, McLean.'

'Sorry, sir, but I just saw a man die and I couldn't do anything to save him. You'll understand if I'm not at my best right now.'

Duguid looked around for something to sit on before leaning against the bonnet of the nearest car. He ran a hand through the remnants of his hair. 'OK. From the beginning. Tell me what happened.'

McLean ran through the events yet again. DCI Brooks ambled up halfway through, so he had to go over it once more. Beside him, Ritchie said nothing, which suited him fine. Had he been the officer investigating this incident, the first thing he would have done would be to separate all the witnesses and get separate statements from them before they had time to corroborate their stories. It didn't really surprise him that Dagwood missed this crucial step, but he expected more of Brooks.

'There'll have to be an internal investigation,' Duguid

said finally. 'I've already put in a call to Rab Callard over in Professional Standards.' He turned to Brooks. 'John, you can take over here.'

'I need to speak to Magda Evans, find out what Buchanan was doing here in the first place.' McLean struggled to his feet, looking for somewhere to put his mug.

'No. You don't.' Duguid's detective brain finally chuntered into life. 'You need to give a statement to DCI Brooks and then you need to go home. You too, Ritchie.'

'I can't go home. I've got to –'

'Perhaps I'm not making myself clear, McLean. Give a statement to Brooks, and then go home. That's an order. I'll see you in the morning.'

Duguid stalked off in the direction of the Range Rover. McLean watched him go, considered finishing his horribly sweet tea. Then a commotion from over by the scaffolding stopped everyone in their tracks.

'Fuck! Catch it!' A whirring sound of rope spinning through a pulley wheel. McLean watched in horrified fascination as Buchanan's body plunged downwards, picking up speed before it smashed into the roof of his bright-red Alfa.

38

A squad car dropped him off at the end of his drive, then disappeared into the late-afternoon city without a word. McLean had tried to get an idea of the damage done to his Alfa, but the area had been swarming with SOC officers and firemen. It was going to be put on a flatbed and taken back to the forensic labs for tests. He just hoped it would be repairable once he finally got it back.

Jenny Nairn looked up from the kitchen table as he walked in through the back door. 'You're home early. Something come up?'

'You could say that.' McLean went to the Aga, put the kettle on. He needed a proper cup of tea to take away the sweet sugar taste lingering from the last one. The shock had worn off now, replaced with a growing anger and frustration. And a right bastard of a headache.

'Want to talk about it?' Jenny had been reading from an old textbook, taking notes in tiny handwriting on an A4 pad. She closed the book from the back, put the pad on top of it, obscuring the cover.

'One of my colleagues died this afternoon. A detective sergeant. He fell off a walkway four storeys up. Hanged himself by accident.'

'Oh my god. Were you there?'

McLean ignored the question. He didn't want to talk about it at all. 'Emma about?'

'Last time I looked she was in the attic. Seems to like it up there. You were there, weren't you. That's why you're home early.'

McLean took the boiling kettle off the hotplate, poured water over the tea bag he'd dropped into a mug. Nodded at Jenny. 'You want one?'

'No, I'm good. And you're avoiding the question.'

'I don't really like talking about work. There's a lot of it I can't talk about, so it's easier not to start, OK?'

'OK. But if you want to talk, I'm a good listener. Just saying.'

'I'll bear it in mind.' McLean hoiked out the tea bag and threw it into the sink, fetched milk from the fridge. 'You know, you can have the evening off if you want. I'm not going anywhere. It'd be nice to spend some time with Emma for a change.'

Jenny paused to consider the offer for all of five seconds before answering. 'Sure. Thanks. I'll do that.'

The stairs creaked under his feet as he climbed up into the eaves, mug of tea held in a steady hand. Under the late-afternoon sun, it was pleasantly warm up here, and still, like being wrapped in a comfort blanket. It was quiet, too, somehow cut off from the endless thrum of the city. As he stepped into the attic, McLean noticed the door to the wardrobe was open and most of the dust sheets had been taken off the larger items of furniture. Emma was lying on the old sofa, bathed in soft sunlight shining through one of the skylights. Fast asleep, she looked like something from a fairy tale, the princess waiting for a brave prince to come and kiss her awake. A book lay open across her chest; he didn't have to see up close to know which one it was. The Conan Doyle copy of Gray's *Anatomy*, formerly belonging to the late Donald Anderson.

Movement out of the corner of his eye. McLean almost jumped, turned too rapidly, stumbling into an old carved hat stand by the door. Hot tea spilled over his hand, and he put the mug down carefully on a nearby trunk, dabbed away the damp with a handkerchief. Mrs McCutcheon's cat eyed him from the shadows, testing the air as if sight alone wasn't enough to convince it of his intentions.

'One of these days, cat, I'm going to get tired of you doing that and throw you out the nearest window.' He didn't really mean it, but felt the need to say something. Mrs McCutcheon's cat stalked past him, casually brushing its tail against his leg on its way to the sofa, where it leapt up and curled itself into a comfortable ball on the arm at Emma's feet. She didn't stir all the while, but as the sun played with the motes of dust in the air above her, McLean fancied he could see shapes forming, people almost. He shook his head and they disappeared, fog in his head from turning too quickly.

And then Emma began to speak.

She hadn't opened her eyes, and her lips barely moved. At first he couldn't even make out the words. Thinking she was waking up, he crossed the attic room to her side, but as he came close, he realized she was still fast asleep. Eyes flickered under closed lids, and her hands twitched, one laid across the book, the other trailing to the floor.

'No, no, no, no, no.' The voice didn't sound remotely like Emma's; more that of a man. McLean reached towards her, meaning to wake her up, but something stopped him. His arm froze as if a thousand tiny invisible hands held him back. Letting out a quiet hiss that was all the more menacing for its lack of volume, Mrs McCutcheon's cat stared him down. Its eyes almost challenged him to try and interfere with whatever was going on.

'Don't touch me. I don't like to be touched.' This voice was plainly that of a woman, but the accent was rich, plummy, English. Not Emma's gentle Aberdeen brogue.

'Please, I can't find her. Has anyone seen her? She was just here.' A child's voice, thick with anxiety. Emma's twitching was more pronounced now, almost a fit, and still the cat sat quietly, as if this were something that happened every day. McLean knelt down beside her, but still seemed unable to reach out and touch.

'You have to help her, Tony. Bring her back and let us go.' This voice shocked him to the core. It was a voice he knew as well as his own; a voice he'd not heard in over a decade. The voice of a young woman dead before her time.

'Kirsty?'

At the word, Emma went stiff, knocking the book to the floor. Mrs McCutcheon's cat rose up on its legs, fur prickling as if someone had passed a thousand volts through it. McLean could only watch as Emma arched her back, her head twisted further than it should surely go. He struggled to reach her, putting all his force into moving his arm.

'You cannot save her. I have her soul. She is mine.' This voice was old, deep. It wired itself straight into the fear centres in McLean's brain. The cat screeched now, wide mouth showing sharp white needle teeth. It looked for all the world like it was going to leap, attack Emma, scratch out her eyes, and as his focus shifted from her to it, so he felt his limbs lighten. The pent-up energy he hadn't realized he was exerting released and he sprung forward at the same instant as the cat, catching it in mid-air. Then gravity took over and the two of them fell on top of Emma in a tangle of arms and teeth and claws.

'Oww. What are you doing?'

Emma struggled up from under McLean, awake now and speaking in her own voice. Mrs McCutcheon's cat shot from his grasp like a bar of wet soap in the shower, disappearing into the shadows so quickly it bounced off the trunk, sending the mug of tea toppling. The crash of shattering china broke whatever spell had fallen, bringing with it the muted roar of the city back into the room. He pushed himself away, sitting down on the floor as Emma shuffled herself upright and yawned.

'What was all that about?'

McLean looked up at her, hair tousled from sleep. For the briefest of moments she was the Emma he remembered, and then the little-girl-lost expression settled back down over her face like a veil.

'You were talking in your sleep.'

'Was I? Oh. There were people all around me. So many people all trying to get my attention.' She scanned the room, craning her neck to see behind her as if looking for them. 'I can't see them.'

'It was just a dream. You're awake now. It'll be fine. You'll be OK.' McLean reached out and took Emma's hand, patted it like he would a child's. That, increasingly, was what he seemed to be dealing with.

*

Jenny Nairn was stuffing her book and writing pad into an old leather satchel when McLean entered the kitchen ten minutes later, cradling the shards of broken mug in one hand. She almost jumped when she saw him, but covered her surprise well.

'I was just getting ready to go out.' A frown crossed her face. 'You're still OK with me having the evening off, aren't you.'

'Yes, that's fine.' McLean dropped the broken pottery into the bin, then pulled out a chair, dropped into it.

'That's good. I've booked a taxi. Wouldn't want to have to cancel.'

'No, you're fine. Could do with another cup of tea though. Bloody cat knocked that one over.'

Jenny gave him a wry grin as she put the kettle on the Aga. 'I'm a carer, you know. Not a domestic.'

McLean struggled to his feet, heading for the cupboard where the mugs lived. 'You're right, sorry. I can get my own tea.'

'Sit down. I'm only joking.'

He did as he was told, grateful for the small rest. Already the incident up in the attic was fading away. True, it had been unsettling, but he'd just imagined those voices, surely. And Emma had always talked in her sleep. At least, he thought she had.

'I really should spend more time with Em. Sometimes it feels like I'm never here.'

'You finally noticed.'

'You could say that. More someone just shoved it in my face today.' He rubbed at eyes sore and tired. 'Times like this I feel like I could sleep for a week, wake up and it's all gone away.'

'Only problem is it never does. Go away that is.'

'How does someone so young get to be so wise?'

'Who says I'm young?' Jenny poured boiling water from the kettle into the waiting tea pot, set it down on the kitchen table. 'But I'll take the compliment in the spirit it was intended.'

McLean watched as she fetched mugs and milk, wondered whether he'd be chancing his arm asking her to get out the biscuits while she was at it. After Emma's strange turn in the attic he felt completely drained; the final straw in a monumentally shitty day.

'Don't forget Em's got an appointment with Eleanor tomorrow morning.' Jenny poured tea into his mug as if she'd known him all her life. McLean found it hard to care about the curious old tradition his grandmother had insisted on, that you couldn't pour tea in someone's house unless you'd known them at least seven years. He just wanted his drink, wasn't really fussed how he got it. He'd have liked a biscuit too, but right now moving was too much effort. When had he got so tired?

'I don't suppose there's any way you could take her for me?'

Jenny leaned her back against the Aga, her own mug of tea clasped in her pale, skinny hands. The smile was gone. 'You think that's a good idea?'

He shook his head. 'Probably not. I just really don't fancy sitting in on another session. The last one didn't go so well.'

'Only because you forgot to turn your phone off. Look, Tony. Emma needs you in there with her.'

'Does she really? Half the time I just fall asleep. I feel like I'm getting in the way.'

'You're not. Trust me on that.' Jenny fell silent a moment, as if in deep thought, then added: 'Why did you do it? Take her in?'

McLean slumped in his chair. He didn't have the energy for this. Jenny just stared at him, her silence demanding the question be answered.

'We had something. Before . . . Well, before. She's got no one else.'

Still the silent stare.

'And yes, dammit. I feel like it's my fault she's the way she is. I need to do everything I can to try and put it right.'

'Now we're getting somewhere. So doing everything means throwing your money at the problem. 'Cause that's what it sounds like when you pay me to take your girlfriend to her therapy sessions.'

'I . . .' McLean started to speak, realized his mouth was open, closed it with an audible click. It was never easy to admit when someone else was right and he was wrong. Jenny's words had raised questions he'd been avoiding for months now; ever since he'd found Emma unconscious, shackled to that dirty bed in Needy's underground chapel. Yes, they'd had a relationship then, Emma and him, but it had only been for a few months. More off than on, if he was being honest. And yet as soon as she'd been taken from him he'd felt like his world had collapsed. Was that because he loved her? Or because of what had happened before, with Kirsty? Christ, it was no surprise he'd lived alone for so long. Life was much easier that way.

The crunching of gravel under tyres outside broke through the whirl of thoughts, any that might have stuck around chased off by a car horn destroying the quiet.

'That'll be my taxi.' Jenny pushed herself away from the Aga, put her mug down and grabbed her bags. 'Think about it, Tony. You feel responsibility for Emma? Go talk to her. Spend some time with her. Help her yourself, don't pay others to do it for you.'

And without another word, she was gone.

39

I walk the drab city streets, scenting the air like a predator. It is not meat I hunt, but the much sweeter taste of hopelessness and despair. There is so much, each person wrapped in their own little aura of gloom. Sometimes it is hard to know where to start, but tonight my trail is clear. The sickly smell of a soul in turmoil guides me to my prey.

On the outside she is carefree, confident, happy even. But the spirit can see through to her core. The spirit knows the secrets of her heart. The failure, the fear, the darkness that has dogged her all her days. The spirit sees her true nature, and through it I know her too.

The world is so much brighter when the spirit enters me. People glow with an inner fire, and everything is pin sharp. I know no doubt when he is with me; anything is possible. I work my way through the crowd, chatting occasionally, charming people, laughing. It's so easy.

'You come here often?' Sure, it's corny. A cliché even. But that's why it works. She looks up, gives me a weary little smile. Contact.

The bar is dark, intimate. Not so noisy that you can't talk, but not so quiet that you can be easily overheard. I buy wine, and she comes with me to my favourite little alcove. I knew she would, even without the spirit guiding me. She is hungry for the happiness of others, clings to it in weary desperation.

She comes here every week, regular as clockwork. I know this because she tells me so, in her soft, bubbly voice. But I also know it because I've watched her for months now, sensing the misery in her, waiting for the spirit to come to me. Waiting for it to confirm what I'd already suspected. We talk of inconsequential things, for that is all she has. Her life has no meaning, and deep inside she knows it. She drinks the wine I have bought her, seeking courage there to admit to the failures that have dogged her. I wait patiently, the spirit coiling behind my eyes. The moment will come. Soon.

She reaches for her glass, then pauses, leans forward. Her hand slips uncertainly across the narrow table, gently brushing my own. At that touch, the spirit surges within me. I have been looking down, demure, but now I catch her gaze, hold it with my own. Her pupils dilate, a shock of electricity between us as I grasp her hand firmly in mine. Then the spirit leaps from me, fills her with its promise. She does not resist, knows that this is the fate she has been seeking. I feel a thrill of anticipation shiver through me.

'You are mine!'

40

McLean watched from the leathery comfort of the sofa as Doctor Austin conducted yet another hypnotherapy session with Emma. Once more, Dave had brought him a cup of rich, black coffee, but rather than savouring it, this time he'd downed it in one. The taste still lingered in his mouth and the caffeine was keeping him at least partly awake.

'Breathe in. Hold. And out. In. Hold. And out.' The Doctor's voice rose on each 'in', kept the same tone for the hold, then dropped with the 'out', rising and falling like waves. It was all but impossible not to get sucked in to the same breathing pattern, but he did his best.

Across the room, Emma sat ramrod straight in her high-backed armchair. She was so thin, she almost disappeared into the dark depths, her pale face framed by her black hair. It had grown since she had woken from her coma, and she'd shown no great desire to get it cut. Now it hung below her shoulders in sharp contrast to the short, spiky chaos she'd worn when first they had met.

'Now, we're going back in time. Just like we did before. Breathe in. Hold. And out.'

Something had changed in the room. McLean couldn't exactly put his finger on it. The air wasn't noticeably colder, but he had a feeling that it should be. He looked across to the door through to the reception room and

Dave. It hadn't opened, and neither had the window. Yet there was a different quality to the air, as if it had been disturbed. As if something invisible had moved through the room.

'You're at college in Aberdeen. It's your first term and you're meeting new friends. Breathe in. Hold. And out.'

New friends. McLean found himself back in Freshers' Week, Edinburgh University in the early nineties. He'd made some good friends then, ended up quite by chance sharing digs with a young Phil Jenkins. He probably ought to give Phil a another call some time. Better yet, he could take some time off, fly over and visit. It was many years since he'd last been to the States. Actually, it was many years since he'd last been anywhere overseas. That trip to Iceland where he'd finally summoned up the courage to ask Kirsty if she'd marry him. He'd met her at university, too.

'Good. You're doing very well, Emma. I think it's time we went back a bit further. To your school days. Sixth form. Breathe in. Hold. And out.'

Sixth form in that dismal English public school his grandmother had insisted on sending him to. He could still hear her voice. 'It was good enough for your grandfather and your father. It'll be the making of you.' Aye, right. And the breaking.

Sixth form at least meant the end of ten years of boarding education. Ten years of being sent away from home to sleep in draughty dormitories, endure the cruel taunting of older boys and the bewildering unpredictability of the teachers. One moment they were all praise, the next screaming at you for some wrongdoing only they could see. Ten years in which he'd learnt to think on his feet, to react rather than plan. Ten years of gut-wrenching homesickness and, yes, the occasional moments of wonder, excitement and joy. By the time he made it to his A levels, McLean had more or less got the hang of private education, but he'd also lost touch with all his Edinburgh friends. Not that there'd been many to start with.

'Back further. To your childhood.'

Is the voice different? He can't tell. It's not important. All he knows is that there is a dark place he doesn't want to go to. But the voice is insistent. He must tread that unused road, back and back and back to the frightened, angry, confused little boy. He is holding on to a hand, staring at the fog as it eddies and swirls in the car headlights. He is holding on to a hand as he stands at the front of a large hall, staring at a pair of pale wooden boxes, raised up on a dais. He is dimly aware they are in those boxes, his mother and father. Sleeping now. But soon the curtains will part and the flames will devour them. He doesn't want to see that. Doesn't want to hear the screams as the plane hurtles out of control towards the towering rock slab of the mountain. He doesn't want to, but the voice is impossible to resist.

'Well, someone's benefiting from these sessions, that's for sure.'

McLean snapped out of his dream with a start that sent his coffee cup tumbling to the thick carpet floor. Luckily for him and carpet both, it was empty.

'Sorry about that.' He stretched, covered his mouth with the back of his hand to hide a yawn. Looking up from the sofa, he saw Emma and Doctor Austin staring down at him, the one with an expression of concern writ large across her thin face, the other seeming rather amused by it all. How long had he been asleep, dreaming of the past?

'How did you get on?' he asked.

'I remembered stuff,' Emma said. 'From school and university. I knew it anyway, but this was like learning how I knew it, if that makes sense?'

'Emma's doing very well, Tony. I think with time we'll get maybe ninety per cent of her memories back.'

'Umm. Great.' He pulled himself up out of the sofa, back creaking in protest, then bent to pick up the coffee cup to more pops and snaps. Doctor Austin took it from him and handed it to Emma.

'Could you take that through to Dave, please. Thanks.' She waited until the door was closed before speaking again.

'I know about Emma's nocturnal visits, Inspector. I can't imagine that's easy to deal with.'

McLean wondered who had told her; Emma herself or Jenny Nairn? It didn't really make much difference. 'An unbroken night's sleep would be nice. Still, there's always your sofa.'

Doctor Austin smiled. 'The night terrors driving her to your bed are all part of her psychosis. She's hiding from the bad memories, and in so doing has repressed everything. But it's still all there, pretty much, and as she drifts off to sleep, it starts to come back. That can be quite overwhelming for someone who basically thinks they're about eight.'

'But you think you can cure her.' McLean tried to keep the pleading out of his voice.

'Emma's not as receptive to hypnosis as most.' Doctor

Austin nodded her head very gently in his direction to indicate exactly who she included in that catch-all. 'I get people like her now and then. It's just a matter of taking the time needed, and we're making progress.' She paused a moment. 'Yes, I think I can cure her. But I must warn you, it will be traumatic. A terrible thing was done to her. It's hardly surprising she's suppressed it so completely. But we need to dig it out and expose it to the light before she can start to rebuild her life.'

'It would be fair to say you and Detective Sergeant Buchanan didn't see eye to eye.'

Really not much later, the taste of Dave's coffee still lingering, McLean sat on the wrong side of the table in interview room three, trying not to feel like a criminal. Across from him, Chief Inspector Callard of Professional Standards was doing a poor job of concealing his contempt. The interview was informal, for now at least. But that didn't mean there wasn't going to be a full investigation.

'I found him obstructive, and I didn't like his methods. I've no idea why he didn't like me, but he hardly tried to hide it.'

'What were you doing at the flat?' Callard had a copy of the initial incident report in a folder in front of him, but had made no effort to look at it since McLean had given it to him.

'You know about Magda Evans being violently attacked?' McLean read Callard's expression to mean he did. 'Well, I was working on the theory it was a warning to the other prostitutes working that area. Probably someone stamping their authority on the place after Malky Jennings was killed.'

'And you went back to her flat to find out what, exactly?'

'Something didn't add up.'

'What do you mean?' Callard's scowl was a permanent feature, but its current severity suggested he had no time for excuses.

'They only did a basic forensic sweep on the crime scene. Photos, prints, that sort of stuff. It should have been sealed up after that, but somehow the message didn't get through. When I went back, the flat was wide open. Anyone could have walked in; probably every Ned in the scheme had done by then. Any forensic evidence we find in there's worth shit. At first I thought it was just a cock-up. Our fault or SEB's, doesn't really matter. It happens from time to time. But I had a set of crime scene photographs printed up anyway. Went around there to see how the flat looked in comparison to how it was originally. Someone searched the place, then trashed it to cover their tracks. I'm guessing they knew Magda had something, money probably, and beat her up when she wouldn't say where it was.'

'Interesting theory. I'm guessing you have an idea who did it, too.' Callard didn't try to hide the disapproval in his voice. McLean had been in this situation too many times now to rise to the bait.

'I'm not prepared to speculate any more, sir.'

'You think it was Buchanan though, don't you.'

'As I said. I'm not prepared to speculate, sir.'

'For Christ's sake, McLean. He's dead. He fell off a

fucking tower block. Snapped his neck. How do I know you didn't push him off?'

McLean leaned forward, rested his arms on the table. Of course it had to happen. The canteen rumours were already swirling. Nothing loved gossip quite like a policeman, and this was Grade A material.

'Isn't it fortunate that there was a witness to the events then, sir.'

Callard let out an exasperated sigh. 'I know you didn't kill him, McLean. You're many things, but a murderer doesn't fit the profile. Professional pain in the arse, yes, troublemaker, yes.'

'If you know I didn't kill DS Buchanan, then why am I under investigation?'

'Because of a little thing called procedure. You remember procedure, don't you? They taught you about it when you joined the force, yes? An officer is dead. You were present when it happened and until my investigation into exactly how it happened and why is completed you will be restricted to an administrative role. Can't risk some shite of a lawyer using your conduct as an excuse to get some scumbag off the hook. Capische?'

'What about DS Ritchie, is she on paperwork only as well?'

'For the time being, yes. So you can imagine just how happy Charles Duguid is right now.' For some reason this brought the slightest edge of a smile to Callard's face. It made him look like a snake with a mouthful of gerbil. He picked up the report and opened it for the first time. 'You'd do well to avoid him if you can.'

*

'McLean. My office. Now.'

He had to have been waiting outside. Hidden just around the corner and listening for any clues, perhaps. There was no other way that Acting Superintendent Duguid could have been in that part of the station at exactly that time. McLean considered pretending he hadn't heard, but the problem with ignoring Dagwood was that it just made him worse.

'Was there anything specific you wanted, sir?' He decided on the annoyingly helpful approach instead. Duguid eyed him suspiciously, then looked around to see who might be listening in.

'Not here. My office.'

It wasn't far, but neither was it so near Duguid might have been just passing. Neither of them said anything until they had reached their destination, Duguid paying particular attention to ensuring the door was closed.

'You're a menace, you know that, McLean?'

'I'm sorry, sir?'

'What part of "go over to the SCU and help out" do you not understand?'

McLean stared at Duguid, looking for any hint that the acting superintendent was joking. If there was one, he couldn't see it.

'Don't pretend you didn't expect me to shake things up there, sir. I'm not stupid. I know exactly why you sent me to SCU and not one of the detective sergeants like Jo asked.'

It stung to admit it, that he was so predictable even Duguid could use him. But that was what the acting superintendent had done when he'd lobbed him at Jo Dexter's team. Rolled a grenade through the open door. Now the man was surprised when it had all blown up in his face. And yet here was Duguid, staring him down with those piggy little eyes as if he really didn't have a clue what McLean was talking about.

'I just don't know why McIntyre put up with you. You're supposed to be helping Jo Dexter's team, not killing them off one by one.'

OK. Count to ten. Silently. Also make sure hands are in pockets so he can't see you clenching them into fists. Ah, fuck it.

'I'm not putting up with shit like that. You so much as suggest anything as ridiculous outside this room I won't think twice about taking it up with the Chief Constable.'

'Don't be so bloody melodramatic, man. It's just a fucking joke.'

'To you, maybe. To me it's an accusation and since we're being blunt it's also fucking unfair. I tried to save Pete Buchanan's life, nearly went over that parapet myself. I'm not naive, I know the lower ranks and uniform are going to gossip and make jokes, sir. I just don't expect it from my seniors.'

'Alison Kydd. John Needham. Now Pete Buchanan.' Duguid counted the names off on his long fingers, bending them over backwards as he did so.

'What of them?' McLean knew what Duguid was doing, but he stood his ground, close to the acting superintendent's desk. For a moment he even considered sitting on the edge of it.

'They're all dead, McLean. All under your command. All in less than two years.'

'What the fuck? Under my command? Remind me again why they put you in charge here?'

Duguid's face reddened. 'Don't you dare take that tone –'

'I'll take whatever tone I bloody well please. I've had it up to here with the lot of you. Stupid gossip and nasty pranks I can take. I've done my best to ignore it because that's the only way it'll ever stop. But you start suggesting I'm some kind of pariah. Some bad luck omen or something. I –'

'I don't need to suggest it, McLean. It's out there already.' Duguid had been standing on his side of the desk, but now he slumped down into his chair. 'Look. Sit down, OK?'

McLean did as he was told, not taking his eyes off Duguid all the while. The acting superintendent looked like he was fighting a losing battle with his temper, but it was a revelation to see him even trying.

'It's the word in the canteen.' Duguid ran a hand through the remains of his hair. 'What do the Americans call it? Scuttlebutt? It's not gossip, really. More a reputation thing. There's constables asking to be taken off plain clothes just so they don't have to work with you.'

'Not much chance of that, the way you keep shifting me from team to team.'

'Well, that'll be one less thing to worry about then. You're off the SCU. Callard insisted, but I was going to do it anyway. Squared it with Jo Dexter. She's having DS Carter to pick up where Buchanan left off.'

God help her. 'What about the Magda Evans case? Is that SCU because she used to be a prostitute, or us because it was attempted murder?'

Duguid gave him an odd look. 'You mean the case that took you and Buchanan to the tower block where he was killed? You think Professional Standards are going to let you go anywhere near it now?'

Of course not. It was a miracle they were letting him carry on working at all.

'No, you can wrap up those three suicides. Collate the forensic and pathology reports. Write them up, close the cases. If you're very lucky I might let you investigate burglaries after that.'

'On my own? Or am I allowed a couple of detectives to help?'

Duguid glowered like a weary schoolmaster, worn down by the bright kid. 'Oh for fuck's sake. You can have anyone who'll work with you. Grumpy Bob, Ritchie, even MacBride. I don't think you'll find many others.'

'Thank you, sir.' McLean stood up, turned to leave. He was almost at the door before he thought to mention something about the malicious rumours, but Duguid spoke first.

'Why are you still here, McLean?'

'I was just leaving.'

'Not here, you idiot. Here. In this job. Why don't you just jack it in? You've got money.'

McLean turned slowly, giving himself time to think. 'I've seen that new Range Rover you've got. Hear your uncle's apartments on the Royal Mile went for a tidy sum, sir. And yet here you are. Still.'

'That's not the same. And my personal financial arrangements are hardly any of your business.'

'If you can't see the irony in that statement, sir, then nothing I say will make any difference, will it?'

McLean didn't wait for an answer. He strode out of Duguid's office, leaving the door open as it had always been in Jayne McIntyre's day, putting as much distance as he could between himself and the acting superintendent before he said anything else he might come to regret.

And yet the question kept coming back: why did he stay? He didn't have to work at all, let alone at this thankless job. He knew the answer, of course. Part of it was he couldn't think of anything else to do. Part was because of Kirsty and the things that had been done to her. He knew he could never catch all the bad guys, but that wasn't going to stop him from trying.

There was another reason why he stayed, though. One which made even less sense than the other two, and yet was so deeply ingrained with his character that he knew he'd never overcome it. That magnificent language, Scots, had a word for it: thrawn. It went beyond the pride that would cut off its nose to spite its face, it was more visceral than that. They wanted him to leave, expected him to quit, and that simple fact was all it took to ensure that he never would.

41

McLean sat in his tiny office, staring at the mountains and foothills of paperwork strewn around. A lot of it was rubbish, he knew that. There were case files in the lower strata that had been left behind by the previous unfortunate occupier of the room, and doubtless many folders that had ended up in here simply because someone hadn't known where they were supposed to be. On the plus side, if he wasn't allowed out into the field then he might at least make a start on clearing the place. Knowing his luck it would take Callard weeks to ferret out what had happened and why, so he'd have plenty of time. Then there was the small matter of preparing a list of his casework for Dagwood to reassign, and the suicide cases to wrap up. Might as well get the overtime sheets squared away as well.

The knock at the open door was DS Ritchie. She still looked pale, as if Buchanan's death haunted her dreams. McLean could hardly blame her; the image of him hanging there, arms limp by his side, one sleeve missing from his jacket was never far from his mind. Like some terrible scarecrow hung to ward off whatever mythical beast fed on the hopes of the dispossessed living in those soulless tower blocks. The noise of the rope whirring through the pulley wheel came unbidden to him too. And the horrible twang as the knot stopped it fast.

'Callard done interviewing you then, sir?'

'For now, aye. Get the impression he's going to drag this out as long as he can, though.'

'Maybe not. Word is the Chief Constable wants it played down as much as possible. Doesn't want anything rocking the boat before the switch-over.'

It made sense. The last thing Lothian and Borders needed was an investigation opening up a nasty can of worms just as the new Police Scotland came into being. Hard enough keeping track of who was supposed to be doing what anyway, without giving Strathclyde another excuse to muscle in on their territory. It wouldn't surprise McLean at all that headquarters were pushing for the whole thing to be wrapped up quickly. A tragic accident, dreadful really. Counselling for all who were involved and the whole episode tidied away. The only problem was Chief Inspector Rab Callard. Professional Standards didn't respond well to being told how to conduct their business.

'They tell you when you'll be allowed back?' he asked her.

'Depends on Callard.' Ritchie grimaced. 'Nothing but paperwork for me. I'd almost rather be down in the basement filing evidence.'

'You don't really mean that, though if you're looking for something to do it might be worth your while asking around about Buchanan. There's a reason he never made it past sergeant. I wouldn't mind knowing what it is before the top brass comes after us.'

'Isn't that a bit . . . I don't know. Callous?' Ritchie asked. 'Won't everyone think I'm just trying to cover my arse. Our arses both?'

'Probably. But a trained detective of your skill ought to be able to ferret out information without too many people realizing what you're doing.' McLean gave her a cheeky grin. He picked up the first folder that came to hand, glanced at the title without really taking it in, dropped it back onto his desk. 'Bollocks. It'll all still be here in an hour. Fancy a coffee?'

The canteen had always seemed something of a last-minute addition to the station. Stuck between the locker rooms and the stores, its windows looked out on a narrow alley and the stone wall of the neighbouring building. It was a gloomy place even on a bright day, but it was always busy. The coffee wasn't bad either, if you liked it weak and soapy.

Shift change meant the place was buzzing when McLean and Ritchie pushed through the double doors, the sound of a dozen or more conversations filling the room. An institutional cooking smell pervaded, which was at least preferable to the more usual odour of unwashed beat constable. As they walked across the room towards the serving hatch, the noise dulled down almost to silence, and McLean could feel the heat of eyes on his back. Beside him, he felt Ritchie tense.

'Ignore them,' he said, just loud enough that the silent policemen nearest could hear. At the counter he ordered two coffees and added a couple of chocolate brownies, since they looked so appetizing. When he and Ritchie turned back, looking for somewhere to sit, every officer in the room was staring at them.

'Very mature. I expect there'll be rude pictures pinned

up inside my locker next.' McLean scanned the room. In amongst a sea of uniforms, over by the window there were a couple of empty chairs at a table otherwise occupied by detectives. DI Spence and DCI Brooks, to be precise. Perhaps not who he would have chosen to sit with, but of Grumpy Bob and DC MacBride there was no sign.

'Mind if we join you?' He voiced it as a question, but was already pushing the seat with his foot, making room for Ritchie. DI Spence gave a little shrug as if he couldn't care less. DCI Brooks was less welcoming.

'You've a nerve coming in here, McLean.'

McLean stared at the fat man, took a bite of his chocolate brownie and washed it down with a swig of coffee. Disgusting, both of them, but he wasn't going to let that spoil the moment.

'I never realized it was the wild west, sir. If I had, I'd have asked DS Ritchie to bring her bow and arrows. Young MacBride does line dancing, I'm told. He could probably lay his hands on some cowboy boots and a Stetson.'

'Don't get cocky with me. A man's dead. Hardly the time to be making jokes.'

McLean studied Brooks. Like many obese men it was hard to gauge his age accurately. The excess fat in his diet kept his skin smooth, and he shaved his head, making it difficult to judge by hair colour. He was chummy with Dagwood, but happy enough to take the piss out of the acting superintendent behind his back, which suggested to McLean that he was younger. That didn't mean he hadn't been another one of Buchanan's friends in high places.

'A man's dead. Yes, sir. I did know. I was there when it happened. I tried to save him.'

Brooks let out a little snort of disbelief. 'Save him? Don't make me laugh. Everyone knows you hated Pete Buchanan, wanted him off the force.'

'Everyone, it would seem.' McLean paused, scanned the room and its gaggle of expectant faces. Like the audience at a particularly cruel comedy act. One where the so-called comedian got his laughs from tearing one of the crowd to pieces in the name of fun. 'Except me.'

Brooks narrowed his eyes, which in a thinner man might have made him look scornful, but in his case made him look constipated.

'Don't play the innocent, McLean. Everyone knows you were boning that prostitute and Pete was going to bring it up with Professional Standards.'

Fortunately for McLean, he'd finished eating his piece of chocolate brownie. Less fortunate for DI Spence, Ritchie hadn't. Had in fact just taken a mouthful along with a swig of coffee, which she duly spat out all over him.

'Oh god. I'm sorry, sir.' She patted ineffectively at the mess with a paper napkin until Spence pushed her away.

'Christ, woman. What's wrong with you?'

Ritchie couldn't answer for a while, struggling to breathe after choking on brownie. 'I'm sorry, sir. But really? To . . . DI McLean? A prostitute?'

'You deny it, then?'

'I'm not sure I'd dignify it with a response at all,' McLean said. 'But I'm intrigued as to where such a ridiculous accusation could have come from. I don't suppose you'd be prepared to tell me who told you?'

Brooks stared at McLean with a look of utter disbelief,

whether at the denial or the request, he couldn't be sure. Fair enough; he'd not readily give up his sources either.

'No. Forget it. I can guess who easily enough, and he's not around to defend himself.' McLean pushed his chair back and stood up. Nodded to Ritchie. 'Come on. There's work to do.'

Ritchie grabbed her mug and plate, scrambling to her feet. 'There is?'

'Aye, there is. And given the way everyone thinks of me at the moment, I'm going to need your help with it.'

It was late when he finally made it home. Jenny Nairn was slumped at the kitchen table, her head resting on a text-book. She stirred as he very gently put down the bag with his take-away supper in it. Looked up at him with bleary eyes.

'You should try that in bed. I'm told it's more comfortable.'

Jenny yawned, stretched and rubbed at her eyes. Considered her textbook and notes, then closed everything up. 'Sorry. I guess Cognitive Behavioural Therapy's not as interesting as I thought it was. Long day?'

'That's one way of putting it. How's Em?'

'Asleep, I think. She went up about ten. Her own bed. Can't promise she won't climb into yours again later though.'

McLean said nothing. It had been a long time since he'd managed a full night's unbroken sleep. Emma's nocturnal visits were regular as clockwork now, every morning at three. And her sleep-talking was getting worse, the voices so different from her own, the language sometimes too.

'I spoke with Eleanor today.' Jenny's words broke into his train of thoughts and it took a while for his brain to catch up. It must have shown on his face.

'You know, Emma's regression therapy?'

'Yes. Sorry. Miles away.' McLean went to the fridge, pleased to find a bottle of cold beer there. The benefits of having someone else living in the same house. 'What did she have to say?'

'She's really got the bit between her teeth. I've not seen her so fired up by a case in ages.'

'That's good. Umm, I think. It's difficult for me to tell how the damned things are going. I just keep falling asleep.'

Jenny laughed. 'Eleanor's voice can do that. She's RADA trained, you know.'

'Is that right?' McLean found it surprisingly easy to believe. There was something very theatrical about Doctor Austin.

'She said she wants to make the sessions more frequent. Said maybe next Tuesday if you can make it.'

An image swam unbidden into his mind; a tiny office filled to the ceiling with paperwork. No hope of any active cases for weeks. Just an endless succession of telling people what to do and then trying to make sense of how they'd buggered it up. 'I think I should be able to manage.'

'OK then. I'll write the details down in the diary and send a reminder to your phone.' Jenny stifled a yawn unsuccessfully. 'Now I think I'll heed your advice. Night.'

McLean wished her good night and watched as she shuffled out of the kitchen. No sooner had she gone than Mrs McCutcheon's cat appeared through the same doorway, leaping up onto the table and sniffing at the takeaway bag in that over-familiar manner of cats.

'That's mine,' he said, which earned him an imperious stare. Fair enough, there was plenty to share.

Later, with the cat happily chasing bits of pilau rice around its bowl, McLean retreated to the library and a much-needed glass of whisky. Emma had left the television on with the sound muted, flickering images of some late-night movie. He slumped down on the sofa, then realized both that the remote was too far away and he couldn't be bothered getting up again to fetch it. Instead, he just let the flashing lights soothe his brain and calm down the endless looping thoughts about Magda Evans, Pete Buchanan, Malky Jennings.

Mrs McCutcheon's cat joined him after a while, smelling slightly of korma. It leapt onto his lap, kneaded at his free hand with its head until he stroked it. The purring came as a surprise; he couldn't remember ever having heard it purr before. It was a deep vibration against his chest, as relaxing as any massage. McLean hadn't really been watching the television, but he forgot it completely, slumped back against the arm of the sofa and stared at the strange shadows cast by the cornicing on the ceiling.

Of course. The ceiling.

He sat up so suddenly the cat dug its claws into his leg in surprise. With a yelp of pain, McLean dropped his whisky tumbler, still half full. It bounced on the rug, sprayed cask strength Talisker all over the antique floor and rolled under the sofa, but he ignored it. Ignored the cat, too, now eyeing him with its more normal deep suspicion.

His phone was in his jacket pocket, on the back of one

of the kitchen chairs. When he dug it out, a message from Jenny had already appeared, noting the time and place of the meeting with the hypnotist. He swiped it out of the way, ready to call DS Ritchie, and only then noticed the time displayed at the top of the screen. She'd probably still be up, sure. But was there anything either of them could really do at this time of the night? And if he was right, then it wasn't going to change before the morning.

Pulling out the chair, he sat down and started to tap out a text message instead.

42

'We're going to get fired. I just know it.'

DS Ritchie hunched her shoulders and shoved her hands deep into the pockets of her long overcoat, shuddering against the chill wind whistling in off the Firth of Forth. Early morning and the noise of the city waking up echoed around the car park at the base of the tower block. Broken glass still glittered on the cracked tarmac where McLean's Alfa had been parked. Just as soon as forensics had finished with it, he'd send it off to the garage in Loanhead for assessment. He had a horrible feeling the insurance company would declare it uneconomical to repair, which meant that he would be digging deep. It was just as well Johnny Fairbairn had come up with a more modern alternative. Even so, he'd parked a way up the street. He didn't want to chance anything to the place now.

'There's worse things than being fired.' He looked up the street for the hundredth time, waiting for the ambling form of Grumpy Bob to appear.

'That's OK for you to say. You're loaded. Me, I've got a new mortgage to worry about.' Ritchie stamped her feet against the cold. 'Can't we wait inside anyway?'

'And you're the one worrying about getting fired? Neither of us should be here, by rights. Professional Standards and Dagwood have both said as much. At least if Bob's doing the looking we've got some small deniability.'

'That's crap, sir. And you know it.'

'You're right. It's crap. But he's got the photos. No point going in without him.'

Ritchie's reply was lost by the arrival of a shiny new pool car. DC MacBride piloted it into the space where McLean's Alfa had met its grisly fate. He and Grumpy Bob both looked up as soon as they got out, rather than greeting McLean and Ritchie. Transfixed by the spot where DS Buchanan had met his end

'You sure you want to do this, sir?' Grumpy Bob asked as he handed over a thick folder. 'Me'n the lad can go over the flat without you.'

It was tempting. He knew that disobeying Dagwood would get him in trouble, but crossing Callard was even riskier. And Ritchie was right. It was fine for him to get himself fired, but her too?

'Well, I've not done anything wrong yet.' He pulled the crime scene photos out of their envelope and leafed through them once again. There was something that had been bugging him since the first time he'd seen the place and it had finally occurred to him last night. A pity he was so bloody slow, really.

'Damn. Nothing here that's any help.'

'What're you looking for, sir?' MacBride peered over his shoulder at the photos as if he hadn't already committed every single one to memory.

'The ceiling. People never look up. Even trained detectives sometimes. Especially when they've got something else on their minds. The floors of these tower blocks are all poured concrete. Nowhere to run services, so they put in false ceilings. Like in offices. Whoever beat Magda

372

Evans half to death was looking for something, and they were back looking for it again afterwards. I thought it was money, the way the cushions were all cut open. Maybe it was, but what if there was something else? And where would you hide something bulky in a place like that anyway?' McLean nodded in the direction of the fourth storey and its precariously low parapet.

'Come on then, lad. Latex gloves, I think.' Grumpy Bob set off for the stairs, closely followed by MacBride. McLean shoved the photographs back in their envelope and stuck them into the report folder. He got two steps in before a hand on his arm stopped him.

'We don't need to go up there, sir.' Ritchie was the voice of reason, only more irritating.

'But what if they find something?'

'My point exactly. What if they find something and we're there? Whatever it is will be useless as evidence. I don't know about you, sir, but I don't want to be some smart-arse lawyer's reasonable doubt.'

McLean had to admit that she was right, even though he hated the thought of someone else going through Magda's flat. Of them missing some crucial detail that only he would be able to see. He shook his head at his own stupidity. How many times had he been told that being an inspector was all about delegation and management?

'OK. I'll leave it to them.' He looked around the windswept car park, feeling the morning chill. Summer was most definitely on the way out. 'I don't suppose MacBride left the car unlocked.'

'I doubt it,' Ritchie said. 'But there's a coffee shop up

the road a ways. Figure you owe me at least a latte and a muffin.'

'I do? What for?'

'How about texting me at half one in the morning? Or dragging me down to Restalrig on my day off?'

'They found Pete Buchanan's prints all over it. Blood matches Malky Jennings. Pretty much a hundred per cent it's the murder weapon.'

McLean sat in the canteen, nursing a coffee and a bacon butty. He'd managed to find a spot in the corner, more or less out of sight of the beat constables coming and going. Afternoon shift time, it was a good place to listen and find out what was going on.

'Reckon he and the whore had a thing going. Jennings hit on her one time too often, so Buchanan beat him to death.'

It wasn't anything he didn't know, of course. It had taken MacBride all of ten minutes to find the loose ceiling tile and the booty stashed behind it. One baseball bat, finest hickory, wrapped in a plastic bag from Matalan. The shape and weight of the bat matched the weapon used to beat Malky Jennings to death and the blood type was his too. DNA analysis would take a while longer to come through, but nobody in the station doubted it was the murder weapon. Several of the senior officers were less pleased about the fingerprints all over it, mostly in blood. It was probably as well Pete Buchanan had hanged himself, however inadvertently. The embarrassment of a detective sergeant of long standing beating a man to death was not something the Chief Constable needed this close to the launch of Police Scotland. It probably helped that Malky Jennings deserved everything that happened to him, but not much.

'Thought I might find you down here.'

McLean looked up into the rotund face of DCI John Brooks. He was in need of a shave, on top at least. A thin fuzz of grey-white hair furred his scalp like an advertisement for hair-restoring pills. McLean started to stand, but Brooks waved his hand for him to stay, pulled out a chair and sat down.

'Spence getting the biscuits in, is he?' McLean glanced over at the serving counter and sure enough a thin detective inspector was chatting with the girl at the till. Brooks scowled that constipated scowl of his.

'A little respect wouldn't go amiss you know.'

'I couldn't agree more.' McLean threw back the last of his coffee with a grimace; it was never as nice cold. The grease on the remains of his butty didn't look all that appetizing any more, either. 'Was there anything you wanted, sir? Only I'm a bit busy.'

'Strange how Bob Laird took it upon himself to go and check out that apartment, don't you think? And taking young MacBride with him, too.'

'I wouldn't know anything about that, sir. Not my investigation.'

'Don't be so bloody clever, McLean. You know as well as I do Grumpy Bob doesn't do anything unless he's told to. Even then chances are he'll have a nap first.'

'I think you're underestimating Detective Sergeant Laird's investigative prowess, sir. He might not move quickly, but his brain's always working away.' McLean was winding Brooks up, but there was a truth in his words too. Grumpy Bob never lifted a finger if he didn't have to, but there were two ways to look for something. You could spend a lot of time and energy turning everything over until you found it, or you could sit and think about it until the obvious hiding place presented itself. OK, so it wasn't Bob who'd done that this time, but he'd taught McLean the importance of not always rushing in head first.

Brooks shook his head, his disbelief all too apparent. 'I know it was your idea, McLean. I just hope to God you weren't stupid enough to actually go there and look for the bloody thing yourself. We might not be able to arrest Pete Buchanan, but I'm sure as hell going to put Magda Evans away. Last thing I want is someone suggesting evidence was tampered with by someone connected to the case.'

'She awake then?' McLean realized he'd not heard anything about the ex-prostitute in days.

'Not yet. She's still sedated, but the doctors reckon they'll bring her out of it soon. Her prints are on that bat too. She'll not get away with this.' Brooks eyed McLean suspiciously as he said this last bit, as if he still harboured suspicions about McLean's relationship with Magda.

'No reason she should. She'll try and play you, though. She played me pretty well.'

'Oh aye?' Brooks raised a single pale eyebrow.

'Yup. We picked her up off that ship, remember. She spun us a yarn about people trafficking, being mistaken for one of the Eastern European pros. I reckon she was doing a runner. Got herself on that boat on purpose. Bang her up for murder; that's the least she deserves. But you might want to ask yourself what was in it all for Pete Buchanan before you send her down.'

'You what?' Brooks made his constipated baby face again.

'I never knew DS Buchanan well, but he didn't strike me as the kind of officer to fall for a prostitute's charms. Sure, he sampled the wares, but this isn't a tragic love story, is it? He was round her flat looking for something. I don't think it was that baseball bat. Or at least not just that baseball bat.'

'What are you suggesting, McLean?'

'My bet's on money. Quite a lot of it, I'd guess. Probably Malky Jennings' stash as well.' McLean stood up, shuffled around the table as DI Spence arrived, carefully carrying a tray piled high with food. 'You might want to ask Magda about that when she can speak. I'd've thought it'd look good on your record if you manage to find a pile of drugs before they get back on the streets.'

43

'Right then, now I've got your attention, let's have a bit of a recap.'

The CID room, early morning. McLean had insisted everyone get in first thing, as chances were good they could have a meeting without being interrupted by anyone more senior than an inspector. Grumpy Bob had grumbled about it, but McLean knew the old sergeant was just playing the part. He might spend the day catching forty winks at every opportunity, but he was always up with the lark.

'Three suicides. All deaths by hanging. All unusual in that the subjects used a method that would break their necks, rather than asphyxiation, and they all used the same knot in the same type of rope. All three were in their mid-twenties, single, white, lived alone. Anything else?'

'All three of them left suicide notes. Textual analysis throws up some similarities, but not enough to prove they were all written by the same person.' DC MacBride was still pink and shiny from his morning shower, but he'd done all his prep work. Pictures of the three victims were taped to the large whiteboard running down one wall of the room, with details for each one neatly written alongside. There were even a few questions highlighted, and lines drawn to indicate where there might have been some connection between the three. It looked a bit like an investigation; just a shame it had taken so long to bring it all together. More so now that they were going to have to wrap it all up.

'Textual analysis?' This from Grumpy Bob, who wasn't pink and probably hadn't showered since yesterday.

'It's technical,' McLean said. 'What about other similarities?'

'Well, you know about the rope. There's the odd blood profiles for Mikhailevic and Fenton.'

'What about Sands? I thought there was something in his blood, too.'

'Initial analysis suggested it, but he'd been dead too long for a decent sample. Doctor Sharp couldn't be a hundred per cent.' MacBride didn't need to consult the report, McLean noticed.

'Same with the knots, I suppose,' he said.

'Actually the forensic expert reckons all three were tied by the same person. Or possibly machine. She's never seen three knots so closely matched, especially given that they've all been, well, used.'

McLean remembered his conversation with Miss Cairns and her fascination with all knotty things. It didn't help, though. Fascinating and unlikely though it was, the identical nature of the three knots was not in itself enough to hang an expensive investigation on. Not when Duguid was trying to control budgets and failing badly.

'So we have three deaths, all with similarities that scream one cause, but nothing that can be proven. That about right?'

'Pretty much, sir.'

'So how are we getting on finding any more solid link between these three?'

Silence filled the room.

'Nothing at all?'

'It's been kind of busy, sir. And this investigation was considered low priority.' MacBride looked embarrassed, even though it wasn't really the constable's fault. He should have been keeping on top of this himself, managing his team properly. Except of course it hadn't been a team, had it. They'd been all over the place and he'd taken his eye off the ball. McLean tried to stop himself from doing the Dagwood response of running his fingers over his face, from forehead down to chin. Failed. A horrible thought crept unbidden into his mind.

'Have we got independent confirmation of each of these victims' identities? Do we actually know these are the people we think they are?'

'Fenton's a positive ID,' MacBride said. 'I got a statement from Constable Stephen. He'd known him for years.'

'What about Sands? He had no immediate family.'

'To be fair, I don't think anyone would be able to identify Sands from his remains. If you recall, he was a bit squishy.' Grumpy Bob reminded them all of something they'd rather have forgotten.

'And Mikhailevic? We get anything back from the embassy? Anyone show his photo to the landlord of the Bond Bar? Or maybe his professor at the college? Did we check his passport with immigration?' All basic steps any detective should have known to do. Maybe Duguid was right to view him with such disdain. McLean couldn't really say he'd conducted any of his investigations well recently. Just when was it he'd started fucking everything up so badly? And why?

DC MacBride stood up, went to his desk and booted up his computer. McLean watched in silence as the detective constable tapped away at keys and scrolled with his mouse. No point asking what he was doing; it would be relevant to the question. It only took a couple of minutes anyway, then he looked up with a worried expression writ large across his round face. 'I think we might have a bit of a problem, sir.'

McLean walked around to the desk and peered at the screen. MacBride had brought up a website for Fulcholme College and somehow managed to find a page detailing the students enrolled in the current year. The thumbnail photographs weren't the most flattering, but it didn't take an ID specialist to see that the Grigori Mikhailevic on the screen was not the Grigori Mikhailevic whose face adorned the whiteboard.

Professor Bain met them in the reception hall with a worried smile. He looked a little more tired than McLean remembered, his thinning white hair unkempt, glasses slightly askew.

'Thank you for seeing us at such short notice.' McLean shook the proffered hand and introduced DC MacBride.

'Not at all. Not at all. Anything for the police.' Professor Bain's face didn't quite match his words. 'You said there had been developments, about Grigori?'

'Could we maybe talk somewhere a bit more private?' McLean nodded at a group of students loitering on the far side of the hall. Another class was obviously just finishing as yet more people streamed out of one of the doors.

'Yes, of course. Please.' Professor Bain didn't lead them to his study, instead directing the two of them down a corridor to the back of the building and an empty classroom. McLean waited until the door was closed before bringing out the photographs he had brought with him.

'I have to admit this is all rather embarrassing. Something we should have checked right at the start of the investigation. Could you just confirm that this is Grigori Mikhailevic?' He handed the first photograph to the professor, who pulled a pair of half-moon spectacles out of the top pocket of his tweed jacket and swapped them with the wonky pair already on his nose before peering closely at the picture.

'Yes. That's him.' He looked again, head bobbing like a nodding dog in the back of a car. 'This is from the college alumni web page, is it not?'

'It is indeed, sir.' McLean took back the photograph and handed over the next one. 'And can you tell me who this is?'

From his expression, Professor Bain recognized the face instantly. True enough, it was a dead man's mug shot, but the reaction was not one of horror so much as resignation.

'Oh dear me. He's dead, isn't he?'

'You don't sound surprised.'

'Poor old Duncan.' Professor Bain handed back the photograph and removed his glasses. 'When you asked me about Grigori being depressed, I thought about him.' He pointed with one spectacle arm at the picture now in McLean's hand. 'Duncan George. Used to be one of Grigori's classmates. You might almost have called them friends. But Duncan … Duncan was difficult. I'm no great expert, you'd need to talk to Eleanor about that, but I suspect he was bipolar. Brilliant for a couple of weeks, then he'd not show up for a month. Or he'd come in late, sit at the back, not contribute anything.'

'When did you last see him?'

'When did I last see him? Now there's a question.' Professor Bain tapped the side of his cheek with a finger, an introspective expression on his face. 'Where are we now, September? Must have been back in the spring, I'd guess.'

'So he'd finished his studies, then? Do you know where he went after graduation?'

'Oh, he never graduated. Never finished. No, like I said, he'd have his moments of brilliance and then drop out. We kept his place open for as long as we could, but when he missed final exams, well, we had to strike him off the register.'

'Didn't you get in touch with his family?'

'The state is his family. Was, I should say. He came here on a scholarship, out of a care home. If I remember right, his parents died when he was four. No other family, and a series of disastrous foster-carers. Poor old Duncan. Life didn't give him much, did it? Tell me. How did he die?'

McLean shuffled the photographs together and put them back in their envelope. Losing his parents at four years old was too close to home to be comfortable.

'Thank you for your time, professor. You've been very helpful.' He held out his hand, and Professor Bain took it automatically, didn't ask the question again.

DC MacBride had stood at the door for the whole interview, and opened it as McLean approached, leaving the professor behind. It was only as he was halfway through that something the doctor had said trickled through. Stopped him in his tracks.

'Your expert on bipolar disorders. Eleanor.' McLean turned as he spoke. 'That wouldn't be Eleanor Austin, would it? The hypnotherapist?'

Professor Bain looked a little nonplussed at the question, as if he couldn't quite work out what connection it had to anything. McLean could hardly blame him.

'Yes. She runs a couple of alternative-therapy courses. Very popular with the students. Do you know her?'

44

'So, we know now that Grigori Mikhailevic didn't kill himself, but Duncan George did. And in Mikhailevic's flat. Any ideas, Constable?'

MacBride was driving, face set in concentration as he tried to get through a snarl of traffic at the bottom end of Leith Walk. The trams had been meant to come all the way down here, so the civil servants in Victoria Quay could get all the way to the airport without stopping. Incompetence that would make Dagwood look like a professional now meant that they stopped a good mile short of Leith, and got nowhere near Ingliston. Even so the roads around the old docks had been dug up and refilled and dug up again. Christ alone knew why. It made any journey fraught.

'Your man back there, Professor Bain, reckoned the two of them were friends. Maybe they were sharing the flat?'

McLean tried to remember the scene. His overall impression was of a space barely large enough for one person.

'It's not far from here, is it. I think I'd like another look.'

A U-turn was out of the question, but MacBride managed to negotiate the side streets in a zigzag route that eventually brought them to the old warehouse development where Duncan George had died. There was no sign of any police presence at the front door, but then it was many weeks on, and the scene had long since been released.

Had Mikhailevic owned the place or rented? McLean realized he knew very little about the case at all.

'I don't suppose we've got a key or anything?'

'I'll find out.' MacBride pulled out his Airwave set and started making calls. McLean got out of the car, walked around the small courtyard. The front door to the development was locked, a series of buzzers for the different flats bearing the names of their occupants. None said Mikhailevic, or even George. He picked one at random and pressed it. No response. Pressed the one below it. Still no response. He was just about to press a third when there was a buzz and the lock clicked open. So much for security.

He pushed through into the dark hallway, breathing in a smell of mould and damp quite at odds with such a new development. Up two flights of stairs, the top landing was high in the roof space, a single, small window letting in too little light from the leaden grey sky outside. He tried to remember which was the right apartment of the two available, settled for the one on his left. The front door had no nameplate or buzzer, just a fanlight above showing an unlit bulb hanging from the open ceiling, and if he took a step back, stood on tiptoes and craned his neck until it hurt, the beam over which the rope had been tied.

McLean stepped up to the door and knocked, then listened hard for any sound of movement within. There was nothing for a while, then a voice behind him said: 'Can I help?'

He almost jumped out of his skin. Turned to see a young woman standing in the doorway of the flat opposite. She had a heavy dressing gown pulled around her and eyes bleary from disrupted sleep.

'Detective Inspector McLean. Lothian and Borders Police.' He showed her his warrant card.

'This about Grigori hanging himself?' The woman nodded her head at the door McLean had just knocked on. 'Only they cleared the place out, what, two weeks ago now? Decorator's been in and all. There's been at least two couples round looking. Reckon it'll be rented out by the end of the month. S'creepy though. I wouldn't live there. Not after, you know.'

'You knew him? Mikhailevic?'

'No' well. Enough to say hi to. I work nights, so I didnae see much of him, to be honest.'

'Anyone else stay with him?'

'There was a bloke, aye. Not all the time, mind, and I'd not seen him in a while. Used to think maybe they were gay, you know. Not that I've a problem with that.'

McLean pulled the envelope with the photos out of his pocket. The picture of Duncan George was quite obviously that of a dead man. Perhaps not the thing you wanted to see just after waking up. On the other hand, it would be confirmation.

'Was it you who reported it?' He nodded his head in the direction of the other flat. The young woman blinked, nodded.

'You saw him, then.'

'Just a glimpse. Didn't notice the door was open until I got inside. I was shutting my own door and I looked across.' She gulped. 'He was just hanging there, like, not moving or anything.'

'Did you see his face?' McLean saw the look of horror passing over the young woman's own face as she relived the moment. 'Look, I'm really sorry to bring this all up again.'

'No, you're all right. It's just . . . No, I didnae see his face. He was hanging wi' his back to the door, like. Gave me such a shock. I phoned you lot and went and hid in my bedroom.'

Downstairs, McLean heard the sound of the buzzer going again. No doubt DC MacBride trying to get in. He selected the photograph of Duncan George and held it up.

'One last thing. The other bloke who came round. Is this him?'

The young woman peered at it like someone who's forgotten to put their contact lenses in. 'Aye, that's him. He deid as well? You think it was a suicide pact?'

'Something like that, aye.' McLean thanked her and let her go back to bed. He doubted she'd get much sleep now.

They were stuck in the traffic jam that was Leith Walk again, this time headed uphill, back towards the city centre and the station. DC MacBride was silent, though it was unclear whether he was deep in thought or sulking because McLean had left him chasing loose ends on the phone. It didn't really matter either way; the quiet gave McLean time to try and marshal his own thoughts.

It was, as his gran had been fond of saying, something of a bugger's muddle. Three deaths by hanging, possibly suicide but increasingly looking like some kind of elaborate pact. Quite how you could force someone to hang themselves without leaving any traces that you'd done so, McLean couldn't begin to fathom. So each of them had to have been willing participants. But only one person had tied the knots, which effectively made it murder.

Then there was the mysterious case of the missing Mikhailevic. Of course, nobody had been looking for him; they'd all thought he was dead. But neither had he turned up at work or college, so either he'd done a runner, or he too was swinging in the wind somewhere.

And looming over everything else was the simple fact that he wasn't supposed to be investigating this any more. He was meant to be sitting in his office, typing up a report that ignored all the complications and drew a line under the point where each case was a simple, tragic suicide. The problem was, his conscience wouldn't let him do that, even before it turned out they'd mis-identified one of the victims. Now the loose ends were getting tangled and out of control.

McLean glanced at the clock on the dashboard. Another day almost gone, unless you were an inspector, in which case it had hardly begun. MacBride would be needing to get back to the station for shift end though. No overtime on this one.

Almost as if he'd known it all along, McLean's unfocused gaze shifted and he realized what he'd been staring at. The shop front hadn't changed at all, still just a small door between a bookmaker's and a chip shop. The faded sign said 'Madame Rose: Tarots Read. Fortunes Told.' Below it, equally faded but somehow something he had missed before, it also said 'Esoteric and Antiquarian Books.'

'You go on back to the station, Stuart. It's near enough knocking-off time anyway.' McLean unclipped his seatbelt and climbed out of the car just as the traffic started to move again. MacBride had no time to question his actions before the car behind started tooting its horn in irritation at the added microseconds of delay. 'See you tomorrow. Briefing at eight, OK.'

The shop door creaked like something from the BBC special effects department. McLean wondered how much business was coming this way. Not much call for a fortune teller in a time of austerity. As he climbed the stairs, his feet brought up a smell of mould and stagnant air, but the reception room was at least warm. There was no one manning the reception desk though. For a clairvoyant, Madame Rose didn't seem to have much idea of who was coming to visit, and when.

'Hello?' No answer. McLean went to the door that opened onto the consulting room, knocked and then pushed it open. It was empty, but the door on the far side was slightly ajar.

'Hello? Anyone about?' This time louder. Still no reply, and then the clumping sound of large feet on loose floorboards.

'Inspector, what a pleasant surprise!' Madame Rose burst into the room like a diva, dressed for the part as well. Even at home, it would seem, the transvestite medium preferred to stay in character. Unless she really was a woman. But no. McLean found himself shaking his head. She couldn't be. He couldn't be.

'I was just passing. Thought I might pick your brains about something.'

'Of course, of course. Any time.' Madame Rose held the door wide. 'Come through to my inner sanctum.'

He'd been in the large room at the back of the building before, but it still surprised him just how crowded the space was. There were shelves on every available wall, and a couple free-standing, all filled with old books. Display cabinets heaped one upon another, their contents too dark to see or too strange to fathom. The desk, arranged under the one window so that it at least had some light on it, was covered in papers, small boxes, things McLean had no name for, and cats. It made his own office back at the station look tidy.

'Perhaps a cup of tea?' Madame Rose didn't wait for an answer. McLean was left standing in the middle of the chaos as the medium disappeared through yet another door. He hardly dared touch anything; there was a fragility about the place that put him in mind of old black-and-white slapstick comedies. Picking up a book would surely set something rolling that would knock something over that would startle a cat that would jump up at something else, and the whole place would be destroyed around him. He was still hearing the comedy sound of a metal plate rolling round and round until it clattered to a halt when Madame Rose came back in bearing a tray.

'Sit, please, Inspector. Don't mind the cats.' She, or he, put the tray down on top of the papers and proceeded to pour tea into mugs. McLean found an old armchair with only one occupant, who looked at him with feline hatred before slinking away to join some of its friends. He took his tea, and then sat down.

'So. You want to pick my brains.' Madame Rose settled into an armchair close by, not the chair on the other side of the desk where he had expected. 'About books? Or other matters.'

Faced with the question, McLean wasn't at all sure. Something had brought him here, though. He remembered a conversation he'd had with Jenny Nairn in the library back at his gran's house.

'Probably a bit of both. Book-wise, I was wondering if you'd be interested in cataloguing and valuing my grandmother's collection. I've no idea what's there, but I suspect some of it's valuable. I'd pay you for your time, of course.'

'I'd be happy to.' Madame Rose beamed a genuinely happy smile. 'As you may have guessed, there's not a lot of call for my other talents at the moment. Everybody knows the future's grim. They don't want to be told it. I'll come around tomorrow morning, if that's convenient?'

'I'll most likely be out.' McLean remembered his shout to DC MacBride about their eight o'clock briefing. 'Emma will be in, and Jenny. They'll probably try and help.'

'Ah yes, Miss Nairn. She's a strange one. And Emma. How is poor Emma? Improved at all?'

McLean shook his head. 'That was the other thing I wanted to ask about. Do you know much about regression therapy?'

Madame Rose said nothing for a while, took a very un-ladylike gulp of tea and wiped the moisture from her lips with the back of her hand. Placed the mug on the side of the desk.

'Is that what you're trying now? To help Emma get her memories back?'

McLean admitted that it was. 'I'm not sure it's working though. We've only had a few sessions. Doctor Austin seems to think it's going well. Can't say I've seen much difference myself. Emma doesn't seem to respond to hypnosis.'

'Some people don't. And I'd be very surprised if Emma did, not in her current state.' Madame Rose leaned forward in her seat, lowering her voice as if there might be spies listening in. 'Hypnotic regression can be useful at times, Inspector, but there are dangers inherent in the therapy. You can go back too far, and if you're not careful, that's where your patient stays. Correct me if I'm incorrect, but isn't that Emma's problem already? She's already regressed to the little girl she was over twenty years ago? How is regressing her further going to help?'

'What about hypnotism itself? You know, to stop smoking, stuff like that? Does it really work?'

'That depends. There's a lot of charlatans out there peddling cheap cures, but if you've got to the point you're looking for a hypnotist to help you give up smoking, you probably want to quit anyway. It's a kind of placebo effect.'

'Always? What about those shows, you know, where they make people in the audience bark like a dog or stand on one leg?'

'You mean those shows where people pay to be entertained?' Madame Rose left the question hanging for a while, then added: 'But that's not what you're trying to ask really, is it, Inspector?'

'I don't know. It sounds silly saying it. But when Emma was being hypnotized, it was almost as if I was the one – what did you call it? Going under?'

'I never said hypnotism doesn't work, Inspector. Just that it doesn't work on everybody. And in the hands of someone who isn't well tuned to the spiritual plane, it can easily go wrong.'

'What do you mean?'

'When you're under hypnosis, you're suggestible. That's how it can seem like a good idea to bark like a dog or stand on one leg. You're open to outside influences, but not just those of the hypnotist. Any perturbation in the ether might influence you. It could be benign and give you a sense of euphoria unlike any you've experienced. Or it could be malign. Could take over your soul and drive you mad.'

Madame Rose's gravelly voice had descended almost to a whisper, and McLean found he had leaned in closer to hear what she was saying. 'But you don't have much belief in souls, do you, Inspector? Just like you don't believe in demons and magic. They don't fit in with your science, do they.'

McLean stared at the large medium for a moment, a strange idea forcing its way through the mess of thoughts clogging up his mind. 'What about suicide?'

'I'm sorry?'

'Could you hypnotize someone to commit suicide?'

'Hypnotize? No.'

'But you're saying there are ways you could persuade someone to, say, hang themselves?'

'Like I said, Inspector. There are forces out there beyond what we perceive as normal. You've encountered them before, even if you won't admit it. I've no doubt such demons could drive a person insane, and what is suicide if not the ultimate insanity?'

As her words sank in, more mumbo-jumbo and not quite the useful insight he'd been hoping for, Madame Rose slapped her overlarge hands on her thighs and pushed herself back into the chair. Startled, McLean looked at his watch. Where had the time gone?

'I'm sorry, I need to get cracking. It's Jenny's night off tonight.'

'Then you'd better not keep her waiting.' Madame Rose stood, and McLean reflexively followed her cue. 'But think about what I've said, Inspector. And what I told you before. There are forces beyond your understanding. You've seen them in action, dealt with them in your own haphazard way.'

'There's a rational explanation for everything, however bizarre.' Even as he said it, McLean knew he didn't really believe it.

'Sometimes the rational is irrational Inspector.' Madame Rose led him out of the room, back the way he had come in. 'You of all people should know that.'

45

She's happy for the first time she can remember. The drink's got something to do with that; more wine than she's been able to afford in far too long. But there's something else, too. A fuzziness that has nothing to do with alcohol. As if something had been weighing on her mind for months, possibly years, never quite resolved. Then this evening she made a decision, and everything is fine.

What the decision was, she can't exactly recall. It's hard to think about anything but what she's doing now. Not the job with its endless weirdness. Not her studies that seem to be going nowhere. Not even the crazy infatuation she's developed with her new boss. She's not falling in love with him, of course. That would be silly. He's far older than her, for starters. And taken, as all the best ones are. But he's fascinating, complex and completely unaware of the maelstrom whirling around him.

Of course, Ellie wasn't happy when she told her, but then Ellie's always been the possessive type. Ellie really doesn't like to share. They might even have had a little argument about that, but nothing serious. And now she's heading home across the city. Walking, the way she likes to.

It's dark, as much as the city ever gets dark. This late there's not so many cars about, and hardly any people. Some fear the city at night, but not her. This is her place.

And anyway, she's made her decision; she's not afraid of anything now.

Not even the beast that roars at her from the top of the hill. Its eyes glow with malevolent fire and she can see within it the writhing forms of the people it has already consumed. They scream in agony, lost souls damnation-bound. Unless she can slay the beast, cut open its guts and set them free.

There is no moment's hesitation. She is in the now and this situation demands action. Fearless, decided, she steps into the path of the onrushing monster.

46

The tinny electronic beep of his phone on its charging stand told him that it was time to get up, but McLean had been awake for a while. Beside him, Emma slept the sleep of a small child, curled up almost foetally, and wearing her heavy fleece pyjamas with the cow print on them. She had a knack for taking up the whole bed, and stealing all the bedclothes. He could ask her not to climb in with him in the wee small hours, but there were times he'd lain awake and listened to her frightened whimpers. Sleep was not a place of solace for her, no escape from whatever monsters plagued her there.

Wearily, he hauled himself out of bed, padded through to the bathroom and began the morning ritual. He'd been mulling over his odd meeting with Madame Rose since about five, the patterns on the ceiling having lost their interest. She, he, whatever, was right about one thing at least. There were times he really did find it difficult to come up with a rational explanation for the evil things that people did. But evil was an adjective, not a noun. And when it came down to it, people did evil things for their own selfish or mad reasons, not because demons were making them do it, or had stolen their souls or whatever else was a simple way of fooling yourself that anything made any sense at all.

Happy thoughts for a grey morning. He wiped condensation off the mirror, then rubbed at his face. Noticed for the first time the dark, saggy folds under his eyes. The stubble on his chin showed flecks of grey, otherwise he might have considered growing a beard. Except that he hated beards.

Shaking his head once more in an attempt to rid himself of his black mood, McLean doused his face in lukewarm water and set about the process of shaving.

Emma was still fast asleep in his bed when he stepped out onto the landing. The mornings were getting darker, and he almost tripped over Mrs McCutcheon's cat, which had settled itself down right in front of the door.

'Guard duty, is it?' he asked and received a withering stare in return. The house was silent, which was unusual. Normally Jenny was up even before he was. Percolator on the stove top and the cereal boxes laid out in the middle of the kitchen table. It reminded him bizarrely of school, although they'd never had percolator coffee there, and cereal had been in huge catering boxes.

But this morning the table was clear, no coffee filling the kitchen with heavenly smells.

He wasn't particularly worried. It had been her night off, after all. She'd probably met up with some friends in a pub somewhere and drunk more than she'd intended. He knew how it worked, had been there plenty of times himself. A quick glance up at the kitchen clock showed he had more than enough time to get his own breakfast, especially with his shiny new car sitting out there on the driveway. Well, new to him anyway, and barely run in. He worried that it might be a little too conspicuous, but it was an Alfa Romeo and it was a GT. That was the closest he was going to get to his dad's old car until it had been fixed. If it could be fixed.

Kettle boiled, McLean made himself instant coffee, then searched through the cupboards for the cereal. There was still no sign of Jenny by the time he'd finished and was putting the bowl in the dishwasher. He was about to go and knock on her door when he heard a noise from the hall.

'Rough night, was it?' he asked before she came in. Except that it wasn't Jenny; it was Emma, still wearing her cow print pyjamas.

'Oh. I thought you were Jenny.'

'She's gone. Not coming back,' Emma said.

'What do you mean, gone?'

'Gone. Left for ever.' Emma's shoulders slumped.

'But she didn't say anything last night. Did she speak to you before?' A flash of anger flared up inside him at the thought Jenny had walked out on the job and left him stranded.

'No. She didn't want to leave. She liked it here. With all the others. She liked you too. A lot. Said you were interesting. But she had to go.' Emma dropped into one of the kitchen chairs, pulled McLean's coffee mug towards her and peered inside. It was still half full, so she drank it. She looked like a little girl trying hard to be brave and not let the tears come.

'When did you speak to her? When did she tell you this?'

'Last night. When all the people came. She was with them.'

McLean stared at the woman sitting in his kitchen. A couple of months of loafing around and eating well had rounded out the skeletal angles from her face, but she was still thin. Her hair was beginning to regain some of its lustre, but there were streaks of grey in it now and it fell down below her shoulders. Lines crinkled around the edges of her eyes as she stared back at him, a curious, questioning frown on her face. She'd been through so much that she had quite literally lost her mind. And it was all his fault.

It occurred to him that he'd not really talked to her for weeks, possibly months. He came home of an evening and maybe had a chat, but it was inconsequential stuff, like talking to a child. More often than not she'd gone to her own room before he got in anyway, their only encounters the wordless ones when she climbed into his bed in the small hours, shivering with fear. He'd fallen into a pattern of treating her like the little girl she appeared to be, leaving the care and companionship to Jenny. It had been a wonderful house of cards, for a while. But now the simplest thing had brought it tumbling down.

'What people were these? When did they come.'

'They always come when it's quiet. Sometimes in the day, up in the attic, the nice ones come and talk to me. But late at night when it's dark, that's when the monsters come. Last night Jenny was with them. She said goodbye. Said she was sorry. Said her mum made her do it.'

He put a call in to the station as he climbed the stairs up to the attic. The phone rang longer than he would have liked before being picked up. No doubt Sergeant Dundas had been busy with his morning doughnut and didn't want to be disturbed.

'You lost another one?' was the sergeant's incredulous reply when McLean explained the situation.

'It's not a joke, Pete. Just a query. Have we got any reports of accidents involving young females in the last twenty-four hours? Hospital admissions. Something serious enough to keep her in overnight.'

A moment's furious one-finger tapping at a keyboard, and then: 'nothing on the screen, sir, but it's been acting up for days now. You want me to put a call out?'

McLean had reached the door to Jenny's room, tapped on it lightly with his free hand. It wasn't serious. Not like when Emma had gone missing. 'No, you're all right, Pete. I'll do it myself when I get in. Might be a bit late till I can find some cover to look after Em. Can you let Bob know?'

'What am I, your private messaging service?' Dundas laughed, said he'd pass it on, then hung up. There had been no response from Jenny's room, so McLean opened the door and stepped inside.

He wasn't sure what he'd been expecting. Jenny Nairn could most simply be described as alternative, so he wouldn't have been surprised if the place looked a little like a protest camp, only with better plumbing. What he found was a room almost identical to the one he remembered as a child. The narrow bed was neatly made, had obviously not been slept in recently. Over by the window, an antique dressing table had been pressed into service as a desk, and Jenny's laptop sat open on it, pad and pen lying beside. A stack of books beside the chair was the only thing in the room that was remotely haphazard. Everything else was neat, dust-free, organized.

But Jenny was nowhere to be seen.

Movement at the door was Emma, peering in but not daring to cross the threshold. 'She's not here.'

'She left her stuff. She'll be back.' McLean pointed at the laptop, noticing as he did so a small leather suitcase under the bed.

'No, she won't. She's gone. Like the others.'

'What others?' McLean hunkered down, his knees popping in protest, and pulled out the case. It was really none of his business, but on the other hand if she was in trouble . . .

'The people, Tony. You saw them. In the photographs.'

McLean had placed the case on the bed, ready to pop open the two old brass catches, but Emma's words distracted him. He turned around, still squatting down, still holding the case, and looked up at her as he opened the lid.

'What photographs?' he asked, but he knew all too well. She looked past him, eyes widening in surprise and let out a little 'Oh.'

McLean looked back around to what was in the case. A woman's wig was scrunched into one corner, grey-brown hair in elegant waves. But it wasn't that which had caught Emma's attention. He reached in with trembling fingers, aware even as he did so that he shouldn't have been touching it, and pulled out a long loop of good, stout, hemp rope.

'I'm OK, really. I can look after myself. Not a little girl, you know.'

McLean glanced at his watch as they walked back down the stairs, leaving Jenny's room and the troubling suitcase behind. It was almost eight o'clock and he should really have been at work by now. He didn't dare leave Emma here on her own, though. Her petulant words only confirmed that. But for the life of him he couldn't think who to call in to babysit.

Babysit. The word stopped him in his tracks, halfway down the stairs and looking out over the hall. When had he started thinking about her like that? She wasn't a baby, she was a thirty-two-year-old-woman. He was under no obligation to look after her if she didn't want him to. No doctor had sectioned her. But what if she wandered off again, stepped out in front of a bus or something? He'd lost Kirsty and that had been too much. Damned if he was going to lose Emma too.

The sound of the doorbell ringing brought him back to himself. Emma was already at the bottom of the stairs and hurried across to answer it. By the time he reached the ground floor, she had let their visitor in. Madame Rose stood in the lobby, rain dripping from her ankle-length coat and the brim of a wide felt hat.

'Ah, Inspector. You're still here, I see. And the delightful Miss Baird.'

'The books are all in here, obviously. You know where the kitchen is. Please, help yourself to anything you want.' McLean stood in the middle of the library as Madame Rose walked slowly around the bookcases. The medium seemed far more absorbed in scanning the books than listening to anything he had to say. Occasionally she would stop, reach up, make a little clicking noise, or a tut. Possibly touch a leather spine with one large, yet gentle finger, and then move on.

'I'll leave you the direct number for the station, as well as my mobile. Should be home by five. You sure you're OK with this?'

Something of his words must have finally got through. Madame Rose stopped her perambulation and looked around. 'What? Oh, Emma. No, of course not. Delighted I can be of help.'

'I'm sure Jenny'll be back before then anyway. She's probably passed out in some friend's front room.'

'Oh, I very much doubt that. Not unless someone spiked her drink, and it'd take a lot to get one past Jenny Nairn.'

'I didn't realize you knew her well.' McLean finished scribbling down the last of the contact numbers he could think of and ripped the page from the jotter on the desk.

'Know of her, Inspector. Miss Nairn has a reputation among the cognoscenti. But I'd hardly say I know her well.' Madame Rose took the proffered notepaper, then turned as if she'd sensed something in the air. 'And here's young Emma, and her familiar too.'

Emma stood in the doorway, Mrs McCutcheon's cat twining around her legs. She'd changed out of her thick pyjamas with the cow print and was wearing what McLean would consider going-out clothes. Faded jeans, long black boots and what he'd always thought of as a sweat-top, but which was now universally known as a hoodie. It was one of his, he noted. Not that he minded. He couldn't remember the last time he'd seen Emma wearing anything other than slouching clothes.

'You sure you're OK with this?' he asked, aware that he'd done so already.

'Shouldn't you be at work, Inspector?' Madame Rose fixed him with a gaze not unlike the one his old school matron had used to such good effect. 'Go. We'll be fine. There's enough here to keep me busy for days. Emma can be my secretary and note-taker.'

47

'Exactly what part of "no active investigation" do you not understand, McLean. You're meant to be on administrative duties only. Not swanning off all over the fucking city.'

Later than he'd have liked, and not the person he really needed to be dealing with right now. McLean stood in the all-too-familiar position on the wrong side of the desk in Acting Superintendent Duguid's office. Downstairs in the CID room, Grumpy Bob and DS Ritchie were hopefully putting some sense of order into the chaos that was the suicides investigation, aided by DC MacBride and most likely hindered by PC Gregg. Ideally he would have liked to have been down there with them, directing proceedings and trying to get his head round all the conflicting facts. Instead he'd not been in the station more than thirty seconds before a terrified young constable had passed on the message that Duguid wanted to see him. McLean had long since given up being surprised at how news of his every movement seemed to spread around the station.

'I was putting together the final report for the three hangings, sir. It turns out that we'd misidentified one of the victims. I thought it important to verify the facts myself. Didn't want to end up compounding an already embarrassing error.'

'Christ almighty. Can you not do anything right?' Duguid

slumped back into his seat, ran a hand through his straggly, greying hair. 'Misidentified how, exactly?'

There wasn't an easy way to tell the tale. Not without making all of them look like a bunch of schoolboys playing at being detectives. He'd barely opened his mouth to speak when there was a knock at the door, which then clicked open before Duguid could make any reply. McLean looked around, expecting to see the sergeant who had been manning the secretaries' desk just outside. Instead he saw the worried face of Grumpy Bob.

'What the bloody hell? Detective Sergeant Laird I'm in a meeting. How dare you just barge in.' Duguid's bluster might have worked on the younger officers, but Grumpy Bob had thicker skin. And less to lose.

'Sorry to disturb you, sir. But I thought this was important.'

'What could possibly be so important it couldn't wait ten minutes, man?'

'Seems there's been another hanging, sir. Same scenario as the three we were already investigating.'

'You . . . What?'

'Mikhailevic?' McLean and Duguid spoke at the same time.

'Not unless he's had a sex change. This one's a woman.'

'Where?' McLean asked.

'Gilmerton, sir.'

A woman. Gilmerton. A chill sensation settled in the pit of McLean's gut. Jenny Nairn's flat was in Gilmerton, wasn't it? He shook his head to dispel the thought. Many thousands of people lived in that area.

'We got a name? Who called it in?'

'No name yet. Big Andy was First Attending.' Grumpy Bob looked at Duguid as he spoke. 'Knew we were look-ing into the other hangings and called it in straight away.'

McLean turned to Duguid, who had gone very quiet.

'It might be nothing, sir. Just a coincidence. I'd like to have a look though, just to be sure.'

Duguid's scowl deepened, then disappeared, replaced by an evil grin.

'Doesn't really matter what I say, does it, McLean? You'll go anyway. Just don't come crying to me when Rab Callard hears about it, eh?'

Once a quiet little mining village to the south of the city, Gilmerton had long since been swallowed up in the expan-sion of Edinburgh. McLean took his new car; it was quicker than any of the alternatives. Grumpy Bob hunched himself uncomfortably in the passenger seat, complaining that it was too low to the ground for a man of his advanced years to get into.

'Leather's a bit posh too, isn't it?' He squirmed around like a child who's wet his pants. Well, at least it would dis-pel the lingering aroma of Magic Tree air freshener.

'I don't know what the problem is, Bob. You're the one's been telling me to get a proper car for years. This one's only a couple of years old. One careful lady owner.'

'Aye and three hooligans who did their best to wrap it round a lamp post, I've no doubt. Goes some, I bet.'

McLean blipped the accelerator and the car shot for-ward quicker than he had expected, accompanied by a very unsubtle V6 roar. He dabbed the brakes before any-one noticed he was exceeding the speed limit, felt the grin he was suppressing as a tightening around his eyes. Then he remembered why they were driving across the city.

'It's just a car, Bob. Four wheels and an engine. Only got it at all because someone thought it'd be funny to phone the local Bentley salesman pretending to be me.'

'Heard about that. Bloody idiots the lot of them. Down here, isn't it?' Grumpy Bob pointed to a side street off the Old Dalkeith Road, lined on either side with 1970s semi-detached houses. A couple more turns brought them to a cul-de-sac currently choked up with squad cars. McLean parked a decent distance away, all too aware of how clumsy even trained police drivers could be in a tight space.

A uniformed constable was rolling out blue and white tape as he and Grumpy Bob approached.

'Over there. fourteen A,' he said as McLean showed his warrant card. He didn't really need direction; there was only one house with its door open and police hanging around like lazy flies. In amongst the cars, McLean noticed Doctor Buckley's green-and-road-grime Volkswagen Golf, so whoever was in charge had at least thought to call the duty doctor. With any luck they'd have summoned the pathologist, too.

Fourteen A was an upper flat, made by splitting the already narrow hallway of number fourteen lengthways. There was barely enough room for one person to walk along the short corridor to the stairs. It never ceased to amaze McLean the ingenuity people found in creating smaller and smaller spaces to live in. Whoever had lived here must have been tiny, though the looming figure coming down the stairs made everything around him seem Lilliputian anyway.

'You're here, sir. Good.' Big Andy Houseman was a dependable sergeant, and no doubt the reason the duty doctor was already here.

'I wondered who was in charge when I saw signs of competence outside. Didn't realize you'd relocated to the sticks.' McLean backed out of the doorway. There was no way he was going to be able to squeeze past Big Andy in the hall. Not without giving him the wrong idea, anyway.

'I like it out here, sir. It's quieter than the city. Well, usually.' The sergeant looked up at the single upstairs window. The curtains had been drawn.

'Have we got a name yet?' McLean asked. Jenny Nairn had been living in as she looked after Emma, but her address was somewhere around here, he was sure.

'Neighbour says she's a Caroline Sellars. Don't know much more about her than that. I've got some constables doing door-to-door round the close, but it seems to be one of those places where people don't talk much. Don't think she'd been here long, either.'

McLean let out a silent breath of relief at the name. 'I guess I'd better go and have a look then. Doctor Buckley still in there?'

'Oh yes, he's still there. Like a bloody kid in a sweetie shop.'

The narrow stairs led up to a narrow landing with just three doors off it. Bedroom, bathroom and living room, McLean guessed. Minimal living. One door was open, leading to the room at the front of the house, and low voices in conversation filtered out. He took the one step that was all he needed to get from the top of the stairs to the doorway and peered in.

She was hanging from the centre of the room, facing away from him towards the window. Like the three young men, she was naked and had gone to considerable lengths to hang herself. A small hatch in the ceiling opened up into the attic space, the stout hemp rope presumably tied to a cross-brace in the rafters above. The room was small; a much larger space that had been partitioned to form the bedroom at the back of the house. Its ceiling was high. More like the old Georgian tenements in the city centre than anything built in the seventies. Caroline Sellars had pulled a dining table across the room so that she would have had enough of a drop to snap her neck, put the noose over her head with the knot running past her left ear, and then stepped off. Her feet were just inches off the floor.

'Inspector McLean. What a pleasant surprise.'

Doctor Buckley greeted him from the other side of the deceased. It wasn't possible for him to hide behind the body, since he was enormously wide himself. McLean had been so distracted by the hanged woman that he'd missed the duty doctor anyway. Now he stepped further into the room, treading carefully so as not to disturb anything.

'It's all right, Doctor. I'm not going to ask you to give me a time of death.'

Doctor Buckley grinned. 'You're learning, then. I can tell you that she is dead, and I can hazard a cause, too. Wouldn't want to trespass on Angus's territory though.'

'Snapped vertebrae?'

'Something like that.'

McLean stepped fully into the room, looking around at a tidy, tiny living space. One wall was given over to kitchen units, with a narrow breakfast bar breaking it off from the rest of the room. The table had been pulled over from a small dining area over in the far corner, if the two chairs facing each other across an empty space were anything to go by. To the other side of the body, a bay window held a small sofa, an old armchair beside it facing towards a gas fire and telly. There were pictures on the wall, some framed photographs of smiling people, a couple of cheap prints of old masters. White IKEA bookcases held a selection of romance paperbacks and dust collectors. All so very normal. Nothing much to suggest a suicidal temperament.

'Was there a note?' McLean directed his question at the uniform constable who had obviously drawn the short straw and been told to watch the body in case it went anywhere. The young lad started, as if he hadn't noticed McLean come in and talk to the duty doctor.

'I . . . I don't know, sir. Haven't touched anything.'

McLean swept his gaze over the room a second time. A note would most likely have been left in a prominent place. On the table, perhaps, or the breakfast bar. There didn't appear to be anything obvious. SEB would probably turn something up.

'Well, I'll get out of your way. I'm sure Angus will be here soon.' Doctor Buckley negotiated his way around the body with surprising nimbleness for someone as large as he was. McLean had images of him getting stuck going down the stairs, having to call out the fire brigade. Dismissed them with a shake of his head. He moved into the space the doctor had vacated and finally got a look at the face of the deceased.

She was young, Caroline Sellars. That much he'd been able to tell from behind. Her shoulder-length hair was glossy black and straight. It partially obscured her face, and the swelling and discolouration caused by the rope further altered her appearance, but there was no mistaking the fact that he had met her before.

48

McLean parked his car in front of Fulcholme College, aware that he had been seeing rather more of the place lately than he'd anticipated. Professor Bain stood in the entranceway waiting for him, half walked, half jogged up as he clambered out of his car.

'I got your message, inspector.' The professor wrung his hands together like nervous, restless snakes. He looked pale in the daylight, as if it weren't his natural habitat. His thin hair glistened at his temples, the strands that protruded from his ears quivering slightly. Since the first time they had met, just a few weeks ago, he seemed to have aged years. Having your students all committing suicide might do that.

'Can we speak inside?' McLean pointed towards the hall and the professor's office beyond. Behind him, Grumpy Bob was looking up at the building, hands in pockets.

'Yes, of course. Please.' Professor Bain led him through a crowd of students streaming out of a lecture and into the relative calm of Room 1. McLean closed the door so that it was just the two of them.

'Caroline Sellars. Tell me about her.'

Professor Bain's shoulders slumped and he collapsed down onto a nearby armchair like a deflating balloon. 'She really hanged herself?'

McLean nodded. Said nothing more. The silence hung heavy for a while before Professor Bain spoke again.

'I can't believe she'd kill herself. She was always so full of life. So bubbly, you know?'

'When did you last see her?'

The professor scratched at his bald pate. 'Yesterday afternoon, I think. She was definitely here on Tuesday. We had a tutorial group. Discussing Keynesian Economic Theory and its application in the current climate.'

'She any good at that stuff?'

Professor Bain shrugged. 'She was good enough. Not bright like Grigori, but she put in the effort, you know. Economics was always her second subject though. She was much more interested in parapsychology.'

'Parapsychology?' McLean emphasized the first two syllables. 'You teach that here?'

'Well, not teach, exactly. It's more of an informal research group. Eleanor runs it in her spare time. Very popular with the students. They come up with all manner of odd experiments.'

'Eleanor.' McLean recalled an earlier conversation with the professor, lost in the rush of everything else that was going on. 'Doctor Austin?'

'That's her. She teaches here part-time.'

'And she runs informal groups?'

The professor nodded, a worried look creeping over his face as his mind made the same connections McLean's had made.

'Was Mikhailevic involved in any of these groups? Duncan George too?'

'I really don't know, Inspector. Shouldn't be too hard to find out.' Professor Bain pulled himself wearily to his feet, headed towards his desk. 'You don't think they . . . ? Some sort of suicide pact?'

'Pact, yes. It's the suicide part I'm not so sure about.'

Grumpy Bob was chatting with a couple of students young enough to have been his daughters when McLean came out of Professor Bain's office. He couldn't tell what the sergeant was saying, but he obviously had their rapt attention.

'Come on, Bob, there's work to do,' he said as he walked past. By the time he'd got to his car, Grumpy Bob had extricated himself and caught up.

'Hot date?' McLean asked.

'Too high maintenance for my tastes.' Grumpy Bob grinned, heading for the passenger door.

'You drive. I've got to make some calls.' McLean pulled out the keys and threw them over. Grumpy Bob caught them with both hands, then looked down at the shiny, sleek shape of the car.

'You sure, sir? I mean, you've only just got it. Wouldn't want to be the first to put a dent in it.'

'It's just a car, Bob. You've driven them before.'

'Aye, but . . .' Grumpy Bob continued to mutter, but did as he was told. McLean climbed into the passenger seat and waited patiently as the sergeant familiarized himself with the layout.

'You get anything useful from the students?'

'A bit. Maybe. Seems the college isn't the picture of love and happiness yon professor chappy would like you to believe. Financial troubles, poor results. There's even talk of some scam selling qualifications so students can get visas. They don't do any studies. Find work, mostly. After a year or two they get a meaningless qualification and permanent residence.'

'What about our suicides?'

'The lot I talked to didn't seem to know much about them. A couple knew Mikhailevic. Thought he might have been in a study group with Duncan George and your Caroline Sellars back there.'

'Let me guess. Parapsychology experiments with Doctor Eleanor Austin.'

Grumpy Bob leaned forwards and started the engine, peered down at the gear stick until he could find reverse. 'See, that's what I'm on about all the time, sir. You send me off on an errand and then get the answer for yourself. Sometimes wonder why you need me about at all. Jesus, you can't see much out of the back of this thing.'

'You'll be fine. It beeps at you if you get too close to anything. Like that.' McLean tried not to tense as an electronic squawking erupted from the dashboard. He pulled out his phone and started tapping at the screen, looking for the name he wanted. Unbidden, it appeared, and it took him a while to realize that it was an incoming call from Doctor Austin herself. The call didn't take long; Grumpy Bob had barely manoeuvred the car to the exit by the time he'd hung up.

'Back to the station, sir?'

'No. Western General. Fast as you like.' He knew now why Jenny Nairn hadn't come home.

49

'They're saying she stepped out in front of a bus.'

It wasn't quite how he'd anticipated his next meeting with Doctor Austin. She'd been waiting at the front reception desk when McLean came in, obviously distraught.

'When did it happen? How is she?'

'Last night. Late, I think. After midnight. She's in the ICU.'

McLean allowed himself to be led in silence through the hospital. That Doctor Austin hadn't answered his second question directly didn't bode well for Jenny's condition.

The all-too-familiar route brought them swiftly to the intensive care unit. A uniform sergeant sat on an uncomfortable plastic chair outside the room where Magda Evans was recovering. He put down his book and stood up as McLean came towards him along the corridor. It was obvious both that he'd been warned not to let the detective inspector anywhere near her, and that he wasn't quite sure how he was going to reprimand a senior officer. McLean put him at ease with a wave.

'It's OK. I'm here for something else.'

'Right you are, sir.' The sergeant nodded and sat back down to his book. Doctor Austin raised an eyebrow.

'One of yours?' she asked.

'Long story. Not important. Tell me about Jenny.'

Doctor Austin started walking down the corridor again.

'She came to see me yesterday evening. We did what we usually do, had a bite to eat, shared a bottle of wine and talked until far too late. She wasn't drunk or anything. Perhaps a bit distracted by her studies. And looking after Emma is hard, as I'm sure you know. She left about half twelve, said she was going to walk to the city centre and then get a cab. I'd have called one for her, but she loved to walk. Especially at night.'

They had reached the main ward of the intensive care unit. Doctor Austin stopped short of the bed where Jenny lay, surrounded by expensive machinery. McLean had seen far too many people in a similar situation for it to be truly shocking any more, but it never ceased to amaze him how small and fragile people were. It was almost impossible to see Jenny in the bed.

Doctor Wheeler was studying the readout on a screen as they approached, and turned when she heard them. It was nice to see a familiar face, but McLean knew all too well what her presence meant. Cranial trauma was her speciality. Brain damage. She looked him straight in the eye and gave the tiniest shakes of the head.

'What's the prognosis?' McLean asked.

'Not good, I'm afraid. There's too much damage to her brain. She'll never wake up. It's a miracle she survived at all, or whatever the evil equivalent of a miracle is. I guess it gives us time to inform her family. Otherwise it's just the machines keeping her body going.'

An involuntary shudder ran through McLean's back as he remembered Emma's words that morning. How convinced she was that Jenny had gone.

'She has no family. Just me.' Doctor Austin's stance was

of someone getting ready for a fight, but Doctor Wheeler just shook her head and turned her attention back to the machines surrounding the bed.

'Jenny's related to you?' McLean asked.

'Not by birth, no. But she was my protégée. She always came to me when she needed something. We were friends.'

'And she has no immediate family?'

'None.' Doctor Austin shook her head. 'Her mum died when she was sixteen. She never knew her father, but she was old enough to be an adult, as far as the law was concerned. Too young to really know what she was doing. She . . .' Doctor Austin paused as if searching for the right words. 'Came to my attention then and I took her under my wing.'

McLean let out a deep sigh. It was never easy. Sooner or later the grief would hit him, too. He was still processing that. He'd not known Jenny long, but she'd lived under his roof for a few months, cooked breakfast for him, looked after Emma. Dammit, he'd liked her, despite her strangeness.

'You said she was your protégée.' Dr Austin's earlier words finally registered. 'You taught her? At Fulcholme?'

Doctor Austin gave a little involuntary start. 'Heavens, no. Not there. I occasionally lecture at the university. Jenny was studying for a PhD. When she could afford to. Grants in her field of study are few and far between. Hence the need to take on work.'

Months and he hadn't known. Had never really bothered to find out. She'd come as a godsend, but how quickly he'd taken her for granted. How easy it was to pay to make the problems go away. Only they never really did, just hid in the shadows and multiplied.

'But you do lecture at Fulcholme still? And run research projects there?'

Again that little start, as if the question were a surprise. 'Yes, I still lecture there. You take the work where you can find it. Might I ask why you're interested?' Doctor Austin's gaze darted away from McLean to Doctor Wheeler, who had her back to them and was most likely not listening anyway.

'It's an ongoing investigation. A couple of your students have ... Well, it's not really the time or the place now.' McLean shoved a hand in his pocket, dug out one of his cards and handed it over. 'Perhaps you could come to the station tomorrow?'

McLean left Doctor Austin and Doctor Wheeler to their silent vigil over the near-departed, went off in search of a nurse instead. You could ask doctors all the questions in the world, but if you wanted to know what was really going on, a nurse was a much better bet.

He found the one he was looking for quickly enough. Jeanie Robertson had looked after his gran in the months before her death, and she was still a part of the ICU team.

'Jenny Nairn? Yes, it's terrible. So young.' Her soft Western Isles accent only added to the feeling that Jenny was dead already.

'Do you know who brought her in? Who saw her first?'

'Well, she was taken to A and E, obviously. But the doctors there moved her up to us as soon as they'd stabilized her. To be honest, it would've been kinder if she'd not made it.'

The second person to make that observation. McLean

could hardly blame them. If there was no chance of recovery, then Jenny Nairn's body was blocking up a bed in intensive care. If there was a slight chance she might start breathing unaided, she was still going to be in a persistent vegetative state for the rest of her life. All that was left was a husk. She'd gone. Just like Emma had said.

'Do you know what happened to her clothes when she came in? Anything else she had with her?'

'They'll be in a locker somewhere. Did you want to see them?'

McLean's head told him no. If there was an investigation into the circumstances of the accident, then he wouldn't be allowed to conduct it. Not given his relationship with Jenny. But there was the small matter of the suitcase in her room. He'd hardly had time to think about that, but the wig, grey like the lady seen with Grigori Mikhailevic; the rope, identical to that used to hang four people. Or by four people to hang themselves, with a little help. He had a hard time squaring that with the young woman who had shared his house these past months, but if she was somehow linked, he needed as much information as he could get before the shit hit the fan.

'I wouldn't mind a wee look at them, if that was OK.'

He followed the nurse down a series of corridors, ending up in a locked backroom filled with all manner of things that had nowhere else to go. Jenny's few personal possessions were in a cardboard box. It didn't amount to much. The clothes she'd been wearing were torn and blood-stained; her phone had been crushed. Only her leather satchel with its collection of textbooks had survived largely unscathed, along with a bunch of keys that would let her into his house and, presumably, her own place in Gilmerton. McLean didn't know the exact address.

'You wanting to take these away?' He was holding the key-ring when the nurse spoke, the impatience barely hidden in her voice. Fair enough, she was busy and he was taking monstrous liberties.

'No. I'll have a constable fetch them once we've opened the investigation. Probably safer here for now.' He closed the lid on the box and slid it back onto the shelf. They'd be questioning the driver and any other witnesses, of course. But there would only be a full investigation if Jenny died. The look on the nurse's face confirmed what he feared, that it would be when rather than if.

McLean thanked the nurse, left her locking up the room. He thought about going back to the ICU for an update on Jenny's condition, but he knew it would be a wasted trip. Emma had told him Jenny was gone. He couldn't begin to understand how she had known, but she was right. Gone and left him with a whole heap of trouble to sort out.

It wasn't until he was halfway to the hospital car park that he realized he still had the key-ring clasped in his fist.

First officer on the scene of the accident had been a Constable Orton. He operated out of a different station, and his shift wasn't due to start for another couple of hours, but he had logged the incident, so McLean was able to piece together something of what had happened.

Jenny had been walking back to the city centre, that much chimed with everything Doctor Austin had told him. The accident had happened on Broughton Street, near the top of the hill. The night-bus driver had been in shock when Constable Orton had spoken to him, and claimed that Jenny had simply stepped off the pavement without warning. She hadn't been wearing headphones like so many others of her generation. Nor was it a particularly dangerous stretch of road. The bus had only been doing twenty, maybe twenty-five miles an hour. But it was a bus.

Paramedics had arrived at the scene within five minutes of it being called in. Constable Orton, aided by a couple more officers who had also arrived by that time, took details from everyone on the bus. Only four people as it turned out, none of whom had seen anything. There didn't seem to have been any witnesses on the street at the time. The bus company had sent out a replacement vehicle and taken the one that had hit Jenny back to the depot, where it would sit in a garage until the police were done with their enquiries. All very simple, all by the book. A tragic accident indeed. But still there was that niggling doubt he found hard to ignore. A grey-brown wig and a length of hemp rope, too.

Closing down his computer, McLean went off in search of the one person he'd really rather avoid.

'Let me get this straight. You want me to ask DI Spence to conduct an investigation into an incident where there's no evidence of foul play? Why can't you look into it yourself? In your own time.'

Acting Superintendent Duguid sat back in his leather office chair, swivelling gently from side to side as he spoke. The desk between him and McLean was spotlessly clean, devoid of all paperwork save a copy of that morning's *Scotsman*.

'Miss Nairn was working for me, sir. As I think I told you already. I can't investigate her . . .' He was about to say death, but managed to stop himself.

'You can't investigate anything, McLean. Not until Rab Callard gives you the OK. Far as I can tell, there's nothing to investigate anyway. Your employee walked in front of a bus. Funny how these things happen to people around you.'

Christ, but the man was irritating. McLean swung his hands behind his back and clasped them together as tightly as he could. It didn't really help, other than to stop him from hitting something.

'I hardly think that's an appropriate comment, sir. She was my employee and my friend, and she had her whole life ahead of her. I owe it to her to find out what happened.'

'You owe it to her.' Duguid sat forward, planted his elbows on the desk, pointed a long, thin finger. 'You, McLean. Not Lothian and Borders Police. Not beyond what we've already done.'

The bare minimum. Probably not even that. It was like dealing with a child, and they'd put him in charge.

'Jenny Nairn's in a coma and she's not going to wake up. She's going to die, sir. Maybe tomorrow, maybe in a month. And when that happens the Procurator Fiscal will want a report. Unnatural death. That's how it works. Don't you think it would be a good idea if we've actually looked into the circumstances? Maybe while the incident's still fresh in everyone's minds?'

Duguid stared at him with piggy eyes, his brow furrowing as he considered McLean's words. It made sense, that was the problem. Duguid knew it, and hated that McLean was right.

'Dammit, man, we don't have the budget to go investigating every incident in the city.'

So it was the money, as always.

'At least have someone speak to the driver, sir. He was in shock when Constable Orton saw him. He'll be able to give us a fuller picture of what happened. It shouldn't take more than an hour. I'd ask DC MacBride, but I can't head this up. Not on paper at least.' He left it there, hanging, in the hope that Duguid would take the bait.

'You're a menace, you know that, McLean?' The acting superintendent pushed his chair back from the desk and stood up, obviously finding it hard to make a decision whilst sat on his arse. 'Very well. Have MacBride interview the driver, draw up a report and submit it to me directly. You are not, repeat not, to sit in on that interview. Understood?'

'Thank you, sir. Yes.' McLean nodded his appreciation at the same time as it occurred to him it might be worthwhile seeing if there was any CCTV coverage. For a moment, he even considered asking before he realized what a stupid idea that was.

'Thank you,' he said once more, and fled from the room.

It was far later than five when McLean finally drove through the gates and parked his new car outside the house. Lights shone from the kitchen window and lit up the lawn around the back, which suggested that someone was home. There had been no calls on his mobile either, so he had to hope everything was all right.

Except that he was going to have to explain to Emma that Jenny was near death and wouldn't be coming back.

Staring out through the windscreen, hands still resting on the leather steering wheel, he realized that Emma already knew. Emma had been the first to know. That was why she had crawled into his bed so early in the morning. That was what she had said when he'd found Jenny missing. He didn't want to know how Emma had known. He didn't want to think about the things Madame Rose had said either, and yet he'd gone to the transvestite medium for help. More than ever, he just wanted to close his eyes and sleep until it all went away. When had it all started getting so hard? So confusing? So overwhelming?

Taking a deep breath, he climbed out of the car and headed into the house.

Emma was sitting at the table as he entered the kitchen. As she saw him, a huge grin spread across her face and she leapt up, embraced him in a warm hug. It was a child's welcome, and somehow that just made him feel even more tired.

'We've been sorting out the books all day. I like Rose. She's funny.' Emma leaned close to his ear and whispered. 'And she's really a man.'

She let out a bark of laughter as if this was the funniest thing she'd ever come across. The noise brought the object of her mirth through to the kitchen. Madame Rose had a pair of horn-rimmed spectacles perched on the end of her nose. His nose. Whatever. The medium peered over them at McLean.

'You're back.'

McLean looked up at the clock on the kitchen wall. 'Sorry, it's a lot later than I realized. I found out what happened to Jenny.'

Madame Rose sank into one of the kitchen chairs as McLean told them the story. Emma fidgeted, as if she already knew it all. In the silence that fell after he'd finished, Mrs McCutcheon's cat came wandering in, leapt onto the table and walked across the middle until it could nuzzle at his hand with its nose.

'I'm so sorry,' Madame Rose said after a while. 'Is there any hope she might recover?'

McLean shook his head. 'I don't think so.'

'I told you she'd gone and wasn't coming back. She said she was sorry.' Emma reached out and stroked the cat's back, making it arch.

'I'll have to sort out all the stuff in her room. Not really sure who should have it, mind you.' McLean stifled a yawn, turning to Madame Rose. 'Can I give you a lift home?'

'I think a cab might be a better idea.'

'You sure?' McLean pulled out his phone and thumbed the screen, looking for the number of the nearest taxi firm. Emma announced out of nowhere that she was bored and was going to watch some telly, flounced out of the kitchen as if the news of Jenny's terrible fate meant nothing to her. Cab booked, McLean pulled out a chair and sat down, the weight of the day finally catching up with him.

'She's a strange one, your Miss Baird. I thought I knew what was wrong with her, but now I think I might have got it all wrong.'

'Oh yes?' McLean wasn't really listening. He could still

see Jenny Nairn's face wrapped in bandages and sunken into a pillow.

'I need to do a bit of research, but I'd like to try something that I think will help. I assume you'll be wanting me to come round again tomorrow?'

That got a bit more of his attention. 'Can you? I'm going to have to find another carer, but that'll take time. Em seems to like you.'

'I like her too. She's interesting. Anyway, we've barely made a dent on the library yet.'

'So what do you reckon you can do to help?' McLean rubbed at his eyes, hoping it might make them easier to keep open. 'Don't say hypnotism, because we've tried that. Electric shocks too.'

Madame Rose laughed. 'Nothing so spooky. I'd just like to take her to a particular place. See what happens.'

'What does Emma think about it.'

'What do I think about what?'

McLean looked up as Emma came back in and walked across the kitchen to the Aga. She put the kettle on before explaining. 'There's nothing on the telly. Thought I'd have a cup of tea.'

'I was telling the inspector about my theory. About the people you see. The ones who come and visit you in the night.'

'Jenny was with them last night.' Emma frowned, the first expression of sadness McLean had seen in her in a while. It didn't last long. 'Rose thinks he knows where the people come from.'

McLean looked at the medium, raised an eyebrow but said nothing.

'It's a theory, but if I'm right it might help.'

'And if you're wrong?'

'Then we'll have gone for a little walk outside. Nothing more.'

That surprised him. 'Outside?' he asked Emma. 'I thought you didn't like going out.'

Lights outside and the scrunching of tyres on gravel stopped Emma's reply. Madame Rose stood up. 'That'll be my cab. They always come quickly when they know it's me.'

50

'If you could just go over it one more time. In your own words.'

McLean stood in the observation booth looking through the one-way glass into interview room three. Detective Constable MacBride was conducting an interview with the driver of the bus that had hit Jenny Nairn. Robert Gurney didn't look anything special. Mid-forties, bald on top, chubbing up as so often happened to people who sat down for a living. He looked pale, like a man who'd not slept well. McLean could sympathize with that; he couldn't remember the last time he'd had an uninterrupted sleep. Even last night when Emma had been so positive, bubbly even after a day spent with Madame Rose, she had still crawled into his bed at half four, shivering and sobbing.

Shaking his head, he focused his attention back on the driver. MacBride was being very patient, giving the man space and time to gather his thoughts. Even PC Gregg, hovering by the door, was keeping her mouth shut. Well, there was a first time for everything.

'Been driving the late bus a couple months now.' Robert Gurney's voice was high-pitched for such a thick-set man. Not helped by the wavering tone. 'Usually that route. Sometimes south to Roslin and Penicuik. There's no' usually that many on the bus by Broughton Street. Tend to pick them up further down.'

'What about pedestrians? Many about at that time? It wasn't all that late, really.' MacBride spotted the digression and gently herded the driver back on course. Like a well-trained sheepdog.

'There's usually one or two spilling out the pubs then. Don't really remember, to be honest.' Gurney had been studying his hands, but now looked straight up at Mac-Bride. 'I saw her, though. She was walking up the hill at quite a pace, that bag slung over her shoulder. She had her eyes set straight ahead, not looking over to see when she could cross. You drive the buses long as I have, you get to read people, you know?' He shook his head. 'Least, I thought so. Till last night.'

Gurney fell silent, and MacBride let the quiet grow as he carefully took down some notes. The interview was being taped and filmed, but there was no reason not to be thorough. Only when he had finished did he speak again.

'I know this must be very difficult, reliving what happened. But if you could just take me through it, step by step. You say Miss Nairn was walking up the hill?'

First mistake. Behind the glass, McLean winced as he saw the driver stiffen. For all they knew he hadn't heard the name before. Speaking it only made it more personal.

'Is she . . . ? Did she . . . You know?'

'She's in intensive care. The doctors are doing everything they can for her. Don't worry about that, Mr Gurney.' MacBride's voice was soft, reassuring. 'You said you saw her walking up the hill. What happened next?'

Gurney's shoulders shook as he sobbed. 'It all happened so quickly. One moment she was coming towards me, not looking at the bus, not even close to the edge of the pavement, really. Then there was just this terrible bang. I never even saw her step off. By the time I'd slammed on the brakes it was too late.'

'Poor bastard. It'll be a while before he drives a bus again.' Grumpy Bob leaned against the one-way glass in the observation booth as PC Gregg led Robert Gurney away. MacBride disappeared from the interview room too, reappearing moments later through the door.

'Sorry about that, sir' were his first words.

'No need to apologize, Constable. That was fine.' McLean still stared through the glass, even though the interview room was empty. He wasn't really all that sure why he'd insisted on the interview now. It was obviously not Gurney's fault he'd hit Jenny; probably not Jenny's either. Sometimes shit just happened. A loose flagstone, discarded Coke can, mistimed step, anything. A lurch to the side, just the wrong moment and splat, you were under a bus. But he needed to know. To be sure. That was his problem, really. He couldn't leave it alone. Wasn't that what everyone always said?

'You know if there's any CCTV coverage of that area?' McLean turned to face MacBride.

'Sure you want to be digging around like that, sir?' Grumpy Bob asked.

'I'm fairly sure I'm not involved in this investigation at all. Certainly not here in this room. That not right, Constable?'

MacBride's eyes flicked between his two superior officers, a look of confusion on his face slowly fading as his brain caught up.

'It occurs to me that following on from that interview, I really should check whether there's any CCTV footage of the area. What do you think, Sergeant?'

Grumpy Bob let out a snort of laughter and slapped MacBride on the shoulder. 'You'll go far, lad. More's the pity.'

The interview room looked very different from the other side of the glass. It was half an hour later and McLean was sitting in the chair previously warmed by the backside of DC MacBride. Taking PC Gregg's part, though less likely to talk out of turn, DS Ritchie sat beside him. Across the small table, Doctor Eleanor Austin seemed calm and relaxed. She stared at him with those wide, grey eyes of hers, very occasionally taking a little break to look at Ritchie or gaze over the room. There was nobody in the observation booth, as far as McLean was aware. Somehow he got the feeling that Doctor Austin would have known if there were.

'You run a course on parapsychology at Fulcholme College. How long have you been doing that?'

'It's not really a course as such. More a module. You can't get a degree in parapsychology, despite what you might have seen on the television.'

'OK. So how long have you been running this module?'

'Four years this August. No, I tell a lie, five years. Time flies, doesn't it, Inspector?'

McLean ignored the question. 'Professor Bain tells me it's very popular.'

'David can be such a salesman. We get a lot of students sign up, that's true. But not many of them stay after the first couple of sessions. They all think it's going to be ghost hunting and mind reading, but the field of para-psychology is more about debunking the myths than anything else. Understanding the state of mind that makes people believe they've seen ghosts. Figuring out the many ways the human brain can be fooled.'

'What about hypnosis?'

'Hypnosis?' The question seemed to throw Doctor Austin for a while. 'Oh, I see. You're thinking about stage shows and the like. No, there's nothing paranormal about hypnosis. It's a well-researched tool and a useful therapy. As I think you're aware, Inspector.'

'But you teach it to your students.'

'Heavens no. I teach them about it, of course. As part of the general psychology course. I don't teach them how to do it. Wherever did you get that idea from?'

'Never mind, it's not important.' McLean shook his head, unsure how he'd strayed from the subject of the interview. 'You taught Caroline Sellars and Grigori Mikhailevic, I understand.'

Doctor Austin settled back, stared straight into his eyes. 'Not in the same class, but yes. I taught Carol and Grigori.'

'What about Duncan George?'

'Duncan was in Grigori's group. They were friends. I was very sad when he left. He had such potential, but he also had very deep problems. He needed therapy, which I would have been happy to give him.'

'Do the names John Fenton and Patrick Sands mean anything to you?'

Doctor Austin stiffened in her seat, and for a moment

McLean saw something like fear flit across her eyes. Then they seemed to widen, pupils dilating as if the lights had dimmed.

'Both of those names mean something to me. But I have to consider patient–doctor confidentiality.'

'You weren't aware that both of them were dead, then?' DS Ritchie asked the question, sparking a momentary flash of irritation in McLean. In Doctor Austin, too, if the look she gave the sergeant was anything to go by.

'Am I under suspicion here?' she asked. 'Should I have a lawyer present?'

'Not at all. We're simply trying to ascertain whether or not there is a connection between a number of recent suicides, Doctor Austin.' Ritchie appeared to be immune to the doctor's stare, much to McLean's amusement. And relief. Now that she was focusing on someone else, the tension he had not realized he was under began to ebb away.

'Well, if that's the case, then why didn't you just ask?'

'I rather thought I just had.' Ritchie tapped her notepad with her pen. She hadn't written anything down yet.

'John Fenton and Patrick Sands were both patients of yours,' McLean said.

'I didn't say that.' Doctor Austin paused, considering her words. 'But yes. They were.'

'How did they come to you?'

'Not "what were they seeing you for"?'

'I didn't think you'd answer that one. Not sure it's really all that important.'

'If you must know, they both came to me through our mutual friend.'

McLean raised a quizzical eyebrow. 'Who?'

'Who do you think? Jenny. She worked with Sands in that god-awful call centre. Nearly drove her mad. John she met in a bar, apparently. He's dead, you say?'

'Did they know each other? Fenton and Sands?'

Again a pause. Doctor Austin tried to fix her gaze on him again, but McLean avoided it. After a brief battle, she gave up.

'They met, certainly. Probably Carol, Grigori and Duncan, too.'

'All of them? Together? Where?' McLean leaned forward. Ritchie, he noticed, had started to write. Doctor Austin gave them a triumphant little smile.

'At Jenny's, of course.'

'She's lying.'

'Yes, but about what?'

McLean and Ritchie had retired to the canteen, Doctor Austin having the dubious honour of being given a lift home by PC Gregg. The coffee was especially bad that morning, but at least it was wet.

'I think she knew all of them. I think she brought them all together. Probably Jenny too. What I'd like to know is what they were doing.'

'What's the story there? I heard about the accident.'

McLean peered into the depths of his mug, saw the bottom clearly through inches of something that claimed to be coffee. 'She won't recover. If there's any fairness in the world, she'll die soon, quietly and painlessly. Mind you, if there was any justice in the world she'd never have stepped in front of that bus in the first place.'

The two of them sat in silence for a while after that,

which suited McLean fine. Only when she had forced down the last of her drink did Ritchie say anything.

'I'm sorry I jumped in a bit, back in the interview.'

'Did you?' McLean frowned as he tried to remember. There was a vague sense of irritation, but he couldn't quite put his finger on why he felt it. Nor could he really recall much in the way of detail from what Doctor Austin had told them.

'You were doing the silent thing. You know? Where you just sit there and stare until the other person feels they have to say something?' Ritchie made a half-hearted stab at it herself, pausing for all of two seconds before adding: 'Only you were leaving it way too long. Almost like you were falling asleep.'

McLean tried not to yawn at that, failed. He really was very tired. 'I didn't realize. Sorry.'

Ritchie suppressed a smirk. 'I was going to say everything all right at home. Bit bloody stupid, really. How's Emma?'

'Remarkably composed.' McLean glanced at his watch, almost two. He could grab some paperwork and take it home with him. Give Madame Rose a break and maybe make a start on finding another home help. 'Think I might go home though. Not as if we're getting anywhere here.'

Ritchie gave him an odd look, as if he'd just said something really stupid. 'You want me to follow up on Doctor Austin?'

McLean almost said: 'Who?' Shook his head to try and dislodge the weariness dragging at him. Maybe he was coming down with something.

'Might be an idea.'

'I'll work up a background on her. See if there's any history.'

A rare lucid thought popped into McLean's head. 'Have a chat with Doctor Wheeler at the hospital. They know each other of old, and aren't exactly the best of friends. Actually, I'll do it. I need to speak to her anyway about Em.'

'OK. You want me to arrange a briefing for tomorrow morning?'

'Good idea. Eight o'clock in the CID room.' McLean abandoned the last of his coffee, stood up to leave. The world dimmed, and he put out a surreptitious hand to steady himself until the blood came back to his head. Maybe he really was coming down with something. That was always a problem if you spent too much time in hospitals.

'On second thoughts, let's make it nine, eh?'

The further he drove from the station, the clearer McLean's head became. Perhaps it was an allergy thing and the pollen filter in the car was clearing the air for him. He'd never really suffered from anything like that before, though. And he was still dog tired; those cats still howling.

Afternoon traffic was relatively light, which made a nice change from commuter-time snarl-ups. Avoiding the city centre and the tram works helped, too. Soon he was parked up outside the house, engine off and just staring out at nothing. It was warm, quiet and peaceful. Comfortable, too, in the deep leather seat. He could just close his eyes and drift off for a moment.

McLean shook his head to clear the cobwebs. A thick wodge of folders sat on the passenger seat, demanding his attention. He could snooze later, perhaps with a dram. First there was work to do.

The first strange thing he noticed was that the back door was locked. He'd grown so used to there always being someone in, it took him a while to remember that he had a set of keys in his pocket. Inside, the kitchen was warm, but silent. Just the tick-tocking of the clock on the wall. He went through to the hall, looked in the library, then checked the front door. It, too, was locked.

'Emma? Madame Rose?' He felt a bit stupid saying the medium's name, but he had no idea what else to call her, him. The transvestism didn't bother him at all; it was not knowing how to treat him, her, whatever, that left him uneasy. Maybe that was the point.

Either way, there was no answer, which meant they must have gone out. Reflexively, McLean checked his phone. There were no messages and no missed calls. Just a couple of texts from Ritchie reminding him to talk to Doctor Wheeler ahead of the briefing. Her subtle way of reminding him about the briefing, no doubt. Had he really been that switched off this morning?

Back in the kitchen, McLean noticed a sheet of A4 paper lying in the middle of the table with an empty mug holding it down. Written in a neat hand that had to be Madame Rose's were the words: *Gone for a little walk outside. Back soon.* The note had been written at half past two, according to the time scribbled below it. A quick glance at the clock showed that he must have just missed them. He raised an eyebrow at the word 'outside'. Emma had shown little inclination for the great outdoors after her excursion to Loanhead, and whilst Jenny had managed to coax her into the garden occasionally, going any further quite obviously filled her with terror. And yet somehow Madame Rose had managed to persuade Emma not only to leave the house, but also the garden. Otherwise why bother locking up? He wondered where they'd gone.

A clattering noise from the hallway distracted him. For a moment he thought it was the front door being unlocked, but then Mrs McCutcheon's cat sauntered in, jumped up onto the table and rubbed its head against his hand. When he absent-mindedly stroked its back, it turned around jumped down and stalked back out again, pausing in the doorway to stare back at him over its shoulder. It looked absurdly like it wanted him to follow it, so he did.

Out in the hall, it strode across to the stairs before checking that he was doing as he was told. It climbed the steps in a series of bounds, stopping at each turn and looking back. When it reached the landing, it stalked purposefully off towards the narrow staircase to the attic and then disappeared into the darkness. Curious, McLean followed all the way to the closed door to Jenny's room.

Pushing open the door revealed the room much as he had left it. The suitcase still lay on the bed, the little dressing table in the window still held Jenny's laptop, the pile of textbooks still built their little Tower of Babel on the floor beside it. He took a step inside, almost tripping over the cat as it twined itself around his legs.

'Dammit, cat. Are you trying to kill me?' He struggled away from the beast, found himself standing right in front of the dressing table. Without really thinking, he pulled out the chair, sat down and tapped at a key on the laptop. The screen came to life, showed the document Jenny had been working on before she had left. Not very good security then. McLean stared at the words, trying to make sense of them. He'd been expecting some essay on Neuro-Linguistic Programming, or whatever it was Jenny had been studying. Instead he found a letter, the address on the top somewhere in Gilmerton, so presumably her home. It began:

Dear Eleanor,
I don't know how to say this without hurting your feelings, and quite frankly I'm not sure I care any more. Time was I thought you were my friend, but I can see now you were only using me to get what you wanted. Just like you used all those others before me.
I

and then the cursor blinked, waiting for something more. It would have to wait a very long time. McLean stared at the words, feeling almost dirty for peering into this private aspect of Jenny's life. It was odd, really. It wasn't as if he hadn't seen many, many secrets revealed in his career as a detective, and yet somehow this was more personal.

He looked briefly at the other items on the dressing table: spiral-bound notebook with scruffy handwriting and doodles; assortment of biros and pencils, all chewed at the ends; a half-finished roll of Polo mints. Sticking his hand in his pocket, McLean pulled out the set of keys he'd taken from Jenny's belongings at the hospital. There was a set for the house, and another set he didn't recognize, though obviously house keys. And there on the screen was an address. Almost as if Jenny had left it there for him to see. As if she were inviting him to go and look.

Behind him, Mrs McCutcheon's cat began to purr, a noise so loud he could almost feel it through the soles of his feet. When he turned to look, it started licking one of its paws. No longer finding him of any interest whatsoever. McLean hefted the keys in his hand, glanced quickly at the partially written letter once more. Downstairs an afternoon's paperwork awaited him, or he could make a trip out to Gilmerton and see what that might turn up. It wasn't really that hard a decision to make.

51

Gilmerton hadn't changed much in years. It was still a drab collection of housing estates, the varied architectural tastes of the different decades marked out in pebbledash and roof tile. There was an older part, though, and Jenny's address turned out to be one of the houses built when it was still a mining village separated from the big city by several miles of farmland.

McLean had assumed Jenny lived in a tiny flat; she had no money, after all. But the house formed the end of a neat terrace and had a large garden at the back, mostly given over to the cultivation of weeds. Not quite sure why he was here, he approached the building as if it were a potential crime scene, peering through the windows and clocking the escape routes. It was a waste of time; the windows were so grimy he could barely make out anything inside, and there were just the two doors. Anyone attempting to escape out the back would have to fight their way through a jungle before clambering over a stone wall into the lane behind.

The front door had two keyholes; a deadlock and a latch. It took McLean a while to find the right keys from the bundle, longer still to realize that the deadlock had not been engaged. Opening the door pushed a stack of envelopes up against the wall, where they joined forces with a growing pile. McLean stooped, picked up one at random.

An invitation to take out a credit card, much like the hundreds that had arrived for his grandmother in the months that she'd been in a coma. He shuddered at the similarities. Would Jenny hang in there for eighteen months or more? Kept alive in the loosest sense of the word by machines that cared nothing for quality of life? Modern medicine had achieved many miracles, but he couldn't help thinking it was stuck in the dark ages where death was concerned.

He noticed the smell when he stood up, and realized that it had been there from the moment he'd stepped inside. Not exactly rot, nor mould, it was something he couldn't quite place. Other than in a box marked 'unpleasant'. The air in the house was stagnant, unmoving. He doubted both that there were any windows open, and that anyone had moved from room to room for a while. Like its owner, the place was stuck in a limbo between dead and alive.

The entrance hall opened onto two small front rooms, then past the stairs to a kitchen and scullery at the back. None of them showed much trace of habitation in recent times. The house was furnished, and generally tidy, but it was as if someone had gone out the front door fifty years earlier and never come back.

Upstairs showed much the same lack of habitation. There were three bedrooms, all small, all kitted out with antique beds and old wardrobes. In the bathroom, the water in the toilet bowl had evaporated away, concentric rings of lime scale marking its slow disappearance. McLean looked out through a dust- and cobweb-covered window, down to the overgrown garden below. He'd missed it before, but there was an old garage at the end, and a gently curving path knocked through the brush leading from the back door. Someone had been down there often enough, even if they'd never bothered with the rest of the property.

The back door had a deadlock and latch like the front. There was also a heavy iron bolt, but it had long since been painted open. As he stepped out of the dead house into the garden it was as if someone had turned the lights and volume back up. Birds sang from the trees, cars whooshed past on the road out the front, and the familiar, reassuring roar of the city bypass covered everything. McLean followed the path through brambles up to his waist, whippy elder bushes and weed ashes that must have been growing for ten years or more, until he finally found himself at the garage.

It was a stone-built structure, tall and narrow, with a steep-pitched slate roof. Probably a coach house in olden days, though it didn't seem large enough to have housed stables. The paint on the wooden door was coming off in thick, curly flakes, but the keyhole glistened in the sunlight where it had been used, regularly and recently. He tried the handle first, found it wasn't locked.

If the smell in the house had been unpleasant, it was nothing compared to the stench that hit him now. This one was all too easily identifiable. He'd smelled it too often before, most recently in a tiny flat in the Colonies. But he didn't need that cue. The body hanging from the beams by its broken neck was clue enough. Sunlight speared through a skylight, dappled by the trees outside. It played upon the naked skin like a weird, moving camouflage.

McLean stepped carefully into the garage, noting the layout. At the far end, double doors would open up onto the lane. There was plenty of space for a car, but like most garages this one was used mainly for storage. The walls were lined with old wooden shelves, piled up with tin boxes, glass jars, rubbish mainly. A workbench stretched under a window whose panes of glass had been painted white. An attempt to stop sunlight fading the paintwork on a brand-new car sometime in the 1950s, no doubt. The obligatory pair of sit-up-and-beg bicycles leaned against a stack of tea chests, tyres flat, wicker baskets almost completely rotted away. An old set of wooden stepladders lay against the wall to his left, resting where they had landed after the deceased took his last, long step. And there was no doubting it was he, McLean saw, as he walked slowly around the body. Decay might have set in, but enough of his features were still identifiable.

Grigori Mikhailevic.

'He loved her so much, but she felt nothing for him. That was his undoing, in the end.'

McLean started at the sound behind him, whirled around. All he could see was an outline, silhouetted by the bright sunshine outside, but he recognized the voice.

'She killed them, didn't she. Lured them in, tied the nooses, made them do it.'

A little girl laugh. 'Jenny wouldn't hurt a fly, Inspector. She was just my huntress. My tool. The spirit's tool.'

He took a step forwards as the figure moved in the doorway. Still the sun cast it in shadow, made him squint to see a face. Then he caught the eyes, glowing like lava in the night. They held him tight, helpless as an infant, pulling him in, dragging him down, down, down.

52

He can't think straight. It's like that time Phil spiked his drink with something he'd cooked up in the lab. Only then they'd both just stared at the wall, trying to work out why the paper was patterned the way it was. For six hours, he thinks it was. Only he can't remember. He's not entirely sure who Phil is, either. Something about a place called America, wherever that is.

He's driving . . . where? Is it a good idea to drive in this condition? He doesn't know, and anyway he can't stop. It's taking all his concentration just to keep his hands on the wheel, keep the car straight.

There's someone sitting beside him, but he dare not look. There's the concentration needed to keep the car on the road, of course. But there's also memories of fire and brimstone, of burning eyes and deep despair, of a man hanging from a rope, his neck broken, his flesh beginning to rot.

Time passes, and he is no longer in the car. Did they crash? He thinks he'd remember that. His parents crashed, so long ago. Smashed to tiny pieces as their aeroplane collided with the side of a mountain. They'd left him all alone, even though they'd promised him they never would. The fires had taken them, burned them into nothing but ashes and memories.

He is in a room. A kitchen. The terrible presence is

beside him, murmuring quietly. He knows this place. His grandmother lived here. And then she left one day in an ambulance, never came back. He remembers the days dragging into weeks, the weeks into months, hope dying bit by bit until finally there was nothing left but despair.

Now he is in an attic room, small, the servants' quarters when people still had servants. A leather suitcase lies on the narrow iron-frame bed and he opens it without realizing he has been told to. Inside lies a coil of stout hemp rope. He reaches in and takes it out.

And finally, where he always knew he would end up. He stands in the middle of an attic, warm like a lover's embrace. The rope is cold in his hands. Cold like the winter's day when they lowered her coffin into the ground. The monster stands beside him, talking to him in words he cannot understand. His fingers know what to do though, carefully folding and twisting the rope, looping it round and round to a count of thirteen. Unlucky thirteen, like his life.

He has to pull an old trunk into the middle of the room, place a precarious chair on top of it so that he can reach up into the rafters, tie off the rope on a stout crossbeam, just the right length. He wouldn't want to hit the floor.

Gazing down, he is aware of movement in the dark shadows under the eaves. Something watches him with patient eyes. Watches the monster as it pulls out his pain, his suffering and loss. Lays it out for all to see. Why would he want anyone to see that? Why would he want to see it himself. He dealt with it, didn't he? Put it all behind him. Moved on.

As he steps back down to the floor, something rushes past him. Commotion, hissing, a flash of teeth and claws and fur. The monster roars: 'He is mine!' A scream like nothing he has ever heard and a tiny body falls at his feet. It gasps for breath, mewling and twitching as he looks down at it. He should go to its aid, but all he can do is stand and wait.

The monster steps up to him, kicks the cat so hard it skitters away across the dusty floorboards into the darkness. Another innocent creature hurt because of him. How much better the world would be without him in it. How much less his suffering.

He feels the hands of the monster on him then, stroking his shoulders, running a finger down the middle of his back, another up the side of his neck and into his hair. He does not fear the monster, yet neither can he disobey it. At its unspoken command he begins to undress.

53

His first rational thought was for Mrs McCutcheon's cat. Somehow it had broken whatever hypnotic trance he had been under, but now it was injured, possibly even dead. The thought of it dying filled him with even greater gloom than the depression that had already settled over him.

McLean struggled to regain control of himself, even as his body continued to respond to someone else's commands. It was almost as if he were watching from outside, only he could see everything through his own eyes, including the noose now dangling beside his head, the bottom of its loop about level with his eyes.

'It will all be over soon. The pain, the suffering, the despair.' The voice behind him was impossible to ignore. It reached into the core of him, pulled out the sadness that had dogged him ever since he had waved his parents goodbye that fateful night, never to see them again.

'No.' He forced the word out through teeth clenched tight. He was done mourning for his parents. He would never forget them, but life went on. The dead held no sway over him.

'Shush now. Calm.' A finger touch on his bare shoulder. When had he begun to undress? Why had he begun to undress? He couldn't remember. There was just the touch, and with it an overwhelming sense of grief. Yes, life went on, but with all the joy sucked out of it by the bad things that lived on with it.

'Climb up, up. You need to get as high as you can.' There was something familiar about the voice, about the person behind it. McLean wanted to shake the fog out of his head, reach up and ram his fists into his eyes until he saw stars. Anything other than what his body was doing. And yes, he wanted to get away from the sorrow, the gut-punching waves of sadness that welled up in him, one after another. But there were better ways than this, surely? Anger had helped in the past. And throwing himself into his work.

'Your anger is all spent, and everyone at work wants you to leave. What will you do without those props? How will you fend off the horrors that have been with you all these years? Better to embrace them, accept them. Take that one step and you will find peace.'

This time the voice was different, all around him, inside him even. McLean struggled against it, but it was too powerful to resist. He had climbed up onto the trunk. And then onto the chair balanced on top of it. The noose was in his hands, the rope looping down towards the floor. All he needed to do was slip it over his head, tighten it just so, and shift it round so the knot pressed against his left ear. That way when his fall was stopped, the weight of his body would snap the vertebrae, killing him instantly. Blessed relief.

'But. I. Don't. Want. To. Die.' Each word was a struggle, each a spasm in his arms as he fought the urge to lift the noose over his head. He was tense now, teetering on the edge of the chair. The floor was somehow miles away, the air between him and the wooden boards filled with darting clouds that shone and shimmered. Not clouds, but ghosts. Souls once trapped, released in a magical fire. Lost now. Searching for a way through to wherever it was they were meant to go. They sensed his ending, flocked to him as if in his despair he might lead them to their goal. Perhaps there would be some benefit in his passing, then. Some final good to come out of the suffering.

His grip on reality slipped away, inch by inch, step by step. Like poor old Pete Buchanan, staring wild-eyed and terrified as his jacket ripped stitch by stitch. McLean almost laughed at the thought that the two of them would end in such a similar manner.

'He said he didn't want to die, you bitch.'

A different voice shattered the bubble that surrounded him. It brought feelings of happiness, excitement, caring. And it had a name.

Emma.

McLean turned around, suddenly back in full command of his body. A single scene painted itself on his eyeballs. Doctor Austin, halfway through turning to see who had interrupted her. Emma with a book in her hands, heavy, leather bound, old, expensive. Sir Arthur Conan Doyle's student copy of Gray's *Anatomy*. She swung it round in an arc, putting the full weight of her body behind it, and as it connected with the hypnotist's face the spell clouding his thoughts evaporated.

Doctor Austin went down like an expertly demolished building, crumpling into a tidy heap at Emma's feet. She looked up at him, triumphant, and he saw something in her eyes that had been missing since the day she woke up.

And then the chair beneath him gave a lurch to one side. McLean had no time to remember whether he'd put the noose around his neck or not. Arms flailing, he fell.

54

A quiet beeping sound roused him from the depths of blackness. McLean was aware of no dreams; there was just nothing and then the slow realization of noise. He tried to move, but something held him back. He was warm though, and the fear had gone. He couldn't remember what the fear had been about. Something to do with his neck; his throat felt tight as if someone had tried to choke him. It was enough to know that it was over. He could relax now and let sleep wash away his exhaustion.

Later, he woke to a dull pain that seemed to run through his entire body. He didn't open his eyes at first, just lay still and listened to the noises. It didn't take long to work out that he was in hospital; the smell was as much a giveaway as anything. It was either that or he'd died and Hell was just like the Western General. With more effort than should have been necessary, he opened his eyes.

He could see that the room was darkened, the overhead lights dimmed and the blinds drawn. It still felt like he was staring into the sun. He blinked until tears ran down his cheeks, blurring everything including the plaster on his leg that anchored him to the bed. When he opened his eyes again, a familiar white-coated figure was leaning over him.

'Back in the land of the living, Inspector? We were beginning to wonder.'

'I . . .' McLean coughed at the attempt to speak. His throat was as dry as a thirsty camel. 'How long?'

'We kept you sedated for a while. Had to get those bones set properly. There's some metal pins in your leg now, will probably be a bit of a pain every time you go through airport security.' Doctor Wheeler gave him a friendly smile, looked at her watch. 'You've been under for about forty-eight hours.'

Two days. McLean let his head sink back into the pillows, tied to take stock of his injuries. His arms were stiff and sore, but unbroken. His left leg was fine, but the right was encased in plaster. Everything hurt, even blinking, and swallowing was such exquisite agony he almost passed out when he tried to clear his throat to speak again. Movement wasn't impossible, just inadvisable for the time being, even if he had the energy. He tried not to think about needing to go to the toilet.

'What happened?' He vaguely remembered driving across the city. Had he been in an accident? Bloody typical to finally give in and buy himself a car, only to wrap it around a lamp post before he'd had it more than a couple of days.

'You fell off a chair balanced on top of a trunk. That's all anyone's told me. You'll have to ask Emma for the rest of it.'

'She's here?'

'Hasn't been away since you were brought in. I think she's asleep in the waiting room. I'll go and fetch her.' Doctor Wheeler paused a moment. 'She's improved enormously, you know. I have to say I had my doubts about regression therapy, but it seems this time Eleanor has actually succeeded at something.'

'This time?' It was painful even forcing out a couple of words.

'I shouldn't really be gossiping.' Doctor Wheeler pulled a chair closer to the bed, dropped wearily into it. 'Who am I kidding? She bad-mouthed me for years.'

McLean kept silent. He might have said he was leaving a space for Doctor Wheeler to fill in her own time, but the truth was he didn't think he could speak even if he wanted to.

'She was my supervisor, when I was studying neurobiology. Gods, that was a fair few years back now.' Doctor Wheeler shook her head in disbelief. 'I thought she was brilliant. To be fair, she was brilliant. But completely self-obsessed. As long as you were useful to her, she'd tolerate you. But if you dared question her. Oof.'

Another pause. McLean looked sideways at the doctor. She was leaning right backwards, head tilted up to the ceiling, eyes closed. For a moment he thought she might have fallen asleep; couldn't find it in him to be annoyed. If anyone looked like they needed a good kip it was Doctor Wheeler.

'She got interested in the whole hypnosis thing about ten years ago. Maybe twelve. I read a couple of her early papers and it looked like she was onto something. But then there was a problem with one of her study groups. A couple of her students committed suicide. There was an investigation. The ethics committee got involved. I was about to head off overseas for a few years. Won a scholarship to study best practice in neurobiology around the world, would you believe. But dear old Eleanor put the kybosh on that. Wrote to the head of the charity that was funding the trip, told him a whole load of lies about me.'

'Why?' McLean forced the word out in a hoarse whisper.

'Because I was the one called in the Ethics Committee. Like I said, she can be a bit self-obsessed. She put her test subjects through the wringer without having any of the obvious safeguards in place. A couple of them just couldn't cope.'

McLean didn't know whether to be grateful that she was telling him this, or annoyed that she'd known it and let Doctor Austin treat Emma anyway.

'Hanged themselves?'

'What . . . ? Oh, no. One of them slit his wrists. John Phimister, that was his name. Poor old John. The other one jumped off the ferry from Rosyth to Rotterdam, somewhere in the middle of the North Sea. Half a dozen people saw him do it. That was Alastair Burns. Quiet chap. From what I recall, neither of them should have made it through the initial screening to be in the test group any-way. Eleanor just fudged the scores to make up the numbers.' Doctor Wheeler straightened up in the chair, looked over at McLean. 'Dear me, I'd not thought about any of this in a while. We patched things up about five years back, when she went into therapy rather than research. She's a brilliant therapist, really. Just not an easy person to like. Sorry, Inspector. You must think me a ter-rible tell-tale.'

'Not at . . .' McLean got no further before his throat gave up in a spasm of painful coughing.

'Rest, Tony. That's what you need. Take it easy and I'll go tell Emma you're awake.'

McLean closed his eyes for a moment, his memory coming back in disjointed chunks, mixed in with the latest information on Doctor Austin. Brilliant or not, the hypnotist hadn't done anything for Emma, so it must have been Madame Rose. The two of them had gone off for a walk. Was that all it took? And regression therapy. He recalled the first session with unusual clarity now. That was when it had all started to go downhill. He'd been tired, sure. Ever since Duguid had effectively doubled his workload. Or was it when Emma came home and started waking him in the middle of the night? But the rot had really set in after the first session with the monster. Doctor Austin.

He tried to sit up and immediately regretted it, winced through the pain lancing through his arm and leg as he looked across at the bedside table for his phone. Of course, it wasn't there, and he wouldn't have been able to use it anyway. He needed to talk to Grumpy Bob, or Ritchie. Even MacBride might understand. Collapsing back into the pillows, he stared up in frustration at the ceiling tiles. He knew now how they had all died: Duncan George, Patrick Sands, John Fenton, Grigori Mikhailevic, Caroline Sellars. Hell, probably even Jenny Nairn.

The problem was that it would be impossible to prove, and worse he'd probably be called insane for even suggesting it.

'Oh my God. Tony. You're awake.'

He barely had time to register the voice before she was

at his side. McLean stared up, his vision blurred by the overhead lights and for a moment thought he was looking at someone else entirely.

'Kirsty?' The word died in his throat. It couldn't be Kirsty; she'd been dead more than a decade now.

'Shhh.' Emma knelt beside the bed, put one hand on his forehead, the other on his chest. 'Caroline told me about your throat. The rope must have crushed your larynx or something.'

Doctor Wheeler hadn't been lying when she had said Emma was much improved. The little-girl-lost eyes had gone and now her face glowed. Unless that was just a strange effect of the lighting. He'd seen it before, but only just realized how much her hair had changed, the spikes become gentle waves of darkest black, shot with here and there a few streaks of grey. That was why he'd thought it was Kirsty come for him. She looked just like her, even down to the mannerisms.

'It's nice.' He lifted a weak hand, took a few strands between his fingers and felt how soft they were. 'Suits you.'

Grumpy Bob was the first to show up from work, once word got out that he was fit for visitors. The old sergeant had brought a bag of grapes with him, which he proceeded to eat without offering any to McLean. Probably be too painful to swallow, what with his neck and everything, was all he gave by way of explanation.

'You any idea how long you're going to be in here for?'

'Day more. Maybe two.' McLean poked at the cast on his leg. 'Don't think I'm going to be back at the station for a while though.'

'Probably for the best. Gives the rumour mill time to burn itself out.'

'Oh Christ. What are they saying?'

'Well, the best one I've heard yet is that you were indulging in some weird auto-asphyxiation erotic thing. Apparently you've always been into that sado-masochistic stuff and the only surprise is you've not hurt yourself this badly before.'

McLean tried not to laugh. Laughing hurt too much. 'What's the worst? I bet it can't top that.'

Grumpy Bob's grin disappeared. 'Aye, well. Mebbe. A couple of folk think the job was getting too much for you and you tried to hang yourself.' He pointed at McLean's neck. 'You might want to wear a cravat or something til that rope burn's gone down a bit.'

Reflexively McLean's hand went up to his chin, fingers lightly brushing the bruised skin just below. He didn't have to guess who those folk were, or what the fallout from their supposition would be. 'I guess I'm going to have to come up with a better story then. I really don't fancy being pensioned off.'

'They'll not do that, Tony. We're short enough good detectives as it is.'

There was an uncomfortable silence then, while Grumpy Bob continued to munch his way through the grapes. In all their years working together, it was the first time McLean had seen the sergeant eating fruit.

'You found Mikhailevic's body? Out in Gilmerton?' Had he told anyone about that? It was all such a blur, he could hardly remember.

462

'Aye, once we'd worked out what you were blethering on about. Almost as bad as the other lad, Sands. The Doc reckons he'd been hanging the longest, which just makes things even more complicated.'

'Not really. He bought the rope, after all.' McLean had already joined up all the dots in his head, but then he'd had a long time to think about it. 'What happened to Doctor Austin?'

'Who?' Grumpy Bob spoke through a mouthful of half-chewed grape.

'Doctor Austin. The hypnotherapist. Emma clocked her a good one with that book.' It was one of the few clear memories McLean had of the whole afternoon of what he was coming to refer to as 'the incident'.

'Oh, her.' Grumpy Bob wiped at his face with the back of his hand. 'She's not going to press charges.'

It took a while for McLean's brain to catch up with this. 'She's . . . what?'

'Way she told it, she could understand why Emma walloped her like that. Thought she was attacking you, whatever.'

McLean dropped his head back into the pillow, spoke to the ceiling. 'She was the one who killed them all, Bob. All of the hangings, probably Jenny Nairn too. They all came through her study groups at that college. She picked them out, marked the ones who were depressed, did something. I don't know how. Made them hang themselves. She nearly killed me too. That's why she was round the house in the first place.'

Grumpy Bob was halfway through scrunching up the

empty paper bag that had contained his grapes, prior to throwing it at the bin and missing. He stopped, mouth hanging slightly open. 'You what?'

'Hypnosis, Bob. That's what she did to them all.'

'Don't be daft, sir. You can't hypnotize someone into doing something that'll harm them. Something they don't want to do.'

Uncomfortable thoughts hovered around McLean's consciousness. He concentrated on the central strand of his theory. Worry about the ramifications later. 'That's the whole point. They were all of them severely depressed. They all wanted to kill themselves. She latched onto that, fed on it somehow.' Like she was being controlled by something larger, more deadly. Something he didn't want to think about.

Grumpy Bob stared at him for a while before saying quietly: 'So how did she get her claws into you?'

'Come on, Bob. Time was you and old Guthrie wouldn't leave me alone for five minutes. Back when Kirsty died. It was subtle, I'll give you that, but you roped all my friends into suicide watch too.'

'Aye but you pulled through, didn't you? You're no more suicidal than my finger.' Grumpy Bob waggled it, just in case, then threw the bag at the bin. Missed.

McLean didn't argue the point. Instead he just stared at the ceiling. 'That's the problem though, Bob. It never goes away. You can bury the past, or lock it away in a little room in your mind. But it's always there. And she brought it all back out. I couldn't work out why I was so tired, so pissed off at everything. I thought it was Dagwood being in charge, and working at the SCU. Pete Buchanan's death didn't help either, but all the while it was Doctor Eleanor bloody Austin messing with my head.'

Another long silence as Grumpy Bob digested the information, weighed it and found it wanting.

'You might want to keep that theory to yourself.'

'I know. Might as well write my resignation letter otherwise, eh? Think I'd rather act my way through a dozen therapy sessions with Matt Hilton.'

'That few? You'll be lucky.'

'Aye, well. It still leaves the problem of Doctor Austin. Who's she going to go after next?'

'I'll get the lad onto firming up that connection between all the victims, then. If they can all be tracked back to her, we'll get her in for questioning.' Grumpy Bob blew out his cheeks, then let the air out in a long low whistle. 'Not sure what we can do about her, though. I mean, how the hell do you prove she did something like that?'

The chair still sat outside the ICU room where Magda Evans was recovering, but it was unoccupied as McLean clumped his way down the corridor, trying to get to grips with crutches. He remembered a time at boarding school, back in the eighties, when one of the boys had come back with his leg in plaster. He'd been the cool kid for a while, deciding who did or didn't get to sign his cast and speeding along on his crutches. Teachers couldn't tell him off and even the bullies hesitated to pick on him, at least for the first couple of weeks. Every boy in the school wanted a broken leg and a plaster cast then. Now, thirty years on, he really couldn't understand why. It was a pain, quite literally.

He paused at the door. The chair looked very inviting, but lowering himself into it for a rest was almost as difficult as standing, and then he'd have to get back up again. Emma was coming to pick him up in an hour or so, after which there would be the fun of stairs to learn about.

Who was he kidding? McLean knew damned well why he'd come this way in the first place, and the fact that there was no police officer on guard was hardly his fault. He knocked lightly on the door, then pushed it open.

Magda was healing, that was about as much as you could say. Her face was still a mess of bruising and cuts, only now the swelling was almost gone, just the colours remaining. Yellow and purple and grey, slashes of dark red hatched with black stitches. She was watching the television hung on the opposite wall, but her eyes flicked across to him as he clumped awkwardly in, up, down, widened in surprise. She barely moved her head, he noticed.

'Wha' ap'n you?' Magda struggled with the words, the stitches tugging cruelly at the slashes to her mouth and cheeks.

'Someone tried to hang me.' McLean reached up for his neck where the rope burn still stood proud. His throat was less painful now, at least for talking. Eating anything solid would have to wait a week or two.

'Why?'

McLean manoeuvred himself to the end of the bed, wedged the crutches up against the frame so he could rest his weight on them for a moment.

'It's not important. I wanted to talk about you, not me.'

Magda said nothing, just stared up at him from her ruined face.

'They told you about Pete Buchanan, aye?'

She blinked her eyes in the most minimal of nods.

'Nasty way to go. Let me tell you.' He rubbed at his neck again. 'Did they tell you about the bat we found in your apartment?'

Another nod, and this time McLean saw the wince of pain that went with the movement. Nerve damage from the attack, likely to leave her in permanent pain. At least that was what Doctor Wheeler had said.

'It was DS Buchanan who did this to you, wasn't it.'

McLean waited for the nod. For a long while Magda just stared at him, then finally she blinked. 'Eff.'

'He killed Malky Jennings too. No, you don't need to answer that one, we know that. I've just been trying to work out what your angle on the whole thing was. Took me a while, but I've had nothing much else to do these last couple of days. So here's my idea of what was really happening.' McLean shuffled slightly to ease the pressure on his wrists. How the hell did people use crutches for more than ten minutes at a time?

'We know you'd had enough of Malky. You tried to get away a couple of times, but that didn't work. The police were no help either. Can't say I've got much time for the Devil You Know approach myself. It wasn't just you, either. All those other girls, the Eastern Europeans who'd been brought over here with promises of good jobs, learning English, sending money back home? Yeah, I know how it goes. So you decided to do something about it. It was bloody clever, too. Get Buchanan on your side. Not sure how, not sure I want to know how. He kills Malky because he thinks he's your protector now. But you keep the bat, hidden away somewhere safe. I'm guessing you've been creaming money off Malky's operation too. Maybe some drugs as well. Am I warm?'

Magda said nothing, just stared at him. Her eyes were all he needed to see though. He could read the relief when he got it wrong, and so far there'd been none.

'You organized the boat, too. Anyone who wants to go home. Something like that anyway. The only problem is we got wind of the whole thing and rounded you all up. I'm guessing Buchanan wasn't best pleased when he found out you'd tried to do a runner. What was the plan, anonymous tip-off as to where the bat was hidden once you'd made it to safety? Drop him in the shit?'

Magda blinked again. 'Aw ee zerrved.'

'You won't find me disagreeing with you there.'

'Appens ow?' Magda grimaced as she tried to form the question.

'To be honest, I don't know. Not my case any more. We've got Buchanan for Malky Jennings' murder, so my boss is happy. But you were an accessory to that, at the very least. I can't see a judge letting you off. I might put in a good word, plead mitigating circumstances. Not quite sure how I feel about being played right now. Still, it's going to be a while before you're fit to stand trial, and there's the small matter of it being a police officer who tried to kill you.' McLean let that last thought hang in the air. He really wasn't sure he could stay angry with Magda Evans. Not after what had been done to her.

'Ugger girls?' This last word gurgled up from deep in Magda's throat like a death rattle.

'Clarice Saunders has taken them under her ample

468

wing. I know everyone laughs at her, but her charity does good work. They'll be given shelter, re-housed, sent home, pretty much whatever they want. No one's going to charge them for being on that boat.'

'Goog.' Magda blinked once more. A single tear formed in the corner of each eye before trickling into the scabs on her ruined cheeks.

PC Jones was back in his seat when McLean let himself out of the room a few minutes later. He looked up, startled.

'Inspector, sir. I didn't . . . You shouldn't have been in there.'

'Relax, Reg. I wasn't in there.'

'I . . . But . . .' He pointed at the door as it clicked shut.

'And you weren't nipping off to the toilet without anyone to cover for you.' McLean smiled, then clunked off down the corridor back to his room.

55

It was a small cemetery, tucked away on a piece of land the property developers would have paid a king's ransom for, were it not for the bodies interred beneath the grass. McLean knew it well from his childhood. Summer days spent exploring the green spaces beyond the garden of his grandmother's house. Out through the little gate in the wall at the back, and you could almost imagine you'd left Edinburgh behind. At least it had been like that back then. Nowadays there was always the roar of traffic, and more and more people. The lock on the gate was rusted solid too, so you had to go around the long way.

Emma led them through the gravestones, once more forgetting that on crutches he couldn't move all that quickly. Not over this uneven ground, for sure. The grass could really have done with a mowing, and the bramble vines seemed determined to trip him at every turn. He wasn't labouring as much as Madame Rose though. The transvestite medium was not built for speed, more of a taxi ride kind of person. McLean got the feeling he was going to have to pay him, her, whatever, a fairly large sum, but it was worth it just to see Emma so much improved.

And now, if the two of them could be believed, he was going to find out how it had been done.

'Here we are. This was the first one.' Emma had stopped

in front of a gravestone, fairly new in comparison to those around it. McLean shuffled an awkward route through the undergrowth until he was standing next to her and could read the words carved into the stone.

In Loving Memory
Rosie Buckley
12-7-1972 25-12-1998
Taken Before Her Time

A cold weight settled in the pit of McLean's stomach. 'Is this some kind of joke?'

'Far from it, Inspector.' Madame Rose lumbered up alongside the two of them. 'This is the final resting place of Donald Anderson's penultimate victim. It took me a long time to track her down, and quite by chance Diane Kinnear is buried just over there.' The medium pointed towards the edge of the cemetery, where it gave way to mature woodland.

'What . . . ? I don't understand. What's this got to do with anything?'

'This is everything, Inspector. This is what has been causing Emma all her problems.' Madame Rose laid a large hand on the headstone, her ornate rings clinking lightly against the granite. 'I have to admit I was wrong, and that's not something that happens often. I thought Donald's book had taken a piece of Emma's soul. Turns out that wasn't the case.'

'They're all here. With me.' Emma tapped the side of her head and twirled her finger like a schoolgirl indicating looniness in one of her chums. 'Well, apart from Rosie and Diane. They're gone now. And the others are much quieter. Makes it easier to think.'

McLean looked sideways at Emma, standing beside him. She reached out and took his hand, a simple gesture but not one he could remember her having done before. They'd not really known each other that long, and were both too old for the teenage infatuation that could not bear to be physically separated for more than a few seconds. It was more like the touch of an old friend, a re-acquaintance with someone he'd loved a long time ago and not seen for years. And as he thought it, so the wild story that Madame Rose was spinning began to take on another layer.

'When you destroyed the book in that fire, you set free all the souls it had trapped down the centuries. Every victim, everyone who tried to read it and was found wanting. They were all in there and they all had to go somewhere. I thought they'd just passed on, gone beyond the veil. Maybe some did, but many of them followed that small piece of Emma back to her. I can't blame them, Inspector. They were scared, traumatized beyond anything you can imagine. Some of them have been trapped inside that book for centuries. They took refuge in Emma, and in the process very nearly killed her.'

He didn't believe it. There was always a rational explanation; that was what he had been trained to look for, after all. But there was no denying the difference in Emma; the slow transformation of the past couple of months. She'd changed as she'd recovered from her time in a coma. His own preoccupations had stopped him from seeing it, perhaps. Now there was no denying how much she looked like her.

'Kirsty.' The word was barely a whisper. For some reason he found it hard to speak. Had he not been propped up on the uncomfortable metal crutches, he would probably have sunk to his knees there in the damp graveyard.

'She loved you so much. She still does.'

'She's in there somewhere, isn't she.'

Emma nodded, and it was a punch to his gut. Never mind what Doctor Austin had done to dredge up his past, with that one simple movement he was transported back to the darkest days, the dawn of the new millennium when only his innate stubbornness had kept him from taking his own life.

'Which is why I have to leave.'

If he thought nothing could shock him more, Emma's words proved him wrong. 'Leave? Why?'

'I have to free them all. I'll never be right until they're gone, and they need this.' Emma pointed at the headstone and its simple, terrible inscription. 'Their deaths were so violent, they need to be reunited with their mortal remains before they can accept what happened and move on.'

'But . . . How many? How long?'

Emma bowed her head, as if the weight of all those souls was almost too much to bear. 'I don't know.'

She came to him in his room that night, as he lay awake staring at the ceiling. The dull ache of his mending leg made sleep difficult, as did the long hours of sitting around doing nothing each day. Enforced rest didn't suit him well.

He didn't look at her, knew the drill. Just shuffled across to one side of the bed to make room. He'd hoped that the night terrors were lessening now; Emma had certainly seemed much more composed, more adult. If not really anything like her previous self. The selfish part of him wondered if this meant she would stay.

Her hand was cold, but not unpleasantly so as it reached through the cover for his chest. She snuggled up against him, stealing his warmth, and that was when he realized she wasn't wearing her thick fleece pyjamas. Wasn't wearing anything at all.

'Em—' A single finger stifled the word before it could escape from his lips. She leaned over, kissed him, her long black hair flowing over his head like a drowning tide.

56

It wouldn't have been a proper day back at work without a summons to Dagwood's office. Still on crutches, McLean had to shuffle his way through the door, but at least standing on the wrong side of the desk wasn't a problem. The acting superintendent hadn't exactly gone out of his way to redecorate Jayne McIntyre's office, but he couldn't help noticing the cardboard boxes piled along one wall, those few personal items that had made their way up to this floor now being packed away again.

'I hear they've finally appointed someone.' He didn't need to point out who hadn't got the job.

'Not for another week yet, so don't push your luck.'

'Actually, sir, it'll be good to have you back in CID. We're always short-staffed and this' – McLean tapped at the cast on his leg – 'well, it doesn't really help. Looks like I'm going to be off active duty at least another six weeks.'

'Way I hear it, you probably ought to be off for good.' Duguid leaned back in his seat. It was always good to hit him with a compliment, put him off guard. 'You wouldn't be the first detective self-destructed under the pressure.'

McLean didn't point out that most of the pressure was due to one particular senior officer. So far the interview wasn't going too badly, no need to jeopardize that.

'I didn't try to hang myself, sir.'

'Well that's not what I heard.'

McLean let slip a sigh. Sometimes it was just easier not to try and hide it. 'I've no doubt you heard all manner of lurid speculation. You probably heard I was screwing that prostitute who ended up having her face cut open. Turns out that was actually your old chum Pete Buchanan.'

Duguid glared, back to his usual self.

'I always wondered why poor old Pete never got promoted past detective sergeant. I mean, he ought to have made inspector at the very least, just for having been around for so long.' Just as McLean had suggested, Ritchie had done some digging into Buchanan's past. It looked like her time in the evidence store and archives had served her well, and no doubt Grumpy Bob had filled in any gaps. The unofficial report that had been sitting on his desk that morning waiting for him had been very revealing indeed. He was glad he'd taken the time to read it through.

'What's your point, McLean?'

'Well, it seems Buchanan was a bit free with his fists as a younger officer. Too many suspects falling down the stairs, stuff like that. "Old School Policing" I think they call it?'

'I'm not going to apologize for anything to you, McLean. Say what you like about Pete Buchanan, he got results.'

'So everyone tells me, sir. The ends justify the means. Evil deeds for evil times and every other fucking homily you care to come up with. It still boils down to the fact that Pete Buchanan was a violent bully who got off on hurting people, screwed the prostitutes he was supposed to be arresting and ended up putting one of them in hospital with injuries she'll never fully recover from.'

476

'I'm supposed to care what happens to some prostitute?'

'Her name's Magda Evans, sir. And for you informa-tion, she was trying to get out of there and take a whole load of other women with her. Can't say I approve of her methods, but props to her for trying something. God knows we'd failed her down the years.'

'And that depresses you. The shit we see every day, the shit we have to wade through just to do our jobs?'

McLean leaned heavily onto his crutches. 'Save the cod psychoanalysis for Professor Hilton, sir. I presume that's why you wanted to see me, anyway. Counselling sessions?'

Duguid had the decency to look embarrassed. 'Waste of bloody time and money, but there's procedure. You'd be seeing him after your involvement in DS Buchanan's death, anyway, but after the . . . incident at your house, I've no option but to suspend you until the shrink gives you the OK. If we can make that match up with your sick leave then it saves a shit load of paperwork, so give him a call. He's expecting you. Quicker you can persuade him to let you come back to work, the better.'

A veiled compliment from Duguid. Wonders never ceased.

'Was that all, sir?' McLean asked.

Duguid stared at him with those piggy little eyes of his narrowed in concentration. 'The hanging cases. Your sui-cide pact. What's happening with those?'

'I've no idea, sir. I've been off two weeks.'

'But you were following up a lead the day . . .' Duguid nodded in the direction of McLean's leg.

'Yes, sir. I was.' McLean paused. He'd had plenty of time to consider the cases, but there was still no easy way of putting it all together. Not without either making himself look like a lunatic or, worse, someone who had harboured a mass murderer for several months.

'And?' Duguid wouldn't let it go. Damn him.

'They all knew each other. All five of them. They'd all had therapy at one time or another from Doctor Austin, so it's safe to say they all had mental health issues.'

'So it's looking like a suicide pact after all.'

'Yes, sir. It does.'

'This Doctor Austin. She was the one round your place the day . . .' He nodded at McLean's leg again.

'Yes. She was working with Emma. Trying to help her get her memory back.'

For a moment McLean thought Duguid was going to ask him who Emma was. The no-longer acting superintendent certainly looked puzzled.

'So that's why she was at your house?'

Tell the truth? Or lie and keep his job? It wasn't hard, really. 'Yes, sir.'

Duguid made a noise that suggested he didn't really believe it but was willing to let it slide. 'Have you interviewed her about the suicides?'

'Like I said, sir. I've been off for two weeks. I'm sure Grumpy Bob will have talked to her though.'

Duguid snorted. 'Not if he wasn't told to, I don't doubt. Get on it, McLean. I want this investigation wound up by the end of the week.'

McLean opened his mouth to protest, then thought the better of it.

'Yes, sir,' he said, and clumped wearily out of the room.

*

'Good to see you back, sir. How's the leg?'

DS Ritchie sat at her desk in the CID room tapping away at a smart new laptop computer. She was all alone save for the five images still taped to the whiteboard. Lines spidered between them, questions now answered, more or less. One name was conspicuous by its absence. He hoped he could keep it that way.

'Sore.' McLean tapped the plaster cast, leaned into his crutches. 'Awkward. Where is everyone?'

'Brooks has got them upstairs chasing actions on his latest investigation. I'm only down here because I've been away at Tulliallan all day.'

'So no one's been working on this.' McLean pointed at the whiteboards.

'Nothing really to work on. We found Mikhailevic where you said he was. PM was pretty clear. He hanged himself like all the others. No sign of foul play. Only difference was he had hemp fibres under his nails.'

Almost as if he could have been the last in the line, were it not for the fact he'd died first.

'It's all written up then?'

'Stuart left it on your desk. The other four as well. Brooks wants it signed off soon as.'

'Him and Dagwood both. They're probably right, too. The last thing the PF wants is a complicated case with no end to it.' McLean shuffled uncomfortably with his crutches, turning himself around so he could leave the room. 'Anyone speak to Doctor Austin? Her name's not up there.'

'Wanted to, but there's a bit of a problem there.'

'There is?'

'Aye. We tried to get in touch with her, but she wouldn't answer her phone. I went to that college she teaches at, and they've not seen her in over week. She's missed a couple of lectures and half a dozen tutorials according to Professor Bain.'

'What about her practice?'

'Stuart went along. Met a nice young man called Dave who's been putting off clients for days and hasn't seen the good doctor since you . . . Well, since then.' Ritchie looked away from him, fascinated by whatever was on her laptop screen.

'You've been to her home, I take it.'

'Us and Dave both. He has a key. She's not there.'

'It's an odd one, I'll grant you. But then nothing about Emma's case has made much sense from the start.'

Doctor Wheeler sat at her desk and stared at him over a mountain of paperwork. It was something McLean had noticed about hospitals, how enormous fat files of papers followed patients around like badly trained pets. Nothing as simple as calling up a record from a central database.

'But she's getting better. You'd agree with me about that?'

The subject of their conversation was sitting out in the waiting room. They had both suggested she be part of the conversation, but Emma had declined. She knew what her problem was, she'd said. Knew what she needed to do to fix it now. If they wanted to discuss alternatives they could do it on their own.

'Oh, she's vastly improved. Yes. I've no doubt she's got the bulk of her memory back. But the story she's concocted for herself?' Doctor Wheeler shrugged her shoulders, raised both hands towards the ceiling, palms upwards in the universal signal of ignorance.

'Is it harmful though? This belief?' McLean couldn't help hearing the desperation in his voice. It filled his every waking moment. He wanted Emma to be better, but knew that as soon as she was given the OK by her doctor she'd be leaving. Off on her mad jaunt around Europe and who knew where else. Who knew how long, either?

'On a scale of one to ten, where one's kind to kittens and ten likes to pull the wings off flies, I'd say she's a three.' Doctor Wheeler flicked through one of the folders, not really reading what was in it. 'Look, I know you want me to stop her going, Tony, but she's an adult, she's healed. I can't stop her doing what she wants to do.'

'That obvious, am I?' McLean shook his head. 'You're right. I'm just being selfish.'

'No, you're not. You're just showing that you care. Let her go. She won't be gone long, I'm sure of that. This is just a part of her brain sorting itself out after the attack. She has to come to terms with what Sergeant Needham did to her. Can't say I'm too happy with the ideas your medium friend planted in her mind, but they've done the job.' Doctor Wheeler paused a moment. 'Started the job, I should say.'

'I just don't want to lose her.'

'You won't.' Doctor Wheeler stared past him, out through the window to the waiting room beyond. 'If there's any sense in her at all, she'll come back. You just need to let her work this out for herself.'

*

He hadn't really expected it to be so soon. Part of him had hoped that it wasn't true anyway, that it would never happen. This wasn't how things were meant to work out. But then life had a habit of dumping on him from a great height.

'You're sure you have to do this, Em?'

It wasn't the right thing to say. There was no right thing to say. They were both standing in the sunlight outside the front door, and McLean couldn't help but notice the dead leaves strewn about the gravel, the green of the trees turning brown and dull at winter's approach.

'We've been over this before, Tony. You know I have to.' Emma reached out and took his hand in hers. Behind them, the little blue and rust Peugeot was packed and ready to go. He'd offered to buy her a new car, but she'd refused. Turned down all his help. This really was something she had to do on her own, apparently. That didn't make it any easier for him to accept.

'At least let me come with you some of the way. I can take a break from work. No one's going to kick up a fuss.'

That at least was true. The first in what looked like it would be an interminable series of counselling sessions with Professor Hilton had not gone well. He'd even had an uncomfortable conversation with Jayne McIntyre in which a year's sabbatical had been mentioned. It was tempting, and the thought of spending twelve months touring Europe with Emma as she worked out her strange therapy had almost clinched it for him. Except that he still had to find Doctor Austin; no way he could let her get away with what she had done.

And Emma had said no. She needed to go alone.

'We've been through this before, Tony.' The tone in

Emma's voice told him he'd pushed just too far. Again. He still didn't know whether to believe Madame Rose's explanation or Doctor Wheeler's. Both were equally far-fetched as far as he was concerned. In some ways it was easier to accept that Emma was somehow carrying the souls of countless victims of an ancient, cursed book. That helped account for the change in her personality as much as her outward appearance, but it brought other, more uncomfortable thoughts to bear. Opened up old wounds long since scarred over if never truly healed.

'Just promise me one thing. OK?'

Emma frowned at him, a half-quizzical expression that sent a shiver up his back. Too similar by far to the way someone else had looked at him when she thought him a fool. 'What?'

'Don't go to Liberton Cemetery.' There. He'd said it. The thing that had been niggling away at him for weeks now. Ever since he'd seen the graves of Rosie Buckley and Diane Kinnear. Donald Anderson's penultimate and third-last victims.

The look softened, and she raised her free hand to his face. 'Not ever?'

He couldn't answer that. It was too much to think about, and anyway she leaned in, kissed him hard on the lips before breaking away. He could do nothing but stand there as she climbed into the car, cranked the engine into life and finally drove away.

57

This city sings a joyous dirge of bleakness and desolation. Its people walk the streets with heavy hearts, shoulders stooped low by imagined cares and worries. Each has their own little piece of misery, clutched around them like a security blanket. An armour of troubles and woes. There is so much for the spirit to feed on. So much work to do.

It has not been easy, coming to this place. I do not know its history or the complexities of its social strata. It's big, too. So much bigger than the place I had to leave. Because of him.

The spirit stirs in me, its displeasure at the memory a tightening in my skull. We lost so much, the spirit and I. The years of preparation, decades of work that went into cultivating that population, everything ripe and ready to be harvested. Then . . .

I shake the thought away. Now is no time to upset the spirit. Now I need it more than ever. We must seek out a new hunter. Someone to trawl this city for the truly lost, to bring them to me so that the spirit might feed and grow strong again.

Time was I hunted for myself. Back when I was young. Back when the spirit first came to me. I have not lost the skill, only the stamina, and so it is that I stalk my prey slowly. He is young, just a few years older than my last one when she came to me. Like so many, his life has not turned out how he expected. He came here looking for fame and fortune, believed the streets were paved with gold. He found out too late that those streets belonged to someone else, that you had to pay just to be allowed to walk on them.

He thinks me strange as he tells me his sorry tale. An old woman who has taken pity on him, the high-finance whizz-kid reduced to selling magazines to strangers just so he can afford to eat. I can see it in his eyes, that spark of life almost extinguished by the crushing weight of his failure. Depression dogs his every step, fuelled by the drugs he took when life was good, but now can no longer afford. The craving chews away at him like rats around a corpse. He will make a fine hunter, this one. He knows the dark and loveless places in this city, has tasted its despair.

I reach out across the table, take his hand. At my touch he looks up, half startled, half knowing this was how it was always going to be. Such hopeless wisdom in those young eyes as they meet my gaze and hold it. The spirit surges through me and into him, meets no resistance at all. I barely need to mouth the words.

'You are mine!'

Acknowledgements

This book might have my name on the cover, but a lot of excellent people have played a part in its making. If I try to name you all, I'm sure to forget someone. You know who you are, and I owe you all a pint.

Having said which, special thanks must go to my agent, the incorrigible Juliet Mushens. Her energy and enthusiasm leave me quite exhausted.

Thanks, too, to Alex, Katya, and all the team at Michael Joseph. A nicer bunch of people I couldn't hope to work with.

I'd also like to thank David and Lesley Spencer for early input, especially with regard to the correct procedure for retrieving a body from a high place. And the gluten-free sausages.

Thanks as always to Stuart MacBride for letting me steal his name for my baby-faced detective constable. I've almost certainly purloined a few more inadvertently.

And thank you, finally, to Barbara. For, well, everything really.

A short note:
It shouldn't really need saying, but this is a work of fiction. There is no Detective Inspector Tony McLean, and there is no Lothian and Borders Police Sexual Crimes Unit. The policy of containment for pimps, prostitutes

and petty drug dealers is entirely my own invention for the purposes of writing what I hope is a compelling story. I have every respect for the uniform officers, detectives, crime scene managers, forensic experts and army of other personnel who do their utmost to keep us safe, often in the most appalling of circumstances and with little or no thanks. I hope that this book merely makes them roll their eyes at my obvious ignorance and the liberties I have taken with the truth in pursuit of fiction.

The *Sunday Times* bestsellin

'His writing is in a class above most in this genre'

DAILY EXPRESS

Inspector McLean series

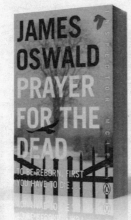

'Oswald is among the leaders in the new batch of excellent Scottish crime writers'

DAILY MAIL

He just wanted a decent book to read ...

Not too much to ask, is it? It was in 1935 when Allen Lane, Managing Director of Bodley Head Publishers, stood on a platform at Exeter railway station looking for something good to read on his journey back to London. His choice was limited to popular magazines and poor-quality paperbacks – the same choice faced every day by the vast majority of readers, few of whom could afford hardbacks. Lane's disappointment and subsequent anger at the range of books generally available led him to found a company – and change the world.

'We believed in the existence in this country of a vast reading public for intelligent books at a low price, and staked everything on it'
Sir Allen Lane, 1902–1970, founder of Penguin Books

The quality paperback had arrived – and not just in bookshops. Lane was adamant that his Penguins should appear in chain stores and tobacconists, and should cost no more than a packet of cigarettes.

Reading habits (and cigarette prices) have changed since 1935, but Penguin still believes in publishing the best books for everybody to enjoy. We still believe that good design costs no more than bad design, and we still believe that quality books published passionately and responsibly make the world a better place.

So wherever you see the little bird – whether it's on a piece of prize-winning literary fiction or a celebrity autobiography, political tour de force or historical masterpiece, a serial-killer thriller, reference book, world classic or a piece of pure escapism – you can bet that it represents the very best that the genre has to offer.

Whatever you like to read – trust Penguin.